Conn fought the bolt of desire spearing a path throughout his body. Her touch spoke volumes—an invitation to taste. Never had he longed to kiss a human like this wee lass. His heart beat loudly, and he found himself unable to move. She was a goddess of the moonlight. It danced off her face and hair, and he trembled before her. Ivy's fingers traced down his cheek and across his lips. He was helpless to contain the growl that escaped from his mouth.

The rush of passion overtook him, and Conn slammed the door on his mind. Grasping Ivy around the waist, he hoisted her up on top of the bridge. Her lips parted on a sigh, and he lowered his mouth to feast on something he dared not take. The first brush of her soft lips against his own ignited a hunger he could no longer contain. Taking her moan deep into him, Conn glorified in the sensation of her mouth—one filled with a honeyed sweetness.

The Fae warrior became just a man for the first time. Something primal burst within him. Emotions he had never felt left him dizzy, spiraling to a physical plane. He craved them all. His lips seared a course down her neck, to her throat, and then recaptured the velvet warmth of her mouth.

Praise for Mary Morgan

"I just love starting one of Mary Morgan's stories. Curling up into a chair, I'm prepared to love her hero and heroine and get a booster shot of time travel."

~Booktalk with Eileen

~*~

"A time-traveling novel of exceptional design, this book draws the reader in and leaves them wanting more at the end."

~InD'tale Magazine

~*~

"Be prepared for an emotional ride that will allow for you to cry, laugh, be sad, happy, confused, elated, and passion filled."

~The Book Junkie Reads

~*~

"Mary Morgan never ceases in delighting the reader with her imagination."

~Dianne Rich

Quest of a Warrior

by

Mary Morgan

Legends of the Fenian Warriors,
Book 1

Quest of a Warrior

Cover Art by *Debbie Taylor*

The Wild Rose Press, Inc.
PO Box 708
Adams Basin, NY 14410-0708
Visit us at www.thewildrosepress.com

Publishing History
First Fantasy Rose Edition, 2017
Print ISBN 978-1-5092-1512-6
Digital ISBN 978-1-5092-1513-3

Legends of the Fenian Warriors, Book 1
Published in the United States of America

Dedication

For Susan Fox and Theresa Baer,
two beautiful women who are
on my Morgan Warriors Street Team.
I required an Irish name for the cat in the story,
and they both thought of Neala,
which means "Champion" in Irish Gaelic.
A perfect name for this feisty feline.
Thank you, Susan and Theresa, with love!

Author's Note

If you need it, a glossary of terms can be found on page 385.

Prologue

In the beginning...when the world was new, Fae and humans lived peacefully together. However, as the centuries passed, fear and distrust evolved. The Fae continued to love the humans, but they believed it was time to safeguard the realms. Therefore, they appointed the Fenian Warriors to guard and protect the domain between mortal and faery. But most importantly, these warriors were to assist the humans.

When evil threatened to destroy a clan, country, or civilization, the Fae council called upon these warriors. Their orders were to steer a new course and aid the mortals. This group of elite warriors had the power to travel through time, called, the Veil of Ages, supporting those in need. They were not to alter the timeline, nor the life strings of a human. To do so, would be catastrophic.

Ancient and powerful, the Brotherhood of the Fenian Warriors was second to only the Fae King and Queen's powers. They have lived among us for thousands of years—watching, aiding, guiding. They could be a professor, lawyer, knight, tavern owner, or a simple farmer.

Whatever was required, the warriors did so without complaint.

Yet, even these great warriors had their weaknesses as with any race—be it human or Fae. Though they have used their powers for good, there were times when a select few deemed it wiser to interfere *without* the knowledge of the Fae council. They twisted the laws to suit their own purpose and changed the course of time.

When three Fenian Warriors left the Brotherhood to aid a clan—the Dragon Knights of Urquhart, they brought the fury of the Fae down upon their heads. Their punishment should have been swift, but the Fae always believed in redemption—even for one of their own.

This is the story of Conn MacRoich. One of the most powerful Fae warriors to be gifted with many powers. His status among the Fae is legendary. He walked among the most ancient of kings and queens, battled alongside the Templars, and sat at King Arthur's round table with the other knights. Robert the Bruce of Scotland granted him lands after the Battle at Bannockburn, and King Brian Boru of Ireland considered him a brother. Such were the tales the Fae bards still weave today.

Yet, in a quest to save the Dragon Knights, he stepped away from the Brotherhood and his own people.

There were whispers that Conn had lived among the humans far too long. Some said he should be stripped of his powers and be made to live out his days in the Hall of Remembrance.

The council heard his account. A sentence was decreed.

In the end, Conn MacRoich was given one final quest to help another. A lost soul whose destiny he altered centuries ago. Furthermore, he must do so without the use of his Fenian magic.

Dare to find out what happened to one of the greatest heroes of Fae and Human. Travel through these pages and be a witness to the tale of a legendary Fenian Warrior.

Chapter One

Beneath the Hill of Tara, Ireland—Late Summer, the season of pleasure and growth in the Fae Realm

"To sit in silence requires a quiet mind and a peaceful heart."

~Chronicles of the Fae

Conn clenched his fists so tightly, the veins threatened to burst, spilling his blood against the walls of his prison. A new day was dawning as the sun's tentative rays streaked through the canopy of trees above him. They teased him as they inched closer—tormenting him with his confinement. Morose gloom weighed heavily on him with each breath he took. It splintered a piece of his soul.

Yet, he found he could not ignore the calling to greet the new day. It was in his Fae blood, seeping into every pore of his being. The land called out to him, and he responded in welcome, no matter the circumstances of his current situation.

Leaning against the crystal wall, Conn gazed upward, his body tensed in anticipation.

He willed the light to brush against the glass rooftop and touch him with its warmth. Watching as the last star blinked from his sight, he could feel the stirrings of rebirth—a new beginning, and he stepped away from the wall. With each step, the pulse of the bare earth surged through the soles of his feet, extending upward throughout his body.

Conn embraced the energy.

His hands unclenched, and he reached outward— stretching as far as he could to capture the flimsy radiance. Minutes passed, but he could sense the time drawing near. As the light shimmered through his fingertips, he absorbed the essence, breathing deeply.

Although fleeting, this moment was enough for him as he eased his hands back down. Collapsing to the ground, he pressed his palms to the earth in reverence. This was his daily ritual—one where he had lost track of how many times he had done so in this dungeon of a room.

An area of space with four crystal walls, the earth beneath him, and a prism of glass above him, so he could witness each new day—each season within his *prison*.

Yet, with each passing hour, day, and month, Conn grew restless and bitter. Bitterness toward those that would still call him family, friend, *brother*. They made him wait in this room, refusing to listen to his account. Ignoring his pleas for a swift and fair trial.

Each day food was brought to him. And each day he issued a request to meet with the Fae council. The Fae guard delivered the same message at the end of day. *"When the Fae were ready, they would summon him. This was a time of reflection, and he should use it wisely."*

Conn dug his hands into the dirt. "Rid me of this anger, Mother Danu. I find it growing daily." Though in his heart, he believed *she* also had turned her back on him, as well as his own people.

Removing his hands, he blew out a sigh and leaned back on his thighs. Closing his eyes, he fought the wave of despair. It left him weak and frustrated of life. In his entire existence this was the first time Conn had walked such a path of emptiness. However, his thoughts did not waver on his decision to join his other two brothers. He had done what he believed to be right. When Fenian Warriors, Liam and Rory MacGregor pleaded their case to assist the Dragon Knights of ridding the world of the evil druid, Lachlan, Conn willingly sacrificed all.

He fisted his hands on his knees. "We did not alter time," he hissed out into the silence. "Only shielded and protected the knights. How could you have expected us to stay hidden and watch as the worlds—human *and* Fae collapsed into darkness? Have we not done the same before? Why is this time so different?"

Conn bowed his head. "If you deem our act unjust, then take *my* life, Mother Danu. Return my life force to the cosmos." Fury erupted within him. Grabbing a handful of soil, he tossed it against the wall. "End this!"

"Do not sit at my feet and ask me to take your life, Conn MacRoich! I give life! Your blood was mingled with mine thousands of years ago. You speak as a human and not Fae. Your time of reflection has ended. The choices you make today will be your new journey. Choose wisely, my Warrior, for the road ahead is unstable. Yet, first, you must address the Fae council."

His body trembled as he slowly stood. The glass dome disappeared, and the tree limbs gracefully made their way down the sides of the walls, absorbing the crystals. The four walls splintered into an array of colorful lights, forcing Conn to shield his eyes from their radiance.

Breathing heavily, he lifted his head to the circle of sunlight streaming down. "I will and always shall be your Warrior, Mother Danu. No matter the path I choose. Thank you."

A soft breeze hinting of roses swept across his face, and Conn inhaled her scent.

"Great Goddess! Did they not give you any fresh clothing?" bellowed Ronan.

Glancing over his shoulder, Conn smiled weakly. Looking down at his soiled, tattered clothing, he replied, "I would assume by your shocked tone that I require new clothes?"

"Aye, most definitely. Ye have been ordered to appear before the Fae council. I thought it best to be the one to deliver the good news."

Conn arched a brow at the man's speech.

Ronan laughed. "And before ye say another word, I am still embroiled in a Scottish clan affair and find I must maintain the language."

Turning around, Conn embraced his friend. "I am happy to see it was you and not an unfamiliar face to escort me to the council."

The warrior leaned back, and his face turned somber. "I made the request on the day they brought ye here."

"Have you given your account of the battle?" asked Conn.

"Aye. The moment I returned."

"And here you stand, *unpunished*?"

Ronan rubbed a hand through his beard, a smile forming on his mouth. "*I* approached the council and gave them *my* terms."

Shocked, Conn shook his head. "*Terms*? What I would have given to be present to see the reaction of the council members—especially the administrator."

"I believe some of them paled," replied Ronan. "One of my conditions was to be your escort when they called ye forth."

"Sweet Goddess," he muttered.

His friend shrugged. "What could they do? I broke nae laws." He placed a hand on Conn's shoulder. "And so I would do so again."

Conn nodded. "Any other conditions I should be aware of? You do realize I may be put instantly to death."

"Nae," reassured the warrior. "Your life— including Liam and Rory's were spared many moons ago from a request made by an individual."

"By whom?" demanded Conn.

"Margaret MacKay MacFhearguis," Ronan uttered softly.

Stunned by the revelation, Conn went to lean against one of the oak trees. "*Why*?"

"She deemed too many had suffered and died. The Fae granted her request immediately. They would do anything for their beloved Dragon Knights, especially the keeper of the Book of Awakening—Margaret."

Conn had roamed the earth for thousands of years and in that time, not one human had pledged to see him safe. On the contrary, they came to him for aid, protection, wisdom, and at times, anger. His heart filled with a deep respect for Margaret, and he prayed the day would come when he could tell her how much the plea meant to him.

"'Tis hard to fathom?" asked Ronan.

Nodding, he moved away from the tree. "Never has this happened in my lifetime."

Ronan chuckled softly. "The humans do surprise us from time to time, aye?"

"Yes, indeed."

"Would ye like me to do the honors with your appearance?"

Conn glanced at him as they moved through the forest. "Absolutely not. You would see me in shimmering clothing."

"Ye wound me," teased his friend. "Yet, ye are to appear in your royal tunic."

"I have a fresh one in my chambers. Surely, the council can wait until I'm cleaned and in proper clothing."

"Not wise to keep the members waiting."

Conn smirked. "Like I care?"

Ronan rolled his eyes. "'Tis your trial."

Emerging from the trees, Conn's steps faltered as the light touched his shoulders. Casting his gaze to the valley below, he inhaled deeply. The Fae realm was buried far below the Hill of Tara, yet, this portion of the kingdom mirrored the one above. Rolling hills in various hues of green surrounded a valley rich with Fae life. Colors so vibrant and opulent, the bucolic scene stole the breath from his lungs. To the east and west marked the ancient waterfalls—one denoting the birth of a Fae, and the other, in the west, a passing of life. He sighed, keeping his sight on the waterfall in the west— *Tir na Og*, the Land of Forever. How many Fenian brothers had he lost to this place? *Too many!*

Slowly lifting his head to the north, Conn let his sight fall on the great palace of the King, Queen, Fae council, and the Brotherhood of the Fenian Warriors. Massive towers shimmered with all the colors of Earth's crystals, along with those from the Fae's homeland—Taralyn.

"How long has it been?" inquired Ronan quietly.

Snapping out of his thoughts, Conn ran his hand through his hair. "One hundred years, ten months, two days, five hours, and thirty seconds." He looked at his friend. "Those are Fae times."

Ronan's eyes went wide. "Ye roamed above for over a thousand years?"

Conn shrugged and glanced away. "There was much to do."

"Then I must warn ye to beware the whispers, my friend." He clapped a hand on Conn's shoulder.

"Whispers?" Shrugging out of his friend's grasp, he made his way down the hill.

Ronan was alongside him in two strides. "They say ye have stayed far too long with the humans. Ye think like one."

Conn halted. "That's absurd!"

"Aye, I ken, but ye have to consider that ye have not returned, if only for a year. These are your people, too."

Ignoring his Fae brother, Conn continued to make his way down the hill. *How dare they whisper behind his back—a great Fenian Warrior. Did he not do everything that was required of him? Repeatedly, he had walked into battles, rescuing those in need. Steering a course of a human life when needed.* He clenched his jaw as he strode more quickly.

Conn could hear Ronan shouting, but he gave no care. His Fae blood boiled. *I will show them all!*

In a brilliant flash, Conn appeared in his chambers within the crystal palace. Stumbling forward, he landed against his writing desk.

"Shit!" he bellowed. Twisting around, he lunged at Ronan. However, the warrior vanished and reappeared on the other side of the chamber.

Ronan's eyes flashed, and he held a hand up in warning. "I will not fight ye, my brother."

Breathing heavily, his hands shook. Great Goddess, what was wrong with him? Anger surfaced so quickly, it blinded him. When he had regained his composure, he asked, "Did it not occur to you that I wanted to walk back?"

The Fae angled his head. "Seriously? Do ye ken how long it would take?"

Conn's mouth twitched in humor. "Months?"

"Aye." Ronan chuckled. He waved a hand in the air. "The council has not stripped your chambers of magic. Therefore, ye can move around freely and do what ye must to appear presentable."

"How kind," he replied dryly, glancing around.

"Ye will find food and drink on your terrace. I will return for ye in one hour."

Conn was tempted to ask if the hour was human or Fae. "Thank you."

Ronan smiled and vanished.

Rubbing a hand over his chin, Conn slowly made his way into his private bathing area, which consisted of a huge garden. A waterfall cascaded down into a pool surrounded by lush foliage. Smells of lavender, honeysuckle, and roses drifted by him. Hummingbirds flitted about, their presence soothing. He had forgotten how peaceful the Fae realm could be, especially his own chambers.

Uncertainty had become his companion in the Room of Reflection, slithering inside him and draining him all those months. The stench of the human world cloaked him, and he shook his head in frustration. Perhaps Ronan was correct. He had stayed away far too long from his own people, albeit his own decision.

But why had he? *A question without an answer.*

Stripping free of his torn tunic and pants, he descended down to the pool. Diving in, the warmth of the water seeped through his tired bones and flesh, cleansing the grime from a battle fought many moons ago. Taking his time, he stroked lazily to the other side, enjoying the caress of the water on his skin.

When he reached the other side, he climbed on top of a polished boulder to warm himself in the sunlight. Crossing his legs under him, he glanced around and closed his eyes. Inhaling deeply, he held his breath and then let it out slowly. Releasing all thought, Conn allowed his body to drift—becoming one with the realm once again. The rich earthiness of the land filled him, and he took what she had to offer. As his body and mind adjusted to the Fae realm, he absorbed the power, but only taking what he required in his healing.

"No matter your path, you are a Fenian Warrior. You are Fae. You are of my blood—far more ancient than the land you sit upon. A new day dawns within you. Though you may not be human, they are to be respected, as well."

With one last shuddering breath, Conn slowly opened his eyes. The trees swayed back and forth, easing all tension from his spirit. "Thank you, Mother Danu."

Slipping back into the water, Conn made his way back to his home. Quickly drying his body with a wave of his hand, he reached for an apple on the table and took a bite. The tartness of the fruit exploded in his mouth, and he let out a moan. Food in the Fae realm was sweeter—another fact he had forgotten in the human world. He wiped away the juices and stepped inside his chambers.

Entering his inner chamber, a haven just for him, he strode over to his giant armoire. Conn traced his fingers over the Celtic spirals etched in maple wood. He had worked tirelessly for months trying to fathom why the humans were fascinated with carving. Soon, he'd found pleasure in creating pieces from any type of wood. However, he would only take from the dying trees and never a living one.

Opening one of the doors, he pulled forth his royal tunic and pants. Quickly dressing, he wandered around the rooms, touching a book or admiring a quartz crystal, until he found himself back on the terrace. Tying his hair back with a leather thong, he opted not to wear shoes. He wanted to absorb as much as he could from his homeland. Lifting the pitcher, he poured some water into a goblet. Sipping the cool liquid, he stood and gazed outward. He filled his mind with every detail, as if fearing he would never return to this place.

Sensing the return of Ronan, he opened the door to his chambers with a single thought.

"Are ye ready?" asked the Fenian Warrior.

Smiling, Conn picked up another apple and stuffed it into his pants. "Yes."

As he made his way out of the chambers, he glanced over his shoulder one last time. "I don't think

I'll be returning," he stated quietly.

"Ye are spouting nonsense. The Fae council will most likely suspend your powers for a thousand years, and ye will remain in the realm to oversee training of new Fenian Warriors."

Conn blinked and looked at the Fae incredulously. "Considering what has transpired, they will not be asking me to train anyone, for fear I would taint them."

Ronan placed a firm hand on his shoulder. "I shall always be with ye, brother."

"I walk this road alone, my friend."

They proceeded to make their way along the corridors of the castle. Quietness settled within Conn as he passed along the many rooms and passageways leading to other areas of the great castle. Too quickly, they approached the hall of the Fae council.

Pausing before the closed doors, Conn turned to his friend. "Have you any news regarding Liam and Rory?"

A frown marred Ronan's features. "None."

Conn snorted. "I suppose my sins are far worse."

The warrior crossed his arms over his chest. "Ye assume—"

"No. I merely state what I already know. It is a path I have chosen. Right or wrong, I shall own the choices. But know this, my friend. Those who seek to condemn me, have yet to venture far from this realm."

Giving his friend a reassuring smile, Conn turned and strode inside the chambers of the Fae council to meet his fate.

Chapter Two

"When truths are revealed, you must bear the burden of the words."

~*Chronicles of the Fae*

Conn stared into the faces of the nine council members. Clasping his hands behind his back, he waited to be called forth. Before his powers were stripped, they would have acknowledged him within his thoughts. However, he now stood waiting for them to summon him forward by spoken words.

In addition, they deemed to make him wait even more as the golden leaflets with information passed from one member to the next in silence.

He had never stood before the council, and his view of the members had only been in passing. These Fae were chosen at a young age to learn the wisdom and laws of their people. Their training was lengthy, lasting decades. Their knowledge also consisted of learning all laws relating to the Fenian Warriors. Only when they had been deemed worthy, and passed numerous tests, would they become one of the nine who would serve for the next ten thousand years. Or until death claimed them first.

The room was unknown to Conn. He had never required their guidance. It was a place where other Fae sought out advice, wisdom, and at times, judgments.

Thick, green ivy covered a long wooden table and wrapped around the legs, the only color in the stark room. The Fae realm was full of many colors, but this place held none. Even the floor was one of gray stone.

He glanced at the white walls and angled his head upward. Even the circular ceiling held no light from the outside. Letting his gaze settle once again on the members, he tried to process what form of defense he would be able to present. How could those who had never ventured far from the realm understand what he had done? They had never encountered the evil druid, Lachlan—a force only he and his other two brothers helped to destroy.

They will not be able to comprehend, so you are doomed. Conn almost barked out in laughter, so ridiculous to think they could, but instead, he smiled, and continued to wait.

Slowly, a female council member stood. "I am known as Seneca. You may come forward to the truth stone, Conn MacRoich."

As he made his way toward the council, Conn glanced down at the massive polished quartz embedded within the stones. He paused. "And may I ask what I'm about to step onto?"

"Since we are unable to read your thoughts, we have only the words you speak here today. The truth stone will ensure that you give us the most accurate account of your transgression."

Conn's fury rose as all humor fled. "Might I remind you, the Fae have stripped my powers. Therefore, if you can't read my thoughts *or* trust my words, this is your problem. Not mine."

Seneca arched a brow. "Might I remind you, *Conn*

MacRoich that you are on trial."

"I am a Fenian Warrior, bound by honor, here in this room to divulge *all* truths."

"All?" another questioned. The Fae rose. "I am known as Tulare." He waved a golden leaflet into the air. "Are you ready to start at the beginning of your misdeeds?"

Resentment and frustration clawed inside Conn. "If the Fae council deems it's necessary to pick apart the life of one of their oldest warriors, so be it."

"Are you a fool to not realize what you have done?" Tulare spat out.

Confused, Conn replied, "I am fully aware of what I have done. Fae and human realms are at peace. Evil has been destroyed."

Tulare started to utter a retort, but Seneca held up her hand. "Enough." Turning her gaze to Conn, she said, "Do you refuse to stand on the truth stone, Conn MacRoich?"

He took a step back. "Yes. I have given my vow as a Fenian Warrior to speak truthfully." He gestured to the stone with his hand. "If my word as a Fae is not good enough, then sentence me now."

"Let him give his account without the use of the truth stone," replied a voice within the shadows of the room.

Conn narrowed his eyes. He knew that voice.

"It has never been done," argued Tulare.

"Do you challenge my decision?"

Hushed silence descended in the room.

The Fae appeared forth from the shadows. "You have not answered my question. Does the Fae council challenge *or* object to my decision?"

"No," stated Seneca.

"If you are all in agreement, you must state your voice in front of the accused. As one."

Each member stated their affirmation of approval, though some murmured the word in disgust.

The Fae smiled. "Good. If you would permit us some time, I would like to confer in private with the warrior."

Seneca gave a curt nod, and the members vanished.

He turned to Conn. "Welcome home, though I cannot say it is a joyous return."

Conn swallowed. "Loran? By the Gods!"

"What? You assumed your friend was dead?" Loran chuckled. "I was ancient when you left and far older upon your return." He tapped a finger to his head. "Though at times, a bit forgetful. Though as an elder to the Fae council, I have no wish in informing them of that bit of information."

Conn embraced his dear, old friend. Stepping back, he gazed over the features of the ancient elder. Lines marred his forehead and gray etched his temples. At the least, Conn believed his friend to be older than the earth they stood upon. "Why are you here?"

Loran rubbed a hand over his chin. "Word traveled the realm quickly when you sealed the doors to all worlds—past, present, and future. The uproar struck a fierce blow to the king and queen. They felt it keenly."

"I was not alone," interjected Conn.

Two chairs materialized, and Loran gestured for Conn to sit. "No. We understood Liam and Rory were there as well. However, yours was the power that locked the realms. They merely closed the doors. Your power is the greatest, Conn. It was a gift given to you specifically from the king on your initiation into the Brotherhood. Did you not consider that they would feel the sharp blade of betrayal when you turned the key?"

Conn leaned forward. "Yes. I knew the moment I locked all within that night. It was the only way."

His friend nodded. "Are you so sure?"

"Yes."

"The Dragon Knights might have succeeded," countered Loran.

Conn arched a brow. "So my trial is not because we brought the MacKays through the veil? It's because I locked the realms?"

Sighing, Loran looked away. "You—your other Fenian brothers never gave us a chance. They would have stood beside you. Your King—"

"He silenced my pleas when I requested assistance the last time the Dark One attempted to enter the human world a thousand years ago! Or have you forgotten?" Conn stood and paced the room. "A terrible battle was fought and many lost their lives." He glanced over his shoulder at the Fae. "This time, I deemed what I believed was necessary for the safety of two worlds."

"When did you become king?" protested Loran. "It was not your decision. Furthermore, your actions through the centuries have been rife with interferences. You bend the law to suit your needs. Some, the king and queen have chosen to look away from—granting you free will. But no longer."

Conn pinched the bridge of his nose to temper his fury. "Are they afraid of what I might do?"

Sighing, Loran stood. "They would never fear their own *son*."

"I am no longer their child," snapped Conn. "When

I took an oath to become a Fenian Warrior, I gave up my rights to inherit the throne. I became one of the Brotherhood. I would never seek to take Abela's claim to the throne, either."

"Sweet Mother Danu," muttered Loran. Rising, he walked over to Conn. He grasped his shoulder. "You have been away far too long. Your sister is now a Fae priestess. She has no wish to become queen."

The blow of Loran's words struck like a knife, tearing into his heart. Stumbling back, Conn rubbed a shaky hand over his face. "*Why?*"

"It is not my story to tell, Conn. You will have to ask her."

"She has passed the ten years of seclusion?" His question was one of shock.

Loran nodded. "Abela has been a priestess for almost one hundred years."

The moment Conn had pledged his life as a Fenian Warrior, he walked away from his Fae family. The years of training and traveling the Veil of Ages had become his new way of life. He never had a wish to stay locked within the walls of the crystal palace, as he had often shouted to his father. No, he was born a warrior, something he and his father did agree upon.

Now to learn his twin—*his sister* had chosen a path of isolation within a deeper part of their world, shocked Conn. Her love and spirit of life always infused others, and he believed she would have made a kind and loving queen. He would have honored her until the end of his days.

But now…

"Can I see her?" uttered Conn softly.

Loran shrugged. "It's entirely up to her. I can pass

20

along a request."

Conn stepped away. "No. If Abela wishes to see me, she'll send the request. I'm sure she's aware that I have returned."

"She dwells deep within the caves," admitted Loran.

Conn's smile was sad when he replied, "We are twins. I felt her brush of power within my mind the moment I returned. I might not be able to communicate with any others, but I shall always have this connection with her."

"Ahh..." murmured Loran.

Fisting his hands on his hips, Conn shook his head. "I cannot believe my parents would allow her to leave the light of the Fae realm and seek such isolation."

Loran crossed his arms over his chest. "Why? It is a great honor to be chosen into the holy community. To be one at times with the land, seeking and learning its knowledge—a great gift, indeed. You chose your path and Abela her own. Your parents were stunned in the beginning, but they have since given their blessing. She is a light among our people, especially during the great fire festivals. They revere her and the other priestesses more than our own king and queen."

Conn glanced at his friend. "Is she happy?"

Smiling, Loran nodded. "Abela's beauty is enhanced by her love of the world below and her people. She is extremely happy and understands the purpose for what she has chosen on this path."

Sighing deeply, Conn made his way to the council table. "Then I am happy for her. Now, tell me what can I expect from this trial?"

Loran brought the chairs over to them with a flick

of his wrist. Sitting down, he motioned Conn to the other chair. "You have several choices. The first, charges will be read and you will be given time to give your account. The second, you waive a trial and proceed to the Hall of Remembrance to witness your offenses through the mirrors of your life. With each, a judgment will be decreed."

Conn snorted. "Those are my only options? You make it sound like I'm guilty no matter if I give my account or not." He leaned his forearms on his thighs. "They may as well pass a verdict, since none of them will listen."

When his friend remained silent, Conn blew out a frustrated breath. He wanted no part of the Hall of Remembrance. His memories were clearly as vivid within his mind. There was no need to have them flash in front of him.

Loran closed his eyes. "They are returning."

"Good. I wish to end this."

As both Fae stood, their chairs vanished. Loran took hold of Conn's arms. "Whatever happens, know you will always have friends here in this realm."

"You honor me with your words, Loran, and I thank you." Embracing his friend, Conn went and stood behind the truth stone.

As the Fae council members appeared within the room, Loran nodded to each in greeting and stepped aside.

Seneca remained standing, waiting for the members to settle into their chairs. Turning her gaze to Conn, she lifted a golden leaflet. "Conn MacRoich, are you ready to hear the charges against you?"

"I am."

Her voice rang out clear and crisp. "Conn MacRoich, Fenian Warrior for the Fae, you have been brought before this council for the crime of using the key entrusted to you to lock and unlock the realms without consent of the King, Queen, or Elders on the earth date of October 31, 2016. Furthermore, knowledge has been presented to show that on more than one occasion, the veil of time was altered. As a result, you have changed the course of an entire generation. These are severe and cannot be left unpunished. The Key of Realms has been restored back to the king. However, the timeline for this clan has had an impact on the destiny of one human." Snapping her long fingers, the leaflet disappeared.

"You may now give your account."

Uneasiness slithered inside of Conn. In all of his time crossing the veil, he had never misused his powers—only for the greater good. Yet, somewhere, somehow, he had failed. And this bothered him immensely.

Conn clasped his hands behind his back. "As a Fenian Warrior, and keeper of the key, I deemed what I believed was right. Sealing both realms kept the evil from escaping into one or the other. Lachlan and the Dark One were vanquished. I will make no apologies. I was given the key, not to protect, but to be used in the event of chaos. As for the second charge, I recall no misconduct within the veil of time…" He paused, dreading his next words. "Yet, I ask to be shown this occurrence in the Hall of Remembrance."

"Granted," replied Seneca. The doors to the chamber opened. "A guard will escort you to the room. The mirrors will reflect the break in time where the future was altered. Darkness will shroud the year, instead of light. Afterwards, we shall announce your judgment."

"I ask for one request before you carry out whatever means of punishment you deem fit for me."

She raised an eyebrow. "Continue."

"I request an audience with the king, queen, and my sister, Abela."

One of the council members gasped, but Seneca held up her hand in warning. "I will pass along your requests, but it is entirely up to them to grant you a meeting."

Conn nodded. "Thank you."

As he walked out of the room, Conn's greatest fear was not the punishment he faced. No, he dreaded that no one from his family would want to see him.

And his heart sank at the possible reality.

Chapter Three

"A missed stitch in time can foretell a different path."

~*Chronicles of the Fae*

The doors closed silently behind Conn, and his gaze traveled the length of the long hall of mirrors. It was a place so infinite, he could not even see where it ended. His life was far too vast. On either side, he witnessed his existence reflected within the glass. Each one recorded a date above the paneled mirror. A story unfolding—a movie of his entire life, including his trial.

He quickly made his way past the most recent images of his life, including the battle against the Dark One with the Dragon Knights. There was only light around the gilded edges of the glass. He would defend his actions until his last dying breath.

One mirror caught his attention, and he moved forward. There he stood, arms outstretched, holding the portal of the veil open for Brigid O'Neill, future wife of Dragon Knight, Duncan MacKay. She had wandered to the standing stones with Duncan's sword and for reasons he couldn't fathom, she opened the Veil of Ages. Yet, without his assistance—*interference*, she would have tumbled into an earlier century and not into Duncan's.

Did he do wrong?

"No," he growled, furious over his own doubt. There was light around the year Brigid stepped through the stones. Therefore, Conn breathed a sigh of relief and continued on his journey down the hall.

With each passing mirror, memories flooded back within his mind. His fists clenched when he came upon the Battle of Culloden. Many were lost on the battlefield. Good Scottish men he had come to know and respect. How he had longed to take the English Duke of Cumberland and his men back through the veil, banish their memories, and have them retreat. But he stood steadfast in the belief that there was a greater cause—one he prayed to see. Besides, he was not allowed to change the timeline based on his own personal beliefs.

Grumbling a curse, he quickly moved away from the horrible image and made his way further back in the timeline of his life. Adventures at sea glimmered, and he smiled, recalling fonder memories and those he met along the way. One of those was, *Grania*—Grace O'Malley. A brave and beautiful sixteenth century Irish chieftain. She rivaled Queen Elizabeth and was one of the most magnificent humans he had ever encountered.

Conn continued his walk along the hall, stopping briefly at those he considered friends, including the Irish King, Brian Boru. "I miss your wisdom and wit, my friend. And those strategic chess games," he uttered softly.

Turning, he froze. The mirror to the left was edged in dark shadows. The year was 936, the battle at Clonmacnoise in Ireland. The King of Munster, Cellachán mac Buadacháin was waving a sword with one hand, and the other he kept firm around a woman's waist. Conn had no problems recalling the memory. His fists clenched watching the scene unfold. The man was a tyrant—one who had slain the father of his friend, Brian Boru.

"Ye ken what I have?" Cellachán bellowed!

"Nae!" shouted the other man. "She is my daughter and promised to another. Dinnae take her, my Chieftain, I beg ye."

"I will take the woman as my slave!" The chieftain's men surrounded him in protection, and the woman gave out a blood-curdling scream, fighting and clawing at her captor.

Conn didn't need to watch what would happen next. Cold seeped into his bones as he watched himself walk through the crowd of men.

"Will ye not give her to me?" demanded Conn.

"I am nae fool," the chieftain sneered. "I ken ye want the lass for yourself. Ye can find another to claim, or bed."

In an instant, Conn's eyes blazed silver and time halted. All remained fixed—the men frozen where they stood. All but the woman.

He held out his hand. "Do ye trust me, Dervla?

The lass nodded.

"Take my hand. I will see ye safely home."

Dervla's hand trembled as she took a hold of Conn's. "What god are ye?" Her question more of curiosity than of fear.

"Nae, not a god, only a friend." As he moved her away from the crowd of men, she yanked on his arm.

"What about my father?"

He tipped her chin up with his finger. "I can only save ye."

The image blurred...faded, but Conn knew what happened next. Her father was killed in a battle—the story of the disappearing girl told in bardic tales.

Conn returned Dervla to her clan. Her future now set on a path to become a powerful druid priestess. However, she decided to ignore the calling and married outside of her clan. Conn had often thought that maybe he should have left her in the care of the brute.

His hand shook as he gently touched the glass. "What should I have done? She was the chosen one." The contact burnt his fingers, and he drew back. And there in the shadows of the trees, he witnessed another young woman, heavily cloaked. Her eyes shimmered with unshed tears as her hands clawed at the tree.

"Sweet Mother Danu!" he rasped. "What have I done?"

"You saved the wrong lass," stated the low voice behind Conn.

He turned abruptly. "Father," he whispered and swallowed. Bowing, he stated in a firm voice, "King Ansgar."

Both men stood apart, neither reaching out for the other. Time lengthened and Conn stared into eyes that bore the same color as his own. Hair the color of golden light was cropped short, and for the first time, Conn saw silver strands around his father's temples. Worry infused his spirit. He glanced over his father's shoulder.

"Your mother will join us shortly. She deemed it would be wise if we met first."

Exhaling slowly, Conn nodded. "I have been away far too long."

"Agreed."

Conn knelt on one knee. "Forgive me, my king."

After several long moments, his father placed a gentle hand on his head. "Rise, my son."

Standing slowly, Conn noticed hurt reflected in his father's eyes. Never before had he witnessed such a display of emotion from him. His father ruled with an iron fist when it came to Conn, but always showed a softer side toward his sister, Abela. Disquiet and guilt settled inside of him. Words failed him.

"Let us move away from this particular event," uttered his father quietly.

They made their way to an alcove off to the side of the mirrors, and his father motioned for Conn to sit beside him on the marbled bench.

Conn placed his hands on his thighs. The time to speak clearly was now. He had no idea when the council would demand him to return for sentencing. "I understand the key of the realms is now in your possession."

"Yes. And before you ask the next question, I support you fully with what you did to vanquish the monster, Lachlan, and the Dark One."

Stunned, Conn turned toward his father. "Truly?"

His father nodded. "It was a destiny...foreseen. Though, I wished you would have sought approval from your king—or the elders."

"But not when I asked you over a thousand years ago? When the evil threatened that time within the mortal realm? I came to you. I could have stopped the Dark One—"

He held up his hand to stay Conn's words. "You would not have defeated him. Yes, you're a Fenian Warrior, but *not* a seer."

Conn felt the blood drain from his face. "Death

would have come to my brothers? Me?"

Frowning, his father shrugged. "I am not disposed to discuss the threads of fate."

"But yet, we are here to argue over another's thread of life."

"A human life," snapped the king. "You are a Fenian Warrior—Fae! Do you not think I understand what happened with the life you saved, but ignored the one in shadows?" He jabbed a finger to Conn's chest. "You had befriended the woman, Dervla. You had *feelings*, and as such, your mind became clouded, unable to see clearly as a warrior. In the end, you failed to see the one human in need of your services. You sought out the light, but the real beauty was hidden in the shadows near the tree."

Breathing heavily, Conn tried to keep his voice calm. "Are we not taught to love these humans? Is it not what was spoken to me from the great elders? From the dragons?"

His father's eyes flashed silver in anger. "Not for a Fenian Warrior! You should have *no* human friends, save only those from the Brotherhood! Is that not what you trained centuries for? Let me remind you, son, you were the one that argued and presented your case before me. You insisted the Brotherhood was your calling. In the end, I relented. I witnessed your determination and believed this was your true path." He shook his head. "Unknowingly, you have spent far too long among the humans and have developed their own traits—*forgotten* what it meant to be a warrior. Indulged in their lifestyle, forsaking your own here. Made rash decisions, which I have overlooked and argued in *your* favor to the council and elders."

Conn stood abruptly. His father's words slashed at his heart, and he had no wish to sit next to the man. "If this human's life thread had unraveled, why did you not summon me back to the council? A thousand years has passed. Why order me to stand trial now?"

His father sighed heavily and stood. Striding to the mirror, he kept his gaze on the scene. "An error in judgment," he uttered softly. "It was your first transgression, and the Fae seer alerted me to the situation. She was unable to see the future clearly for this human and the generations that followed. Therefore, I asked—no *requested* that the knowledge be kept silent."

Stunned by his father's declaration, he walked to his side. "You've kept this secret hidden? For me?"

The king glanced at him. "For my son."

"Yet, once the key was used in the great battle with the Dragon Knights, your father had no choice but to stand aside and let the council review your deeds," stated a soft voice behind him.

Conn turned. Emotions overcame him, and he struggled to get the word out. "*Mo…Mother.*"

She cupped his cheek, tears streaming down her face. "It is so very good to see you, my son."

Closing his eyes, he let her love fill him as she embraced him. Conn's hardened warrior armor cracked open, and the Fae prince emerged. Holding her close, he inhaled her scent—one of honeysuckle. Emotions that had stayed in, controlled and locked away, were now set free with her simple touch. "I have missed you," he whispered.

She drew back. Casting her gaze over his features, she smiled. "I thought never to see you again."

He placed his forehead on hers. "Forgive me."

"Shh...no need. You have requested to see us, and I feared you would not have a chance to speak with your father and me."

Conn kissed her cheek and moved away from his parents. "The life of a warrior can leave one feeling numb. Perhaps that is why I stayed away. I did not want you to see me as an unfeeling Fae." He rubbed his eyes vigorously and then glanced at the shadowed mirror. "Although, there are those that would argue I let out sentiments toward the humans."

His parents each came to his side, and he felt their strength seep into his bones. "Remember, Conn, you chose this path of a Fenian Warrior. Your deeds have saved thousands," stated his father.

Glancing at the king, Conn nodded. "Thank you for believing in me. For keeping this secret. Although, I deem more was wrought by not bringing me forward to the council at the time of my error. We could have solved this at the time of *my* indiscretion."

The king gestured to the mirror. "The loom of fate had already unraveled. To attempt a repair of the damage could have altered another life. I fully expected a time would come when all would be revealed."

"Let us remove ourselves from this scene of your life," suggested his mother.

As they made their way further back within the centuries, the queen waved her hand in an arc and light shimmered on the path in front of them. "Before you are escorted back to the Fae council your sister wishes to speak with you."

"Why did you let—"

His mother placed a finger on his lips. "It is

Abela's journey and not yours to question. Did she not fully support you when you left to become a warrior?"

Swallowing, Conn nodded slowly. His sister never uttered one negative comment when he had made his announcement to the family about joining the Brotherhood.

"But I did cry," added a soft feminine voice—one filled with song.

Conn turned at the sound of his sister speaking. She was a vision to behold. Where his hair was blond with silver streaks, his twin's was as black as ebony, cascading around her in soft waves. Her eyes blazed with the many colors of different gems, instead of the lavender of their people. This was not the sister he'd left a hundred years ago. She had grown from Fae royalty to become part of the Mother Danu. He stood mesmerized.

Holding a silver staff in one hand, she smiled at him. "Come forward, Fenian Warrior."

Making a slight bow, he proceeded to walk to her.

The room opened up to reveal a crystal cavern of many colors. Two oak trees stood as sentries, their branches swaying gently. The air was warm and inviting, luring Conn forward. Her power enveloped him, and he found it difficult to breathe. There was so much beauty to absorb. Lights shimmered before his eyes, and he felt the need to be free from his body.

She raised an outstretched hand. "Relax, Brother."

"Too much..." Conn wiped a hand across his brow. "The power is tremendous." Taking her hand, he embraced his sister in a hug.

"You are in the womb of the Mother," she uttered softly.

"Abela," he whispered and placed a kiss on her cheek.

She stood back and gazed into his eyes. "Walk with me."

They wandered along a path filled with wildflowers, and the cavern opened up to reveal a world filled with birds, animals, and trees. Several hummingbirds flitted near his sister, and she smiled at them. With each step, his body began to ease from the strain of the past few months. Glancing in all directions, he was in awe of the majestic beauty surrounding them.

"And here I thought the Fae realm was remarkable," he commented.

"You've been away far too long," chided Abela.

Conn glanced sideways at her. "So I've been told."

She chuckled and for a brief moment Conn saw glimpses of the sister he had left a century ago.

Neither spoke as they continued to amble along the soft path. The rich scent of earth filled him.

Abela led him to a bench overlooking a waterfall. As they took their seats, he leaned back, studying his sister. He only had one burning question. *Why?*

Sighing deeply, she kept her gaze outward. "You forget, Conn. I can read your mind. Why did I choose this life? Is that your burning question?"

"Yes. You loved your life in the Fae realm. Each day was filled with joy—a new party to plan, a garden to organize, flowers to bundle. But this—" He flung his hands upward. "It might be serene and the most stunning place on this planet, but I never thought my sister would seal herself off from her own family and people."

The air cooled around them. "Remember, you have

not set one foot in this realm for over a hundred Fae years. I am no longer the young woman you remember." She turned fully toward him. "The day you left was one etched on my spirit. I cried for days, since I knew that during your training our link—*our bond* would be severed." Abela turned her head away. "Afterward, I needed to find a purpose to my life, too. My heart guided me to the temple of the Mother Danu one day, and I've never regretted my decision to become one of her priestesses. On no account did I ever question your *calling*, so I ask that you respect mine, as well."

Conn reached for her hand. "I'm sorry. I never knew."

She shrugged. "How could you? And you never came back, which made it only worse for us. I longed to share my journey and hear about yours."

"Are you happy?"

The smile she gave him radiated over her entire body. "*Yes*. Mother and father came to see me quite often after I passed the solitary time period. They love to share what's happening in the cities. There will come a time when I shall venture out of here. Yet, for now, this is where I will remain. I am here to serve *Her*."

"We both have chosen our own paths, though who will claim the throne?"

She touched his hand. "When the time comes, I'm positive our king and queen will choose wisely."

Abela stood and angled her head to the side as if listening to someone. "Father states the Fae council has requested your return." She turned her gaze toward him. "Are you ready?"

Standing, Conn grasped both her hands. "You pass

no judgment on me?"

"Never," she whispered. "I have honored and respected the warrior you have become. Your name and deeds have spread throughout the kingdom. Regardless of what has *or* will happen the people adore you."

He kissed her hands. "I will miss you."

"Kneel, Fenian Warrior," she commanded in the voice of an ancient being.

As he knelt before his sister, she placed her hands on his head, and he closed his eyes. "Where your path leads, is your choice Conn MacRoich. Choose wisely, guard, and protect those in your charge. This will be your greatest challenge. Learn to listen with your heart—your Fae heart."

I love you, Brother. Be well. Look for me in the soft breezes of the rowan and oak trees, or the kiss of rain upon your cheek. I will always be there for you.

When Conn opened his eyes, he found himself kneeling on the floor of the Hall of Remembrance—all alone. His father and mother were gone. Standing slowly, he placed a fist over his heart. "Be well, too, Lady Abela."

Turning around, he walked out of the hall fully prepared to face whatever judgment the council decreed.

Chapter Four

Cork Airport, Ireland

*"The light of illumination often is found in the
remote darkness within a heart."*
~*Chronicles of the Fae*

Horrible things always happen during
thunderstorms. Lightning can strike anywhere, sparking
a wildfire and destroying all in its path. Torrential rain
can wreak havoc on body, mind, and soul. Not to
mention what it can do to the land. Rivers can swell and
spill out onto the terrain—forcing many to flee as their
homes are washed away, including those of the animal
kingdom.

The mere thought sent a shiver of unease down
Ivy's spine. What a poor welcome from the land of her
ancestors—this Ireland.

Bringing the fur-lined hood of her coat more firmly
over her head, she peered out into the busy airport
traffic and tried to stay out of the fierce storm's path
while huddled in a corner outside the building. Yet, the
wind was relentless and managed to spray her with
water repeatedly.

A couple emerged from the warmth of the terminal,
bumping into her. They looked her over like some kind
of specimen. "An apology would have been nice," she

muttered as she watched them dash out into the sopping mess.

Wiping a hand over her face, she mumbled a curse. Maybe she should return inside and book a flight back to San Diego. There were no rainstorms in her hometown, only sunshine and sea breezes. The simple thought lifted her sagging spirits. *Why did you agree to come? What a foolish notion.* All because some lost relative—an uncle—decided to leave you everything in his will. The only condition? She must come to Ireland and claim her inheritance.

"He most likely left me some run-down shack in need of repairs," she uttered in disgust.

Ivy glanced over her shoulder at the ticket counter inside. Though the idea of going back home was tempting, she couldn't. For one, she didn't have enough funds in her bank account. And the second, Ivy could never resist an intriguing opportunity, especially one handed to her. When the envelope arrived that warm summer morning, Ivy never imagined the endless possibilities of how her life would change. Her hands had trembled while she ripped open the sealed wax and read the lawyer's letter.

Fate had stepped in and presented her with a gift.

Her job at the local museum was ending, and her search to find anything in her related field of history proved to be daunting. Everywhere she applied they all wanted the same—a PhD attached to her resume. No one cared if she had a Master's Degree in Ancient History. Nope! Not one. After the death of her parents, she had sold the house and paid off their enormous debts. She moved into a tiny studio, barely making ends meet. Her job had become her friend, lover, *and* family.

Now that it was gone, she prayed a new prospect would present itself here in Ireland. If not, she would sell everything and return to San Diego.

"If it's a crumbled shed, I'll spit on your grave, Uncle Thomas."

A black jeep zoomed past her, spraying her with more water. "Damn!" she hissed, wiping the water out of her eyes for the umpteenth time that morning.

Just as her vision cleared, the same offensive vehicle backed up alongside her. The driver rolled down the window. "Would you be *wee* Ivy Kathleen O'Callaghan?"

"*Wee*?" she protested glaring at the man. "I'm Ivy O'Callaghan. Are you Mr. Casey, the attorney?"

The man shrugged. "Sorry, but that's what your Uncle Thomas would call you." He jumped out of the car. Giving her no time to utter another retort, he grabbed her two large suitcases, opened the back trunk, and shoved them inside as if they weighed nothing. Opening the side door, he waved her forward. "Best to get inside, the storm is heading this way."

"And what do you call this?" Quickly entering the vehicle, she pushed back her hood and snapped the seatbelt in place.

"A light summer shower," he answered, after getting in beside her. His eyes held mirth when he nodded to her. "I'm Peter Sullivan. I work for the local newspaper at Glennamore. Mr. Casey asked if I could fetch you from the airport. He'll meet you at the office. There are a few documents that need to be signed before he gives you the keys." Taking off his cap, he ran his hand through his hair. Placing the cap back on, he gave her a wink. "Ready?"

She tried not to roll her eyes at the man, but failed miserably. "Yes."

"How was your flight?"

Ivy glanced out the window, trying to get a sense of Ireland, but the rain blurred her vision. "It was long."

Peter chuckled. "Aye. Most definitely. However, there's always a movie or two to keep you entertained."

"I read during most of the flight."

He slammed his palm on the steering wheel and Ivy jumped. "This is why you'll be perfect to run the store." Peter pointed a finger at her. "I figured any relative of Thomas O'Callaghan would surely keep their nose buried in a book, so the bookstore is in capable hands."

The man was insufferable. His only redeemable quality was his good looks. He certainly did not make a good first impression when he called her *wee*. Yet despite the remnants of a headache from the long trip, Ivy grew curious. Turning her head toward him, she asked, "Why would you say that? For all you know, I could be a video gamer and hate reading."

Peter arched a brow. "The O'Callaghans of Glennamore have always enjoyed a good book." He suddenly swerved. "Sweet Jesus! Some people don't know how to drive."

Ivy closed her eyes, though briefly. *I'm going to die before I get to see this place. Angels and Fae protect us.*

"As I was saying, your people were known to have a great appreciation for the spoken word. Many were *seanachies*—storytellers, including your own uncle. May he rest in peace."

Puzzled, Ivy asked, "You seem to know more

about my relatives than I do. How did my Uncle Thomas know about me?"

Peter frowned. "Did you not know the man at all?"

She shook her head. "My parents never mentioned him—or any relatives. They said they were all dead."

Peter's gaze grew serious. "Your uncle adored you. Spoke all the time about his *wee* niece in America. In fact, the entire village knows all about you. Each time he received a new school picture, Thomas would show it off to all. He was quite proud of you."

Stunned, Ivy could barely register his words. "But why would my parents keep this from me?"

"Cannot explain. I'm as confused as you are now that I've heard your account. But I'm certain your lawyer, Mr. Casey can sort all this out for you."

Ivy rubbed her nose. "I suppose…yet, it's weird to find out that others knew all about me."

"Don't worry. You're liked here in the village. Remember, you're an O'Callaghan."

"Hmm…"

For the next hour, Peter filled her in on the daily life in Glennamore village. It was a quiet, seaside town that had survived for centuries, where most of the villagers could trace their lineage back to one of the Irish chieftains. Even Peter boasted of being a descendent. Ivy tried hard to retain all the facts and stories, but there were too many details. Between the tapping of rain on the windows, the movement of the car, and the man's chatter, she soon drifted off to sleep.

The car jolted to a stop, and Ivy rubbed her eyes vigorously. "We're already here?"

He chuckled. "Sorry it was only a short nap."

As Peter got out of the car, Ivy glanced around at

her surroundings. Smiling slowly, she opened the door and gazed at the scenic postcard picture village. Standing, she breathed in the crisp, clean air, grateful the rain had turned to a light mist. The wind whispered against her cheek as if in welcome.

Shops dotted each side of the street, their doors painted in different colors. People ambled along in slow movements, unlike the hurried folk she was accustomed to back home. The road sloped downward toward the hills, where sheep grazed peacefully, and Ivy was sorely tempted to run down and greet them. A sense of peace engulfed her and for a moment, she blamed it on the lack of sleep and jetlag. Quickly tossing the idea aside, she looked over her shoulder. Peter was leaning against the vehicle and smiling at her.

She arched a brow. "What?"

"You've already fallen under her spell." He gestured outward. "The true Ireland. The land speaks to you, *O'Callaghan*."

"The town *is*…charming." She shielded her eyes as a shaft of sunlight pierced through the gray clouds. "Where is my uncle's store?"

"Down around the bend in the road. You have quite a view of the hills, trees, and river from *your* home and store."

She frowned. "I keep forgetting it's all mine."

Peter nodded behind him. "Let's go get those papers signed, so you can see everything."

Smiling fully, she followed Peter to one of the largest buildings. Upon entering, the foyer was paneled in rich dark wood. On a table in the center was a huge bouquet of flowers. Passing by the arrangement, she inhaled their heady aroma. Making their way up the stairs, she marveled at the painted carvings on the wall. *Stunning!*

As if reading her mind, Peter stated, "Scenes from mythology."

"I recognize them," she uttered in a shocked tone. "This one is Bricriu's Feast." Walking to the next one, she pointed. "And this one is the birth of Cuchulainn—the son of the Celtic God Lugh. The details are amazing." Her gaze traveled along the rest of the wall. Dashing closer, she burst out, "Oh, my…Deirdre of the Sorrows. It's amazing how the artist captured her sadness."

"Aye. Not one of my favorites, though," remarked Peter.

"These should be in a museum. Are you not fearful of them being knocked down from the wall? Or stolen? Why are they here?"

Peter leaned near her. "They say this building was built on sacred ground owned by the druids and then later claimed by the monks. These are in honor of those men from long ago. No one would dare tempt fate by taking them."

Ivy gave the man a sidelong glance. "Then the artist wished to mock the monks for stealing the land?"

He rubbed his chin. "Don't think so. Legend states that the druids *became* the monks."

"Fascinating," she whispered. "How old is this building?"

"Many centuries."

"Well, bless my soul," shouted a booming voice at the top of the stairs. "If it isn't *wee* Ivy Kathleen!"

Ivy tried hard not to grimace and turned fully toward the man with a beaming smile. "You must be

Mr. Casey."

The portly man made his way to her on the landing. "At your service."

As she held out her hand to give the man a handshake, he surprised her by enveloping her in a hug. Taken aback by the overt affection, she patted him and took a step back. "Um…good to see you, too."

The man beamed. "You have the looks of an O'Callaghan. 'Tis a pity that Thomas never had a chance to see you."

Before Ivy had a chance to respond, the man steered her up the remaining flight of stairs and into a large oval office overlooking another portion of the hills. Bringing her to an oversized chair near a blazing fire, he then brought over a nearby table.

"I'm perfectly comfortable sitting at your desk, Mr. Casey," stated Ivy as she removed her coat.

He waved her off. "That's for legal business." Taking her coat, he placed it on a peg by the door. "You are family and Thomas had requested specific details of this transaction."

"But—"

"And please call me Sean." He chuckled warmly, tugging at his suit jacket. "You make me feel like an old man with Mr. Casey."

Peter snorted. "Well, you're not exactly young, now are you?"

Sean gave her a wink. "Ignore the young lad. He's always spouting nonsense."

Peter tipped his hat to her. "I shall fetch you within the hour to take you to the store and your home. Be wary of this old man. I hear he's an outrageous flirt."

"Thanks, Peter," she replied, trying hard not to

laugh.

As the door closed softly, Ivy settled back within the chair and watched Sean gather several sheets of parchment paper and a pen.

"Before we get to the details of your inheritance, Thomas had one request."

"Besides traveling an ocean and residing in the village?"

Sean set the papers down. "Yes." Sitting down next to her, his gaze grew somber. "Thomas adored you, Ivy Kathleen. From the moment he knew of your birth, he made preparations for you. His land has always remained with the O'Callaghans, and since he never married, you were his sole heir."

Ivy held up her hand. "I'm sorry, Mr. Ca...*Sean*, you have to understand that I never knew about my uncle. My parents told me all my relatives were dead. So all this news comes as a total shock." She rubbed a hand over her temple. "And I've only learned—through Peter—that the village has been keeping up with my life through pictures and reports sent to my uncle. What I would like to know is who sent them?"

The man folded his hands over his stomach. "Your mother," he stated quietly.

Her mouth gaped open in shock. Swallowing, she asked, "Why the secrets?"

"Because, my dear, your father wanted nothing to do with this place *or* Ireland. There was bad blood between the brothers—Thomas and Patrick."

Ivy leaned forward. "So Uncle Thomas is my father's brother?"

"Correct. Patrick was born here."

A weight of sadness leveled like a stone against

Ivy's chest. All these years and not one peep about a long lost relative in Ireland. Her father had mentioned on more than one occasion how he hated the island, even saying once that he hoped it would sink into the Atlantic. "What happened," she uttered softly.

A look of sorrow passed over the man's face. "I'm sorry to say that whatever it was, Thomas kept it locked within his own mind and heart. Never mentioned his brother's name again. Though, he spoke fondly of Sara."

Tears welled up within Ivy's eyes, and she did her best to keep them from spilling forth. Wiping her nose, she reached for her purse and pulled out some tissues. "Sorry," she mumbled, wiping at her nose.

The man patted her knee. "Och, my dear. My heart breaks to know how this news comes as a shock, but you have to understand that they—Thomas, Sara, and Patrick loved you fiercely. I wish I could fathom why your parents fled Ireland several years after your birth, or why your father and uncle never spoke to each other again."

Ivy wiped away her tears. "Yes, I know I was born here, but my parents never said why they left. They took their secrets to the grave with them and a part of me is now angry."

"What is done is in the past. You cannot change what happened. Move forward, Ivy Kathleen."

Tempering her irritation, Ivy nodded. "What was my uncle's request?"

Sean pulled out a pair of glasses from his front pocket. Placing them on, he handed Ivy the parchment sheets. "Before you sign, Thomas wanted to make it perfectly clear that if you should decide not to remain in

46

Ireland for one year's time, the entire property—bookstore and his home will be donated to the village. All claims from you would become null and void. Furthermore, you are not permitted to sell the property to anyone."

Ivy glanced at the man over the documents. "Seriously?"

Sean let out a sigh. "Your uncle was adamant about this request."

She glanced down at the papers, the lettering in a flowing script. "So I'm only the caretaker? Not the owner?"

"From the moment you sign your name, you will become the rightful owner. Furthermore, if you change your mind, the property will automatically revert to the people of Glennamore."

You have no choice, Ivy. You're almost penniless and have no home to speak of. You didn't renew your lease on the studio and moved what little you had into a storage facility. What do you have to lose by staying for one year?

"I didn't come all this way *not* to take up residence and make this work. As everyone keeps telling me...I'm an O'Callaghan."

Sean smacked his hand on his thigh. "You have true grit and the spunk of one, too!" Lifting the pen from the table, he handed it to her.

Taking the item, she tapped it against her mouth as she read the documents. *Nothing like signing your life away, right?* Ivy almost burst out laughing. It was all as Sean had stated and it only took her a few moments to read through the two pages. Quickly signing her name at the bottom, she let out a long sigh.

Sean took the papers and dropped them on his desk. Going to a large cabinet, he opened it and drew forth a bottle and two glasses. Making his way back to her, he placed the glasses down. "Now to fully seal the deal."

"Is this the way business is conducted in Ireland?" she asked dryly.

He winked at her. "Of course." Filling both glasses, Sean handed one to her.

Taking the offered glass, she sniffed the contents. "Whiskey?"

The man held his glass up. "The best single malt in Glennamore. May the leprechauns and fae strew happiness wherever you walk each day. And Irish angels smile on you all along your way."

Ivy bit the inside of her cheek to keep the laughter from bubbling forth. By all accounts, she thought the man was most likely a leprechaun himself.

Lifting her glass, she replied, *"Sláinte!"* Sipping the whiskey, Ivy embraced not only the fiery liquid, but also her new journey in Ireland and the hope of new possibilities.

Chapter Five

"Looking through a rose colored prism will open your world to epic possibilities."
~*Chronicles of the Fae*

"I'm gobsmacked!" Ivy stepped out of the car and stared at the brick bookstore. She glanced at Peter and seeing the man wince from her expression, Ivy shrugged. "Sorry, my dad used to use this slang term all the time."

"Don't apologize. I can tell you're impressed with The Celtic Knot Bookstore."

She turned her gaze back to the building. "Extremely. It's larger than I had expected. And what a perfect name. I love it!" Pulling forth the large key, she was giddy with anticipation of seeing what lay behind the double wooden doors.

"Ready?"

"Yes," she replied smiling fully.

"Lead on, Ivy Kathleen."

The gravel path led to four stairs. Quickly climbing them, her hand trembled as she placed the key in the lock. Turning it once, it gave with a loud click. Pushing the door open, the smell of books assaulted her senses. She inhaled deeply. "You can't get this smell from reading a book on a tablet."

Walking fully inside the bookstore, her gaze

traveled along the many shelves, filled in perfect order with books. A massive polished wooden counter stood to the left. One lone cash register rested regally on the desk. Ivy feared the item would be out-dated, but she pushed aside any fears and absorbed her surroundings. As she made her way slowly over the hardwood floors, certain ones creaked in welcome, and she smiled. There were sections on gardening, travel, fiction, science, biographies, cooking, arts, history, and her favorite, mythology.

Standing on tiptoe, she could make out another room. Etched above the entrance was the saying, *For those that long to return to Neverland.* "The children's area?"

"Aye," replied Peter. "Wait until you see it, too."

"Look at all the overstuffed chairs, as well. It's almost like a library." Touching the spine of one of the books, she asked, "I never thought to mention, but did my uncle do well here? Make a profit? If I was someone, I believe I'd want to curl—" She dashed to the end of the room.

"Is something wrong?" Peter rushed to her side.

She pointed. "There's a fireplace in here!"

The man frowned and rubbed his chin. "Aye. Helps to keep the place warm, since the heating is ancient in this place."

Ivy couldn't contain her excitement. "But it's fabulous! I love it!"

"It's good to hear," he responded, smiling. "And to answer your earlier question, your uncle had a thriving business. He had visitors from the other villages—many asking for special orders. Would you like to see the rest of the store?"

She rubbed her hands in glee. "Lead the way!"

Peter took over the tour, quickly showing her Thomas's office and storage area. There was an upstairs loft, where authors would come and do signings and readings. Her excitement overtook the lack of sleep and little food she'd had as she went from place to place inside the store, brushing her hand over books she longed to peruse later.

"It's more than what I could have hoped for, Peter." She now rested against the front counter, surveying her new place. "I can hardly wait to see the cottage. It must be a wonder, too."

Peter scratched behind his ear. "I believe your uncle gave no care for the place, since he spent most of his time here."

Ivy's shoulders sagged. "I knew it was too good to be true. Show me the place."

He led her out the front and circled down a path around the building. Trees bordered the lane and when they emerged forth, Ivy halted.

"You call this a cottage?" She scanned the house, noting two large upper and lower windows.

"We do here. The upstairs was added in the late fifteenth century and became an inn for a brief time in the sixteenth and seventeenth century."

She grimaced. "Is it habitable?"

Peter glanced over his shoulder at her. "It's not as a bad as it looks."

She pointed to the roof. "It's drooping on one side. And several window panes are broken." Yet, she couldn't help but admire the roses blooming in front of the cottage. Ivy wandered slowly to the front of the place and pulled out another large key. "Needs some paint, too," she muttered.

"It only requires your loving touch. In addition, there's a stable in the back. I don't know if you fancy riding, but your uncle loved horses. He always wanted to have a few, but never had the time to make a purchase."

"How old is this place, Peter?"

"Thomas would boast that it was at least six hundred years old. Of course, there have been upgrades over the centuries."

Ivy unlocked the door and hesitantly pushed it open. Stepping inside, she glanced around the place. Though the outside needed some repairs, the inside was surprisingly clean. Stairs leading to the second floor were on the left, but it was the library that drew her attention. Volumes of books with spines of warm russet and brown lined many of the shelves. Glancing to her right she spied a sitting room. Two large chairs flanked the fireplace, along with a small sofa in front. The bay window seat captured her attention. Ivy could see herself curled up with a good book and cup of tea.

Making her way down the hall, she peered inside the large kitchen, her eyes wide with delight.

"Wow! It's wonderful. I love the cream-colored walls. And they kept the hearth open. I can only imagine the meals being prepared centuries ago. Looks like my uncle used it as a drying rack for herbs. Oh, look! There's an Aga stove!"

Peter edged past her, entering the kitchen. He coughed into his hand as he stood in front of the stove. "There's a problem."

Ivy groaned, her joy slipping away. "I'm afraid to ask."

He held his hands up. "Your uncle was meaning to have one of the local handymen stop by. The Aga stopped working many months ago. Therefore, he started to take his meals at the bookstore. It was his first home."

Stepping into the kitchen, Ivy dumped her purse on the wooden table and pulled out a notepad and pen. "First on my list: fix the Aga. Second, find someone to thatch the roof." She glanced up at Peter. "Any other problems before we finish the tour?"

"None other...that I know of."

"Could you give me some acceptable recommendations?"

He nodded. "Roof or Aga first?"

"Both please."

"Will do. I'll place those calls after I bring in your luggage."

Moving out of the kitchen, Ivy left Peter, and made her way upstairs to the bedrooms. Two rooms appeared as if they were being used for storage, but the third was obviously her uncle's room. A large chest of drawers set against one wall and the bed, though small, was inviting. Another bay window looked out toward the hills where the river flowed gracefully southward. A few sheep were grazing, and Ivy could see the remains of a ruined castle. Smiling, she left the bedroom and entered the only bathroom, noting there was no shower. "Guess I'll have to learn to wash my hair like the people here. Sitting in the tub." She chuckled softly.

Checking inside the hall closet, she took note that her uncle cared less about organizing linens, towels, and such. It was a mess and sorely needed tending to, along with the repairs.

When she stepped back into the sitting room downstairs, Peter was outside talking on his cell. Walking over to the hearth, she peered into eyes she knew so well sitting on the mantel. It was a picture of her and her mother. She recalled the vacation memory fondly and tears welled within her eyes. "What happened?" Her question more a plea, and Ivy closed her eyes wishing someone would reach out from beyond the grave to answer her.

"Are you all right?" Peter asked softly.

Rubbing her eyes, Ivy nodded. She tapped the picture frame. "Strange. All these years I never knew the man existed. How lonely for him."

Peter stepped near her. "If he was, your uncle never mentioned a word. I have to return to the newspaper, but Norm will try to be here within the hour to check out the Aga. I have a few calls into Tim Stevens, the local thatcher. I'm positive he can re-ridge the damaged area. If he's not available, I'm sure he can recommend someone. I'll check back with Sean, too."

"Thanks Peter. I would have called them myself, but I really appreciate it."

"A pleasure, Ivy Kathleen, though why don't you give me your number." He pulled out his cell and waited.

She arched a brow. Reaching for his cell, she typed in her phone number and handed it back to the man.

Smiling, his fingers flew over the keypad, and Ivy heard her phone ping with an incoming text. "Now you have mine. I'll ring you later to see if all went well with Norm."

It's only business, Peter Sullivan and nothing more. "Thanks, again."

Watching him sprint down the path, she closed the door and leaned against the wood for support. Sighing deeply, she closed her eyes. Sleep beckoned like a siren, but her stomach protested loudly. Opening her weary eyes, she pushed away from the door and made her way into the kitchen. Flinging open cabinets, she found cans of sardines and crackers in one, another held canisters of tea and sugar. Dumping the sardines in the trash, she sniffed at the crackers. "Most likely stale." Tossing those into the trash as well, she opened the small fridge. Nothing.

She rubbed at her gnawing stomach and went to fill the kettle for tea. Leaning against the counter, she gazed outward at the bucolic scenery. *What was this feud with your brother, Uncle Thomas? How sad. I really want to know what happened. I wish I had known you.* So lost in her thoughts, she nearly jumped out of her skin when she heard the soft feminine voice behind her.

"Hello, Ivy Kathleen?"

"Good grief. I thought I was hearing ghosts of the past," Ivy blurted out.

The woman laughed, the sound filling the kitchen. "I'm sorry. I should have knocked harder. I didn't think to wait longer for you to answer. I've brought you a casserole from the pub. Thought you could do with a hearty meal."

Ivy smiled at the woman. The delicious aroma drifted past her. "Gosh, it smells heavenly."

Moving to the counter, the woman placed it on the wooden board. "Good to hear, since there's nothing to eat in this place." She thrust out her hand. "I'm Erin O'Reilly. I run The Seven Swans Pub along with my brother, Mac."

Grasping her hand, Ivy nodded. "Your timing is perfect. I'm starving. I just put water on for some tea. Do you want a cup?"

"Tell you what. Why don't I prepare the tea and you help yourself to the enchiladas."

Before Ivy could utter a protest, Erin moved past her, taking out several cups, a plate, and silverware. Handing them to her, she watched the woman prepare some tea.

"Lovely teapot," remarked Ivy as she scooped out a large portion of the food. "I love the shamrocks."

Erin rubbed her fingers over the china pot. "I believe Thomas mentioned that it belonged to his mother—your grandmother."

"A pity I never knew them," she stated. Taking her plate to the small table, Ivy went and retrieved the cups and sugar. She slumped down on the chair, shaking her head.

"I agree," commented Erin, bringing the pot of tea with her. Sitting down across from Ivy, she poured some tea into their cups. "He refused to talk about the issue with anyone." She tapped her finger to her chest. "Kept it locked away. Though whenever a package arrived from America, he would beam with pride and shared all with the village."

"Was it *always* about me?"

Erin took a sip of her tea. "Always. Not a word about your parents. Only you."

Rubbing her temples to ward off an impending headache, she tossed aside the questions that tumbled through her mind.

"Eat," urged Erin. "I'm sure you'll unlock the

secret."

Ivy glanced down at her plate. "Looks delicious. Never expected to eat enchiladas on my first night in Ireland."

"We try and mix up the menu at least once a week with something *not* Irish."

Taking a bite, Ivy closed her eyes and savored the many flavors. "Mmm…"

The woman chuckled. "I can assume you like the dish?"

Opening her eyes, she smiled. "It's scrumptious." Digging in fully, she continued to eat the food, while Erin chatted away.

"Now when you get settled in, you can pop in at the pub. The others would love to meet you. We've grown to love the stories about Ivy Kathleen."

Ivy arched a brow. "You do realize how strange this all seems to me? Especially, how you all keep calling me Ivy *Kathleen*. Ivy is just fine."

She waved her hand outward. "Thomas called you that fondly, so it's one name that has stuck." Placing her teacup down, Erin added, "Your uncle used to call me Erin Marie. It was a habit of his to call everyone by both their names. And if he knew your confirmation name, he would call you by all three." She leaned in close and whispered, "I kept mine a secret from the fox."

"What was it?" asked Ivy taking another bite of her food.

Erin sat up straight. "My lips are sealed."

Ivy almost choked on her food. "Seriously?"

"Humph! The spirits still have ears, and Thomas might be lurking. I don't need to hear him calling out my entire name in the middle of the wee hours."

Clamping a hand over her mouth, Ivy tried to contain the fits of laughter. When she managed to get herself under control, she took a swallow of tea. "I like you, Erin Marie."

"Likewise, Ivy Kathleen."

Ivy waved her fork over the casserole. "Don't you want something to eat? There's plenty."

Standing, the woman shook her head. "No. It's all for you." Walking over to the chalkboard hanging on the wall, she picked up a piece of chalk. "Here's the number to the pub, along with my cell. We're across the street from the bookstore. Difficult not to see the sign. I can take you to the market for supplies."

"Is it far? I can walk or did my uncle have a car?"

"It's located at the other end of the village. Thomas has a car, but I'm afraid to tell you that it hasn't worked for some time. He would walk to the market or have Mac drive him there, depending on what he needed." Erin nodded to the fridge. "As you can see, he barely had any food. I cleaned out what little he did have in the house after his passing."

Ivy stood slowly. Not once did she ask how the man died. Or where he was buried. "What happened to him?"

A frown skittered across the woman's face. "I'm sorry. I thought you were told. He was run over by a car one early evening after he left the pub. Clearly a hit and run, since the bastard never stopped to check on him."

Ivy placed a hand over her heart. "How horrible. Didn't anyone see it happen?"

"Not a soul."

Though the food and tea had warmed her spirit, Ivy

felt a chill creep up her spine. Lights danced before her eyes, and her vision became clouded. There was no stopping what would happen next, and she prayed she could remain focused and standing.

The room filled with the screeching of tires, and she watched in horror as her uncle crossed the road, softly whistling a tune. Ivy stood in the road, unable to stop the turn of events she was witnessing. The sunlight was fading quickly in the west as the car barreled down the road, her uncle unaware. The scream lodged in her throat when the car impacted her uncle, tossing him like a rag doll high into the air. He landed with a sickening thud on the road, the car careening onward.

The image vanished as suddenly as it appeared, and Ivy found herself on the floor, trying to take in deep calming breaths.

"Ivy, Ivy Kathleen...can you hear me?" Erin's soothing voice cut through the fog within her mind.

"All...ri...right," she stuttered.

"Did you have a vision?" asked Erin, wiping away a strand of her hair from her brow.

Blinking several times, she looked at the woman in shock. "You know?"

"Aye. It runs in the family. Your uncle had them."

Ivy slumped back against the cabinet doors. "What land have I fallen into?"

Erin extended her arms wide. "Why a land filled with faeries, leprechauns, and Irish people with the gift of sight."

Ivy rolled her eyes. "A strange land...this Ireland."

Both women burst out in hysterical laughter.

Chapter Six

*"To weave a broken thread, you must first seek out
the untruth."*

~*Chronicles of the Fae*

Seneca's voice rang clear in the hall. "Your deeds
are many, Conn MacRoich—legendary. However, you
have bent too many laws for a purpose we see as
human, not Fae. We will pass judgment on this one."

Grumblings from other council members echoed
within the room. Seneca held up her hand to silence the
outburst.

She turned her gaze to Conn. "You have witnessed
the break in the veil?"

Conn stood before the Fae council, gazing at each
member. "I have noted the event."

Closing her eyes, she lifted her staff high. "The
Mother has spoken." Upon opening them, she
continued. "She has given you a quest. The descendants
from this specific branch of the O'Callaghan have
drifted from their true course in history. There were
many great healers—some blessed with the gift of
sight. However, they chose to hide in fear and distrust.
There was none to guide them. When you saved the
wrong woman, you—Conn altered their history."

He arched a brow. "You want me to return and
save the lass hiding among the trees? Done."

Seneca's smile sent a chill down Conn's spine. "If it was so simple, anyone could undo what you have done." She slowly shook her head. "No, you must thread a new fate into the O'Callaghan of the *present*. She—Ivy Kathleen is the last of her family. Her parents wove distrust and fear into her at a young age. You must show her the light of her gift."

How difficult could it be, he mused. "I will show her the path of the Fae," he announced.

"I am not finished," protested Seneca. "Once you are taken from this realm, you will be on your own. No powers will you be granted, Conn MacRoich, except those within your bloodline. You are not permitted to seek out other Fenian Warriors for assistance. The only knowledge you have is your own and of the humans."

His anger simmered below the surface. "And how am I supposed to bring light—transform the mind of a human? What you ask of me—"

"Beneath you?" she interrupted.

He shifted his stance. "You did not let me finish. Must I become human to guide her? Why not grant me my full powers—those of a Fenian, so that she may travel a new path?"

"Because this journey is not only for the O'Callaghan woman, but for you, as well."

"For what purpose?"

Seneca sighed. "Only you can find the answer, Conn."

"And if I fail?"

The room became eerily quiet and several of the Fae members lowered their gaze. "Then death will come to you both," stated Seneca softly.

Conn feared if he spoke, his words would bellow

throughout the kingdom. *Fools, all of them!* Why didn't they let him slip back through the Veil of Ages and undo the injustice? No, they treated him like an apprentice.

Did not the Brotherhood have their own rules? A code of conduct? Temper the burning rage, brother. Abela's voice whispered gently within his mind.

Conn exhaled. "How long do I have?"

"Until Samhain—when the doors to both realms are open. If your quest is not completed—"

"Yes, as you have stated. I am aware of the dire consequences." He bowed.

Turning around, Conn waited until the massive doors were opened. There to greet him was Ronan and one other—Taran, another Fenian Warrior and friend.

Conn smiled at both of them. "I now have *two* to escort me?"

Taran stepped forward. "Did you really think I would let any guard usher you out of the Fae realm?" He leaned near Conn. "Let us make our way from the prying eyes of the council members."

As they moved along the corridor, Conn paused. "It is good to see you, Taran."

The Fenian Warrior clamped a hand on Conn's shoulder. "Did you believe that any in the Brotherhood would abandon you? We stand as one—always. Besides, we all harbor bitter feelings upon learning that the Fae council has decided to make you the example for all to see."

Conn narrowed his eyes. "Explain."

"Let us make our way out of the castle. We can continue this conversation at the southern gate."

The moment they stepped through the crystal gates

of the palace, Ronan waved his hand and all three vanished. Appearing at the trees near the southern gate, they walked forward. At the base of a rowan tree, Conn noticed his clothing and shoes were for the human realm.

Folding his arms over his chest, Conn waited for Taran to give his account.

"You should have seen this coming, my friend," stated Taran.

Ronan chuckled. "He does not understand."

Taran rolled his eyes. "Seriously?" He gazed at Ronan and then back to him.

"Spit it out," demanded Conn.

"You're the prince. What better way for them to show the other warriors that even the most elite are not protected."

"Enough!" He turned his back on the warriors. "When I accepted the binding rings around my arms and the Brotherhood emblazed my chest and back with the ancient tattoos, I no longer became royalty. I gave up all claims." Conn stormed over to the entrance between his homeland and the earthly realm. "There is not one among us that hasn't tampered in one way or another with the threads of fate on the loom of humans."

Stripping free of his Fae clothing, he heard their gasp when they witnessed his back no longer was marked with the sacred tattoos. They had been removed the moment he was sent to his prison. Now, only his arms reflected the ancient symbols of his Fae lineage. Those could never be taken from him. Slipping into his human clothing and shoes, he glanced over his shoulder and looked at his friends. "As you can see, I no longer bear the markings of the Brotherhood."

"Yet, you will always be the prince. It's in your blood," argued Taran.

Ronan scratched behind his ear. "Aye, I cannae deny your statements, Conn. I am not judging ye, although, it was not I who stayed away from the Fae. Moreover, the council placed ye on a higher standard than the rest of us. Ye may not like the words I speak, but 'tis truth."

"What was the outcome of the council?" asked Taran.

Conn snorted. "I must guide the descendant of the one I did not save. She has the gift of sight, but hides in the shadows."

"And how do you propose helping this human without your powers? Without being able to manipulate time?" Taran demanded.

"Unsure." He gestured outward. "I venture forth into this world with only the knowledge I possess and my Fae blood." Glancing at the warriors, he added, "And I am to have *no* contact with anyone from the Brotherhood."

"A true quest, indeed," uttered Ronan softly.

Taran spread his hands wide. "You were always on a quest from the moment you were initiated as a warrior. Now, a greater one is given to you. Go forth— conquer, save, learn, and then return to us once more."

Conn fisted his hands on his hips and gazed outward. The veil shimmered, but for the first time in many centuries, he had no desire to enter the human side. "I have no idea where this woman dwells," he protested.

"Look to the village of Glennamore. 'Tis our

parting gift to ye," replied Ronan.

The tension in his shoulders eased. He knew the village well, since it was where he made a wrong choice over a thousand years ago. Turning fully toward his friends, Conn placed a fist over his heart. "Honor, wisdom, and strength to you both."

In a flash of dazzling lights, he passed through the realm to the land above into the human world.

****

The late August heat seared like a burning knife through his head and several times, Conn had to find relief under a tree. The blistering sun was merciless, and he longed for a cool breeze or rain shower to squelch the agonizing pain. The moment he had stepped through the veil from his home to the Hill of Tara, he had experienced a wave of dizziness. Never before had the heat, cold, rain, or snow bothered him. Was this his punishment, too? Or a side effect when they stripped him of all powers? Regardless, he prayed in time his energy would return.

His mouth was parched, and he longed for a cool stream to slake the heat from his body and mind. He glanced up at the sky. "Did you make me human?" If he weren't so exhausted from walking, he would have laughed at the absurdity.

Leaning his head against the cool bark of the tree, he concluded he had walked for three hours based on the direction of the sun. He tried to hitch a ride, but the small country road was devoid of any drivers.

If only he could make it to his apartment in Dublin. There he would be able to get transportation to this village of Glennamore. But he couldn't fathom the length or the correct road to lead him there.

He looked down at his hands. "I am Fae, *not* human."

A leaf fluttered down and brushed against his cheek. He plucked it up and twirled it between his fingers. The colors, though muted, glimmered in the late afternoon light. Releasing his hold, he let it glide to the ground, where it transformed immediately into a vivid shade of green.

Hope surged forth within him. "Could it be possible? My body may lack my warrior powers, but my blood is of the ancients," he growled. "You cannot take what is already mine."

Closing his eyes, he placed both hands upon the ground. "Hear my plea those within the animal kingdom. Seek me out, for I require your aid. I am lost and need your guidance and transportation."

The energy surged forth—burned through his veins and out his fingers.

When he opened his eyes, his vision became clouded. Conn stood slowly on shaky limbs as he used the tree for support. Wiping a hand across his brow, he realized the simple attempt to communicate magically had left him weak. Nevertheless, he knew the message was sent when the cry of a hawk pierced the silence of the hot afternoon.

Smiling, he moved away from the tree and followed her movement. She circled high on the wind, but her meaning was clear. Conn followed the direction of the bird, and with each step, renewed strength filled his being. Shading his eyes from the glare of the sun, his smile grew broader. A horse stood grazing in the field off the side of the road.

Moving slowly toward the animal, he knelt on one

knee. Using the language of his homeland, he spoke softly. A light breeze blew the hair from the nape of his neck, and he waited. The horse shook his head—clearly a sign that the beast did not intend to leave his lush meal.

Conn rubbed a hand over his chin. "Then I shall wait." Sitting on the ground, he placed his hands on his bent knees.

The horse stomped his front hoof in obvious agitation.

"I have no plans on claiming you. I merely require you to take me near Dublin. Would you deny this Fae warrior?"

This time the horse turned its back on Conn.

He smiled, since the animal reminded him of one he owned many centuries ago. A fierce beast, his Brutus. Conn didn't know which was worse—his foul temper or the stubborn attitude. The horse gave no regard to his position in this world, and many a time they both butted heads. Conn smiled at the forgotten memory. "Should I tell you a wee story about one of the greatest warhorses that lived?"

The animal glanced over his shoulder.

"Curious? Well, the majestic animal stayed by my side during many battles, especially the one at Culloden in Scotland. He charged forth with no fear—a fine leader for the other horses. Though a stubborn brute, he was my friend until he took his last breath in my arms."

Conn watched as the horse turned around and trotted slowly toward him. He remained sitting on the ground and lifted his hand up. "His name was Brutus, and I am called, Conn MacRoich, Fenian Warrior for the Fae. Greetings."

The animal nudged his hand in welcome.

Standing, he patted the animal. "I thank you for your service."

Mounting the horse, he surveyed the area. "Take me as close as you reckon to the southern part of the city."

When the horse refused to budge, Conn rolled his eyes. "*Please?*"

Instantly, the stubborn beast took off, racing across the meadow and heading toward the hills. Conn gripped the animal firmly, issuing a curse as the scenery blurred. He focused ahead and noticed they were heading east. He only prayed the animal was not leading him astray. *Brutus would be proud of you, my new friend. His stubbornness was his strength, as is yours.*

As the setting sun dipped low behind them, Conn marveled at the animal's endurance. Never once did it lessen its stride—swift and steady the horse galloped through the countryside. When the first sign emerged on the road in the far distance, he urged the beast onward. Soon, Conn could make out the wording and relief coursed through him. Dublin was only eight kilometers away.

They galloped past the sign and continued at a steady pace until lights from the city glimmered in front of them. The animal eased in his pace and took Conn over a hill and down past another road. When he deemed they could go no farther, Conn gave the horse a gentle pat. The main road lay ahead of them and it was one he knew well.

The horse's steps slowed, and he wandered over to a tree a few feet away from the road. Conn dismounted and surveyed his surroundings. Since he knew the area, he surmised he had at least an hour to make it to his apartment, which was located on the outer edge of the city.

Turning around, he stroked the horse's mane. "I thank you for your service today, mighty beast. May the Fae guide you back to your home."

The horse nudged his shoulder and gave a low snort.

"Yes, I would be honored to call on you again, if I should need your service. Be well, my friend."

Chuckling softly, Conn gave the animal one final pat before heading toward the city. The last rays of sunlight vanished into the night as he traveled on the road. The first star winked down at him, and he nodded in reverence and continued on his journey. His body returned to a normal rhythm. Though his Fenian powers were gone, the blood of the Fae poured through his veins—rejuvenating him.

An hour later, Conn took two steps up the brick stairs to his apartment. Lifting the potted container of herbs, he drew forth the key embedded within the soil. Sealed by magic decades ago, the herbs maintained their health—never requiring water or trimming. A perfect place to keep his key hidden.

Stepping into his home, he closed the door gently and leaned against the wood. Sighing deeply, he pinched the bridge of his nose. The days—*damn*, the months had taken a toll on him mentally. He was now a man caught between both worlds and for the first time, Conn felt lost.

"You are a Fenian Warrior for the Fae," he muttered to the empty room.

Quickly shoving aside his doubts and weariness from his trek across the country, he went into his kitchen and pulled out a beer from the fridge. Popping the top with one finger, he guzzled deeply, savoring the Irish liquid. Wiping the back of his mouth with his hand, he wandered into the den.

Sinking into his chair behind his desk, he glanced around the room. Pictures of ancient maps, some of battles, towns, and castles, covered most of the walls. A few of them were quite valuable, but to the untrained eye, just simple drawings. His handiwork, which began centuries ago, now came back to haunt him. He had spent many hours jotting down precise notes and etchings, transferring his work onto parchment and then later within frames. There was no thought process to his work, only a desire to become one with the memory of the time period.

He sipped more of his beer and his focus settled on one particular etching. A map of Waterford in the tenth century. Narrowing his eyes, he slammed his beer on the oak desk. It was the beginning of his time spent with Dervla.

Standing he walked over to the map. Tracing a path with his finger on the glass along the roads, he snarled. "Were you a pawn in your father's game, Dervla? Or were you the mastermind? They say you married outside of your clan. Why?"

Questions without answers, and Conn required more information.

Instantly, he smiled. Walking back to his desk, he moved the chair aside. Turning around, his fingers glided under the painting of his friend, Cuchulainn and his hounds, until he found the small latch. With one touch, the painting opened to reveal a safe on the wall. His fingers deftly turned the combination lock and soon it opened. Pulling forth his passport and cash, he sealed everything.

Reaching for the large satchel he kept on the nearby couch, he stuffed the items inside and proceeded to go into his bedroom. Dumping the bag onto his bed, he rubbed a hand over his face. He would pack light, since there was only one place he could seek out more information. As soon as he acquired what he needed, Conn would return to Ireland.

His laugh turned bitter. "You may have forbidden me to have contact with the Brotherhood, but you didn't say anything about dealing with a Dragon Knight and a Bard for the Fae."

Pulling out his cell phone, Conn proceeded to make arrangements for his trip to Scotland—more specifically, Aonach Castle.

Chapter Seven

"Heed the wisdom of a child, especially those who have witnessed the ancients."

~Chronicles of the Fae

The brisk, Highland air stung Conn's face as he maneuvered his motorcycle through the hills near Aonach Castle, but he gave no care. The Great Glen was filled with a majestic beauty of both—past and present centuries. He had seen this land in peaceful and turbulent times. The latter he had dealt with only last autumn when he and the Brotherhood had helped the Dragon Knights defeat the evil druid Lachlan, preventing him from bringing forth a monster that would have destroyed both realms.

Conn was now returning to a place he once called home.

Making his way around a bend in the road, he slowed his vehicle and pulled over to the side. There among the trees, Conn could partially see the standing stones. The very spot where evil had been vanquished. He closed his eyes and reached out with his Fae senses. Smiling, he opened them. The place had been blessed, most likely by Margaret—*Meggie* MacFhearguis. She was the sister to the Dragon Knights and now married to Adam MacFhearguis.

Starting his bike, he took off toward the castle. A

renewed sense of purpose filled him. Onward he traveled—passing familiar landmarks. No signs were posted for Aonach. Adam and Meggie deemed it a place where outsiders were not welcomed, especially to a home where magic dwelt within. Their original plans included a bed and breakfast with horseback riding through the scenic area as part of the package. However, after much discussion they decided to open the castle to the many cousins of the MacKay and MacFhearguis clans, disregarding their original idea.

Turning his bike from the main road, Conn took the narrow path leading upward toward the castle. Twisting and turning along the road, he ducked under heavy pine branches, never slowing his speed. The engine noise frightened several deer along the outside path, and they dashed away. Soon the area cleared, and the road leading to the castle opened before him.

Riding slowly through the gates, he braked suddenly at the scene in front of him. Jamie MacFhearguis stood in a cart—Meggie and Adam's son. He held a wooden sword high as his father deflected his blows with his own sword.

Turning off the engine, Conn's mouth gaped open in shock at the lad. In ten months, he had grown more, making him appear older than his mere three human years. He frowned as a chill swept over him. The Order of the Dragon Knights was stronger—both physically and magically. It would not be needed for another thousand years when the Dark One would once again try and enter the human realm. Or would it happen sooner this time?

Getting off the motorcycle, Conn rubbed a gloved hand over his chin and shoved the uneasiness aside. He was not a seer. Furthermore, he was on a quest of another matter. Removing his gloves and helmet, he smiled at the scene before him. Putting the items on the back of his bike, he shouted, "Should not the lad be fighting in the lists?"

"Conn," yelled Jamie, leaping off the cart and dropping his sword. Running over to him, he jumped into Conn's outstretched arms.

Conn laughed. "You have grown, Jamie. Or is it James?"

The lad snickered. "Only my mama calls me James and that's when she's mad." He pointed to the motorcycle. "Cool bike."

Placing the boy on the ground, he stated, "Bought it this morning in Inverness."

Adam approached slowly. "'Tis strange to see ye traveling thus."

Shrugging, Conn crossed his arms over his chest. "Since I am without powers, I had to do as any human would have done. Besides, I'm prone to keeping a motorcycle or two, especially in Ireland." Brushing a hand over the sleek metal, he added, "Love the speed you can get from these vehicles, especially away from the cities."

"Ye are well, then?" asked Adam.

Conn saw the uncertainty in the man's eyes. "For now. And you? If I recall, my last memories were of your death."

Adam smiled broadly, bringing Jamie to his side. "Aye. I am well." He held his arm outward and Conn embraced the forearm in an ancient warrior tradition.

"Conn MacRoich! Is it truly ye? Since when do ye use the front entrance? Ye usually appear without notice," shouted Meggie, ambling along as she clutched her abdomen.

His heart lurched at the sight of her coming toward him. He would be indebted to Margaret MacFhearguis for the rest of his life. Embracing the pregnant woman, he held her firmly.

"'Tis good to see ye, Conn," she uttered softly. "And alive."

Conn swallowed. "I owe my life to you."

She gazed up at him. "It was the least I could do. Without ye, Rory, and Liam, we would not have been able to defeat Lachlan. Ye risked your lives for us." Standing on tiptoes, she kissed his cheek. "Thank ye. I never got to say those simple words."

Emotions swirled within Conn. Releasing Meggie he took a step back. "You and the Dragon Knights will always have my loyalty, strength, and support."

She frowned. "Why are ye here, Conn?"

Adam came forward and placed an arm around his wife. "We thought to never see ye again. If ye have nae powers, then what do ye want from us?"

"Do ye wish to work for us?" gasped Meggie, her eyes wide.

"I may have pledged an oath to you, but I would surely never work as a hired hand," he replied dryly. "I am here to see Archie regarding historical information."

"Ye seek answers to help on your quest," stated Jamie as he retrieved his wooden sword.

Conn rubbed the back of his neck. "You are a wise one, Sir James, and correct."

The boy snorted. "*Laird* MacFhearguis to ye."

"Enough," protested Meggie, trying her best not to laugh at her son. "Let's move inside to the Great Hall, where I'm sure Conn can give his full account."

"Do ye think ye could take me for a ride on your black beast?" asked Jamie.

Conn gazed into the amber eyes of the wee Dragon Knight. "Have you mastered riding your horse?"

Jamie lifted his chin. "I am learning. Da takes me out each morn after my chores."

"When you can master the first jump, I will take you on my bike."

The boy's eyes turned to glowing amber in a second. His inner dragon came to life before Conn's eyes.

Adam chuckled. "Jamie has mastered several jumps on his own."

"Scared me so, I almost had the babe right there," proclaimed Meggie, brushing a lock of hair away from her son's face.

Conn looked at the lad. "Truth?"

Jamie's smile spoke volumes—a mix of the ancient and the child.

"Then after the evening meal, I shall take you down to the loch."

"Yippee!" he squealed in delight, thrusting his sword upward and running toward the castle.

Conn kicked up the kickstand on his bike and pushed it forward. He watched as the lad disappeared inside, shouting a war cry in Latin.

Glancing around, he noticed several new improvements. The horses' stalls had been enlarged, as well as the smithy area. Curious, he asked, "Have you hired a blacksmith?"

Adam glanced sideways at him. "Nae. I find solace in the forge." He pointed to it. "Ye can put your beast over near the place."

Conn arched a brow. "Having problems adjusting in this century?"

Shrugging, Adam replied, "Nae, only wished to bring my knowledge to this time period."

"It helps to soothe and connect him with the past," interjected Meggie over her shoulder.

Chuckling softly, Adam nodded. "Ye ken I like to make my own swords and shoes for the horses."

"I still have difficulty getting him into any car," she added.

"They are naught but loud, smelly beasts. I prefer Ciar over any of those," he argued gruffly.

Meggie laughed. "Have ye smelled Ciar lately? The horse needs a bath in the loch."

Adam sprinted forward and swept Meggie into his arms.

"By the hounds, put me down! I weigh a ton with the extra weight from the babe." She smacked playfully at his chest.

"I deem I should take ye for a swim in the loch, *wife*." He nuzzled her neck. "And ye will never be too heavy for me to lift." Adam silenced any further outbursts with a kiss.

Conn quickly glanced away and went to park his bike outside the smithy. Making his way to the entrance of the castle, his steps stilled and he turned around. For a moment, he envied the tender scene of husband and wife. *What would it be like to have another in his life?* The thought stunned him, and he clenched his hands. *You are a Fenian Warrior, not some sappy human.*

Quickly turning his back on the couple, he stormed into the Great Hall. Glancing around, the faces of the

MacKay Dragon Knights stared back at him from their places on the wall. Though they were long dead, these great warriors would always be alive within his heart. Clasping his hands behind his back, Conn strolled down the length of the wall and around the other side.

When he stood in front of the tapestry of Duncan MacKay, he nodded. "Though you and your brothers were angry at me for many years, I'm happy to have sent your wife, Brigid to you. Peace and long life in the land of *Tir na Og*, Duncan."

"You made a wise decision on the day you sent Brigid to meet her destiny," uttered the male voice behind him.

Conn turned and smiled at his friend. "Do you never age, Archie McKibben?"

"Have you not seen the gray at my temples? Being the Bard for the Fae can be trying." The man laughed and went to embrace Conn.

"I can empathize," agreed Conn.

Archie stood back and gazed at him in confusion. "I have heard the account of the Fae council, but why are you here? I thought you were to stay—"

"My instructions were there would be no contact with the Brotherhood. Nothing was mentioned about other Fae, or Dragon Knights," interrupted Conn.

Archie pointed a finger at him. "Tread carefully, my friend."

"Are ye ready to explain?" asked Adam, strolling in with Meggie on his arm.

Meggie gave her husband a kiss. "I'll go see to some food and drinks."

"I'll be along shortly to help ye. And we have wine already on the table."

"Where are your other MacKay relatives?" asked Conn. "Surely you're not doing all the work so close to your birthing?"

Meggie waved him off. "Ye men—regardless if ye are human or Fae, ye seem to believe I'm a fragile piece of porcelain simply because I'm carrying a babe. Lena left for Inverness for a few days and the others—Bruce, Lucas, and Scott are purchasing some more horses in Glasgow."

Conn walked over to Meggie and lifted her hand. Placing a kiss along the knuckles, he said, "I would never insult the sister and wife of a Dragon Knight."

She winked at him. "I never knew ye could be so charming, *Fae*."

He released her hand and smiled. Turning back around, he went to the table by the large hearth. Adam poured some wine into a mug and handed it to him. Sitting down, Conn swirled the liquid and waited as Archie took his seat. He sipped the wine, savoring the fruitiness on his tongue.

"Are you making your own?" he asked over the rim of his cup.

Adam nodded. "Another task I am working on."

"You've been busy, Dragon Knight." Taking another sip, Conn placed the mug on the table.

"Verra," he laughed. "Let me go tend to Meggie, before she burns or drops something."

Watching as the man made his way out of the hall, Conn leaned his arms on the oak table. "As you know, I've been sent on a quest as part of my sentence from the council."

"Yes. We all heard the proclamation," Archie said softly.

Conn leaned back and folded his arms across his chest. "Apparently, I saved the wrong woman at a pivotal point in the timeline. She was unknown to me at the time. Hidden and not considered important. Or so I was told."

"You relied too much on the woman, Dervla, and her own words," argued Archie.

"Yes, I understand that now," he snapped.

"Then what do you require of me?"

"All knowledge of this O'Callaghan woman. I need to read your scrolls, maps, any and all pertinent information."

Archie took a large swallow of his wine. "Which woman? Past or present?"

"Both."

Smiling, his friend put down his mug. "So you have determined that they might be linked—from the moment the threads split?"

Conn nodded slowly.

"You do realize how frail these threads are? If you succeed with one—"

"Then I might be able to close the gap in the veil and help to heal the past without affecting the timeline for any of the descendents."

"You risk much, Conn." His friend leaned forward. "Why not simply help the lass in the present on her journey?"

Reaching for the pitcher, Conn refilled his mug. "Because I owe both, and I know it can be done." He held up his hands. "I may have been stripped of my Fenian powers, but I am still a Fae—a prince. With the right knowledge, I will be able to forge the link between the two women. All I'll need is to see the records from that time to determine what needs to be done. You have the accounts, so it's only a matter of reading through them all."

Archie glanced into his mug. "What you're attempting has never been done. To weave the life strand from present to past is one only spoken of in theory."

"I've had plenty of time to consider the hypothesis."

"Have you considered that you will need the lass in the present fully aware of what you'll be doing? She must consent." Archie leaned forward. "In addition, if you weave a new thread, you could tamper with the current lass's timeline. Have you even thought of that possibility?"

Conn knew the risks as he rubbed a hand across his forehead. "I owe both women a chance for this opportunity."

Archie slammed his palm onto the table. "For the love of Mother Danu, you risk much!"

"A Fenian Warrior never does anything halfway." He pounded his chest. "I live and breathe by a code of honor that is unspoken. I may have been stripped of my powers and markings, but I am a trained warrior—from the instant I pledged my vows. I owe them *both*!"

Nodding slowly, Archie asked, "What if you're unable to do so?"

"If I fail on either account, then death will surely follow to the O'Callaghan woman of the present. I have nothing to lose."

"Only your life. For death will swiftly claim you, as well."

"Nae!" shouted Meggie, bringing in a basket of

bread. Coming over toward them, she slammed the item down. She glared at Archie. "My one and only request to the Fae was to spare Rory, Liam, and Conn's lives. I willnae hear such talk."

Conn rose and placed a comforting arm around her. "And they will always honor your wishes, Meggie. This is entirely different. I have chosen this path to set things right—past and present with a certain clan. I was fully aware of the consequences when I accepted this quest."

She shook her head as tears misted in her eyes. "Surely ye can find another way?"

He tipped her chin up with his finger. "That is why I am here. I must heal the past, before I can weave a new thread on the loom in the life of another."

She snorted and wiped at her eyes. "Ye speak in riddles only a Fae would understand."

Conn arched a brow. "And you comprehend as a human." Glancing up, he saw Adam and Jamie striding forth, their arms loaded with food items. Giving her a kiss on the forehead, he released her, whispering, "No tears, Meggie, or your husband would certainly demand my head in the lists."

"Aye, he would like training with ye before ye take your leave. Do ye think ye could do so?"

Conn groaned. "Do I have a choice?"

She pinched him on the arm. "Nae. How long are ye planning to reside here?"

"For as long as necessary to obtain the information I seek."

"Good. Ye can begin before dawn tomorrow."

"You're a demanding woman, Margaret MacKay MacFhearguis."

She motioned for Jamie to put his items on the side

table. "My husband and child would agree with ye."

For the next few hours, Conn explained in detail the events of his situation and the knowledge he required from Archie. In turn, Adam and Meggie filled him in on the improvements to Aonach—from expanding certain rooms, to meeting more MacKay descendants. The conversation grew tense at times, especially when Meggie's brothers were mentioned. Her eyes misted with unshed tears, and on several occasions, Adam would wrap his arm around her shoulders and whisper in her ear. Though Meggie had assured him that she accepted living in this era, she still grieved for her brothers from time to time, as well did Adam for his own family.

The afternoon grew late and Meggie yawned. "Excuse me, but I cannae sit any longer." She leaned against Adam and rubbed at her side. "I swear this one kicks far worse than Jamie did when he was inside me."

Adam placed a hand over her swollen abdomen. "'Tis a strong, fighting lad."

She glanced at him skeptically. "Could be a lass, ye ken."

Her husband roared with laughter. "Did not the Great Dragon tell ye otherwise?"

"What does she ken," she grumbled, though her mouth twitched in humor.

"The Great Dragon knows everything," argued Jamie, stuffing another apple tart into his mouth. "Did she not tell ye that I would have many brothers?"

"Truth?" asked Conn, smiling broadly.

Shrugging, Meggie replied, "We shall see. I like to leave the door open for other possibilities."

Standing, Conn motioned to Jamie. "Let us go visit

the Great Dragon."

His eyes grew wide with excitement. "Can we go on your motorcycle?"

Conn glanced at Adam and Meggie. "Will you permit me?"

"Do not ken why ye cannae take him on a horse," grumbled Adam, helping Meggie stand.

Meggie rolled her eyes. "Of course, Conn." She touched her husband's cheek. "They're only traveling down the path to the loch. No harm shall come to them."

Jamie shouted and dashed over to his mother and father, embracing them both. "Thank ye!" Releasing his hold, he ran out of the Great Hall.

Nodding to both, Conn took his leave and found Jamie examining his bike. "Much like racing a horse through the Highlands," he stated, lifting Jamie into his arms. Settling them both on the motorcycle, he started the engine.

"Are ye not going to wear your helmet?"

"Not here. Only when I travel far distances. And since I do not have a helmet for you, we will go slow."

Placing a firm hand around the lad's waist, he maneuvered the vehicle out of the bailey and across the bridge. The soft glow of twilight settled around them, and Conn could see the loch in the distance. Light splintered and danced along the water's edge. He could feel the power all around him—his, the Great Dragon, and the wee Dragon Knight. The boy laughed out loud, as Conn sped them faster down the path. The cool evening wind slapped at their faces, and Conn smiled.

As they neared the loch, Conn made a sharp left turn on the road, following his Fae instinct. Soon, he sensed *her* presence and continued down the path. A hawk appeared from a nearby tree, swooping low in greeting. Jamie roared in delight and waved.

Onward they traveled along the path leading closer to the Great Dragon. Making another turn around a bend, he slowed as he drove under a canopy of thick pines. Ducking under some branches, the area opened up fully. Coming to a stop, he turned off the ignition and placed Jamie on the ground.

"That was magnificent!" exclaimed Jamie. His fingers trailed along the metal. "When I am older, I am going to have one of these."

Making their way down to the water's edge, Conn removed his boots and knelt on one knee. The Great Dragon had already whispered her greeting when the first brush of power touched his mind. Lifting his head, he watched as Jamie transformed from boy to Dragon Knight in a flash. The fire blazed in the depths of his eyes more powerful than any he had ever encountered—more so than the MacKay Dragon Knights.

"Do you come here often, Jamie?" he asked, standing slowly.

"Aye, Fae Prince," the lad responded in a low voice—ancient and full of wisdom.

Clasping his hands behind his back, Conn moved forward and stepped to the water's edge. The cool water was soothing. "So she has shared my heritage with you."

"And your sister's," he added. "Two shall weave the thread upon the loom and one shall break the other."

Stunned, Conn glanced over his shoulder at him. "Are you speaking with the Great Dragon? Does your knowledge come from her?"

Jamie stood gazing outward. "Nae. There are many. The others that have gone before her."

"The many?" he whispered. Uneasiness slithered inside of Conn.

The boy nodded slowly. "The timekeepers."

"Dragons of the past," stated Conn and glanced upward into the early evening sky.

"Aye, and they have issued ye a warning. Only follow the path of the stars to the beginning. If ye stray, they will come for ye."

Conn placed a fist over his heart in reverence. "I understand, ancient ones."

Chapter Eight

"Beware the shimmering eyes of a Celt."
~Chronicles of the Fae

"Lovely summer rain," Ivy groaned. Pulling the hood of her jacket over her head, she felt brave enough to cross the street without fear of any visions threatening to spill forth. After her last vision several days ago, she would only venture to the bookstore by the back entry. It took all her courage to walk through the woods to the market yesterday and back home. She did not want to witness her uncle's death again within her mind.

Quickly darting across the street, she glanced up at the wooden pub sign and smiled. Pushing open the door, she stepped into the warmth and heavenly aroma of food. Glancing around, she noticed more carved paintings like the ones she'd seen in the building where Sean Casey worked. She instantly recognized the legend they were telling. None other than the Children of Lir.

Moving her way to the bar, she placed the clean casserole dish she was returning to Erin on the counter and removed her jacket. Shouting erupted at the other end of the pub where four men were gathered around a dartboard—each boasting that they were the winner. Ivy turned her head to get a better look at the men. The older ones were making barbs at the younger man, as he shrugged.

"Ye had the board rigged, right lad?" demanded a stout balding man.

"Now, Seamus, you wound me. Accusing me of malicious practices in my own bar," protested the young man.

The other men snorted and made crude remarks, as the accused held up his hands. "I am deeply offended."

"Ye can make it up to us by letting us have drinks on the house," suggested the man called Seamus.

Ivy hopped onto a nearby stool to watch the lively debate.

"I've already given you a free round, Seamus. For the love of Mary—"

"Do not bring our Lord's mother into this debate," argued the elderly man.

"What's happening?" asked Erin, emerging from the kitchen with a tray of soup bowls.

"It would seem someone has been accused of cheating so that free drinks can be had for all."

Erin snorted and leaned close. "It's a weekly occurrence with those three. They come in daily, drink and get a bite to eat. Afterwards, it's a game of darts. But for reasons I have yet to determine, they pick one day a week to inform my brother that he's done something to the gaming board." She waved her hand about. "From tampering with the darts themselves or slamming a door to sway the board on the wall."

Ivy gave her a sharp glance. "Seriously?"

"Yes. And what's worse, is my brother turns a blind eye. Feigns this ignorance and in the end, he's buying them a round of pints." She pointed a finger at the man. "It's a good thing I love him, or I would fire him immediately."

Smiling at the group of men, Ivy muttered, "Positively wicked of them."

Erin nodded her head in agreement. "Aye, the whole lot of them, including my *wee* brother."

"He doesn't look small to me." The words flew out of Ivy's mouth.

Erin burst out laughing.

A hushed silence ensued as all male eyes turned toward them.

The younger man arched a brow at Erin and then slowly gazed at Ivy. Retreating from the group, he made his way toward her. Leaning against the bar, his eyes never left Ivy's, when he asked, "Is this our new neighbor, Erin? You never mentioned how pretty she is."

Ivy almost choked on his remark. Instead, she thrust out her hand. "Yes, I'm Ivy O'Callaghan."

"Ivy *Kathleen*," he corrected. Stepping forward, he took her hand and placed it on his chest. "You've stolen my heart already."

"I have no problem returning it to you," she countered, trying to free her hand from the devilishly handsome man. His green eyes raked over her face, as he leaned closer.

"Oh for the love of angels, Mac! Stop trying to charm her, or she'll never step foot inside the pub again," complained Erin and moved away to serve the soup to a nearby table.

Ivy stole a glance at Erin and then back to the man. "Now that we made our introductions, *Mac*, do you think I can have my hand back?"

His smile turned predatory as he lifted her fingers to his lips. "Welcome to Glennamore."

She fought the smile forming on her face as he released her hand. She turned toward Erin. "I have a question about the name of your pub."

Mac stepped in front of her. "Perhaps it's a question only I can answer."

Ivy narrowed her eyes. "Why Seven Swans for the pub?"

"Go on, Brother. Explain away," shouted Erin over her shoulder.

The man shrugged. "For the Irish tale of Lir's Children."

Ivy tapped a finger against her lips. "If I recall the legend, there were only four, not seven children. Do you have a certain insight to the tale?"

Erin returned and stood next to her. "Even the *pretty* American knows the tale."

Mac rubbed the back of his neck. "Seven sounded better than four."

"I never agreed on the name," she argued, looking at Ivy.

He pointed a finger at his sister. "You forget I won the coin toss, so it was final."

His sister rolled her eyes and walked away.

"Is it really you? Our own Ivy Kathleen." The man called Seamus barreled up to her, embracing her in a big hug.

Surprised by the man's outburst, she replied, "Um…yes, it is."

Soon, others came forth, all greeting her with hugs and words of endearment. They all were extremely grateful she had returned to Glennamore to run the bookstore and take over the property. Before she knew it, someone had placed a pint in front of her. Gazing up over the crowd, she noticed Mac leaning against the post behind the bar. She lifted her pint, and he winked at her.

Several hours later, Ivy finally begged off telling another story about her life by saying she had to return to the house. They relented only if she would return tomorrow. And she had agreed.

The pub had filled as soon as they found out she was there. Trying hard to remember their names, Ivy gave up after being introduced to far too many to count. For reasons she found difficult to comprehend, she was being treated like a long lost celebrity. Each person asked the same questions, and she patiently answered them all.

Scooting off the barstool, Ivy looked around for her coat, which had disappeared.

"Leaving us so soon?" Erin smiled and tossed a towel behind the bar.

"Good grief," she uttered quietly. "I've never talked so much at once in all my life. Have you seen my coat?"

The woman put an arm around her shoulders moving her away from the bar area. "A bit overwhelming, but they mean well. Yes, it's hanging on a hook by the front door."

Ivy shook her head. "Sorry, I'm sounding disrespectful. Everyone's been so nice."

"It's a shock, so I understand." Erin released her hold and stood back. "When are you planning on opening the bookstore?"

"Next Monday. I wanted to be available for the

workers."

Frowning, she asked, "You haven't heard from Norm or Tim?"

Ivy's shoulders slumped. "Yes, to both. They can't take care of the Aga, roof, or the other repairs. They're too busy, so they've offered to send for someone from the neighboring village. Norm said he would also see if Sean knew of any other help."

Mac walked over, carrying Ivy's coat. "I can take a look at the Aga."

Erin snatched the coat from him. "Absolutely not! I'm not running the pub by myself, while you attempt to fix her precious Aga."

Mac ran a hand through his hair. "Shameful, you telling Ivy Kathleen that I'm not good enough to lend a hand."

She jabbed a finger at her brother's chest. "I can see clearly where you'd like to lend that hand, dear brother."

Putting a fist to her mouth to stifle the laughter, Ivy turned when the front door to the pub blew open. The cold blast of air lashed across her face, but she gave no care. Her mouth became dry as the man stood there blocking what little light remained in the sky. His silver-blond wavy hair whipped around his chiseled face shaded by a light beard. Yet, it was those eyes that bore into hers—holding her captive. Were they silver or ice blue? She blinked several times, and swallowed.

The giant stepped into the pub and closed the door. Ivy's gaze traveled the length of him as he made his way past her to the bar. She couldn't help but follow him with her eyes. He was sinfully dressed in all black—jeans, boots, leather jacket opened to reveal a black tee. He was magnificent.

"Sweet Brigid," whispered Erin. "Have the Vikings invaded Glennamore again?"

The woman's words snapped Ivy out of her lustful trance. She looked at her friend. "Vikings in Glennamore?"

Mac placed her coat over her shoulders and chuckled. "Do not fear, they were banished many centuries ago. I'll go see what the *Viking* wants. I'm sure he's only passing through and needs a pint and some food. There's nothing in Glennamore to raid."

The room blurred, and Ivy brushed a hand over her brow. "Not a Viking," she uttered softly.

Erin placed a hand on her arm. "Are you all right?"

Ivy lifted her head. The gorgeous man leaned against the bar as Mac made his way to him. "I said he's not a Viking."

Erin smirked. "You could have fooled me."

The man straightened as Mac pointed a finger directly in Ivy's direction.

Ivy was unable to move, the words tumbled free as if spoken by someone else. "He's an ancient Celt."

The stranger immediately glanced her way, shock registering across his face as if he had heard her spoken words.

"Good Lord, you're as white as a sheet, Ivy Kathleen."

She barely heard Erin's words. The Celt moved toward her, a frown marring his handsome features. A tremor slithered down her spine as she lifted her head up to meet his gaze.

"Ivy O'Callaghan?" The soft burr of his voice brushed over her face, and she couldn't determine if it

93

was Irish or Scottish.

Her mouth stayed dry, making her unable to acknowledge the man's question. Nodding slowly, she took a step back. Then the Celt smiled, and Ivy thought she would melt right there on the floor. How could anyone look that gorgeous?

Erin nudged her. "Forgive my friend, Ivy Kathleen, she seems to have lost her voice."

Recovering her wits, Ivy replied, "Sorry. I'm done telling stories about my life in the States."

The Celt arched a brow. "Not interested in your stories. Sean Casey sent me to inspect your repairs."

"You know Sean?" interrupted Erin.

Smiling, the man nodded. "Most of his life. I'm Conn MacRoich."

Ivy frowned. *Scottish?*

Conn glanced at her as if hearing her thoughts. "I don't want to interrupt your meal, so I'll return tomorrow."

"No, I'm...done. Yes...well...you can come back later." *You can't even talk to the man without stumbling over your words.*

"She was just about to leave when you blew in here," stated Erin.

"Good. I'd like to take some notes of what I'll need," replied Conn.

Grabbing Ivy's arm, Erin propelled her out the front door. "Take the sexy Viking and show him what needs to be fixed," she whispered.

Ivy's face burned. "He's *not* sexy," she fibbed.

"'Tis a sin to lie." Erin gave her a pat on the arm and brushed past Conn.

Ivy grunted. She didn't need to look behind her to

see if Conn was following. The man oozed a presence of raw masculinity. Ivy could feel it ripple across her own senses. Quickly making her way across the street, she led him down the path to her cottage. The cool breeze helped to settle her silly nerves. *You're acting like some besotted idiot, Ivy!*

Dashing to the front, she pulled out her keys and entered the place. "I'd like to have the Aga working," she said, pointing to the stove as she walked into the kitchen. "There's an issue with the faucet in the bathroom sink, plus the roof needs thatching and several windows require new glass panes." She kept rattling off the list of repairs, not even bothering to see if he was keeping up with her. "Oh, there is one more item, but I don't know how good you are with cars. It won't start. I hope it isn't costly, but no worries, since it's on the low end of priorities that need fixing."

"I can assure you, I can handle any task you ask of me," he responded in a low voice.

She turned abruptly. He stood mere inches from her, invading her space and making her head spin. Tilting her head upward, she marveled at the color of his eyes. "I believe you can," she whispered.

"Name the first item you want repaired," he said with a smile.

She lifted her hand and pointed. "The Aga."

"Tell you what. Why don't you make me a list of the order of repairs, and when I return tomorrow, I'll start on the Aga and proceed from there."

"Deal." Thrusting out her hand, she added, "Thank you."

The man held her gaze as he took her hand in his large one. The touch seared a path up her arm and spread throughout her body. For a brief moment, the room faded and she found herself gazing across an open field at him. Breathing deeply, the room came back into focus.

Releasing her grip, she pulled away and made her way to the front door. Stepping outside, she waited until he followed. Locking the door, she turned to him. "If you—"

"I'll be here at seven a.m.," he announced.

"Good, an early riser." *What the heck was that vision all about? You almost swooned in front of the man.*

His eyes flashed in humor. "Always." Giving her a slight bow, Conn strode off down the path.

Ivy placed her palms over her cheeks to cool the burning fire. Never in all her life did she behave so foolishly in front of a man. Although, she believed this man was no ordinary individual. Waiting until he was gone from her view, she walked toward the bookstore, trying to figure out Conn MacRoich. There was something peculiar about him. Her gift of sight had shown her something and several times, he responded as if he had read her thoughts.

"Impossible," she muttered. She picked up a twig and tossed it far, releasing the tension in her body. She pursed her lips in concentration. "I wonder what your ancestors looked like in a kilt." Letting out a giggle, her steps slowed.

"I shall be on guard against you, Conn MacRoich. I will not fall prey to those mysterious eyes again."

Chapter Nine

"Egos of Men and Fae have been known to start wars."

~*Chronicles of the Fae*

Stepping once again inside the Seven Swans Pub, Conn surveyed the surroundings. There were customers at the bar chatting with the man he'd noticed with Ivy when he first entered the establishment. Seeing a booth in the far back, he made his way to the table. Removing his jacket, he dropped down against the soft cushions and sighed. Stretching out his legs, he glanced at the menu. In truth, he simply wanted to drink his meal away.

His senses were still reeling from the encounter with Miss Ivy O'Callaghan.

She may have whispered the words, *ancient Celt*, but they echoed loud within his mind. No one had referred to him as a Celt. No, they always assumed he was of Norse blood, or a damn Viking, intent on pillaging their town. The moment their gazes locked, he thought her to be the most adorable sprite he'd ever seen. Her short, wispy blonde hair only highlighted her vivid aqua-colored eyes, reminding him of the ocean on a calm day. Although Conn never cared for the current fashions, he found himself staring at her form of dress—her tartan mini skirt and tight sweater made his mouth dry. In addition, the boots she wore only accentuated her shapely long legs.

Tossing the menu aside, he rubbed vigorously at his eyes. "She's only a woman. A *human*," he muttered. By the hounds, he should have requested a visit to the Pleasure Gardens before he left for the human world. There he would have found release with one of his own.

"Having a difficult time deciding what you'll be eating?" asked the woman who now stood before him.

Opening his eyes, he placed his hands on the table. "I'll take a pint of your best Irish stout and the Vegetarian Shepherd's Pie."

The woman placed a coaster on the table. "Do you have a place to stay while you're doing the repairs on Ivy's place?"

He arched a brow and leaned back. "Yes. I'm staying with Sean Casey."

"Good. I'm Erin O'Reilly, part owner of the Seven Swans. Let me go fetch your pint and put in your food order."

As she walked away, Conn tried calming his restless spirit. Any other time, he would have enjoyed the solitude, but now, he would dearly welcome the counsel of a fellow warrior.

Erin returned and placed his pint on the table. She leaned against the other side of the booth. "Funny thing… I've never heard Sean mention anything about you, Conn MacRoich."

Reaching for the glass, he guzzled deeply. "Ahh…perfect." Gazing up at her, he replied, "Do you want to hear something funnier, Erin O'Reilly?"

She nodded, though a frown marred her features.

Conn leaned forward. "He's never mentioned *you*

either."

Erin quickly recovered and straightened. "Well I guess we weren't important enough for him to talk about."

He lifted his glass and nodded in acknowledgement. "If you would be so kind, I'll take another pint."

She smiled fully. "Thirsty man. I'll go see to your dinner." Taking the empty glass with her, she quickly walked away.

As Conn waited for his pint and meal, his thoughts turned once again to Ivy and her lineage. After going through volumes regarding the O'Callaghan clan with Archie, he couldn't fathom that one misstep in time would lead to such a miserable group of people. They often hid among the shadows, attempting to seclude themselves from others. Their gifts were extraordinary and they chose to squelch any within a family or clan that carried the gene. Centuries flowed, but the O'Callaghans retreated farther away from society.

He smacked his fist on the table. "Bloody fools," he hissed.

"I thought I'd find you here." Sean chuckled and dropped down in the booth across from him.

Conn tapped his fingers on the wood. "Did I invite you to share a meal with me?"

The man rubbed a hand over his chin. "Already had my supper. Thought I'd stop in for a pint."

"Is there something you wish to discuss with me?"

Sean turned and waved at the man behind the bar. "I'll take a pint and a shot of whiskey, Mac." He focused his attention back toward Conn. "I can tell by your foul mood you have met Ivy Kathleen."

Crossing his arms over his chest, he replied, "My mood has nothing to do with the wee lass."

Erin brought over their drinks, placing them on the table. "New or old friend, Sean?"

Smiling, the man pushed the dram of whiskey toward Conn. "Positively *ancient*."

She rolled her eyes. "Exactly what Ivy stated. Would you like something to eat?"

"No thanks. The pint will be all."

As the woman walked away from their table, Conn pointed to the dram. "What's this for?"

Sean took a sip of his pint. "How long have we known each other?"

"From the day I saved your life in Kintale Bay, which would make that over fifty years."

Closing his eyes, Sean remarked, "I was a foolish lad of only ten." When he opened them, he added, "So I know you well."

"From one encounter?" challenged Conn.

"You forget, *Fae*, the conversation we had that day on the shore."

Conn leaned forward. "You dare to unleash my anger by calling me thusly? Do I call you *human*?"

Sean roared, causing several in the pub to glance their way. "Forgive me, and I have seen your anger. On the day you rescued me, your fury was evident. You were extremely pissed at the men who were supposed to be watching over me. They let the boat drift farther out into the sea as they drank on the shore. They were so drunk that the lashing you gave them has always haunted them. Sadly, both departed several years later."

"Good riddance," stated Conn. "Did they ever mention me to others?"

"And be scorned by the people of Glennamore? No, they kept quiet about the strange giant with silver eyes that blazed."

Sighing, Conn lifted the dram and inhaled the peaty aroma. "You were wise then, Sean Casey, and wiser now. I'm happy to see that the Gods favored your life well."

"Aye. Thanks to you, my friend." Sean lifted his glass. "*Sláinte.*"

"*Sláinte mhath.*" Conn drained the glass and placed it on the table.

"Can you tell me why you are here? You mentioned it had to do with the O'Callaghan family, but why *Ivy*?"

Conn glanced at Erin as she approached with his meal, ignoring the man's question. She set the steaming plate of food in front of him. "Would you care for anything else?"

He shook his head, reaching for a fork.

"Give a holler if you do," she said, and walked away.

Scooping out a huge chunk of vegetables, he took a bite. Closing his eyes, Conn savored the intense flavors.

"They say Erin has a secret ingredient she puts in her Shepherd pies. Many have tried to weasel it out of her, but the lass is firm on keeping it private," uttered Sean quietly.

Opening his eyes, he nodded. "Damn good. I believe she uses wild mushrooms and green garlic. There's a mixture of spices I'm sure I can name, but I'll keep her secret."

Sean took a sip of his pint. "Sweet Brigid. She'd most likely have your head if she heard you mention one word."

Shrugging, Conn took another mouthful. He had to admit the woman was an excellent cook. Reaching for his pint, he took a long swallow. Could he possibly share his reason for being here with Sean? Perhaps the man could assist him—help him see the real Ivy O'Callaghan. He placed the glass down. "To answer your previous question, I'm here to assist Ivy on a search for her true identity."

Sean narrowed his eyes. "What does that mean?"

Conn waved his fork in the air. "She is…*gifted* and hides behind a wall of her own secrets. Some are even in this village. No one can tell the lass why her parents left Ireland."

"Then she carries the traits like her Uncle Thomas, who spoke to me about his sight of seeing things before they happened, or events of the past." Sean drained his glass. "We spoke of this only once, but he never mentioned the discord between his brother. He was distraught over their leaving in the beginning. But when the first letter arrived with pictures, Thomas felt it was his duty to share everything about his niece living in America."

Reaching for his pint, Conn drained the rest of his beer. "So there is no one in this village that can explain why her parents left?"

Sean frowned and scratched behind his ear. "He had many friends, but did not like to discuss the bad blood with his brother, Patrick."

Conn concentrated on his meal, letting his thoughts settle on which direction to take with Ivy. He had no plan whatsoever. Nowhere to start and his gut soured. Shoving his meal aside, he concluded the path would eventually reveal itself. For now, he would work on the repairs at Ivy's cottage.

Sean smacked his hand onto the table. "There might be one who could shed some light on the O'Callaghan brothers."

Eyeing the man skeptically across from him, he replied, "Continue."

He pointed a finger at Conn. "There was a lass who was fond of both brothers. However, when Patrick started seeing Sara, the woman turned her sights to Thomas. 'Tis a pity nothing more happened. She would visit the village a few times a year to visit relatives, but Thomas refused to see her again."

Leaning forward, Conn placed his hands on the table. It was a small slice of information and he would gladly accept the morsel. "Where is this woman?"

"Anne Fahey is her name. She moved away after Patrick and Sara left for America. Bought a small place up north in Kindale."

Conn smiled. "It's a start."

Turning sideways, Sean waved to the bartender. "Bring us two drams of your best single malt."

****

The new dawn brought the promise of another clear day as Conn maneuvered his motorcycle down the path to Ivy's cottage. After several more drams of whiskey last evening with Sean Casey, he had as much information as required. There was a mystery to the O'Callaghans and this woman, Anne. It niggled down his spine this sense of secrecy. Until he could meet with this woman, he pushed aside any further thoughts.

Turning off the engine, Conn got off the bike and made his way to the front door. Knocking several times, he waited. After several moments, he peered in the front window. Glancing up at the sky, Conn knew the hour, so he frowned in confusion. Was the lass prone to sleeping? Did she forget?

He walked around to the back of the house. Unprepared for the vision in the early morn's sunlight, his steps faltered, and he froze. There in the garden stood Ivy, the light shimmering around her in a hazy glow. Today's outfit was a flowered mini rose-colored dress, and he could make the outline of all her shapely curves. Smiling, he noticed she wore no shoes. Her hair blew in soft waves around her face, reminding him of those from his own Fae realm.

Conn stood in a trance watching her as she tilted her head up to let the sun's warmth touch her face. Time slowed, the rhythm of the land pulsed all around them, and it frightened him. "Who are you, Ivy Kathleen O'Callaghan," he whispered.

Her head turned toward him with eyes that blazed from another time and held his own—ancient and powerful. His sprite was in another time. Conn held out his hand, "Come back, Ivy," he commanded softly.

She blinked in confusion, and placed a hand over her brow. "I'm...so...sorry."

Ivy swayed, and Conn was there immediately, placing an arm around her waist. The mere contact blazed a path of longing throughout his body. Instantly closing off the emotion, he tipped her chin up to meet his gaze. "Are you unwell?"

Her eyes grew wide from his touch. "Lost...track of time."

Regretting his next move, Conn released his hold on her and took a step back. "I would imagine one would lose all sense of time coming into this stunning garden, especially in the early morn. Your beauty only enhances the place."

She quickly turned away, but not before Conn caught a glimpse of the blush staining her cheeks. "You must think I'm foolish being out here without shoes, too," she said moving toward the house.

"No. I find it enchanting. You can feel the heart of the land through your skin."

Ivy paused and looked over her shoulder. Giving him a smile, she nodded. "I do it each morning and evening. Would you like a cup of tea before you start on the Aga?"

"Coffee?"

She laughed, the sound reminding Conn of bells. "Sorry. I don't like the stuff. I was brought up on strong tea."

Conn shrugged. "Then *strong* tea will do."

Laughing once again, Ivy made her way into the cottage.

He hastily knelt on one knee and placed his palm upon the ground. "Where did the lass go?" He closed his eyes reaching out with his Fae senses. Trying to grasp a thread of where her essence traveled to, he blew out a frustrated breath when the vision refused to open for him.

Standing, he gazed at the garden. A profusion of flowers, herbs, and vegetables all grew in abundance. They were pleasing to the senses, and Conn marveled at the place. "Beauty everywhere."

Making his way into the house, he stood in the arched entrance of the kitchen. Ivy had donned a pair of socks and she was busy preparing the tea and muffins.

She gestured him over to a chair. "I've bought some blueberry muffins. Would you like one?"

"Of course," he replied taking a seat. The small chair creaked under his weight, and Conn feared this would be another project—fixing broken chairs.

She quickly set everything down in front of him. "If you need anything else, I'll be at the store."

He arched a brow. "You're not eating?"

"Well, umm… I have tons to do, since I'm opening the store in a few days." Ivy bustled about, and Conn watched her every movement. "I need to look at the inventory sheets, monetary ledgers, go to the bank, and—" She burst out in laughter.

Leaning forward in his chair, Conn folded his arms on the table. "Extremely humorous, I'm sure."

"No, sorry." Ivy leaned against the table. "Do you want to know a secret?"

By the hounds of Cuchulainn, Conn wanted to know all of her secrets and unravel those waiting to be whispered into his ear. "Do tell," he encouraged in a low voice.

Ivy leaned closer. "I don't have a clue what I'm doing."

Instinctively, Conn reached out and placed a hand over hers on the table. "Trust your inner guidance. And when chaos surrounds you…smile."

Her rosy lips parted, inviting Conn to taste. The call of desire so potent, his vision blurred. Snatching his hand back, he stared into her aqua depths.

"Sage advice," she whispered and moved away from him to grab a pair of boots. She quickly put them on and stood. "I checked your motorcycle and didn't see any tools."

"Sean told me that your uncle kept a shed full of the necessary items," he replied, and then added, "I'll make an initial inspection and determine what further supplies I will require."

Ivy reached for a sweater from the back of one of the chairs and a muffin with her other hand. "Great! I sure hope you can get the Aga working." His eyes followed her out of the kitchen. "I would love to start baking my own food." Her voice trailed off as she left the cottage.

The moment the door closed, Conn's shoulders slumped. What the bloody hell was wrong with him? Why did a mere slip of a lass almost cause him to lose control? He gritted his teeth and then pounded his fist on the table, the result causing the chair to splinter beneath him.

His arse hit the ground hard. "Damn! Now you can add another repair to your list, sprite."

Laughter bubbled up within Conn, and he roared with its release.

Chapter Ten

"The dating game of unwanted men awaits those who have sealed off their hearts to love."
                              ~Chronicles of the Fae

Ivy stood transfixed outside her uncle's office in the bookstore. The place was arranged and neatly in order. Her gaze drifted around his room. Beautiful floor-to-ceiling bookcases contained old and rare books, and others looked to be more recent. To the left hanging on the wall were various maps. Stepping inside she moved closer, and noticed they were of the village of Glennamore—some had dates as old as six hundred years. "Amazing," she muttered.

Glancing to the other wall, she let out a small gasp. The wall to the right was covered in framed photos of herself. She swallowed hard, willing her feet to move closer. A mirror of her life gazed back at her. Tears misted her eyes as her fingers brushed over the one where her mom was holding her as an infant. Born premature, they warned her parents that she might not survive. But Ivy proved them all wrong. When someone told her no, she balked and did it anyway. Walking at ten months, she embraced the world around her.

Once, she remembered a doctor telling her mom that she would need surgery for her eyes and glasses afterward. Again, Ivy stormed out of the office and ran to the park. There she knelt before a giant tree and said a silent prayer that the faeries would heal her eyes. Within six months, Ivy's vision cleared and the doctor proclaimed it a miracle.

As her gaze traveled the many years of her life on the wall, she choked out a sob. So many precious memories that her mother shared with someone she'd never known. The faces haunted her and anger infused her spirit.

"Why?" she blurted out. "Someone explain all of this!"

The ticking clock on the wall mocked her outburst, chiming the hour. Rubbing her eyes, she went over to her uncle's large desk and started opening drawers. Pulling forth the books and ledgers, she stared at them. "These are now mine and I don't know what to do," she uttered quietly. Gently turning the pages, she gazed at the handwriting. Detailed and organized, Ivy was pleased with what she saw. Each month showed good sales for the year—a good sign.

Setting them aside, she opened a side drawer. Keys dangled on a large ring holding them all in place. She picked them up, the weight heavy in her hand—three keys, all of them looking positively antique.

"Great. Where and what do you open?" Putting them back in the drawer, she discovered a book meant for orders and other pertinent information on the store in the second drawer. Leafing through the pages, everything appeared to be going smoothly at the bookstore. She noted an incoming order from Galway due to be shipped out at the end of the month. It was a collection of travel memoirs from a new author, and a few books on the geography of Ireland. Peering inside the other drawers, she came across miscellaneous items. There was an array of pens, quills, ink, parchment, leather journals, and writing tablets. Yet, what Ivy couldn't fathom was why her uncle didn't keep everything on a computer.

Pulling out a tablet and pen, Ivy started to make lists. Number one, ask Sean Casey if her uncle had a laptop somewhere. Perhaps it was behind the counter at the front of the store. Number two, what were all the keys for? Number three, incoming shipment at the end of the month. Number four, check with the bank manager regarding cash used in the store. Did her uncle have a specific amount?

Tapping the pen against her mouth in thought, Ivy's mind started to drift. Running a bookstore was not her expertise. No, it was history and mythology. Images of Conn swirled in front of her again. He had approached silently in the garden while she was attempting to put the pieces of an image she had seen earlier within her mind. She could actually visualize the landscape of Glennamore from long ago. Rolling hills dotted with trees, and for a brief moment, Ivy could hear the water from a nearby stream. Never before had her visions been so powerful. It was as if she had traveled back in time. They were so vivid, until Conn MacRoich arrived.

A gorgeous male specimen standing there staring at her. Each time she saw him, he sent her pulse skittering, as if he could read her every thought. Ivy could imagine him posing for one of her art classes. His muscles rippled when he walked, and she was not blind to his physique. He would have made an ideal subject for her nude life drawing class.

Snorting, Ivy glanced around the room in embarrassment. "Get a grip. You're daydreaming too much about the man." However, her face heated with the idea of what he would look like without any clothing.

Slamming the door on her lustful thoughts, she stood and made her way to the front counter of the store. Lifting the latch on a side entry half-door, she stepped behind the counter. One lone cash register with a sales pad rested on top. Underneath, the counter were bags with the logo of the Celtic Knot Bookstore. Pens were neatly stacked off to the side, along with more tablets. The counter was worn, but beautiful. The wood's luster glistened in the early morning sunlight. She placed a hand on top, trying to get a feel for the place. After several moments, she gave up and moved on with her inspection.

Finding nothing more, Ivy moved away from the counter and wandered the bookstore at a leisurely pace. Contentment filled her as she trailed her fingers along the spine of several books. It was truly a lovely little store—filled with books, some authors she recognized, and others who were new to her.

For the next hour, Ivy perused the store, making mental notes of authors she would want to check out and writing down those she thought might make a good addition to the store. Weaving her way along the back, she smiled when she entered the children's section. There was a small place in the back by the window with a table and comfortable chairs—all in warm, muted colors. Her mind started spinning with ideas to expand and add to the area. Quickly jotting down her plans, she smiled.

Taking a step back, she tried to envision what the room would look like with a faery house for the girls and a train depot for the boys. There could be special events and a Children's Hour for storytelling. Almost jumping for joy, she heard someone shuffling around out front.

Turning around, she gave a startled cry. "Who the hell are you? And how did you get inside?" she demanded more brusquely than intended.

The man held his hands up. "Sorry, didn't mean to frighten you. We saw the door to the store was open and thought business had resumed."

Ivy narrowed her eyes, believing she had locked the door when she entered earlier. "*We*?" The man blocked her exit, and she tried to peer over his shoulder.

"I'm here with Peter Sullivan. My name is Mike Banister. He told me you were a pretty wee thing."

"Nice to meet you, but the store is closed." Shoving her way past the man, Ivy quickly made her way to the front. Approaching the counter, she eyed Peter skeptically as he leaned against the counter.

"Good morn, Ivy Kathleen."

"Is there something I can do for you, Peter?"

He moved away from the counter. "Noticed the door was open and making sure all is well. But now that you've asked, care for a pint at the Seven Swans?"

Smiling, she moved toward the door. Opening it wide, she gestured with her hand outward. "As I told your friend, the store is closed. I'm catching up on everything here. Lots to do. Come back in a few days, when I hope to re-open for business."

"Perhaps another time." He gave her a wink as he stepped outside. His friend, Mike nodded to her as he followed behind him.

Watching as they made their way down the path, she shook her head. "What games are you playing, Peter Sullivan?" she whispered.

Closing the door, she bolted it once again. Slowly making her way to the counter, she stared at the side. The small half-door was open. Obviously, Peter was searching for something. Squatting down, she straightened the bags and other various items. "What were you looking for?"

Standing, she pushed the button to open the cash register, only to find it empty. Already getting a sense of her uncle, she surmised that he had most likely removed the cash for the day when he went to the pub that fateful night. Sighing, she moved away and continued adding more items to her list.

Yet, she couldn't stop thinking about her uncle. Sinking down in one of the overstuffed chairs, she gazed around. This was his store. His life. She wanted to find a way of honoring him. Had there been a funeral?

Ivy jumped out of the chair. "Yes!" She loved where her thoughts were leading. Excitement filled her, until she heard the clap of thunder outside. "Blast! Not more rain. It was sunny moments ago."

Running to the door, she opened it wide and gasped. Mac O'Reilly stood on the front steps. "Excited to see me?" The man chuckled low.

"No," she burst out. Seeing the change in his expression, she added, "Sorry, but I was hoping that the rain would stay away for one day."

"Ahh..." He glanced upward. "This is Ireland. One moment the sun is shining down upon your face—"

"And then the sky opens up with showers," she interrupted.

"Aye!" The first drop of rain landed on his head, and Ivy burst out in laughter.

"Come on inside before you drown."

"'Tis only a light summer shower," he responded stepping inside the store. "It'll soon pass."

Ivy left the door open. "Is there something I can help you with?"

"Making the rounds and thought you'd like to have lunch at the pub."

"Umm...thanks. I think I'll pop in later to grab something, especially for Conn."

Mac folded his arms over his chest. "Conn?"

"He's the man working on my Aga and will be doing the repairs on the cottage. You met him last night at the pub."

"The Viking?"

Ivy laughed. "He's not a *Viking*."

Mac snorted in disgust. "Doesn't look like the kind of man who fixes things."

No. He looks like a hunky male model, chiseled from the Gods. "He's working on the Aga, so we shall see."

Turning to leave, he said, "Come by anytime."

"Thanks, Mac. Hey, do you know if there was a funeral for my uncle?"

"Sadly, he wanted none. His body was cremated."

"And his ashes?" she asked softly.

Mac ran a hand through his hair. "Follow me." He led her to the back of the store and over to the history of Ireland, specifically the village of Glennamore. Pointing, he declared, "There is where you uncle sits."

Glancing upward, Ivy saw the green urn residing between two books. She glanced sideways at Mac. "Why is he here?"

"He's waiting for you. Didn't Sean tell you?"

She glared at the man. "What?"

"Damn him," hissed out Mac. "He should have told you. Maybe he was waiting for the right time." Placing a hand on her shoulder, he continued, "One of your uncle's requests was for you to scatter his ashes throughout Glennamore—his land."

Ivy shivered. Recalling how she buried her parents' ashes in the Pacific, she didn't relish doing it again. Sighing, she looked at Mac. Her previous idea took on new meaning. "Before I do so, I would like to have a wake for my uncle on the re-opening of the Celtic Knot. I want to honor his life, since he didn't have a funeral. I believe he would have approved."

Smiling broadly, Mac nodded. "A great idea."

"Do you think you can provide the food and drinks?" She shifted slightly. "Of course, I would pay for everything."

"Absolutely. And don't fret about the money. I'm sure I can think of something. Say have a drink with me other than the Seven Swans?"

What is up with the men in this village? "I would feel more comfortable paying, Mac."

He moved closer. "Are you afraid to have one drink with me?"

"The beer truck is here with our order, Mac," stated Erin behind them. "Do you think you could go let them in at the back?"

Mac glanced over his shoulder. "Yes. Be there shortly." He turned toward Ivy. "Come see me later and we can discuss the arrangements for the food and beer."

"I'd like to add some bottles of whiskey, too," she added.

"You might have to have two drinks with me."

"I'm paying for this," insisted Ivy and moved away from him.

Both women watched him leave and finally Ivy grabbed Erin's arm. "What is wrong with the men in this village? They act like they've never seen a woman before."

Erin's eyes went wide, and then she burst out in laughter. When she calmed down, she replied, "Let me explain...*you* are fresh blood, Ivy Kathleen. Most of the women here in the village have grown up with these men. Those that are still single view the current male population as the brotherly kind, and for good reason."

Ivy shook her head and moved to the front counter. Placing her tablet and pen down, she watched the rain spattering against the windows. "Not interested in dating. There's too much to do with the store and cottage."

Erin strolled over and leaned her arms on the counter. "Don't let them bother you. They may be cute, but they're only men with one thing on their minds."

Ivy gave her a sideways glance. "And it isn't marriage?"

Erin snorted. "They view the ring as a sign of prison." She nudged Ivy. "They like the occasional tumble."

"So I've gathered. I'm not hanging a 'sex for a night' shingle out anytime soon."

Pushing away from the counter, Erin placed an arm around Ivy. "Honestly, they're not that bad, but I foresee someone else in your future."

Ivy shrugged out of Erin's embrace. "Don't know what you mean," she lied.

"How's your *Celt* doing over at the cottage?" asked Erin as she made her way to the door.

Feeling the heat creep up into her face, she turned away from the woman. "Don't know. But he'd better have that Aga working soon." Ivy waved a hand over her head as she headed for the office.

Glancing over her shoulder, Ivy could still hear the woman's laughter as she dashed out of the store and across the street.

The next several hours were spent going over every detail of the accounts, making a couple of phone calls to Sean, and checking in with the bank. Everything had been immediately transferred into her name the moment she signed the papers. Shocked by what the bank manager had told Ivy was in the account, she had to ask him to repeat the figure again. Stunned by the vast amount, she could only nod and mumbled a word of thanks before departing the bank.

Stuffing the statements into her purse, she walked along the narrow sidewalk. Her parents had left her with little money and debts to pay after their premature death. She'd expected the same with her uncle. However, the day was proving to be one full of surprises.

Warm sunlight touched her face, and Ivy lifted her head. Pushing back the hood of her jacket, she smiled, grateful the rain had eased. Heading toward the Seven Swans, her stomach growled the moment she stepped inside the pub. Waving to Erin, she made her way toward her.

"Are you here for lunch?" asked Erin, wiping down an empty table.

"Yes. I'm starving. What's the special today?"

"Beer-battered fish and chips," she responded, moving past her.

"Sounds heavenly. I'll take two orders."

Erin paused. "A date with the Celt?"

She glared at the woman. "He has to eat, too." Pulling out a chair, she sat down.

"Of course, of course," she replied, slipping into the kitchen.

Fifteen minutes later, Erin returned with a large bag. Placing it on the table, she said, "I've added some malt vinegar, napkins, and extra chips.

Standing, Ivy reached into her purse and asked, "How much do I owe you?"

Erin shook her head. "On the house today."

"Absolutely not," argued Ivy. Retrieving a twenty euro, she tried giving it to the woman.

"Next visit, Ivy. Consider this part of Glennamore's welcoming."

Ivy's shoulders slumped. "You've already done so much."

Erin reached for the bag of food and shoved it into Ivy's arms. "Wait until I put my order in for specific romance books." The woman smiled broadly.

"Are you serious?" she asked. "You could give me your list now."

She steered Ivy toward the front door. "Next visit. I like this one particular author. She writes steamy catering romances."

"I'll hold you to it, too," Ivy tossed out over her shoulder walking across the street.

"We can also discuss plans for your uncle's wake. Mac informed me of your idea. Positively wonderful!" Erin shouted back.

When Ivy approached her cottage, she heard shouting in a strange language, and her steps quickened. All the windows had been flung open, along with the front door. A strange smelled assaulted her as she ran inside and toward the kitchen.

Skidding to a halt at the entrance, she stared at the man standing in front of the Aga and speaking foreign words. His hands were fisted at his sides, and he had removed his shoes, standing barefoot on her kitchen floor. She scrunched up her nose at the smell. "What happened?"

Conn looked over his shoulder—his gaze primal. His face was smudged with black streaks, making the color of his eyes stand out more. He quickly turned away. "Bloody thing is fixed, though I cannot say it cooks properly."

Ivy stepped cautiously inside the room. Setting the food on the table, she removed her purse and placed it on a chair. Peering around him, she looked at the charred lump. "What was it supposed to be?" she asked, while keeping her gaze on the item in the oven.

He raked a hand through his hair. "I was attempting to warm one of the muffins from this morning. A simple task, you would think."

Trying hard to keep from smiling, she angled her head to the side. "How long did you keep it in there?"

Shifting his stance, he replied. "A good hour."

Clamping a hand over her mouth, Ivy nodded and turned away. Doing her best to stifle the laughter, she finally turned back around. "I believe the Aga is working properly."

Conn blinked in obvious confusion. "Seriously? How do you know?"

Reaching for a towel, she removed the burnt muffin and tossed it into the sink. "Trust me, I know these things. And if you ever need to heat a muffin again, you only need five minutes."

His eyes grew wide, and Conn scratched the side of his face. "Amazing."

"Why don't you take a break and eat some lunch with me." Ivy moved to the table and removed the food from the bag. "Could you grab a couple of plates from the cupboard, please?"

"You brought lunch?"

His tone surprised Ivy. "Yes. You need to eat, too." She glanced up to find him staring at her. "Go clean up in the bathroom. Your face is covered in grime."

He didn't say a word as he exited the kitchen and returned a few minutes later, retrieving two plates for them. Sitting down at the table, Ivy handed him a napkin.

"Thank you," he replied softly. "What are you doing?"

Her face took on sadness, but then quickly vanished. "I'm writing a list for my uncle's wake. I found his ashes sitting on a shelf in the Glennamore section of the store. Something Sean Casey forgot to mention." She gave a slight shudder. "Anyway, I have to scatter his remains across our lands. But first, I would like to have a proper send-off when I re-open the Celtic Knot."

"Indeed. I believe he would be pleased."

"Eat," she said, pointing to his plate.

"Only if you join me. Your list can wait."

Ivy let out a groan when she took the first bite. "Holy moly!" she exclaimed between mouthfuls. "It's so much better than in America. The fish is so fresh and moist." She continued to eat, the warmth of the food bringing a sense of peace within her. Wiping her mouth with a napkin, she noticed Conn hadn't eaten. He sat staring at her, his intensity heating her face. "What? Food still on my face?"

He leaned forward. "Do you always eat with such *pleasure*?"

"I...um...well it's go...od," she sputtered, embarrassed by his question.

Chuckling softly, he stood. "Let me get you some water."

Frustration seethed inside of her. "Why aren't *you* eating?"

The man shrugged, bringing her a glass of water. "I'll eat the chips, but will pass on the fish."

Realization dawned on Ivy. "You're a vegetarian?"

Conn nodded, reaching for a chip and sitting back down.

"Why didn't you say anything?"

"I didn't want to appear rude."

Ivy gaped at the man, unable to say anything else.

When the first drop of water landed on his head, Conn narrowed his eyes and glanced upward. "Eat your meal quickly, Ivy, for I fear the roof is next on my list for this afternoon."

Chapter Eleven

"Tread carefully toward wee beasties with sharp claws."

~*Chronicles of the Fae*

Drenched in rain, muck, and sweat, Conn did his best to patch up the leak in Ivy's roof until he could return and thatch the place properly. What had possessed him to become her handyman? With a snap, wave, or thought, he could repair almost anything with magic. Not that he didn't mind the manual labor, but his hands itched to use Fae magic on the roof. Unfortunately, a human would not comprehend the repairs in a matter of moments. The Aga was easy, only a minor part needed to be fixed.

Swearing softly, he quickly made his way to his motorcycle, only to find Ivy leaning against the seat. "Is there something else?"

He watched as she trailed her fingers along the leather of the seat, wishing they were on his own skin. "You ride without a helmet?"

"Yes," he answered slowly.

"I've always wanted to ride one, but they seem frightening. I much prefer a horse than a vehicle."

Her response stunned Conn. But then everything about Ivy had him in a state of wonder and puzzlement. "They are both to be feared and respected, though at least a motorcycle will not talk back to you."

She giggled and moved away. "True. I used to own a horse—Daisy, and she was as stubborn as a mule. Mind you, she did have a good temperament, but it was her way or the highway."

Fascinated by her story, he moved closer. "I've never heard the expression about the highway. But if I understand your meaning"—he arched a brow—"she was mighty obstinate with having her own way."

"Sorry. I forget most here don't know American slang." She twisted the ends of her sweater.

"I am a quick learner, Ivy."

"I imagine you are, Conn."

"What happened to Daisy?"

Sighing, she kicked a stone away. "She broke a leg. It was too severe to repair. I loved her dearly, even as she took her last breath with her head in my lap."

All Conn wanted to do was embrace the sprite. Bring comfort to her as she recalled the painful memory. Yet, he kept his hands fisted by his side.

Removing his keys, he mounted the bike.

She glanced upward. "Looks like you'll have a dry trip back to Sean's place. Stars are shining and no threat of rain. Thanks so much for getting the Aga working and patching the roof."

What would it be like to have Ivy riding with him through the hills of Glennamore? His mind screamed at him to remain silent, but the words uttered forth of their own free will. "Would you like to take an evening ride with me tomorrow?"

Seeing the startled look on her face, he waited, holding his breath and fearing her reply.

"Are you sure it wouldn't be any trouble? You'll

probably be exhausted after working all day here."

"I can guarantee you, Ivy, I will be hale and hearty for an evening ride."

Conn could see the hesitation in her eyes, but then she replied, "Then I'll take you up on your offer. But only if you're not too tired."

Smiling broadly, he added, "See you in the morn."

She stood back as he started the engine. Moving slowly down the path, Conn was sorely tempted to look back in his side mirror at the lass who made him react in the most peculiar ways. Breathing deeply, he ventured away from the village—away from the aqua-eyed beauty. He needed to cleanse his body, especially the fire that burned within.

And the icy waters of the lake beckoned him.

****

Conn peered over the rim of his coffee mug at Sean. "Is there a library on the history of Glennamore?"

"No," answered the man while reading the newspaper.

"Then how does one find any information on the village?"

"Celtic Knot."

"Of course," responded Conn dryly.

Sean put down the paper. "What knowledge are you seeking?"

"Family ancestors, battles—anything related to the village." He sipped the strong liquid, making mental notes for items he would require today at Ivy's cottage.

"Thomas kept all pertinent information at the store." Sean scratched behind his ear. "You could say he was the keeper of knowledge, especially the generations of the villagers. Are you speaking of anyone in particular?"

"O'Callaghan."

The man chuckled and picked up his paper. "Should have guessed. There's a section on the village in the Celtic Knot. I'm sure Ivy Kathleen has already seen—" Sean tossed down the newspaper. "Sweet Brigid! I never told her about her uncle's ashes. Completely slipped my mind. I should go out there this moment." The man stood abruptly, but Conn held his hand up.

"She found out yesterday and is making plans for a wake at the re-opening of the store."

Sean let out a groan and collapsed back into the chair. "A wake is exactly what Thomas would have approved of. Though, I must make my apologies later."

Conn stood and placed a hand on the man's shoulder. "I'm positive she harbors no ill feelings toward you."

"'Tis shameful of me, no matter what you say."

Before leaving the kitchen, Conn reached for an apple and tossed it into his backpack.

"Dinner at the Seven Swans?" asked Sean, picking up the newspaper.

"Other plans," he shouted over his shoulder, stepping outside.

Breathing deeply, he glanced upward. "Thank you, Mother Danu for this beautiful day." Kneeling, he placed a hand upon the ground. "Grant us this day without rain." Standing, he smiled, since his final request was for Ivy. Sunshine and a promise of a ride on his bike.

Maneuvering the motorcycle down the path, he turned left and sped down the main road toward the village. Conn had only driven a few miles when instinct had him slowing down. Veering sharply off the main road, he slowed to a stop. Idling the bike, he put his foot down on the ground and cast his gaze inward toward the forest. A thread of recognition flared within him.

Turning off the engine, he got off the bike and walked along the dirt path through the dense copse of trees. Screams ripped through his mind of memories of long ago. The clang of steel echoed within the silence, and his hand longed to hold a sword. As he stepped over a fallen log along the path, a chill of familiarity shot through his blood.

Conn's pace quickened, intent on reaching his destination. Halting in front of a giant yew tree, the air hummed with energy. Glancing in all directions, his vision of another place and time shifted. In the distance was the very place he stood between the mad King of Munster and Dervla. Every detail of the memory now etched in his mind after visiting the Hall of Remembrance.

Gritting his teeth, he swung back around toward the tree. His hand shook as he brought it outward and laid his palm on the rough bark. "Grant me your wisdom of the ages, wise one."

Images tore through his mind—the passing of years within the ancient being, until the one he sought came forth. Keeping his focus steady, Conn could almost hear the lass's breathing on the other side of the tree when she came into his view.

Her head was bent, as she held the cloak firmly around her, while the other hand clawed at the bark. When a scream rent the air behind him, she lifted her head. Conn's heart slammed into his chest at the sight before him. Eyes that he knew well stared back at him. Her mouth opened in shock.

"*Ivy?*" he asked in a strangled voice. Removing his hand from the tree, he reached out toward her.

Instantly, the scene vanished and Conn slumped to the ground. Gasping for breath, he attempted to slow his body's reaction from being ripped through the vision so swiftly. Absorbing the healing energy from the land, he waited a few more moments before endeavoring to stand.

Whispers of ghosts from long ago haunted him as he gently touched the tree. The woman was the image of Ivy O'Callaghan—from the dimple in her cheek, to the color of her hair. The only difference was Ivy's eyes were aqua, and her ancestor's ones mirrored the green hills of Ireland.

Walking around the yew tree, Conn traced a finger lightly over the place where only moments before he had witnessed the lass's hand digging into the tree. "Who were you?" he demanded.

However, the forest responded in silence, unwilling to give up its secrets.

Bowing before the majestic ancient, he whispered, "I thank you for your memories."

Striding quickly back to his motorcycle, Conn made another mental note to heavily peruse the Celtic Knot and all pertinent information on this ancestor.

Twenty minutes later, Conn drove down the path to Ivy's cottage. His nerves were wound tight from earlier, so he relished the tasks he had planned today. Driving to the side of the cottage, he turned off the ignition, dismounted, and reached for the bag of supplies off the back of his bike. Stepping away, he strode to the front of the cottage and halted. What was that infernal howling?

Dropping his backpack at the front door, he moved around to the back of the cottage. Shielding his eyes from the early morning sun, he could barely make out Ivy standing in front of a rowan tree. As he approached her, she turned around. She shook her lovely head indicating not to come any further.

And the howling intensified. Conn's gaze traveled upward.

"Oh, please, won't you consider meeting me halfway. Once you're in my arms, I can untangle you from the mesh," she pleaded.

Conn folded his arms over his chest. "The animal doesn't believe you."

"Hush," hissed Ivy.

"If you come down here, I can feed you some fish." She held her arms out wide.

"Blah. Not to the animal's taste."

Ivy glared at him over her shoulder. "I had the poor cat almost climbing down until you came barreling forth on the scene."

Conn arched a brow. "I don't *barrel* anywhere."

"Whatever," she snapped.

She turned her attention back to the trapped animal in the tree. "Now, as I was explaining, I can offer to free, feed, and give you a proper place to sleep. But you must let me help you."

"In addition to a small bowl of cream once a week, too," Conn added dryly.

Ivy turned and faced him. "Are these your demands, or the cat's?"

Conn chuckled low. "You have no idea what I would demand of you, Ivy."

Her face took on a rosy glow, and she quickly spun around toward the cat. "Yes, you may have your cream. Satisfied?"

"And a warm rug in front of the Aga, as well," stated Conn.

"Absolutely," she responded sarcastically.

Conn gestured to the cat. "Jump," he commanded.

The cat let out a long meow and jumped into Ivy's outstretched arms. "That wasn't so bad," she murmured to the animal.

Conn stepped toward them. "Here, let me free you." The cat let out a hiss, and he pointed a finger at the offending sound. "Need I remind you that I bartered some extra conditions for you?"

The cat turned its head away and Conn proceeded to remove the netting from the animal's leg.

"Shh…" cooed Ivy, stroking its head. "He's not really all that mean. You're a gorgeous calico cat, my friend."

Removing the last of the offensive material, Conn held it up. "Fishermen's netting. Curious how the animal made its way from the fishing shore."

"How far?"

"Several kilometers," he responded, tucking the netting into his pocket.

"In miles, please. This is all new to me."

"Two-and-half miles."

She snuggled the cat against her chest. "You poor thing. You must be famished from your journey."

"She most likely got trapped while savoring the fresh catch of the day," stated Conn.

Ivy tilted her head to the side. "She?" Then her eyes narrowed. "Is this because you view females stubborn and assumed it was a *she*?"

Taken aback by her comment, Conn shrugged. He knew the cat was female from the moment he started speaking to the animal. In addition, all the requests were made by such animal and not him. He was doing his best to handle the situation as a mediator. In truth, he found the feline to be quite stubborn. "If you don't believe me, check for yourself."

"Horrid man." She turned to the cat, "Let's go find something for you to eat, and then you can accompany me to the bookstore." Ivy gave a slight smile to Conn as she passed by him.

"Ungrateful beast," he muttered, though he returned her smile.

Conn watched the pair disappear around the corner of the cottage and rubbed a hand over the back of his neck. The morning had been an interesting one. However, it was the evening he eagerly awaited, and work beckoned.

Making his way to retrieve his backpack, a truck came charging down the road. Stepping quickly aside, he narrowed his eyes at the driver. The man slammed on his brakes, coming to a halt a few feet from Conn. Jumping out of the truck, he went around to the back and opened the doors.

"Are you the one doing the repairs on Thomas' cottage? I have panes of glass for the front window."

Conn strode forward. "Yes, I'm the one mending *Miss O'Callaghan's* cottage."

"Yes, yes," mumbled the portly man. Reaching for the box, he handed it to Conn.

"Do you have an invoice?"

The man waved him off. "Paid for by Thomas several months ago. They were specially made to match the others in the cottage."

"Thank you," replied Conn and walked toward the cottage.

Entering, he almost collided with both females—who looked at him as if he was the offending person.

"Glass panes for the window."

Ivy set the cat down. "Oh, so quickly?"

"It would seem your uncle had ordered them several months ago."

She shivered and rubbed her hands together.

"Are you all right, Ivy?" Conn placed the box on a nearby chair.

She gave him a weak smile. "Fine. I'm fine."

Without thinking, he grasped her hands within his, rubbing his thumb over the vein in her wrist. "I despise that word. It is often used when the person wishes not to state their true feelings."

Ivy swallowed and met his gaze. "Why do you care, Conn MacRoich?"

The words tumbled free from him once again. "Because I do."

Chapter Twelve

"Secure your heart if you venture under a heady mix of stars."

~Chronicles of the Fae

Slumping down at her desk, Ivy massaged her temples. The headache had started early that morning and by noon had traveled down the back of her neck. "Too many visions," she mumbled, closing her eyes. Instead of blocking them, she attempted to draw them forth and brought along the headaches associated with them. "Foolish, Ivy. You should have waited until after the opening of the store." Opening her eyes, she stretched her arms over her head.

Glancing to the side, her new-found friend was curled up among the blankets Ivy had placed within a small box, purring contently. "Ahh...a nap sounds heavenly right now. Take an extra hour for me." The cat lifted its head, yawned, stretched, and went back to sleep.

Shuffling her paperwork into a neat arrangement, Ivy ran her finger down the lists in her notebook. Everything had been ordered for the wake. Phone calls had been made, even the dreaded one to Peter Gallagher of the Glennamore Daily Dispatch. He assured her that the entire village would be there.

Standing, she peered out the window. In two days,

the bookstore would be re-opened. She planned to keep the same hours as her uncle had, every day, except Sundays. Leaning her head on the cool glass, she smiled as several sheep ambled along the grassy hills. Peaceful, content—a place she longed to walk along when time permitted.

Sitting on the ledge, Ivy continued to gaze outward. A road weaved around the trees, and Ivy's thoughts turned toward her evening ride with Conn. What had possessed her to say yes to him? Or even go out to see him off that evening? She was another person around the man. Not the shy introvert her parents often chided her for being. No, she became bold whenever he was near—drawing forth another woman.

"He was probably being nice. And now is burdened with taking me for a ride." She laughed at the ridiculous statements. Ivy could hear her mother chastising her for thinking herself unworthy, as she often told her.

"Why are my eyes so large, Mama? And I don't like the color," pouted Ivy, *turning her head away.*

"Dear, beautiful child. They mirror those of your ancestors. You are special, my wee Ivy."

"I don't want to be special," she complained, *twisting her fingers together. "The other children make fun of me. The older ones said you must have put bleach on my head for my hair to be so blonde."*

Her mother walked around in front of her and knelt. "They're jealous, because they've never seen a faery before."

Ivy giggled. "I am not a faery, Mama."

Her mother trailed her fingers over Ivy's cheek. "Every person on this planet is special, Ivy, some are blessed with gifts—"

Ivy placed a hand over her mother's mouth. "Shh…if Father heard you, he would be angry."

Her mother placed a kiss in Ivy's palm, before taking it into her own. "Do not fear him, Ivy. He may not believe in the old ways, but do not, I repeat, do not cower in front of him." She squeezed her hand and stood. "Besides, he's at work and not at your school."

Ivy glanced around. "He doesn't like me to talk about…you know." She gazed up into her mother's eyes.

"Do not hide from who you are, Ivy Kathleen. Ever. Now, let us go greet your teacher."

Ivy sighed as the last remnants of her memory faded. "I so miss your wisdom, Mother."

Rubbing her eyes, she moved away from the window, only to be startled by the pounding at the front door. Quickly moving toward the entrance, she was grateful for the two windows opposite the door. Peeking outside, she noticed two teenagers chatting and laughing.

Unbolting the door, she put on her best smile and said, "The store will be open in a few days. Please return at that time."

Their smiles transformed into ones of shock. The girl recovered first. "Hello, I'm Nan Sullivan. We're here to help you out."

The boy stepped forward. "I'm Roger Griffin."

Now it was Ivy's turn to act stunned. "Help?"

They both nodded in unison.

"My brother, Peter, mentioned that The Celtic Knot was re-opening and I—*we* were hoping we could have our jobs back," stated Nan.

"You worked for my uncle?"

"Sure did," replied Roger. "It wasn't much, but we enjoyed choosing a free book once a month."

"Really," Ivy replied with humor. Fully prepared to check out their stories, especially when one of them was kin to Peter Gallagher, she added, "Why don't you come in and give me all the details. I'll need to write down your available hours."

Both followed her quietly to the counter. Ivy reached for the pad and pen and jotted down their names. Glancing up, she noticed their solemn looks. "Is this the first time you've been here since the death of Thomas?"

"Yes," replied Nan. "I keep expecting to see him walking down the lane, or sweeping the front steps of the store. Never spoke ill of anyone. And he always made time to listen. He was the nicest man in the village."

"Agreed," stated Roger quietly.

Sorrow for a man she never knew left an ache in Ivy's heart. "Sadly, I never knew my uncle. Thank you for sharing your view of him. You'll have to tell me more stories when you're working here."

"You'll let us keep our jobs?" asked a stunned Roger.

"Why wouldn't I? I can't do this alone and welcome any and all assistance." Pushing the pad and pen toward them, she added, "If you write down your availability and what my uncle paid you—besides letting you have a monthly free book, I would be grateful."

Nan reached for the offered items. "You're wrong, Ivy Kathleen, we're the grateful ones. We feared you wouldn't want to hire anyone."

"Or worse, close the bookstore," added Roger.

"Nonsense. I happen to love books, so owning a bookstore is perfect. I've also noticed how important this place is for the village of Glennamore, too."

"Who's the furry sham?" Roger nodded to Ivy's new friend perched on one of the chairs.

"*Sham*?"

Nan laughed. "Your *friend*, Ivy Kathleen."

Ivy rolled her eyes. "I must order a dictionary of Irish slang." Strolling over to the cat, she picked up the purring animal. "Rescued her from one of the trees by the cottage. One of her paws was tangled in a fisherman's netting."

"She's a beauty," commented Nan, stroking her head. "A perfect mascot for the store. Have you named her?"

"Not yet."

"Give her a name soon, or she'll return to the forest," teased Roger. "I've written down my information. I hear there's a wake tomorrow, so if you need any help, I can come in the afternoon."

Ivy placed the cat back on the chair. "Perfect, Roger. I'm going to open the store at five for the wake. It's more a celebration of my uncle's life in the village. The Seven Swans is catering."

"Ooo...great food," stated Nan. "Do you need help setting up the place?"

"I would love some. Thank you both for stopping by."

"Good. We'll see you tomorrow."

Walking them to the door, she watched as they made their way across the street. Grateful for her unexpected visitors, Ivy realized just how important this wake was going to be—not only to honor her uncle's memory, but for the people. In only a short time, she was finding that Thomas O'Callaghan had been a central part of this village.

****

When the clock in the office chimed five-thirty, Ivy couldn't believe the hour. She'd spent all afternoon organizing and familiarizing herself with the Celtic Knot. Her new part-time helpers were true to their word, since she found records of their hours and pay; including the books that each would choose. Her uncle was a kind and generous man, and Ivy was determined to keep the tradition ongoing.

"Well, *Miss Ivy Kathleen*, you've got the food, drinks, music, invites, and help all done. In addition, the store is in perfect order and ready to open. Are you ready to face an entire village?" She chuckled softly and scooped up the cat into her arms. Holding the animal in front of her face, she asked, "What are we going to name you?"

The furry feline batted playfully at her nose.

"Ahh...but it must be a noble name. For you were brave to not only face me, but the giant man."

Suddenly, Ivy recalled her evening ride with Conn and bit her bottom lip. "I shouldn't pester him for a ride. He's most likely exhausted from everything." She tucked the cat against her body. "We'll send him on his way. In truth, I don't have time for silliness. Or men."

Bolting the door to the Celtic Knot, Ivy made her way slowly to her cottage. Perhaps the man had already left for the day. For a brief moment, sadness engulfed her thinking he would have gone. When she turned the corner and saw his motorcycle parked to the left of the

137

cottage, Ivy's heart started to beat faster.

The light by the cottage door was illuminated, basking the place in a soft, welcoming glow. She noticed the new window panes had been installed and smiled. Tossing her worries aside, she entered the place. A candle burned on the hearth.

Placing the cat on the floor, she continued to move throughout her cottage. Everything was tidied and the place cleaned from Conn's work in the kitchen, but his looming presence was missing.

Frowning, Ivy went out the back kitchen door in search of the mysterious man. There in the fading sunlight, Conn sat in silence on a fallen log. The man appeared in a trance with his head lifted toward the last light of the day and his eyes closed. A magnificent male specimen.

Ivy remained motionless where she stood. Caught in the same mesmerizing spell of the early evening.

A breeze brushed her cheek, and Conn opened his eyes and turned his head toward her. With that one look, Ivy believed he knew everything about her.

Who are you Conn MacRoich?

"Are you ready for your ride?" The soft burr of his voice caressed her, and Ivy shivered as if he touched her with his words.

Tossing aside her worries, the bookstore, and all else, Ivy nodded. "Let me go change out of my dress. I'll be right back."

Without giving him time to respond, Ivy dashed back into the cottage. Rummaging through her closet, she yanked out jeans and a pink T-shirt. Hastily changing into the clothing, she quickly stole a glance at herself in the mirror. Her hair had a mind of its own, so there was nothing she could do about the wavy, wispy mass. Pinching her cheeks to bring out some color, she dabbed some gloss on her lips. Satisfied, Ivy grabbed a brown velvet jacket from the closet as well as her boots.

Stepping into the kitchen, she narrowed her eyes at the cat sitting on one of the chairs. "Yes, it's dinnertime, but you're not allowed on the chairs." Scooping the animal into her arms, she placed a kiss on her head and set her on the ground. "Until I can get to the market, you'll have to be content with some left-over chicken and rice from the Seven Swans."

The cat's response was a deep purring. Ivy chuckled softly as she prepared the meal. Placing the food in a bowl, she set it next to the animal. "Don't get used to all these fancy meals. Cat food is on the list for tomorrow."

The happy feline rubbed against her leg.

"You're so welcome." Giving one final scratch behind its ear, Ivy put on her boots and jacket. Making sure to blow out the candles, she reached for her keys out of her purse, and locked the back door.

Making her way around to the front, her steps slowed. Conn stood leaning against his bike. Excitement flared within her as she moved toward him. "You won't go too fast?"

Conn held out his hand to her. "Never with you, Ivy."

She slipped her fingers within his—warm, strong— filling her with peacefulness and a promise of something else. He squeezed her hand and then smiled.

Releasing her, Conn got on the motorcycle and gestured for Ivy to sit behind him.

As Ivy settled in, he turned partway. "Wrap your

arms around me. Tight."

Nodding, she complied. Conn was a massive muscular rock. She snuggled against his back, inhaling his scent. *Oh my goodness!* The man smelled divine—woodsy mixed with leather. She was too close. Her senses were spinning. Lights danced before her eyes.

"Ivy?"

"Yes," she mumbled in a strangled voice.

"Breathe."

Grateful he couldn't see the embarrassment on her face, she let out a long breath.

The rumble of his laughter made her want to smack him. "Stop," she chided, though started to giggle over her own behavior.

Conn started the engine and leisurely maneuvered the bike down the path and onto the main road. Slow and steady, he drove toward the fading light glinting off the hills. Ivy inhaled the crisp air, relishing the sensation. Glancing upward, she could see the first star of the evening. Smiling, she hugged him more tightly. Joy infused her spirit.

The ride was exhilarating—a quite tranquil journey on an Irish road.

True to his word, Conn made no attempt to speed up. Instead, his pace slowed as they weaved their way around the hills, taking them farther away from the village. The only time she'd experienced the same rush of adrenaline was on a horse. Yet, someone else was guiding her now, and she treasured the brush of the wind on her face and the heat of the man in front of her.

Onward they traveled, the sun finally sinking in the west behind them, leaving the glow of the motorcycle's light in front of them. She had no idea where they were headed, but in truth, she had no worries. Being with Conn felt safe—a new concept for Ivy to ponder later. Why him? Why now? Perhaps it all had to do with the magic of the land. Ireland was steeped in myths and legends. Her mother had told her the stories often—a ritual at bedtimes. She could recite them all to this day.

Sadness weighed on her heart. *You should have shared more, Mama.*

Approaching a stone bridge over the river, Conn slowed the vehicle and brought them slowly to the top of the bridge. Turning off the engine, he turned his gaze eastward. "She rises to greet the evening. Would you like to get off and watch?"

Ivy leaned her head to the side. She gasped and got off the motorcycle. Clutching her hand to her chest, she gazed at the glorious sight in front of her. The moon was slowly rising over the tops of the trees—big and full. "I've never witnessed it so close," she uttered softly. "It's huge." Lifting her hand, she could almost touch the light coming forth from the giant mass.

"Truly a magnificent sight when you are away from the city lights," stated Conn.

"My mother and I would always watch the full moon rise each month. It was our quiet habit." Ivy smiled at him. "Thank you for bringing me here."

He leaned his arms on the stone wall, but his gaze stared outward. "There is magic everywhere, Ivy. On the dew of a flower, in the scent of a rain shower, even in the gifts we all possess."

She stepped closer to him, startled by his declaration. Could he be unique? "Yes, but one must be careful, too."

"Why?" he asked.

"People can be ignorant and naïve. Hate is generated for those that are different."

Conn stood fully. His eyes blazed with that of the moon, but Ivy did not fear this man. "You cannot let others dictate who and what you are."

"It's difficult." She swallowed, wanting to blurt out everything to him about herself. She was tired of hiding in the background, frightened what others would think of her gift.

However, her body swayed to a different rhythm. One as old as time. She didn't care if they'd only met. All she could think of was the *man* in front of her. He oozed raw masculinity, even when he walked. Powerful. Intense. And Ivy desired him—to taste his full lips. Her only fear would be, if one kiss were not enough.

In the soft moonlight, Ivy reached up and touched his face.

Chapter Thirteen

"Intoxication can unleash the beast within a Fae."
~Chronicles of the Fae

Conn fought the bolt of desire spearing a path throughout his body. Her touch spoke volumes—an invitation to taste. Never had he longed to kiss a human like this wee lass. His heart beat loudly, and he found himself unable to move. She was a goddess of the moonlight. It danced off her face and hair, and he trembled before her. Ivy's fingers traced down his cheek and across his lips. He was helpless to contain the growl that escaped from his mouth.

The rush of passion overtook him, and Conn slammed the door on his mind. Grasping Ivy around the waist, he hoisted her up on top of the bridge. Her lips parted on a sigh, and he lowered his mouth to feast on something he dared not take. The first brush of her soft lips against his own ignited a hunger he could no longer contain. Taking her moan deep into him, Conn glorified in the sensation of her mouth—one filled with a honeyed sweetness.

The Fae warrior became just a man for the first time. Something primal burst within him. Emotions he had never felt left him dizzy, spiraling to a physical plane. He craved them all. His lips seared a course down her neck, to her throat, and then recaptured the velvet warmth of her mouth.

Ivy wrapped her arms around his neck, and he deepened the kiss. When her legs went around his waist, he was the one to moan. His body burned to delve inside her—give her all that he had by spilling his seed deep within her. He wanted to claim her for his own. Show her the moon and the stars with every kiss—every touch.

Their kisses were ones of seeking—each exploring the other. Conn slipped his hand under her shirt while his mouth continued to cover hers hungrily. With trembling fingers, he brushed them over her taut nipple through the lacy material. Breaking free from the kiss, he gazed deeply into her eyes. One to never ask—always taking, he surprised himself by saying, "I want to taste you here. Will you grant me this?" he asked while fondling her breast.

Her breathing was labored, but the smile she gave him was a moonbeam of promises. Removing her jacket, she placed it next to her. Lifting her shirt over her head, she undid her bra and dropped it onto the ground. Leaning forward, she whispered, "Kiss me anywhere."

"Are you sure, Ivy? I may ask—*demand* more of you." He trailed a finger between the soft mounds, pale in the luminous light.

Conn watched as lust infused her eyes. "For every kiss you take, I will give back to you on your body. And you can start by removing *your* clothes."

His cock swelled even more with her brazen words. What would it feel like to have her lips on him? Stripping off his own jacket and T-shirt, his gaze raked over her body.

Arching a brow, he cupped her full breasts, heavy in his hands. Yet, he kept his eyes focused on her face. "You are a rare beauty, Ivy."

Ivy shuddered from his touch.

Ever so slowly, Conn bent his head and feasted on the soft ivory flesh. She quivered beneath him, urging him on with her gasping pleas of more. He complied. His lust grew along with the size of his cock, straining to be released.

After grazing his teeth across one nipple, she curled into him and moaned. He inhaled her scent, filling him with a passion he'd never experienced in his lifetime. It was a mixture of the land—sweet and primal, and he ached to possess Ivy.

Lifting his head, Conn crushed her to his chest, recapturing her mouth with savage intensity. She speared her fingers into his hair, deepening the kiss and sending them on a spiral of ecstasy.

"You're intoxicating, Ivy," he whispered along the side of her neck.

"I've never felt this way. It's almost like...magic," she murmured as her body arched against him.

Magic? The human world crashed all around him. His mind screamed at him. What the hell was he doing? By the Gods, he was here to help the lass, not take her up against a stone wall. Her body was like a siren's call—from her voice to the hands that roamed over his skin.

The sound of a lone wolf's cry startled her, and Conn felt her shiver. "Nearby?" she whispered against his chest.

Conn glanced to the left. "Yes," he lied, gritting his teeth. The animal was miles away and posed no threat.

She lowered her head against his chest. "You should take me back home."

"Agreed," he stated softly. Kissing the top of her head, he gently lifted her off the top of the bridge and onto the ground. Turning from her, Conn tried to ease the pain from his swollen cock, along with the one within his heart. Retrieving her shirt and bra from the ground, he silently handed them to her. Turning back around, he gathered his own clothing. The magic of the moment now shattered.

Raking a hand through his hair, he glanced over his shoulder to find her already dressed. Guilt at almost taking her left Conn frustrated and disheartened. He knew the lure of the full moon. Her power, especially with the Fae was one he had ignored. Buried. Warriors had no need for sex. Only in the Pleasure Gardens of his homeland.

Confusion settled within him as he climbed on the motorcycle. When he felt her arms circle around his waist, desire threatened to spill forth once again. Breathing deeply, Conn fully slammed the door on the emotion.

Starting the engine, he took off more quickly than intended, and heard Ivy's gasp. His mood so foul, Conn could not fully utter the apology that formed on his lips.

The scenery passed by them in a blur and soon they were approaching the cottage. The moon shone brightly over Ivy's home, enfolding it in a serene glow. Maneuvering the vehicle to the front, he turned off the engine. She quickly got off the bike.

Remorse riddled through Conn. He owed her an apology for his actions. However, the words remained frozen within all the other emotions. "Ivy," he said in a hoarse voice.

She stood in front of him. Placing a finger on his lips, Ivy shook her head. "Don't you dare say you're sorry for what happened out there, Conn MacRoich. I have never felt so free in all my life. Thank you for the ride, though I believe we should only remain friends. Deal?" She extended her hand outward.

Stunned, Conn blew out a frustrated sigh. Grasping her offered hand, he reluctantly replied, "Deal, Ivy O'Callaghan."

"Good." She released his hand and added, "I'll be at the Celtic Knot early, so I'll leave the key under the mat for you."

He followed her with his eyes until she softly closed the front door. Conn remained for several moments. The lass had surprised him once again, and he tried to reason why this mere slip of a human female had his guts twisted inside out.

Even now, her taste lingered on his mouth. "Good-night, Ivy," he whispered into the darkness and started the engine.

By the time Conn reached the home of Sean Casey, he wanted to do only one thing. Parking the motorcycle, he bounded the steps. Pulling out his keys, he unlocked the door. Light glowed from the library as he made his way in that direction. Walking inside, a blazing fire greeted him, but no Sean. The man had most likely found the comfort of his bed.

Moving to a large cabinet behind Sean's desk, he opened the maple doors. Sean had one of the finest collections of single-malt whiskey, and Conn was going to sample an entire bottle, or two. Reaching for a glass, he pulled down a 21-year old bottle. "Excellent," he murmured. He strode over to one of the leather chairs and sank into its embrace.

Pouring a hefty amount, he downed the fiery-amber whiskey in one swallow. Refilling his glass, Conn continued to belt the drinks back. Nevertheless, the burning liquid did nothing to soothe the ache and longing he felt within his body. "I should have never touched you, Ivy. You're now under my skin, and I don't know how to get rid of you." He gazed into the whiskey glass as if it held a solution to his current dilemma.

Tossing back the liquid, he continued to drink, hoping that numbness would overtake his senses. When he had finished the bottle, Conn wiped his mouth with the back of his hand. Walking slowly to the cabinet, he reached for another bottle. Not bothering to refill his glass, he guzzled deeply. Wandering back to the chair, he sat and stared into the flames.

"Remember, a Fae's emotions are heightened. We are not like the humans. We feel more. We taste more. We desire more. Furthermore, as a Fenian Warrior, you must master and hone these feelings. This will become your greatest challenge. Being around humans can make you weak."

Conn looked at his fellow warrior, Aidan Kerrigan. "You're older than I, so do share how you were able to chain off all emotions."

Aidan clasped his hands behind his back. "As your mentor, I cannot tell you how, only that you must. Each warrior is different. We, a select few, are chosen as the keepers between the Veil of Ages. It is an honor to be selected. You are now one of us. To walk the path of a Fenian Warrior, one gives up a great deal—for a greater cause."

Conn arched a brow. "I have already given up my heritage."

"Do not include giving up heir to the Fae kingdom to the list of grievances, for it sounds like one to me," he scolded. "Find a way to shield your heart. Strength, courage, loyalty, and honor. Use these words to build a fortification around yourself. Always remember, you are a Fae among the humans."

As they continued on the path, Conn glanced at one of the oldest Fenian Warriors. "I will not fail you."

Aidan chuckled. "There is no failure within the Brotherhood. Only lessons to be learned. Remember my words when I am gone."

"You are leaving?" asked a stunned Conn. "I have only been training for twenty years with you."

His mentor clasped a hand on Conn's shoulder. "Aye. Leaving for Scotland. Glasgow in particular. There is trouble festering, and I have been ordered to investigate. Your training will continue with another."

"Return to the Brotherhood soon. You are required here."

Aidan shrugged, gazing off into the distance. "There is something—an unease within me. I almost have a sense that I will not be returning quite so soon." He let out a sigh, and added, "Continue your training, my brother. Our paths will cross once again."

Conn shuddered at the long forgotten memory. Aidan Kerrigan, the oldest and most powerful Fenian Warrior—a friend and mentor to many, never did return to the Fae realm. Instead, he renounced his heritage as a Fae warrior. All for the love of a human female. And in doing so, brought down the wrath of his own people.

"I miss your wisdom, old friend."

The flames snapped and Conn glared back. "I will shield my heart from you, Ivy. If I do not, I fear only harm will follow."

****

Ivy paced back and forth at the entrance to the Celtic Knot. In a few minutes, the doors would be flung open for her uncle's wake. Her nerves were wound so tight, she found it difficult to breathe. The entire day was spent in preparations and now there was nothing to do but wait. Everything was ready. The food was displayed on a long folding table to the left of the counter. There was a mixture of appetizers, fruit, and breads. Mac had brought over Irish stout, punch, and bottles of Thomas' favorite single-malt. Again, the man refused to take any money from her. All was in order. Perfect.

Therein lay the problem. Her mind started to shift to the one man she had pushed aside with the massive workload, and now there was nothing left to do.

Sleep had eluded Ivy after her evening ride with Conn. She'd never sought the comfort of her bed, instead sitting before the fire and gazing into the flames. What made her become so bold with the man? When he dropped her off at the cottage, his look of remorse was written all over his face. But for the rest of her life, Ivy would treasure the memory of making out with Conn MacRoich under the light of a full moon. A kiss that almost went all the way. Did she feel ashamed? Not for a moment. And this bothered her. Finally blaming it on the heady power of the moon, she'd arisen and greeted the new day earlier than expected.

"Are you all right?" asked Nan, touching her shoulder.

Blinking several times, Ivy nodded at the girl. "Yes. I believe it's time." Stepping toward the doors, Ivy unlocked them. Opening them wide, she was unprepared for the sight that greeted her.

Dozens of the villagers were lined up waiting to enter. "Oh, my—welcome. Please do come in out of the cold." She cast a glance over her shoulder at Nan. "Do we have enough food?"

The girl's eyes went wide. "Plenty."

As the villagers entered, each greeted Ivy with a nod, kiss, or embraced her in a huge hug. Overwhelmed by the kindness of these strangers, joy infused her spirit to know that they came to honor her uncle. She deemed it a wise decision to open the store in celebration for him.

Moving along the crowd, Ivy chatted with several of the women. They seemed pleased she was staying and told her to seek them out once she was settled. Seeing Sean walk in, she waved to him as he walked over to the bar area.

She wandered near two young girls and bent down. "Have you seen the faery lights in the children's section?"

They giggled in response. "No," replied the older girl.

"Follow me," ordered Ivy.

Entering the room, Ivy stood back and gestured them inside. An audible gasp came from both of them.

"So pretty," whispered the younger girl.

"Are you sisters?" asked Ivy leaning against the door jam.

"Yes. I'm Becky, and this is my younger sister, Mary."

Ivy smiled at them. "Pleased to meet you both. Feel free to come anytime."

Mary pointed to the corner. "Look. It's a train." She glanced at Ivy. "Does it move?"

Chuckling softly, she replied, "Yes."

It was all the encouragement the young girl required and she scampered over to the toy and turned it on.

"Mary adores train sets over dolls," chided Becky.

Ivy shrugged. "Then make sure you show her the books on trains."

Soon, other children entered the room, and Ivy silently left them alone. Tonight was one of joy, renewal, and friendships. Making her way to the table, she noticed her uncle's ashes had been moved to the front near the cash register. A glass of whiskey set next to the urn. But something else was missing. There weren't any pictures of the man.

Striding over to the counter, she motioned for Mac to pour her a small amount of whiskey. Turning toward the crowded room, she lifted her glass high and gazed at the people gathered. "Thank you all for coming here this evening. I'm sure my uncle would heartily approve of this celebration of his life, especially having it in his beloved bookstore. Even though I didn't know the man, in just a short time, I have discovered how well loved he was in Glennamore. I encourage you to share your stories of my uncle with me, for I have none." Holding her glass toward the urn, she said, "May your days be filled with peace, love, and many books to read. *Sláinte!*"

"And a good bottle of whiskey," add another.

"Aye!" roared the crowd, their words mixed with laughter.

Seeing Erin walking toward her with another tray of food, Ivy cleared an area on the table. "Smells divine."

Erin placed the tray down. "One of your uncle's favorites. Mini sausage and cheese stuffed in puff pastry."

"I'm salivating," commented Ivy.

Reaching for a napkin, Erin plucked one off the tray and handed it to her. "I bet you've not eaten anything all day."

"Ha! You're wrong," scolded Ivy taking the offered morsel. "I had tea and toast."

Erin rolled her eyes. "When? At daybreak? Mac mentioned seeing the lights on in here at four a.m."

"Nope. Tenish." Stuffing the food into her mouth, Ivy closed her eyes and moaned.

"By the sound, I believe you like them?" Erin laughed.

Opening her eyes, Ivy snatched another one from the tray. "They're delicious! But I'm afraid I'll eat them all standing so close to the table."

Erin waved her hand dismissively. "Eat. There's plenty back at the pub." She peered over Ivy's shoulder. "Nice crowd. Don't see your sexy man anywhere. Is he coming?"

Ivy choked on her food as the heat crept up her neck and into her face.

"Mac, hand me a bottle of stout."

Turning away from the woman, Ivy reached for a napkin and wiped her mouth.

"Here, take a sip," ordered Erin and placed the beer in her hand.

Ivy guzzled deeply. "Thanks. Spicy sausages," she replied weakly.

Her friend leaned near. "They're mild. Thomas didn't like them hot."

Ignoring the woman, Ivy was about to take another sip when Conn entered the store.

"Ahh…speaking of the sexy man," teased Erin and nudged her.

Ivy followed his movement as everyone parted when he entered. Most nodded or smiled as he strode to the counter. He took an offered dram from Mac, touched the urn in reverence, and then tossed the drink back.

Friends. We're only friends. Stop ogling the man!

"Are you all right?" Erin touched her arm.

Snapping her gaze to the woman, Ivy noted the concern on her face. "I'm fine. It's been a long week."

"You should wait to open for a few more days."

Ivy smiled. "No. I want to open on Monday."

"Well, tomorrow is Sunday, so rest and recharge."

Ivy squeezed her hand. "Nothing planned but sleep, reading, and eating."

"Good. Have another bite," she encouraged.

Waving her off, Ivy immediately sensed Conn's looming presence next to her. It prickled along her spine as she turned slowly to meet his gaze. "Good evening, Conn," she uttered softly.

"Ivy," he breathed her name in a whiskey-laced murmur.

His smile disarmed all the barriers she had built overnight. The room was too confining. Ivy needed fresh air. Not waiting for a response, she mumbled an apology and pushed past him. Stumbling down the steps of the store, she almost collided with a man.

"So sorry," she apologized.

He steadied her with his hand. "Precisely the woman I came to see. From my contact's description, you must be the new owner."

"Excuse me?" Ivy tried to free herself from the man's grasp, but he kept it firmly around her arm. The look he gave her certainly was not one of friendship. Coldness emanated from those dark eyes.

"Word has traveled that a relative of Thomas has come to stake claim on his land—property that should by rights be mine. I am here to offer you a price you will not want to refuse."

Ivy lifted her chin. "Not a claim. An inheritance and I can't sell the place even if I wanted to. Please release your hold on me."

The man's smile sent a tremor of unease through her. "There are always *loopholes*, Miss O'Callaghan."

She was not going to be intimidated by this stranger. "I will not ask you again to release your grip."

He snarled at her and leaned closer. "What is a wee thing like you going to do?"

"Nothing, because I'll snap the arm from your shoulder and feed it to the nearby wolves," growled Conn, stepping into her view.

Releasing his grip, the man slowly backed away. "Remember the name of Dunstan—Eric Dunstan, Ivy O'Callaghan, and my offer."

Ivy watched as the man made his way to his car and rubbed the sore spot on her arm. As soon as he drove off, she spat on the ground. "Insolent man!" She glanced sideways at Conn. "Thank you. I'll have to ask Sean if he knows the idiot. I think we've made our first enemy here in the village."

"Enemies can be slain," Conn stated, keeping his gaze outward.

Chapter Fourteen

"Broken rituals shall cause a Fae to become unbalanced."

~*Chronicles of the Fae*

Flexing his muscles in the fading light of the day, Conn leaned against a pine tree and waited until Ivy had locked the door on the Celtic Knot. Each day had been the same for the past few weeks—rising before dawn and making sure Ivy's steps led her safely to the bookstore and back home again. From the moment Dunstan had made himself known to Ivy, he—Conn MacRoich had silently become her protector. He had done so all without her knowledge, since she surely would have berated him.

Days and nights became a blur—each busy with their own work. Weeks drifted by, and all the repairs to the roof were done. A job Conn had relished, since thatching was something he had done many a time over the centuries. Old pipes had been replaced with new ones, and he fixed the gate leading to her garden. He would never forget the joy on her face when she saw what he had done to the broken down bits of wood. Conn carved a new one from fresh oak, and she almost wept in his arms.

The moment engraved forever in his memory.

The lights went dark in the store, and Conn slipped

under the heavy branches to wait. Soon, Ivy appeared. However, the lass did not venture onto the path toward the cottage. He let out a hiss as she made her way across the street to the Seven Swans. Tempted to follow the lovely-eyed lass to the pub, Conn stepped forth from the trees. Her hips swayed to a rhythm that called out to him, luring him to go after her.

His steps stilled, and he raked a hand through his hair. "Not tonight, Ivy O'Callaghan." He deemed another would most likely see her safely back to the cottage. She did have her share of admirers making this another reason why he should not follow her into the pub. He might be sorely tempted to take a fist to one of them. Especially to Mac O'Reilly.

Tighten. Release. Breathe. Yet, his hands clenched once more as he turned away from her.

Making his way to his motorcycle by the garage, Conn started the engine and took off for the main road. Increasing the speed, his mood worsened the farther he went. Would he ever rid himself of this fixation over Ivy?

Deciding it best not to be on the road, Conn veered in the direction of Sean's place. Within moments, he came upon the dwelling and brought the motorcycle to the side. Shutting off the engine, he got off and quickly sought the refuge of the home and its owner.

Warmth enveloped him when he walked into the library. Sean was leaning over some scrolls, a dram of whiskey by his side.

"Interesting research?" Conn wandered over to the cabinet and removed a glass. Bringing it to the table, he set it next to the bottle.

Sean kept his focus on the scroll. "Not keeping Ivy

Kathleen company this eve?"

"I'll step aside for the other followers in her group."

The man glanced at the glass. "You've returned without even one bottle to replenish the ones you've drank?"

"My next trip into town."

"Humph! Don't expect me to fill your glass. Your hands are not broken."

Smiling, Conn did just that and bent over the desk. "O'Callaghan lands?"

"Aye," muttered Sean.

Taking a sip of the whiskey, Conn pointed to the frayed parchment. "I take it Ivy has contacted you about Dunstan."

Sean removed his glasses and rubbed the bridge of his nose. "I can tell you for certain, there are no loopholes to claiming her land."

"Yet, here you are studying *said* lands."

Slumping down in his chair, Sean refilled his glass. Rolling the tumbler in his hands, he nodded. "His family has made allegations over the centuries, though it faded over time. Bloody fools, the whole lot of them. They wish to see all the land—from the hills to the coast in their name. Their account is one where an O'Callaghan chieftain took over the lands by killing their kin. It's an outrageous story. If they did their own lineage, they would conclude that the O'Callaghans have always been on this land."

Conn took a seat across from his friend and stretched out his legs. "Why now? Surely Dunstan must comprehend that Ivy is an O'Callaghan and has every right to the ownership."

"Cannot say why the man has aspirations of getting his claws on the land. He came into his own inheritance a few months before Ivy Kathleen, so he might be one of those who simply craves the power of owning all the land around here. His father cared only for the next drink and a woman to fill his bed." He slipped his glasses back on his face. Pointing to the scroll, he added, "You can see only a stream separates the borders between O'Callaghan and Dunstan's lands. I've heard he hired an attorney, but Dunstan was told there is no validation."

"Apparently, the fiend is a lunatic. Or are you concerned there is more to all of this?"

Sean tossed back his drink. "Yes. I would like to bury this ridiculous claim—one that surfaces every hundred years. It is madness."

Standing slowly, Conn walked to the blazing hearth, his blood churned at the memory of seeing Ivy being held against her will. "I seek to banish this notion of his claim, as well. He frightened Ivy with his raving comments."

"Sweet Jesus! He threatened her? She never mentioned being scared of Dunstan."

Conn gave him a sideways glance. "I fear what he would have done to her, if I had not come forth. I doubt his words frightened her as much as his grip. The wee lass stood her ground as he held her firmly."

His friend rubbed his jaw. "I could tell she was upset, but on the phone it's hard to see one's face. Bloody bastard!"

Finishing his drink, Conn walked over to the desk for another. "Why didn't the man come forth after the death of Thomas? Again, why wait until now?"

Sean shrugged and leaned back in his chair. "He may have been away on business. Although, I now hear the man never ventures far from his own lands. He owns many horses and tends to them, so I assume this is why he wants her land. On another note, have you been to see Anne Fahey?"

"No. I am considering taking Ivy with me. The lass continues to ask questions of the villagers."

Sighing, Sean shook his head. "So I've heard. Do you think it wise to take her out to see Anne?"

"She deserves to know everything. This is a part of her life."

"Her parents had secrets—ones that might be best left buried."

"I disagree," argued Conn. "She already lives in the shadows. To seek out the truth will bring light and closure. And it could aid in my plan for her."

Sean snarled. "You now have to deal with a thorn called Dunstan, as well."

Taking a sip of the amber liquid, Conn tried to calm the fury rising within him again. "If you come across anything, let me know. Ivy does not need to be troubled. I will keep a watchful eye on Eric Dunstan."

Arching a brow, Sean put down his glass. "Are you now her protector? Or is there something more?"

"No," he lied. "My path with Ivy is far too important for this kind of distraction with Dunstan. Furthermore, I have no wish to see the lass upset. She is settling in well in her new home."

The man continued to stare at him in silence. How could Conn possibly explain to his friend this fascination with Ivy? It was an overwhelming desire to protect *and* claim her. What he required was a conversation with one of his Fenian brothers. Draining his glass, he set it on the table. "I shall leave you to your research. Do inform me if you come upon any further information."

Striding out of the room, Conn could hear his friend chuckling softly.

****

Greeting the new day in silence and meditation among the trees, Conn absorbed the energy of the land as he knelt. Lifting his head, his gaze traveled upward through the branches, wet from the early morning rain shower. Light shimmered off their limbs as the sun rose slowly into the sky. Peaceful, calm, cleansing—an entire night spent outdoors. When sleep eluded him, he concluded he had become soft around a certain woman. Therefore, he left the comforts of his bed and sought out the training of the land.

The warrior stood.

Shutting off his emotions, he sealed all thoughts pertaining to Ivy, except those necessary to safeguard. No longer would he fall under her spell. He was a Fenian Warrior. Not a human. Lustful feelings could be controlled—eliminated. They were not for him.

Breathing deeply, Conn walked out of the woods, ready to assist his charge.

An hour later, he pulled around the back of Ivy's cottage. Getting off his motorcycle, he decided to look at Thomas's car. If his plans included taking Ivy to see Anne Fahey, they required a vehicle other than his bike for the journey. Furthermore, she needed something for her own personal use, and Conn hoped it was something easily fixed.

His hand stilled on the garage door. Soft cries came

from the back of the cottage. Frowning, he quickly made his way to the weeping person. Conn froze, mind and body numb. The sight before him ripped him apart. Ivy was on her knees rocking back and forth.

Rushing to her side, he could see instantly what had caused her grief and tears. The beautiful garden—one filled with flowers, vegetables, and herbs had been torn to shreds, including the garden gate he had built. Glancing in every direction, the place held a savage destruction he couldn't fathom. "Ivy," he said in a strangled voice.

She lifted her head, tears streaming down her face. In her arms were her cherished roses—petals strewn everywhere. "Why?" Her voice choked on the simple question.

Seeing Ivy in torment, Conn's shields—his defenses dissolved, the warrior slumped down next to her.

Ivy glanced down at her hands clutching the petals. "They destroyed everything, even the beautiful roses in the front. And I only recently scattered my uncle's ashes beyond the garden. It's horrible."

Stunned, Conn muttered a curse. Why had he not noticed the flowers were gone when he drove up to her place? Had he shielded himself off from all, including the land? Guilt plagued him for leaving Ivy alone last night. This was his fault.

"Cruel, mean—an insult to the land," she sobbed, flinging the petals outward.

When he placed a gentle hand on her shoulder, she flung herself into his arms. "I am sorry, Ivy." His hand caressed her back, murmuring words as ancient as the land they sat upon. Cradling her quaking body, Conn let her pour out her sorrow in his arms.

When clouds gathered once more, and the rain threatened to spill down on them, Conn lifted her into his arms and walked into the cottage. Taking her to the couch by the hearth, he placed her down. Reaching for a blanket off the back, he draped it over her shoulders.

Kneeling in front of her, he wiped away a tear from her cheek with his thumb. "What can I do for you?"

Ivy hiccupped. "A cup of strong tea, please?"

He smiled and reached for her hands, placing a kiss along her knuckles. "Done."

Stepping into the kitchen, Conn's hands trembled. Fisting his hands on his hips, he could only think of one person who would have the balls to rip apart her garden. *Dunstan.* But why? He tossed the idea aside, for it made no sense.

He filled and put the kettle on, and then reached for a cup. Within moments, the water heated and he prepared her tea. Stepping back into the room, he noted her face held sorrow.

Handing her the cup, he asked, "Do you need a wee nip of something stronger?"

She rewarded him with a small smile. "Thanks, but whiskey won't help ease the pain." She took a sip of her tea, and added, "However, I might need a bottle later this evening."

"I will gladly purchase the finest for you, too." Conn sat down beside her. "Did you not hear anything during the night?"

Frowning, she held the cup against her chest. "No. Usually, I keep the bedroom window open a crack for fresh air, but by the time I returned home, I was exhausted and climbed into bed."

Conn nodded toward the cat ambling their way. "What about the lady of the keep?"

Ivy chuckled softly. "Ahh…said lady has a name."

He arched a brow. "Do tell."

The cat jumped onto the back of the couch and perched herself behind Ivy's shoulders.

"Neala. It's Irish for—"

"Champion," he interrupted.

"So the *Celt* knows the Gaelic?" Smiling, she sipped more of her tea.

"Among other languages. I commend your choice of name for the feline."

Ivy glanced behind her. "Thanks. And to answer your question, she was snug under the blankets all night, so she didn't hear anything either." She turned her gaze back to Conn. "Why would anyone do this? Do you realize how old that garden is? My shock has turned into anger, because the damage that was done cannot be replaced."

"Nevertheless, the harm can be replaced with new seeds. The land can be healed, Ivy."

She narrowed her eyes. "Who are you? Sometimes the words you speak are incredible."

"Remember, one who is *ancient*," he teased.

Her lip twitched in humor. "Now you're making fun of my words."

Instantly, Conn drew her free hand into his. "I don't jest."

Ivy's lips parted, and her tongue darted out, tempting Conn to taste. "Can you tell me something?" she asked softly.

His heart raced as he traced a path within her palm. "What do you wish to know?"

Placing the cup on the table, Ivy scooted closer to him. "When you were holding me in the garden, what language were you speaking?"

Conn swallowed, feeling the breath of her words against his face. "Why?"

She grasped his other hand. "Ever since I heard you speaking those words that day you were working on the Aga, I longed to find out."

He was compelled to tell Ivy, tired of hiding in his own shadows. If he was going to bring her out of her darkness, he had to step forth from his own. "An ancient language, older than the Celts. From a race who invaded Ireland thousands of years ago."

Conn could see the conflict within her eyes when she spoke. "My mother taught me all about the history of Ireland, so what race are you speaking of?"

"Tuatha De Danann," he uttered softly.

"The Shining Ones?"

"Yes."

"You do know that they're revered here in Ireland? The *Fae*?"

"Of course," he intoned evenly.

Silence followed for several moments. Neala proceeded to clean herself, as if bored by the entire conversation.

Ivy bit her lip and cupped his chin. The contact seared a path across his face. Leaning forward, she brushed a feather-light kiss on his cheek. "Thank you for bringing light *and* humor to me, my friend. Perhaps one day you will share the truth." Moving off the couch, she folded up the blanket. "I'm off to open the bookstore. I'll worry about cleaning up the garden later." Taking her teacup, Conn watched her saunter

166

into the kitchen with Neala following her mistress.

Smiling slowly, Conn stood.

The first seed of hope had been planted. Now, he would wait for the first leaf of knowledge to appear.

Chapter Fifteen

"Celt or Fae? A question often asked by the elders."

~*Chronicles of the Fae*

"Faerytale mush," muttered Ivy, opening a box of books. "Impossible. Ludicrous. Does the man make up stories as he goes along?" Checking off the items from her list on her clipboard, she continued her rant. "Do I look like a fool, Conn MacRoich? The *Fae* language was never written down. Some would say that the race never existed." Her voice continued to rise as she spoke.

Removing the books, Ivy placed them on the worktable. "I believe the next time I see you I'll ask you to spell out some of those fabricated words."

She tossed the empty box onto the floor. "You say you don't jest, but isn't that what you were doing earlier this morning? Ha! I'll find out the truth."

Pausing, her face heated. "Do I really want to know the truth about you? Perhaps you're from another time and place and will disappear when all the work is done."

When she called him a friend earlier, Ivy almost gagged on the word. Yes, the man had become a friend, but she ached for so much more. She refused to throw herself at Conn, since it was her rash decision to remain

168

only friends. Although, when he approached her in the garden, Ivy knew her hero had arrived. He brought the golden light, along with his strength and comfort. "I'm just having a crush on my Celtic fantasy. You'll leave like they all do in my dreams."

"Who are you speaking to, Ivy?" Nan's eyes were wide as she glanced around the workroom.

Ivy waved her off. "Don't worry. No ghosts in here, only the ramblings of a frustrated bookstore owner. And thanks for coming in early. I didn't want to be alone in here."

The girl moved inside the room. "You should be at home, Ivy. I can manage the store."

"I'm fine. Really. My grief has taken on the stage of anger." Ivy gathered some of the books into her arms.

"It was horrible what they did to your place." Nan retrieved the rest of the books and followed Ivy out of the room.

"You've got that right, but we don't know if it was a random act of violence by one or others." Ivy walked over to the history section and began placing the books on the shelf.

"Did you call the Garda?"

"Police? Yes. They'll be out later this afternoon." Turning around, she retrieved the books from Nan and started to arrange them neatly in their place. "Though, I don't think they'll find anything. It's a complete mess. I just want to clean it up, and soon."

"Thomas loved the garden," the girl replied sadly.

Ivy leaned against the bookcase. "Tell me what he liked about it the most."

Nan closed her eyes for a moment. When she

opened them, a smile lit her face. "He called them his friends. Loved seeing the growth burst forth with new foliage in the spring. Thomas had a true green thumb." Her eyes glowed with delight. "Do you know what his secret was to getting them to grow, especially his vegetables?" She tapped a finger to her mouth. "Maybe I shouldn't say."

"You must share," urged Ivy. "Remember, I'm an O'Callaghan."

The girl laughed. Looking around, she leaned closer, and Ivy was drawn in by the secret she was going to confess. "He would talk to them—once in the morn and again in the evening."

Ivy shook her head and smiled. "That's no secret to me, Nan. I've been speaking to plants my entire life. My mother taught me everything about nature. You should have seen the looks people have given me over the years when they've come upon me speaking to a flower, or greeting a tree."

Nan clamped a hand over her mouth to stifle the laughter.

Ivy peeled her hand away. "It's all right to burst out in glee inside the store. It's not a library."

"Oh, Ivy. I'm happy you've decided to stay in Glennamore." The girl surprised her by embracing her in a hug.

Sighing, Ivy whispered, "I am, too."

The bell at the front signaled an incoming customer. Both looked around the bookcase. "It's Mrs. Fraser. I'll go see if I can help her with anything," stated Nan.

"She loves paranormal romance, right?"

Nan rolled her eyes. "Definitely. Hey, you're good.

Only a month here and you already know their likes."

Ivy winked. "I have a marvelous staff to help me."

Nan placed a hand over her heart. "Thanks."

Stepping out of the history section, Ivy meandered over to the mythology section of the store. The shelves were filled with Celtic legends, Gods and Goddesses, tales of heroes, battles, and their deeds. Her fingers trailed along the spines until she came upon the history of Ireland. More specifically, the different invasions. Pulling out the large tome, she wandered over to a back chair and opened the book. Skipping to the contents, one chapter caught her gaze. The one on the Tuatha De Danann. Flipping to the chapter, she read the opening line.

The Tuatha De Danann, the people of the Goddess Danu, were one of the great ancient tribes of Ireland. They were also known as the Shining Ones, or the Fae. According to a significant manuscript, The Annals of the Four Masters, it states that they ruled Ireland from 1897 B.C. to 1700 B.C. Although, many believe they dwelled within the land thousands of years before the first recorded evidence was documented.

Over time, the race vanished. Many believe they descended within the hills, streams, and mountains of Ireland.

"Fascinating," whispered Ivy. "But this is nothing new."

She settled back in the chair and spent the next hour poring through the book. There was no mention of a written language, only a footnote comparing it to a complex melody of words. Flipping to the back section of the chapter, she let out a gasp. An image of the Fae, painted by the renowned artist, Bradon Finnegan in

1460 was a look she had seen often on someone. There were three men in the picture—each standing near the hill of Tara and gazing outward. Yet, it was the man standing off to the side that captivated Ivy. Hair as silver as the moon and eyes that flashed with the brilliance of many crystals. His stance spoke volumes— power and wisdom. Ivy brushed a hand over the picture. The painting was titled, *Meeting of the Warriors*.

"Conn?" The resemblance was uncanny. Goosebumps prickled across her skin.

She quickly turned the page, only to find out there were no more. "No," she uttered with conviction and slammed the book closed. But one name remained in her mind. Who was this Bradon Finnegan?

Shelving the book, she checked on the store and found Nan chatting with several customers. Ivy wandered over to the art section. Scanning the shelves, she pulled out one on Irish painters. When she opened the book, her senses began to tingle. Not bothering to look up, she asked, "Has the Garda arrived?"

"Yes. I gave them an account, but they wish to speak with you."

"Thanks, Conn." She turned to face the man. Yep. *Not only a Celt but also a Fae? Nah, only Irish superstition.* She waved to get Nan's attention. "I have to speak to those *visitors*."

Nan nodded and gave her a knowing smile.

Conn kept pace with her as she headed out the door and down the steps. "Are you following me?"

"I have a proposition for you."

Ivy slanted a sharp glance at him. "I'm intrigued. Anything to do with the garden?"

Pausing, he grabbed her elbow. "It has to do with your parents. Sean believes there is someone outside the village that could help you understand the rift between your uncle and parents. I thought we could take a ride to visit this person."

Ivy gaped at the man in confusion. "Excuse me, but *why* would Sean speak to you about my family?"

Releasing his grip on her, he replied, "Because I asked him. Did you not say we were *friends*?"

I'm beginning to hate that word. "Yes." She jabbed a finger into his rock solid chest. "But friends ask before poking around the sensitive subjects of others. You could have asked me first. It's been frustrating from the moment I found out everyone in this village knew so much about me and my life in the States."

His gentle laughter rippled through the air. "True. Am I forgiven?"

Ivy bit her lip to hide the mirth. By the saints, the man was sinfully gorgeous when he smiled. She turned away from his stare and walked toward the cottage. "It will have to wait until tomorrow." Ivy halted, recalling the recent weather report. "Rain is expected for the next several days."

"Not to worry, I have fixed your uncle's car," he shouted over his shoulder as he made his way ahead of her.

"Conn MacRoich, you're a miracle worker. Or blessed by the Fae." She stifled the laughter and quickly made her way to the waiting police officer.

****

A soft rain greeted Ivy as she glanced out the front window waiting for Conn. All arrangements had been made at the store. Nan and Roger's shifts would overlap for coverage—both thrilled that she was taking some time off. Furthermore, Ivy assured them there would be a hearty meal at the end of their shift at the Seven Swans. Erin had insisted when she found out Ivy's plans, though Mac frowned when he heard Conn was escorting her to Kindale. Apparently, he had misgivings about the *Viking*, as he consistently and arguably called Conn.

"At least there will be distance between us on our journey." She gazed outward. Her face heated recalling the image of Conn without his shirt that night under a full moon weeks ago. She touched her lips, his touch invading her dreams and consuming her thoughts. "Friend or lover, Ivy? What do you want?"

She wasn't ready to answer her own question. Not yet.

When she saw him approach on his motorcycle, she dashed to retrieve her boots and give Neala one more scratch behind her ears. "Watch over hearth and home, my lady."

Neala purred loudly, rubbing against Ivy's hand.

Quickly putting on her boots, she grabbed her purse and hastily made her way to the garage. Ivy halted. Gone were the black jeans. Today, they were blue and a white shirt under the leather jacket. His hair hung in soft waves around his shoulders, instead of being tied back. Why did he make her mouth go dry? She blinked. "Good morning."

He nodded and smiled. "Good morn, Ivy." He lifted his hand into the air. "Should I call upon the Gods to clear the rain away?"

Ivy glared at him. "Are you jesting again?"

He walked to the passenger side of the car and

174

opened the door for her. "I told you, I don't jest, especially with you."

"Then, yes. Today I would enjoy sunshine on our trip," she challenged.

Conn closed his eyes. The air warmed around them, and Ivy became spellbound by the silence that followed. Slowly, he opened his eyes. "Done." He gestured for her to take her seat inside the car.

Bemused, Ivy complied. Snapping the seatbelt in place, she waited.

Her mysterious Celt entered and secured himself. Starting the engine, he smiled.

"What was wrong with the car?" she asked, determined to bring her focus to a rational conversation.

He patted the dashboard. "It only required a new battery. An easy solution."

Ivy looked away. "I do hope you're saving all the receipts. You haven't shown me any since you started working on the cottage."

As he maneuvered the vehicle out of the garage and onto the main road, Ivy frowned when he remained quiet. She knew he must have already spent a great deal with the repairs.

"Conn?"

His mouth twisted wryly. "There are none."

Ivy shook her head disapprovingly. "I will *not* be indebted to you. I can't believe—"

"Not a single person would give me a receipt. They informed me that it was their parting gift for Thomas," he interrupted.

"Seriously? You're kidding."

His hands clenched on the steering wheel. "Can you not accept a gift, Ivy? Must you always deem I'm teasing or speaking untruths?"

Shocked by Conn's tone and formal words, she stared at him. "Is this you losing control?"

His mouth twitched in humor. "I find myself doing so many times around you."

"Oh…" Ivy quickly averted her gaze when he glanced her way.

"Does this offend you?"

"No," she blurted out, regretting saying anything. Silence should have been her choice.

His laughter filled the car—warm and sexy, like hot chocolate. Or honey smothered on hot male buns. *Your mind is positively wicked, Ivy. Change the subject now!*

"When I spoke with Sean last evening, he said Anne Fahey left Glennamore not long after my parents left for the States."

"Apparently, her attentions toward your uncle were not reciprocated, so she left the village."

"Hmm…there's more to this story. Sean was hesitant with his facts. Yet, he did say he would send her an email to alert her we're coming."

"Why would you believe there was more?" he asked softly.

Ivy turned her gaze back toward Conn. "Gut instinct."

"Has it always been thus? Do you rely on your intuition?"

"Yes. But what about you?" Ivy could see a muscle twitch in his jaw. What secrets did this man hide?

"It is in each of us—this ability to sense the truth. Although at times, I have been wrong. My *gut*," he glanced sharply at her, "has steered me in an erroneous direction. I have recently faced consequences I've made from those rash choices."

Ivy shrugged nonchalantly. "We're not perfect, Conn. We're flawed as humans."

"Some more than others," he added with mock severity.

"True," she uttered softly. Sweeping her gaze outward, she almost shouted in glee. "Your gods heard you. Look at the sun shining over the ocean!"

"Always," he responded with a smile.

"The view is stunning. I've missed the ocean." She sighed, leaning back against the seat.

"It's only a few kilometers from your cottage. You could walk there," suggested Conn.

"I've been busy lately," she replied dryly. "But I plan on getting some walks in when I return." Ivy cracked open the window and breathed deeply of the salty sea breeze.

"Tell me about your life. Was it a happy one? Were your parents content living in America?"

Ivy snorted. "Only if you share yours."

"Nothing much to tell."

She kept her focus on the waves. "Conn MacRoich, I believe you have a lifetime of stories to share."

Once again, his laughter filled her. "And it would take more than a lifetime to tell you, Ivy O'Callaghan."

Chapter Sixteen

"If one seeks to open Pandora's Box, they must possess the strength to close it as well."
~Chronicles of the Fae

Conn sent out a prayer of thanks to the Gods for pushing back the storm clouds and letting the sun burst forth. He would do almost anything to see a smile remain on Ivy's face for the duration of their journey. The lass had endured too much emotional upheaval from the moment she arrived in Ireland. This latest trauma—her glorious garden, tested his endurance to keep calm. He longed to rip apart the villain. Yes, he deemed there was only one person responsible. The human scent lingered, but he dared not utter a word to Ivy. How could he explain? If only he had all of his powers, Conn would hunt down the person and do what they had done to her heart—when they destroyed her garden.

He flexed his hands on the steering wheel. Stealing a glance at Ivy, her mouth was parted as she stared outward. The ocean had its own healing, soothing properties. Seagulls flew gently past them, and he caught her slight smile. She looked peaceful, and he ached to brush back a strand of hair from her cheek.

Quickly averting his gaze, Conn concentrated on the road. Once again, he rebuilt his shields, doing his best to seal off his emotions from this female. In truth, Conn was finding it extremely difficult to maintain them. Each day, he grew weary of building the walls all over again. Could there be something wrong with him? For a brief moment, he considered reaching out to a Fenian brother. *Screw the consequences. I require their wisdom.* Yet, he knew none would answer his call.

"Are you all right, Conn?" Ivy inquired softly, placing a gentle hand on his arm.

Slamming the door on his thoughts, he glanced down at her tiny hand. Her touch soothed the conflict between warrior, Fae, *and* man. "Processing past deeds," he replied, pulling off the road and onto a narrow path.

"One of these days you'll have to share more than clipped sentences with me. Friends do share their troubles, too."

Friends. He almost spat out the word. Conn wished for more and this bothered him immensely. No matter how he tried to deny his feelings, the desire haunted him day and night.

Seeing the sign to Anne Fahey's home, he turned onto the lane. Bringing the car to a stop in front of her place, he turned off the engine. "Are you prepared?"

Ivy kept her hands clenched together. "I don't know if I want to find out. Maybe I shouldn't delve into my family's secrets."

Conn studied her concerned profile. "Remember, they're now your secrets to keep locked or to set free. Nonetheless, if you don't ask, you'll always fret over not finding the answers."

She lifted her gaze to meet his. "You always say the most profound things. Thank you." Letting out a sigh, she undid her belt and exited the car.

Conn followed and placed a comforting hand on the small of her back. The simple gesture seemed to calm them both as they climbed the steps to the woman's house. Ivy stole a glance at him before knocking on the door.

They didn't have to wait long. The door opened to reveal a stunning older woman. Conn guessed her to be no more than fifty, but shadows haunted her eyes. She drew her hand to her chest and tears misted her eyes.

"Sweet Brigid," she gasped. "*Ivy*...Ivy Kathleen O'Callaghan?"

Nodding slowly, Ivy smiled. "Yes. And you're Anne?"

"Sorry, yes. Please do come in." She moved aside to let them enter.

Ivy gestured toward him. "This is my friend, Conn MacRoich."

Anne stood transfixed in the small corridor. "You're the spitting image of your father, Ivy."

Frowning, Ivy countered, "I never saw the resemblance, but thank you."

"No. No, you would not," she mumbled. "I have some tea and sandwiches in the front room." Not giving them time to respond, Anne made her way down the hall and disappeared into the room.

Conn arched a brow. "Odd."

"Definitely. I don't look anything like my father," she whispered.

He waved her onward and then followed Ivy into the room. The place was small, yet, cozy. A window framed one side of the room, its view of the trees spanned as far as the eye could see.

The woman busied herself with filling teacups and plates with tiny sandwiches, and stealing glances at Ivy. When they were settled, Conn sniffed the tea and hesitantly took a sip. A good glass of whiskey or a pint would have been his desired drink of choice, but tea would suffice.

"Thanks so much for seeing us on short notice, Anne," commented Ivy, sipping her tea.

Anne smiled weakly. "It came as a surprise when I found out Thomas left you the store. I had no idea he had kept in contact with you."

"He didn't," she corrected. Ivy placed her cup down. "You see, Anne, I never knew anything about my uncle until I received a letter from Sean Casey telling me I had inherited his estate. It came as a complete shock—one that I'm still coming to terms with. Apparently, it was my mother who wrote to him."

Anne rubbed her brow. "Oh goodness. Very distressful, indeed."

Ivy stole a glance toward Conn and shrugged.

Ask your questions, Ivy

As if hearing his unspoken thoughts, Ivy asked, "Can you tell me why my parents left Ireland, Anne?" She hesitated, but continued, "I want to know everything. There were too many secrets, and I believe it's time to find out the truth."

The woman gave a nervous laugh. "Secrets? Truths?" Standing abruptly, she moved to the window. Rubbing her hands over her arms, she shook her head. "Where do I begin?"

"I've always found that it's best to start at the beginning," suggested Ivy.

Nodding, Anne kept her gaze on the trees. "I have

never spoken of this to anyone, Ivy Kathleen." She turned and faced them. "Not until this moment. Everyone, except me, is now gone from this world, so there is no harm in telling you. Nevertheless, be forewarned, for what I'm about to tell you will alter everything you've been led to believe."

"I can face anything, especially the truth."

Anne tilted her head. "Really? You may think otherwise afterwards. Even your opinion of me and your parents could change."

"Do you not deem it best to unburden your secrets?" asked Conn.

She clicked her tongue. "It no longer matters to me." Anne pointed a finger at Ivy. "However, it will change her life."

Ivy stood and pounded a fist against her chest. "I have lived most of my life hiding my own secrets, Anne. Enough!" Walking to the woman, she grasped her hands. "I'm a grown woman of almost thirty, so I think I can finally hear the truth."

Anne cupped her chin. "Then the truth you shall learn." Leading Ivy back to her chair, the woman went to a cabinet and pulled forth a bottle of whiskey. Bringing it back to the table, along with three glasses, she poured some in each. "Before I make a toast to the departed, I will start at the beginning."

Leaning back in her chair, Anne closed her eyes. "We were all so young and foolish years ago. Good friends...good lovers." She opened her eyes, and Conn witnessed hatred mixed with sadness within them. Lifting her glass, she drained it quickly and set it back down. "Your mother was my dearest friend, Ivy. Nevertheless, all that changed when she fell in love with the man of *my* dreams—the man I longed to marry one day. Thomas O'Callaghan."

Ivy gasped. "What are you saying?"

Anne held up her hand to halt Ivy's words. "Please, hear all of my account first."

Conn placed a comforting hand on Ivy's shoulder.

"Continue," urged Ivy.

"As I was saying, your mother had set her eyes on the man I talked incessantly about for months. Never once did Sara mention she had developed feelings for Thomas. She let me ramble on. I should have known, since she didn't encourage me to seek him out. Silence was her response to my gushing comments," she snapped. "Then one evening, I caught them both holding hands and laughing in the park. I was furious. I went and sought out Patrick. For, you see, he was in love with Sara, and I thought—*believed* she was dating him. All this time, I spilled forth my secret crush to my best friend, only to find out she betrayed me." She gripped the sides of the chair. "Oh, she claimed they had been secretly dating for six months, since she knew her mother wouldn't approve. Thought Sara deserved better." She sneered. "Your mother's excuse for not telling me was that she didn't want to hurt my feelings and hoped I would seek out someone else, especially since Thomas would never return my affections."

Anne leaned forward, wringing her hands. "But she was wrong. Thomas *would* love me. All I required was a plan. I immediately sought out Patrick. He was livid when I told him. Vowed to beat the crap out of his brother." She laughed bitterly. "And he kept his vow. Took out his fury on his brother's face, breaking his nose and several teeth."

Conn felt Ivy shudder under his touch.

The woman folded her arms over her chest. "In the end, it was I who went to lend comfort. For you see, I had my own plan. I tended to Thomas's wounds, soothing his own anger with my words, hands, and some drugs that I bought to help him sleep. I know revenge is wrong, but I was desperate to have Thomas as my own." She sniffed and reached for her napkin, wiping her nose. "I knew word would reach Sara, so I waited until I heard her car approach. As Thomas lay in his bedroom, I stripped my clothing off and tossed on one of his T-shirts over my head. When your mother came bursting into the house, I was the first person she came upon. My hurt was so deep that I concocted a lie involving Thomas and myself, though I elaborated and told her we had been sleeping together for several weeks. Of course she didn't believe me, but Thomas was incoherent and only wanted to sleep. So when Sara called out to him, he yelled at her to get out, believing it was still me."

Anne stood and went to her desk. Opening a drawer, she pulled out a picture frame. She ran a finger down the front of the glass. "I loved him dearly. In the end, we both lost Thomas. In spite of that, Sara always had a piece of him with her."

"But my mother married my father—Patrick," stated Ivy. "Why would she do so if she was in love with his brother?"

"She had no choice," responded Anne flatly.

The truth slammed into Conn and his hold on Ivy tightened. "Whose picture are you holding?"

Her lips thinned. "The only man I ever wanted in my life." She moved slowly across the room to Ivy.

Turning the picture around, she added, "Your father."

"No." Ivy's hand shook as her fingers touched the glass. "*No*," she uttered with more conviction. Jerking free from Conn's grasp, she stood.

"That's *not* my father. He's my uncle!"

Conn also stood, though he kept his hands clasped behind his back. "The similarities are there for anyone to see, Ivy—from the eyes, dimple in the cheek, and hair coloring," he stated softly. "You cannot deny the resemblance."

She glanced up at Conn, and he could see the pain reflected in her eyes. "It can't be... This is shocking news."

"Your mother was pregnant when she came to the house that evening. Her only recourse was to seek out Patrick."

Ivy glanced sharply at the woman. "He married her knowing she was pregnant with another man's child?"

Anne shrugged. "He loved her. Although, I believe, he didn't know she was carrying a child at the time they got married, which was the following week. Shortly afterwards, she found out the truth—knowing I fabricated the lie and Thomas was innocent."

"When did he—*Patrick* find out he wasn't the father?" demanded Ivy.

"Shortly after your birth. The image of his brother was all over your features."

Placing the picture on the table, Anne sat down. "Patrick thought it best to leave the village. He had no wish to see Thomas and Sara reunited. He also made sure his brother never saw you before they left."

Ivy's faint smile held a touch of sadness. "But he did come to know all about me—*my life*. My mother

185

made sure to keep him updated."

"Was Patrick a good father to you?" asked Anne, brushing away a piece of lint off her sweater.

"He provided a roof and put food on my plate, so yes," responded Ivy bitterly. "In truth, the only love I received was from my mother. At times, I feared the man who I thought was my father."

Conn could sense the fury mixed with sadness within Ivy. "When did you leave Glennamore?" he asked, trying to bring the conversation to some closure.

She quickly glanced at the photograph and swallowed. "When Thomas said he never wanted to see me again. He found out from a mutual friend what I had done. I could no longer stay in a place where he might choose another to marry."

Ivy clenched her hands. "He never did marry. Apparently, the only woman he loved left." She shook her head. "I hope in time I can forgive you, Anne."

The woman stood to meet Ivy's hard stare. "I don't want your forgiveness. I would do it all over again."

Sighing, Ivy reached for Conn's hand, and he squeezed her fingers. "Thank you for telling me the truth. At least my mother had a part of Thomas with her always. You were left with bitterness."

Anne glared at them. "Beware, Ivy, when cupid's arrow strikes you. I pray it's with someone who can love you back."

The woman's words haunted Conn as they made their way out of Anne's home.

Chapter Seventeen

"Once a woven love knot has been spun, the bond cannot be undone."

~Chronicles of the Fae

"What a wasted life—full of remorse and bitterness," snapped Ivy as she continued to stare outward toward the ocean as they sped along the road. "I'm stunned, confused...*angry.*" She refused to let the tears fall. Once they did, she feared she would never be able to stop the flow.

"Obviously, the woman will continue with her obsession with a man that was never hers to begin with. She wasn't strong enough to move forward in her life. Her feelings were not of love," declared Conn.

Ivy turned toward him. "She's demented."

"A touch," he agreed.

"All these years..." She blew out a frustrated breath. "To think I never knew the man who was truly my father."

"You said you feared your father—*Patrick*. Why?"

Where should she begin? How she ached to explain all to Conn. Rubbing at her temples, Ivy couldn't get enough air. The scenery was a blur, and all she wanted to do was run along the ocean—have her feet touch sand and water. "Stop the car," she pleaded. "I need to get out and walk. It's too confining."

"Where?"

"*Anywhere*," she ordered, trying to maintain her composure and not become a blubbering idiot in front him.

Gripping the handle of the locked door, she held on until Conn could venture off the main road. Clenching her eyes shut, she tried to take in deep calming breaths. Anxiety clawed at her, fracturing her mind and spirit.

"You can exit the car, Ivy," he spoke softly.

She didn't need to be told twice and bolted from the vehicle. The blast of sea breeze slapped across her face as she made a sprint down to the ocean. Stopping halfway, she removed her boots and ran parallel along the waves.

Blissful freedom. If only she could fly, she would venture far off into the horizon. When she could no longer run any farther, she slowed her steps and faced the rolling waves. A calming rhythm to quiet her racing heart. Here is where she let the tears fall freely.

"Collect my sorrow Manannán mac Lir and transform my tears into crystals," she uttered quietly to the God of the Sea.

"I have faith he has heard your request," stated Conn behind her. His voice was a soothing balm on her wretched nerves.

Ivy kept her focus on the rise and fall of the waves. "My mother used to bring me to the ocean when the arguments became fierce in our home. I knew *he* didn't much like me, though I tried so many times to gain his favor in anything. All I wanted—*craved* was some kind of approval."

"Your father?"

She sucked in a breath. "*Patrick* is not my father.

The veil of truth has been shown." Ivy picked up a stone and tossed it far. "No wonder he hated me. I wasn't even his real daughter."

Conn spun her around to face him. Taking his thumbs, he wiped away her tears. "You were his kin. He should have loved, cared, and protected you." Placing a gentle finger under her chin, he held her gaze. "The man was a coward—taking your mother and you away from your heritage."

"My *mother* could have stopped him, though," she argued. "I loved her tremendously, but I'm a bit angry with her, too. Why didn't she divorce him and return to Ireland?"

Conn frowned, his handsome face suddenly solemn. "Questions without answers."

Grasping his hand, Ivy held it tight within her own. "You asked if I feared him. The answer is yes." Her lip trembled, but she gave no care. The time had come to strip away the layers of secrets. "I have a gift, Conn. One where I can see the past or future. Sometimes it comes without warning, and there's nothing I can do, especially when meeting someone new. Or, a vision will start with an aura—flashing lights and I go into a trance. My mother did her best to protect me from him, but he hated the outbursts."

Ivy scanned his face, but no trace of shock or disbelief shown. "He hated that I was different. Called me a freak of bad genes. Now I know why."

"Because you inherited your gift of sight from your biological father," confirmed Conn.

She placed her head on his chest, warm and safe. "He vowed to beat me if I couldn't control them, though my mother made sure he never laid a hand on me."

His arm wrapped around her shoulders, drawing her closer to him. "Bastard," he growled.

Clinging to his jacket, Ivy gazed up into his face. "The past is gone. I cannot undo what has already occurred. Nevertheless, I can make sure the future is not one cloaked in shadows. I have you, Conn, to thank for listening, *encouraging* me to share."

His hands cupped her face. There was an invitation in the smoldering depths of his eyes, and she found herself spiraling into an unknown abyss.

Ivy was tired of living behind a shroud of lies, especially with the man in front of her. She was a fool to think he could only remain a friend, when she desired so much more. *Can this friendship mean more? I've never wanted—needed another man like I do you.* Her heart screamed at her to utter the words, but her mind kept her tongue silent.

Conn bent his head near her ear. "Ivy, *ghrá—* love," his breath hot against her cheek.

Moaning softly, she leaned closer, her lips searching his. He captured her mouth, hot and demanding. Ivy returned the kiss with a hunger that belied her outward calm. Reaching upward, she delved her fingers into his silky strands, deepening the kiss. His tongue stroked the inside of her mouth, sending her senses reeling. The roar of the ocean a distant hum as Ivy clung onto him needing to feel more. He tasted of the woods—wild and free.

God, how she desired this man. She wanted to break down his walls and bring him comfort—soothe his demons and share his worries.

In one swift move, Conn lifted her into his arms,

his mouth trailing a path along her neck. "Tell me to stop, Ivy," his words came out in a strangled voice.

She pulled on his bottom lip with her teeth. "No."

Desire flared and slashed within his steel blue eyes. "Are you prepared to accept all I give you?"

"I crave your touch everywhere. You've haunted my days and nights." No longer letting fear guide her, Ivy traced her finger along his chin, and added, "Claim me, Conn MacRoich, for I am all yours, and I'm tired of denying what I feel for you."

Words she couldn't comprehend poured out of the man as he carried her across the sandy beach, grabbing her boots along the way. He walked past her car and strode into the forest. Ivy remained silent, watching his profile—raw and sensual. There was no going back. Their destiny now set. He continued to move with fluid grace through the dense foliage. At times, the tree limbs seemed to lift all on their own to let them pass through. But Ivy didn't care, for the magic of the land surrounded them. Her blood burned to be with Conn.

Leaning her head on his shoulder, Ivy watched him take them deeper within the trees.

Thunder rolled in the distance, and Conn's steps hastened to a partial clearing. Slowly, he brought her feet to the ground, his hands firmly on her back.

He released her and cupped her face. "I will take you here upon the land—in the light. The grass will be your bed and the flowers your pillow. Your pleasure shall be mine." His hand moved under her dress to skim her thighs. "And mine will be yours." He kissed her tenderly before walking around to her backside.

Ivy trembled. Above the trees, the sky brightened. Warmth and desire surrounded her, seeping into her toes and curling up within her body. She yearned to be free from her clothing. To touch her skin with his. She slipped the jacket free from her body. Easily pulling the dress off over her head, she heard his soft hiss, and smiled.

She shivered as he trailed his finger down the length of her back, stopping at the tattoo just above her lace panties. Conn's presence loomed behind her, his breath hot against her neck. "You're not wearing a bra?" The burr of his voice a heady sensation.

Ivy's breathing was labored as his finger moved around the lace. "No," she uttered softly.

His fingers tugged at the material, and she groaned from the friction over her sensitive core. "A Celtic knot suits you."

"You approve?" she asked softly.

His laughter breathed warm against her skin. "Have you not seen my own?"

Peering over her shoulder, her breath hitched as she gazed into his eyes. "They're stunning," she answered, staring into his brilliant depths.

Conn turned her around to face him. He had stripped his shoes and shirt off, revealing a muscular body chiseled from the gods themselves. She tilted her head to the side to gaze at his tattoos running down the length of both arms—from shoulder to wrist.

He placed his hands on her hips. "You are a vision, Ivy. More stunning than I ever imagined."

She arched a brow. "So you've imagined me...*naked*?"

His gaze raked over her body. "Yes."

She traced a path on one of the Celtic tribal tattoos, the heat flooding her face. "I've often wondered what you would look like without clothes, too. I thought of you posing nude for a drawing."

"Truly?" His smile was hot and seductive.

Ivy glanced back at his tattoos. "What do they all mean?"

Placing his head on her forehead, he replied, "My lineage."

"Can you share more?" Ivy placed both hands on his chest.

"After I make love to every inch of your body." He then smothered her mouth with demanding mastery causing her knees to become weak.

Conn drew the breath from her lungs and then gave it back to her mingled with his own. Breaking free from the kiss, her vision was clouded with passion. He left her aching for more.

Taking a few steps back, his gaze was one of promises to come as he slowly removed his jeans. Tossing them aside, he waited. Ivy tried to look away, but the sight of him lured her forward. A perfect male specimen. Her Adonis come to life. A man like no other and Ivy wanted him not only for today, but always.

"Are you afraid?" His voice whispered low as he held out his hand to her.

Ivy slipped her fingers within his. "Never when I am with you."

Their lips met, and she felt buffeted by the winds of a savage harmony. His hands roamed over her skin, inciting a roar of sensations that begged to be satisfied and released. When his fingers squeezed her nipple, Ivy groaned. He broke from the kiss only to feast on her breasts. She swayed to a rhythm powerful and intense, not knowing how much longer she could remain standing.

"Your smell is intoxicating, *mo ghrá*." He fondled one breast while his other hand glided over her abdomen to her curls. His finger slipped inside Ivy and moved back and forth, taking her to an entirely new height of urgency.

"More, Conn," she pleaded rocking against his hand.

He nuzzled her ear. "What have you done to me?"

Ivy couldn't respond, his fingers making slow sensuous circles. The blaze of desire built with each movement—so close to flame. She watched in a lust-filled haze as he knelt in front of her. When he stopped, she groaned in frustration, and his lips descended to capture her torment in her most private area. The touch of his mouth sent a shockwave throughout her body and stars flashed before her eyes. His tongue teased, coaxed, sending her on a wave of ecstasy more powerful than anything she had ever experienced.

Scooping her up into his arms, Conn brought her down upon the soft grasses. She could feel the length of his arousal large against her side. "Take me," she whispered. "Now."

"Once I take you, there will be no other," he stated firmly.

"Hmm…you're sounding medieval." Ivy skimmed her hands across his abdomen until she reached her destination. Grabbing his swollen erection, she squeezed, eliciting a growl that vibrated across the land.

Conn had only wanted to soothe Ivy—a chaste kiss of healing on the beach. Yet, the fire of something more raced through him, burning the blood within his veins. Now, he would give her something he had never given before to a woman. Himself. His heart. A binding pledge that he had vowed never to give to anyone.

Nudging her thighs apart, he continued to stare into eyes that had mesmerized him from the moment they met. She opened fully for him. The moment his cock touched her sweet entrance, he thought he would die. Groaning, he slowly thrust into her, and she welcomed him inch by inch into her warm body. His arms shook trying not to spill his seed, tasting her ivory breasts, and moving in a dance more ancient than his ancestors.

"Conn...oh, *Conn*," she whimpered.

He knew her release was near, and he waited. Time stilled, their breathing became labored, and then the wave of pleasure shattered through them both sending their bodies in exquisite harmony with one another. The world spun, tilted, and Conn roared as the release poured out of him and into Ivy.

A cool breeze drifted over the lovers, as they lay tangled in each other's arms. Conn brushed a lock of hair away from Ivy's eyes. The sun streamed down around them, casting a glow on her beautiful features. She was lovelier than any in his own world.

A lone tear slipped down the side of her face.

His heart froze, fearing he had hurt her. "Why do you weep?"

Her eyes fluttered open. Reaching up, she placed a hand on his face. "Tears of joy. I never knew that making love—*real* love could move your soul."

"*Mo ghrá*," he said softly, caressing her body with his fingers as his mouth devoured her sigh within him.

He wanted to be her confidant. Her champion— slay any and all demons for her. But most of all, Conn wanted to be her lover. *Forever*.

Chapter Eighteen

"A path not chosen, but taken, will be fraught with sharp curves."
~*Chronicles of the Fae*

When the first drop of rain landed on Ivy's breast, she giggled. A sound he found enchanting. She was his sprite of the forest. As another splashed on her cheek, he kissed the water from her face. She wiggled under him, and his cock swelled at the invitation. Nuzzling her breasts, he murmured, "If you continue to move sensually, I'll be forced to take you again."

"In the rain?" she asked, opening for him.

"Are you afraid of a little water?" he teased, tracing a path along one breast with his tongue.

"Bah! Bring it on," she encouraged, wrapping her arms around his neck.

Thunder rolled directly over them as Conn thrust deep within Ivy. The sky could have opened with hail and lightning, but he was lost in the arms of the most bewitching woman he had ever met. She was the sun, moon, stars above him, and the earth beneath Conn. As he roused her passion, his grew stronger. Moving in a primal dance, the liquid fire built inside of him, and he captured her cries and mingled them with his own— shattering into a million pieces. His release so strong the ground shook beneath them.

Moments passed before Conn could focus. Trying to calm his racing heart, he shielded Ivy from the torrential downpour. Her eyes were closed as he kissed her swollen lips. "Unless you want to be knee deep in mud, I believe we should get out of the rain."

Her eyes flickered open. "Come back to the cottage with me?"

"Will you feed me?"

Ivy arched a brow. "It depends on what you're hungry for."

"You have wicked thoughts, lass."

"Only when I'm around you."

Conn stood and reached for Ivy's hand to help her stand. "Not true. I want to hear more about this proposal of painting me in the nude."

Her face turned crimson, but she didn't look away. "Those thoughts don't count. Also, I don't recall saying anything about a proposal."

"Yet, you have intrigued me," he responded dryly.

As Conn gathered their wet clothes, he moved them under a large pine to shield them from the rain as they attempted to dress themselves. Ivy's dress clung to every curve, and he was tempted to strip her of the fabric and make love to her once again. Instead, he placed his leather jacket over her shoulders.

"Warmer?"

She smiled fully at him. "I was never cold."

Grasping her hand, he pulled her toward him and kissed her soundly. Then Conn scooped her up into his arms and headed back to the car.

"I can walk, *Sir Knight*," she mocked, tracing a finger down the side of his face.

"I like holding you."

Conn could feel her gaze, but he kept his focus on the land. Soon, he stepped out of the forest, made a steady path to the car, and helped Ivy inside the passenger side. Slipping in next to her, he fumbled for the keys. Moments later, they were headed back to Glennamore.

By the time they returned to the cottage, the sky had turned black, and the rain had turned into a vicious storm. Conn maneuvered the car near the front entrance and Ivy dashed out. When she was safely inside her house, he drove to the garage and parked the vehicle. Sprinting back to the cottage, he stripped free from his boots and left them outside the front door.

Stepping inside, Conn made his way to the hearth in the sitting room and placed kindling and wood inside. Wiping his nose, he looked around for matches. Seeing none, he grumbled a curse. Taking a quick glance over his shoulder, he turned back around. Flexing his fingers, he let the sparks dance off onto the wood. Instantly, the blaze took hold. Warmth and light flooded the place, and he smiled.

"How did you start the fire?" demanded Ivy, towel drying her damp locks and looking adorable in black leggings and a sweater dress that hugged all her curves.

"Matches," he lied.

She gaped at him. "I have none. It was on my list to purchase at the market."

"Found one lying nearby." He stared at her, daring her to challenge him.

"Lucky find, since I cleaned this place only yesterday." Ivy moved into the room and stood in front of the blazing heat.

Conn shrugged dismissively.

Slumping down in a chair, she lifted her bare feet to the fire. "Ooo…feels heavenly."

He remained standing. "No socks?"

She wiggled her toes. "Nope. I've always hated them. I only wear them with boots. My mom—" Ivy paused and looked away. Sighing, she continued, "She told me that it started as soon as I could walk. She'd always find me running around without shoes and socks. My feet were constantly dirty." Ivy glanced at him and laughed. "Said I was a child of the Fae."

Amused, Conn only nodded.

Ivy jumped up. "I'm sorry. Here I'm babbling on about me and have changed into dry clothes, but you're sopping wet. Give me your clothes and I can put them in the dryer."

"Eager to have me out of my clothes, *ghrá*?"

She swallowed. "Yes, but food first. And I need to find something for you to wear." Tapping a finger to her mouth in thought, she then darted out of the room. Returning a few moments later, she handed Conn a plaid blanket. "I think it's large enough to cover your…um…you know, your body."

He leaned down near her ear. "And only you would know how large."

Ivy's eyes went wide. "Really? No others?"

None that were human. "Not as important," he clarified.

Taking the offered plaid, Conn chuckled as he made his way into her bathroom. Stripping his clothes free, he wrapped the material around his waist. Proceeding out of the bathroom, he found the small closet with the washer and dryer. Placing the items inside, he turned it on.

The aroma of food enveloped him as he entered the kitchen, and his stomach protested.

Ivy laughed. "Hope you're hungry for leftover vegetable soup and beer bread." She glanced over her shoulder. Her mouth hung open, and then she snapped it shut. "Magnificent," she muttered.

"Did you make it?" He peered over her shoulder, inhaling deeply.

She snorted in disgust. "Of course. I don't eat *all* my meals at the Seven Swans. It will only be a few more moments. If you don't mind, I'd like to sit by the fire and eat. There's a fake fur rug in my bedroom, which is located on the far right of the hall. Would you mind fetching it and placing it by the fire?"

He kissed her behind the ear. "With pleasure."

Leaving the kitchen, Conn hastened upstairs. When he entered her bedroom, he froze. In the corner of the room, set an easel, but it was the drawings on her dresser that captured his eye. Stepping closer, he brushed his fingers over the likeness of himself. A chill went through his body. The image was from long ago— the time when he took the oath of a Fenian Warrior. He stood before the crystal pillar and pledged his vow.

"Sometimes my imagination grows wild," she uttered softly from the entrance.

"When did you draw this?" he asked, keeping his eyes fixed on the drawing.

"The day after we met." Ivy walked inside the room. "I believe it's one of your ancestors."

You're wrong, Ivy. You have captured me at one of the most pivotal times in my life. "You have a powerful gift, lass." He glanced at her sideways.

She hugged her arms around herself, moving

closer. "I know. This one was extremely intense."

What will you do when you find out they're one and the same? Can you accept the Fae along with the man? Frustration slithered inside of Conn, but he quickly banished it. "Your talent at drawing is rare, as well."

Smiling, she turned the sketch over. "I studied at the Art Institute in San Francisco. However, my true passion was history, so I left and got my degree in ancient history." Lifting her head, she added, "And now I'm running the Celtic Knot."

He placed a gentle hand on her shoulder. "An admirable quality, too. I would like to hear more about your life." Reaching for the fur, he walked out of her bedroom and descended the stairs.

"Oh no you don't, mister." Ivy poked him in the back. "You said you would share more about your life."

Conn dumped the fur before the fire and grasped her around the waist. He kissed a path along her neck. "I believe my words were *after* I made love to every inch of your body."

She pushed against his chest, though her eyes held desire for him. "No. Not one more kiss shall I grant you until you offer some morsel about yourself. Or two."

Ivy dazzled him with her determination. Lifting one of her hands from his chest, he kissed each finger. "You win."

Reaching up on her tiptoes, she kissed him, lingering, savoring every moment. Breaking free, she whispered, "Food first."

He watched her saunter into the kitchen and return with two bowls. Handing them both to him, she strolled back to retrieve the bread and two bottles of beer.

They settled down in front of the blazing hearth and ate their meal in silence. Conn savored the richness of the broth—heavy with herbs and vegetables. Tearing off a piece of bread, he sopped up some of the liquid. "Delicious."

"Just an old recipe," she stated between mouthfuls.

"All praise to the cook, too."

Conn placed his bowl down and reached for the beer. Taking a long swill, he gazed into the flames. Contentment and anxiety clawed at him. How much of his life did he want to share with Ivy? And where did one begin? Wiping his thumb around the rim of the bottle, he said, "My mother and father are still alive. I have one sister—a twin, though her hair is as black as night. I was raised in a place near the Hill of Tara. I have spent my life working at various jobs and positions—more as an advisor. I was schooled at the finest in the land."

"Interesting. Never married?" she asked, wiping the crumbs from her mouth with a napkin.

"The opportunity didn't present itself." He hesitated briefly. "In my line of work, there is no room for a wife *or* a relationship. I am always moving from one place to the other."

"Hmm…and now?"

Conn raked a hand through his hair. "I am at a crossroads in my life."

"Am I a passing fancy until you set off on your new path?" she asked softly.

He glanced sharply at her. "No."

Her faint smile held a touch of sadness. "Good. Though I feared you'd be gone come morning."

Frowning, Conn reached for one of her hands.

"This is new to me, Ivy. I am not one to bed a woman and leave the next day." He shook his head, unable to explain further. How could he tell her that he only sought sexual pleasures in his own realm? Furthermore, they meant nothing to him, only a release.

She brought his hand to her lips and placed a kiss inside the palm. "I believe you've shared enough for today."

His eyes roamed her face and a sudden urge to take her on the fur overtook him. "You are more beautiful than the stars."

Scooting closer to him, Ivy brushed away a lock of hair from his face. "I am only one and there are many brilliant ones."

"Ahh...but your beauty outshines them all."

Blushing, she withdrew from his touch and stood. "There is something I've longed to do and I mentioned it in the woods. Stay right where you are."

Swallowing the last of his beer, Conn followed her movements out of the room. Cleaning up the area, he placed the bowls and bottles on a nearby table.

Ivy returned carrying a large sketchpad and pencil. She had stripped free of her leggings causing his mouth to become dry. Her sweater dress barely covered her bottom, and his fingers itched to renew the path from her ankles to the secrets hidden under the material.

Tossing down several pillows, she made herself comfortable. "I would like to sketch you."

Conn arched a brow seductively and tugged at the plaid. "With or without?"

Eyes that blazed with desire held his own. "I'm afraid I wouldn't be able to draw anything if I remove your plaid. Besides, I can already see your desire for other artistic activities."

He threw back his head and roared with laughter. "Later, *mo ghrá*."

Flipping back the cover, she smiled. "Definitely."

"And the pose?"

Gesturing with her hand, she replied, "I don't like forced poses, and you have a strong profile. So turn back toward the fire, with one knee bent and arms clasping the knee."

He eyed her skeptically. "Anything else?"

Ivy tapped a finger to her mouth. "Please stay silent."

"Your wish is my command." Turning his attention to the flames, Conn let his mind drift. An entire life had been spent learning rules and preparation. He was a chiseled and hardened warrior, not one for softness. His world was unknown to Ivy—she a mere lass that slipped under centuries of training. Why did he let it happen? He had walked blindly into her life, unprepared for the consequences. Words from an old friend came back to haunt him. Did not his mentor, Aidan Kerrigan, warn him to always be on guard with the humans? Nonetheless, the Fenian Warrior ignored his own guidance and *married* a human.

Conn stole a glance at Ivy. Her hand glided over the paper, while she bit her lip in concentration. Turning his sight once again to the flames, he realized that none of it mattered anymore. When the heart of a Fae opens to true love, there is no turning back. Bleakness and despair will follow if a Fae fights against the inevitable.

However, another realization slammed into him. What about the lass from centuries past? Did she not deserve a chance of freedom and love? If he changed one thread on the loom, would it change Ivy's fate?

His fists clenched. Conn had never considered his plan thoroughly. His mind and heart screamed at him—a battle of rights and wrongs. To undo an injustice, he stood the risk of losing the one woman who had captured his heart—Ivy.

There had to be another way.

"Conn?" Ivy's soft touch splintered through his dark thoughts.

He blinked and grabbed her around the waist. Desire drummed in every cell of his body. It built like a storm—a dizzying current racing through him. The thought of losing her fractured a part of his very soul.

She angled her head toward him, the glow of the firelight illuminating her features. "What troubles you?"

"Battles yet to be fought," he responded and then took her mouth with savage intensity.

Conn let out a groan when her tongue darted inside, dueling with his. The kiss spiraled through his veins, and he battled not to take her swiftly. Slipping one hand along her thigh, his fingers brushed against her soft curls, eliciting a cry from Ivy. He stroked between her folds, teasing, tormenting her. Her pleas turned to whimpers and Conn tried to be gentle, but his blood roared within his body.

Breaking free from the kiss, Conn tossed aside his plaid and swiftly removed Ivy's dress. She reached out to touch his swollen cock, but he tossed her back on the fur rug. "No," he growled in protest.

He leaned over her, his love—all his. Words spilled forth—ancient, claiming her in a ritual as old as time. Ivy lured him forward with her own words and outstretched hands. Searing a path down her neck with his lips, he thrust deeply inside of her. Her heat surrounded him. Withdrawing slowly, he slammed back into her. The pleasure so exquisite, he cared not if the world around them had burned to ashes.

When the wave crested, Conn soared, taking Ivy's passion and desire with him. Stars opened and moonlight cast her glow on the lovers. Her cry of release echoed his and for several moments, the world dissolved around them.

As Conn held Ivy's quaking body, he whispered the sacred words in an ancient language—words he vowed to never speak, and he hoped she would comprehend the meaning, for he could not utter them in her language. *Until the mists descend and I depart from this life to the next, you shall have a part of me. I weave my love freely—heart to soul, soul to heart. I bind you with these words to me always. We shall walk in the land of forever as one love.*

Pain sliced through his chest, leaving him temporarily unable to breathe. When the last remnants faded away, he rolled onto his back, bringing Ivy against his side.

The flames snapped, the only sound in the room. Conn's eyelids grew heavy, beckoning his body and mind to slumber.

Right before sleep lured him away to its peaceful abyss, Conn heard her soft whisper echo in the room, "I love you."

Chapter Nineteen

*"Removing the Fae-colored glasses will illuminate
the truth."*
~Chronicles of the Fae

Go away.

Her body was warm, sated, and blissfully content.
Nevertheless, something kept swiping at her nose. Too
tired to move, she willed it to vanish. It did not belong
in her peaceful world of dreaming. Contentment filled
her being, and Ivy desired to remain happily in this
beautiful realm.

When the beast dared to intrude once more, her
hand flung outward, smacking away the soft, furry
creature. "Leave," she uttered, but found her voice
lacking a more commanding tone.

Then said feline started to lick her face.

"For the love of Zeus, be gone." Ivy turned away
from the departing, purring animal and tucked herself
closer to the hard, hot male body.

"Zeus was a demi-god according to the Goddess
Danu. He boasted of powers that he never had. A bit of
a show-off, so I've been told," murmured Conn as he
nuzzled her neck.

"What?" Ivy laughed and slowly returned to the
land of the living. However, she found herself slipping
into a pleasurable rift as Conn's fingers traced a path

207

over her breasts, lingering to fondle each softly.

"Truth," he replied in a husky voice as his hand swept down her abdomen. "Apparently, he had limited powers, but liked to claim otherwise. Taunted the other Gods and Goddesses."

Ivy let out a moan when he flicked one finger over her sensitive core. "You're just full of make-believe stories."

His hot mouth descended over hers, silencing any further conversation. Yet, their desire was short lived by the pounding on the front door.

"Bloody bastards," growled Conn, removing the blanket from their naked bodies and standing.

The pounding continued, and he started to make his way to the door.

Ivy stood instantly and pulled on his arm. "You can't answer my door without any clothes on."

He shrugged and glanced around the room, obviously looking for his clothing.

"They're in the dryer, remember?" she hissed, reaching for her sweater dress.

She stumbled to the door, and Conn yanked her back. "I refuse to let *you* open the door half-naked."

She rolled her eyes. "Barbarian."

Dashing into her bedroom, she shouted over her shoulder, "I'll be right there!" Tugging on her leggings, she ran back to the door.

Flinging it open, she faced the glare of none other than Mac O'Reilly. "Good morning," she greeted in her most cheerful voice.

The man took in her appearance, and Ivy fought the urge to run her fingers through her hair and straighten her dress. Keeping the door partially closed, she waited for him to speak.

"Are you ill, Ivy Kathleen?"

Almost choking on laughter, she shook her head. "Never better. Was there something you needed, Mac?"

"I was concerned—"

Ivy almost let out a groan when Conn appeared behind her. His presence loomed over her. The man was so close, the heat poured off his body and onto her back. She fought the urge to jab him in the stomach with her elbow, especially when he fully opened the door revealing their love tryst.

Mac's gaze darkened. "What are *you* doing here? I thought all the repairs were done."

Conn put a hand on Ivy's shoulder. "None of your business."

Ivy smiled sweetly up at Conn, though her eyes held daggers. "Could you give us a moment?"

His reply was a kiss on her lips. Giving her a wink, he then strolled away.

Turning her attention to Mac, who now had his fists clenched, she said, "I'm sorry, but there's no need to be concerned. Thanks for checking. Conn is taking care of a few minor repairs."

"Erin and I grew *concerned* when customers came in for lunch asking why the store was closed. They feared you were feeling ill."

The blood drained from Ivy's face. "What time is it?"

"Almost noon," clipped Mac.

"Damn," she muttered. "Thanks. I'm sorry. Long day yesterday. If anyone comes asking, tell them the store will be open within the hour."

"Yeah, right." Shoving his hands into his pockets,

he stormed off down the path.

Closing the door, Ivy bolted into her bedroom and yanked clothing off hangers. Pulling out underwear from her dresser, she almost collided with Conn on her way to the bathroom.

"No time for a meal?" He held a slice of toast in one hand and a cup of tea in the other.

Ivy nodded. "I've never overslept in my entire life." Taking a bite of the offered food from his hand, she shook her head in frustration.

"You were exhausted," he countered.

"Humph!" Taking in his appearance, she scowled. "You could have at least put on a shirt when you came to the door."

Shrugging, he tore off a piece and plopped it into her mouth. "The man needed to know his place. You are mine."

"Do you hear yourself, Conn? You're acting like a medieval cave man."

"For your information, medieval men did not live in caves," he responded dryly.

"Infuriating man," she complained and walked into the bathroom.

Conn immediately opened the door and handed her the mug. "We don't want the Mistress of The Celtic Knot grumpy without her morning...ahh...I mean *noon* tea."

"Oh, for the love of Brigid," she snapped, though Ivy's mouth twitched with humor as she closed the door on his smiling face. "And don't forget to feed Neala, too!"

****

No sooner did Ivy open the Celtic Knot than Erin

came walking across the street. Knowing her brother, Ivy would bet everything she had that he spilled what he saw earlier to his sister. Erin had a grin on her face that made the Cheshire cat in Alice in Wonderland's story tame.

Handing a mystery novel to Mrs. Thompson, she hastily started to make her way to the back of the store, when the woman grabbed her arm.

"Are you sure this is the author's latest? The plot sounds awfully familiar."

"It's the most recent." Snatching the book from her hands, she flipped to the publication page and pointed. "See, it came out three months ago." Snapping it shut, she handed it back to the woman.

"Goodness! I never thought to look inside." Smiling, Mrs. Thompson gathered her other items and brushed past Erin.

"Hello," greeted Ivy, picking up some magazines off a nearby table.

Erin said nothing as she followed Ivy to the magazine rack. After several moments, Ivy glanced over her shoulder. Her friend stood against one of the bookcases, arms crossed over her chest.

"As you can see, I'm hale and hearty. I just overslept." Filing the last magazine, she moved away from the woman.

But her friend was quicker and stepped in front of her path. "Overslept?" She pinched Ivy.

"Ouch!" Rubbing her arm, she glowered at the woman. "What?"

"Don't you mean you were preoccupied with a tall, sinfully gorgeous hunk of a man? All night long?"

Images of Conn flashed within Ivy's mind and her

face heated. "Gosh, your brother is horrid. He's most likely telling the tale to everyone who enters the pub."

Erin laughed and linked her arm through hers. "Nope. Only me. He came storming into the pub and straight into the kitchen. The first thing he reached for was the largest knife, cursing the man's name."

Ivy's eyes grew wide. "Tell me you didn't let him leave?"

The woman tugged on her arm. "My brother has a fiery temper, but he would never go after someone in a rage. He is pissed it wasn't him in your bed. Although, he generally does care about you, even though you won't date him."

"Definitely not like a sister," she stated flatly.

"Hell, no! Because then he would certainly take a blade to Conn's balls. You should see how he treats the men I decide to date. Lately, I've been meeting them in the next village. I love my brother dearly, but he can be a pain in the ass and overprotective."

Both women burst out laughing.

Ivy blew out an exasperated sigh. "You should have come and checked on me, not your brother."

"I was on the phone. Didn't have a clue until Mac poked his head into the office and said he was running over to the cottage to check on you. Mentioned several customers were wondering why The Celtic Knot was closed."

Ivy peeled herself away from her friend's grasp. "As you can see, I'm fine. Next time, I'll set the alarm."

"So, was it a lovely evening with the Viking?"

She was sorely tempted to toss a book at Erin. "Extremely." Striding to her office, Ivy went and stood by the window.

"Will there be more *lovely* evenings?" asked Erin, sinking down in a chair.

Not prone to discuss her personal life with anyone, Ivy kept silent. She never had close friends and only two boyfriends in her life. Sharing intimate details with someone was something foreign for her. Not even her own mother had known when she had sex for the first time. Ivy had lived a life keeping her own secrets tucked within—safe and secure. Yet, with Conn, she took the first step in peeling back a piece of herself, and a part of her longed for a girlfriend to share confidences, compare notes on life—particularly men.

"I'm sorry, Ivy. I didn't mean to pry. Thought maybe you wanted to talk about it."

Seeing the forlorn look on Erin's face, she moved away from the window. Leaning against the desk, Ivy drew in a long breath and released it slowly. "It was the most magical night of my life, Erin. I think I've lost my heart to the man."

Erin jumped up and clasped Ivy's hand. "I *knew* he was meant for you. The stars and the Fae have aligned perfectly for you both."

Ivy snorted. "*Fae?*" Stepping around the desk, she sank down in the chair and opened a drawer. "Ireland is an extremely superstitious country."

Arching a brow, Erin pointed a finger at her. "Best be warned, Ivy Kathleen, that your house sits on land approved by the Fae centuries ago."

"That was hundreds of years ago. Don't tell me people actually consult them in the twenty-first century?" Pulling out the monthly journal, Ivy paused.

"They sure do," argued Erin.

Deciding not to debate the subject, Ivy withdrew

the ancient keys. Placing them on the desk, she asked, "Do you have any idea what these are for?"

"Ahh…you found the puzzle Thomas was working on." Erin drew up a chair and sat down. "He found them in a box buried in the garden a few months before he died. They were deep under a tangle of foxgloves. Told me that he stayed away from the area, since the flowers are special to the Fae—"

"Good grief," grumbled Ivy. "Reminds me of the painting."

"As I was saying, Thomas decided they were intruding on the herb area. Therefore, as he started pruning the foxgloves, he stubbed his foot on a large stone. When he removed the item, he found the box. He'd only mentioned it to me." Erin pointed to one of the larger keys. "This was the original key to the cottage."

Ivy traced her finger over the cold steel. "Amazing. But how did he know?"

"He kept the hardware pieces in the garage. Always wanted to re-do the oak door and use them, but he didn't have the key." Erin tossed her long braid over her shoulder and leaned across the desk. "Your uncle searched the entire cottage and store hoping to find what they unlocked. Sadly, he never had a chance to ask anyone in the village, and I simply forgot about them. Although, he could have found their purpose and didn't have a chance to mention anything. We were all very busy the few weeks before his death."

Picking them up, Ivy decided to ask Conn about them. He gave the impression as an expert handyman, so he might know what they were used for. Instantly, pain shot through her arm and slammed into her head.

White lights flashed before her eyes. Fighting the wave of nausea, Ivy clutched the keys to her chest, spiraling to an unknown place within her vision.

"Ivy Kathleen?" Her friend's voice called out to her from far away.

Standing in the meadow, Ivy could see the three men in a comical conversation. One of them laughed and smacked the other on the shoulder. In the center was another man at an easel, waving his paintbrush at them and demanding they stand still.

"Ye ken we are waiting for another. Do ye not wish him to be in the painting?" asked the tall, striking man with auburn hair.

"Aye, of course. Will I be honored by any others?"

"Nae," replied the other giant of a man with hair as black as night. "Remember, 'tis only for ye, Bradon. Ye have been chosen to paint us."

Bradon nodded. "It does nae matter. No one will believe me. I only wish to capture the light around ye."

The man with black hair approached him. "What ye do today, will be remembered. Your name shall be revered by the Fae. Your skill is extraordinary, and you have been chosen."

"I thank ye," stated Bradon and moved back to his easel. "I hope your other friend arrives soon. The light is fading."

The dark-haired man rubbed his chin in frustration. "By the hounds, can he never be on time, Liam?"

"The warrior keeps his own schedule." Liam snorted and leaned against a tree.

"Ye ken I had other duties, Aidan Kerrigan," protested another man strolling forth from the trees.

"About bloody time you arrived, Conn."

Ivy gasped, her hand reaching out to him. As he turned toward her cry, their gazes locked and the vision clouded and receded.

Numbness and blindness surrounded her. Ivy fought the inky blackness and struggled to return to the voice calling out to her. Desperately fighting the wave of pain, she took in deep breaths, trying to calm her racing heart.

Warm, soothing arms were wrapped around her as Ivy managed to crack open her eyes. Dumping the keys on the desk, she wiped her trembling hands on her skirt.

"For the love of Brigid, what happened?" demanded Erin, handing Ivy some tissue.

She waved her off. "Thanks, I'm all right."

"A vision, then?"

Goosebumps broke out on Ivy's arms. "Definitely."

"Do you want to talk about it?" Concern filled her friend's voice.

"You'd think me crazy. What do you know about Bradon Finnegan?"

Erin blinked and stood back. "He was a famous artist, born here in the village. When fame took over, he left. Near his final days, he requested to have his ashes sprinkled near an old oak tree up in the hills. The place was a favorite—one where he painted many landscapes." She sighed. "The priest was furious when Bradon requested to be cremated and damned his soul to Hell. But the villagers loved him. He used to stay at Castle Lintel. You can see the ruins from the store. Bradon did many paintings of the castle and surrounding landscape."

Looking back down at the keys, Ivy frowned. "I saw him painting on a hill, surrounded by trees. Do you think one of these belonged to him?"

"You don't know, do you?" Erin shook her head and smiled. "Bradon Finnegan is a cousin to the O'Callaghan clan. Not only was he born in your cottage, but he also lived here briefly. His paintings are stunning. Some are on display at the museum in Dublin."

Ivy narrowed her eyes and stood. "Stay here." Walking out of the office, she made her way to the history section. Retrieving the desired tome, she stormed back into the room. Opening the book, she flipped to the one of the painting by Bradon Finnegan.

Placing the book on the desk, she pointed to the page. "The man that painted this picture is my ancestor?"

Erin nodded. "Yes."

"Is this painting—*Meeting of the Warriors* in Dublin?"

"Wow! I've heard of this painting, but have never seen a picture." Her friend's shoulders slumped. "Sadly, no one has been able to find it. The item was stolen soon after he died. If it's ever recovered, the painting could be worth almost a million dollars."

She stared at the woman in shock. "You're kidding, right? I knew he was famous, but why would it be worth so much?"

"The village council tried to buy one from a collector many years ago. Unfortunately, the price was too steep—a half-million dollars. After the collector died, it went to the museum in Dublin. Bradon Finnegan had a way of capturing the light in his work.

Many people believed he was gifted with magic. He filled his landscapes with animals along with men and women from Celtic mythology. His work is sought after by collectors in the art world."

Glancing back down at the painting, Ivy's world was fast becoming a mix of the real and surreal. *Conn may resemble a Celtic God, but he's not...right? Stop! Crazy life you spiraled into when you accepted the invitation to come to Ireland.*

"You know the blond man bears a striking resemblance to Conn."

"Must be an ancestor," mumbled Ivy, closing the book.

"You'll have to ask him," teased Erin, a smile warming her eyes.

Ivy's hand trembled over the keys, fearful of more visions. Finally picking them up, she looked at Erin. "More secrets to unlock."

Chapter Twenty

"A well fed garden will not only honor the Fae, but reward your soul."

~Chronicles of the Fae

Dark clouds loomed overhead as Ivy scurried from the Celtic Knot in the lingering twilight. Quickly entering her home, she dumped her purse on the table. Greeting a sleeping Neala curled up in the corner of the sofa, the feline rewarded Ivy with loud purring.

"Another day filled with surprises, my furry friend. I've learned I had a relative who was a famous artist. Imagine that?" After giving her another scratch behind the ears, Ivy made her way into the kitchen.

Frowning, she gazed out the window. Candlelight spilled forth from the garden area. "Conn," she whispered on a sigh.

Uncertainty had filled Ivy as she approached the cottage earlier, fearing Conn had left. She didn't extend an invitation to stay for dinner. No words were uttered between them about tonight. In fact, she just assumed he would want to stick around, since obviously she wanted him to stay.

Her hands gripped the counter. "Foolish, girl. You've fallen for the man."

Trying to steady her rapidly beating heart, Ivy walked out the back and into the garden. The scene was indeed one out of the faery tale books. Beauty in the soft fading light, illuminated by the candles. He must have spent the entire day in the garden cleaning and painting. Fresh flowers were everywhere, along with budding herbs. Even the garden gate had been repaired and painted. Her eyes misted with unshed tears.

"It's magical," she uttered softly.

Moving forward, she noticed her Celt kneeling on the ground. Again, she heard him speaking in a strange language—words that were soothing, luring her to him. The man wore only his jeans and nothing else. He was in complete harmony with the land, and the air hummed with new energy.

"How can I ever thank you, Conn?"

His hands stilled on the ground. When he glanced over his shoulder at her, his eyes blazed in the gloaming. "My gift to you deserves no thanks. I wished to heal the land *and* your heart."

Her lip trembled as the tears slipped down her cheeks. *I love you Conn MacRoich.* Biting her lower lip, Ivy reached out her hand to him.

He stood slowly, wiping his hands on a cloth. "I tried to recall the placement of everything, though come spring we shall see what happens. Some of the broken shoots, especially the vegetables may strive forth."

Ivy linked her fingers within his, warm and strong. His strength filled her. "Yes, but for now, I'll enjoy the autumn beauty of new growth, though they're heading for winter, and I fear they may not survive."

Conn drew her toward him and lowered his head. His lips sought hers, and she welcomed his touch. It was a kiss that left her body burning for more. When he broke free, he glanced upward. "I've said a prayer for their endurance through the harshness of winter's hand."

Ivy leaned against his chest. "You're the most fascinating man I've ever met. Even your words reflect the unique quality about you."

He brought her hand to his lips and placed a kiss along the knuckles. "Remember, *ancient*."

"That reminds me, I wanted to ask you a question about one of my relatives...and possibly yours."

Releasing her hand, Conn started to blow out the candles. "You have me intrigued."

"Are you staying for dinner?" she asked, fearing the answer.

"Yes. And the night."

Ivy wanted to jump to the stars with joy. Her skin prickled with anticipation as they both entered the back door to the kitchen. "Why don't you go clean up and I'll start the meal."

"What's on the menu?" Conn asked, his eyes roaming over her body.

She turned away from his intense stare, as if he wanted to feast on her. Pulling out a frying pan, Ivy busied with the preparations. "Hope you like grilled cheese sandwiches. They're one of my favorites." A sense of guilt plagued her. The man deserved a full meal, not some simple fare.

His breath was hot against her neck. "Make mine with extra cheese and some dill."

She nodded, unable to form any cohesive words. His presence made her a jumbled mess—one where she was finding herself tumbling out of control with Conn.

As his footsteps receded, Ivy let out a long held breath. Peering out the window, she could see an owl perched in a nearby tree. "Hello, any sage words of wisdom on love?"

Neala rubbed against her legs, and Ivy almost let out a screech. "For the love of the saints, you could announce yourself."

The cat immediately started to purr.

"Humph! Must try harder my friend." Ivy shook her head in humor and started making their cheese sandwiches.

Conn entered as Ivy was setting the table. "Do you want water? Beer? Wine?" She paused. "Wait, no wine, only beer."

He moved to the fridge. "Beer will suffice. You?"

Ivy smiled. "I'll take one, too, please."

Sitting down at the table, each dove into their meal. The warm, gooey sandwich was one her mom made often for her when she was young, and Ivy never grew tired of the comfort food.

"A combination of cheeses?" questioned Conn between mouthfuls.

Wiping her mouth, Ivy nodded. "Mozzarella and gruyere. I like it cheesy. Grabbed the last block of gruyere from the market the other day."

"I can't recall the last time I had one."

"You approve? Seriously?"

"Of course." He reassured her with a smile. Reaching out, Conn grasped her hand. "Remember, I don't jest."

She held up her half of the sandwich. "I remember the first time my mom made one of these for me. It was after my first vision. I was only four. It frightened me so much I wouldn't speak. She coaxed me back to the land of normality with a cheese sandwich and cup of cocoa." Sighing, Ivy placed the food back on her plate. "If I could talk to her this very minute, I would ask her why she didn't divorce him and move us back to Ireland."

Conn squeezed her hand before releasing it. "She must have had her reasons."

Clenching her fists, Ivy shook her head in frustration. "It's not like it was fifty, sixty years ago. We're talking only a few decades."

"You forget. This is Ireland. Divorce is frowned upon, even worse several decades ago."

She snorted in disgust. "My mother was not Catholic. Yes, there's a piece of the religion drilled into me by my *stepfather*, but my mother shared her belief in the Celtic ways with me. That's why I don't understand."

"No matter her beliefs, your mother did what she thought best for you." Conn took a sip of his beer. "Did your mother have any gifts?"

Ivy frowned in concentration. "Funny you should mention the possibility. I often thought she did, especially when she had that far-off look. However, when I questioned her one time, she flatly denied having any clairvoyant abilities."

"A question to ponder another day," suggested Conn.

Reaching for her bottle of beer, Ivy peered over the rim at him. "I have a question for you."

Conn gave her one of his smoldering looks. "Which I will endeavor to answer."

She took a sip and leaned back in her chair. "First question. Did your ancestors live in this village?"

His heated gaze vanished. "No. Never."

Ivy took another sip and nodded slowly. "All right. Second question. If they never lived in this area of Ireland, how did an artist by the name of Bradon Finnegan happen to paint the very likeness of you hundreds of years ago?"

Conn's expression changed to one of cold steel. "Since many believe I have the looks of a Viking, any other blond-haired man could resemble me."

Stunned, Ivy glared at him. "Really? That's your answer? Poppycock!"

He placed his hands upon the table and leaned toward her. "Then pray tell, what do you *believe*, Ivy?"

Placing her beer on the table, she crossed her arms over her chest. "I can't form any conclusion, since I keep stumbling over one secret after the next." She kept her gaze steady on his. "For instance, today I learned that the renowned artist, Bradon Finnegan, was a distant relative. Erin told me all about it earlier after I showed her one of his paintings. Did you know it's titled, *Meeting of the Warriors*?" For a split second, Ivy could have sworn Conn's eyes flashed to silver.

She leaned forward. "I had a vision today and you were there." Pausing, Ivy studied his face, trying to read the man. He was as impenetrable as a stone fortress.

"Continue," he ordered, his tone almost a growl.

"One of the men—an Aidan Kerrigan, called the one who could have been your twin, *Conn*."

Instantly, Conn's features softened. Reaching for his beer, he pointed it at her. "You, *mo ghrá* have an overactive imagination. It's one that slips into your dreams."

"I wasn't dreaming," she corrected. "I was in a vision trance."

He waved her off dismissively. "Even so, visions cannot always be interpreted accurately."

Ivy looked at the man incredulously. "For your information, I take my visions seriously."

"As you should. But you've been under a tremendous amount of strain with all this knowledge. Any of it could have a factor on your images."

The man's words made Ivy doubt everything. Could he be correct? Her vision fabricated by everything that had happened to her since she landed in Ireland? Then again, she had experienced turbulent times and it never interfered with her gift of sight.

Rising, she dumped the rest of her sandwich in the trash. Swallowing the last of her beer, she gazed out into the night sky. "You're wrong, Conn. What I saw were images of the past. I can't explain why, nor do I really care. You say it couldn't be your ancestor, but then, you can't be positive either."

Silence greeted her, but Ivy knew he was right behind her. The man had stealth-like moves. His heat radiated around her, making her feel safe, warm, and loved.

"What purpose would the vision serve, Ivy?" asked Conn, his arms slipping around her waist.

"Have I ever told you I love to solve puzzles?"

He kissed the back of her neck, causing her to shiver. "No. What kind do you enjoy?"

His lips caressed the sensitive area behind her ear, and Ivy moaned. "Life puzzles. Trying to figure out the pieces of my visions. They have helped me see things in a clearer light."

"Then I shall do my best to help you solve them."

Ivy angled her head around to meet his gaze.

"Interesting."

Conn turned her around to face him. Cupping her chin, he traced a path over her bottom lip with his thumb. "A challenge."

Before she could utter a reply, his mouth swooped down to capture hers, igniting a firestorm of desire. All previous thoughts dissolved, leaving Ivy aching for Conn's touch. The room could have burst into flames, but as long as she was in his arms, Ivy was safe—floating on a current of passion.

****

The glow of stars faded to make way for the dawn of a new day. Conn watched as one slipped effortlessly into the next. His body hummed with energy—a call to greet the land. But a certain lass was curled against his chest, softly snoring. He didn't have the heart to leave. In truth, he craved her more than the new dawn. Conn wanted to take Ivy once again. He'd spent almost the entire night exploring her body in a loving, pleasurable way, and finding those places that drove her wild. Images of her body spiraling into ecstasy made him hard again.

Nevertheless, Conn let her sleep. His mind dwelled on their conversation last evening. In all his lifetime, no other human had managed to see into his past. However, that didn't trouble him as much as finding out Bradon Finnegan, friend to the Fae, was an ancestor. Thank the Gods the painting she talked about was missing. She'd probably want to inspect every detail. *Ahh...Bradon, you would have adored your descendant.*

Glancing down at her lovely features, Conn let out a sigh. His duty to bring her out of the shadows was almost complete. A shift in her aura had deepened to reflect the change. Ivy didn't sense it yet, but soon she would be on a path of light. The loom of life was a tangled mess in Ivy's world, and Conn was knotted in there with her. It was his journey as much as hers and with each unraveling piece, his fate moved closer to Ivy's world.

Yet, he had neglected another. Conn was determined to set the path right for Ivy's ancestor. There had to be a way, but his mind was unable to map out any cohesive objective.

Ivy stirred in his arms and desire rolled through him. Muttering a curse, he kissed her forehead and slipped quietly from her bed. Picking up his clothes from the floor, he cast one more glance over his shoulder at his sleeping beauty.

His quest might be ending, but Conn was not ready to leave the woman who claimed his heart. Furthermore, his next decisions could alter both worlds.

Dressing quickly, he shut the bedroom door softly. Making his way downstairs, he strode out of the house. His steps took him on a path he had grown familiar with—one where he now sought to seek advice.

Brushing past tree limbs and through the brush, he continued onward. The first light of dawn became a beacon as it fell across the sky in welcome. Conn embraced the energy, absorbing it through his body. Early morning birdsong heralded the arrival, and he smiled.

Quickly making his way to a place among the trees, Conn stripped his shirt and knelt. Lifting his head upward, he closed his eyes. "Stars, moon, and sun, so the cycle continues around the land. Greetings, Mother Danu."

He waited patiently, no longer aware of time. Minutes slipped into an hour and still he waited.

A faint whisper touched his cheek. *"You seek answers to your questions, but there are none. For you have them all within your heart."*

Conn snapped open his eyes, keeping his hands fisted on his knees. "I have not yet asked the question."

"Beware the path you are on. Beware the love you have allowed to enter your heart. Beware the quest to right an injustice to ease the guilt."

"It is my destiny to make it right," he argued, fighting the urge to shout.

"Beware the loom of fate. You try and mend a string on the harp and another may break."

He wiped a hand over his brow. "I do not understand."

"Go tend to your garden, my warrior."

Confused by her words, Conn placed his hands upon the ground. Anxiety clawed at him. Why was it so difficult? Scooping up a handful of dirt, he brought it to his lips and then flung it outward.

Standing, he reached for his shirt and walked slowly away, his mind now uncertain of the path ahead.

An acorn fell from the tree and landed on his head. He froze.

"You planted the seed, now follow your heart."

Conn chuckled as he plucked the acorn from the forest floor. "No, Ivy planted the seed of love within my heart."

Whistling softly, he made his way to Ivy's garden. Halting in front of the gate, he smiled at the sight. The seedlings had grown more overnight. Though the air crisp, he had magically sealed off the flowers and herbs from any harm. Entering the place, he walked softly through the garden, chanting ancient words. The new life greeted him in return.

Reaching outward with his hands, the power surged out of him, gliding over the land. His spirit now renewed, until he heard Ivy's bone-chilling scream.

Chapter Twenty-One

"When walls crumble, seek the source of the loose stone."

~Chronicles of the Fae

Almost taking The Celtic Knot's front door off its hinges, Conn ran into the store and headed for the office. "Ivy!" he bellowed.

"In the office," she responded angrily.

The moment he spotted her, he breathed a sigh of relief. Placing his hands on her shoulders, he peered into the office. "Only this place?"

"Yes," she snapped. "Stupid bloody idiots. What a hellish mess! *Why?*"

Conn moved past her and inspected the room. "Someone was looking for something in here."

Ivy threw up her hands in frustration. "What? There's no money in here. The safe is in the side closet. There is absolutely nothing of importance in here, unless you count the books." She tiptoed inside and pointed to the bookcases. "They pulled them off the shelves and dumped them onto the floor. Some of them are very rare." She started to pick one up when Conn reached for her hand.

"Again, I believe this was a search for something. The Garda should be notified immediately."

She clenched her hands. "So much for a peaceful

day."

"How did they enter the store?"

"Back entrance. The bolt has been cut."

"*Mo ghrá*, are you sure there's nothing missing?"

"Yes, I haven't removed anything—" Ivy paused and looked up at Conn. "Yesterday I pulled out three old keys that I had found stuffed in the back of a drawer my first day at the shop. I showed them to Erin."

Rubbing his chin, Conn glanced around the place. "Where are they now?"

Ivy walked out of the office. "I took them home with me."

Following the lass to the front of the store, he watched as she opened her purse and withdrew the keys. "Erin knew about them. She said the larger one was the first key to the cottage, but my uncle couldn't determine the use of the others. Do you honestly believe someone thinks these are of value?"

Conn narrowed his eyes. "What time does the Seven Swans open?"

"Not for two more hours."

He maneuvered her toward the front door. "I'll call the Garda, but you go home."

She shook her head. "I'm all right. I'm going to keep the store open. No one is going to frighten me away."

Conn wrapped his arms around his warrior lass. "Any help today?"

Ivy lifted her head, and Conn noticed the shadows under her eyes. Tonight he would stay away from her bed and let her sleep. "Only Nan," she answered softly.

He kissed her tenderly. "Good. I don't want you to be alone today. I'll go place a call to the Garda."

****

The man stood silently within the thick cluster of trees down the road from the Celtic Knot. Several officers had arrived and walked around the place, and he studied their movement. Not concerned with the law, he focused on the one person he wanted to see. Fury boiled inside him when he found no trace of the keys in her office. Pitiful it had come this far. He hated resorting to tactics like these. They were beneath him. He'd prefer a rougher assault. Better to go for the jugular and dump the body somewhere.

Perhaps Miss Ivy O'Callaghan would trip on her way across the street resulting in the same loss of life as her uncle. Or wander down a path and become lost and confused in the woods. No evidence. No trace of her existence. "Vanished into thin air, the newspapers would say of the poor woman."

He chuckled low at the thought, and then sobered. First, he needed those keys. It was important.

He straightened when he saw Ivy emerge from the Celtic Knot. Keeping his gaze focused on her, he raked his dirk against the bark of a tree in slow, methodical slashes. She spoke quietly to the officer.

"Pretty Ivy. You require a real man. Maybe I'll show you what I can do, and then I'll carve lots of pictures onto your body."

Noticing her pale features as she spoke to the officer, he snarled. "Good, little mouse. Be scared. Scurry back home to America or suffer at my hands."

The Viking came striding out front as if he owned the place. He despised the arrogant man from the moment he stepped foot in Glennamore. How simple it would be to put a bullet through his smirking face.

Since when did he become protector of the bitch? He spat onto the ground in disgust.

"Yes, maybe *several* bullets for you as you speed off on your bike." The man raised his index finger and thumb forming them as a gun. "Bam, bam, right through your heart."

Content with everything, the man turned and stalked back within the forest, planning his next strategy in case the persistent Ivy O'Callaghan refused to leave on her own accord.

****

After Conn had inspected the back entrance, he deemed it was a male who had broken into the Celtic Knot. Though he wasn't able to determine the exact person with magic, it was now time to pay a call on Eric Dunstan. First, he required some information.

Folding his arms over his chest, Conn's gaze drifted across to the Seven Swans. Their sign was lit open for business. He started to move steadily toward the pub, when a certain sprite dashed up and grabbed his arm.

"Not without me, you don't," ordered Ivy. "I told the police...Garda to come find me here when they're done. I have questions, too."

He placed a hand over hers. "Afraid I'll rip a limb off someone?"

Her laughter was music to his ears. "Yep."

Upon entering, all eyes turned toward the couple, and Conn tightened his grip on Ivy. His intent was clear. Ivy was his woman.

Erin was the first to approach. "Sweet Brigid, what happened? We saw the Garda vehicles."

"I came in this morning to find my office trashed,"

replied Ivy.

"It seems as if the person was searching for something of value," interjected Conn.

The woman's mouth dropped open in shock. "Was anything taken?"

Mac moved alongside his sister. "What could they want?"

Conn looked at the man skeptically. "Indeed. Perhaps they were curious about a set of ancient keys?" He released his hold on Ivy, only to wrap an arm around her waist.

Ivy jabbed him in the side.

"The keys you showed me yesterday?" asked a stunned Erin.

Mac made a disgusted sound. "Who would want those rustic items?"

Conn glared at the man. "You know about the keys?"

"Yes, I told him," answered Erin. "I'm sorry, Ivy, was I supposed to keep it a secret?"

Ivy reached for her friend's hands. "No. But did you tell anyone else?"

Erin cringed. "Everyone in the bar last night."

"I was there," proclaimed Mac, placing a hand on his sister's shoulder. "Seamus and his friends were in the back playing darts, but there were only two at the bar when Erin talked about doing some research on the computer to help out Ivy."

"And these two individuals?" asked Ivy.

"Mike Banister and my brother, Peter," announced Nan from behind them.

Conn and Ivy turned around to face the young girl.

"Oh, Ivy, he's a mess," sobbed Nan. She moved

toward them hesitantly.

"Let's move to the back of the pub," suggested Mac.

"Agreed," Conn stated.

When they were all settled at a large table, Ivy reached for the girl's hand. "What happened?"

"I swear my brother had nothing to do with your office, Ivy. Please believe me. He took a beating from Mike Banister, because he wouldn't go along with him. He lured Peter into thinking there was going to be some fantastic story about the lost relics of a certain clan and a treasure worth a lot of money."

Conn drummed his fingers on the table. "Let me guess. Clan Dunstan?"

The girl's eyes grew wide. "Yes. How…did you know?"

He sneered. "Eric Dunstan made threatening advances toward Ivy the day of her uncle's wake. It would appear Banister is working for him."

"Filthy bastards," growled Mac.

Ivy glanced at Conn and then back to the girl. "And Mike and Dunstan thought the keys were to these relics?"

Nan nodded. "Peter refused to participate any further." She wiped her nose. "He came to like you. After he heard about your garden, Peter was furious."

"Where is he now?" demanded Conn.

Her eyes filled with unshed tears. "He left. Packed everything and told me he would call when he got to Galway. Peter was the only family I had," she sobbed out.

If Conn ever saw the man again, he would strangle the bastard. How could he leave his sister? Did he not consider she might be in danger as well?

Ivy squeezed her hand and looked at those gathered at the table. "No, Nan, you have family here in this village. You won't be alone, I promise you."

She laughed nervously. "At least I'll be turning eighteen in a month. If not, I'm afraid they would have removed me from my home."

"It will never happen," stated Erin soothingly. "Remember, I promised your mother before she died that Mac and I would look after you, too."

Nan smiled weakly. "Thank you."

"You know you'll always have a job at the bookstore, and I can give you extra hours if you want," remarked Ivy.

The girl's lip quivered. "I was afraid you would fire me."

Smiling, Ivy shook her head. "Not going to happen. Your brother's actions had nothing to do with you."

"Oh, Ivy, thank you."

The two women stood and embraced each other.

"Now, do you want to help me clean up the office?" suggested Ivy.

"Would love to."

Ivy surprised Conn by leaning down and kissing him. "See you later."

"Of course," he replied and followed her movement out of the pub.

"You two an item?" asked Mac.

Conn turned his attention to the man. "Yes. She is mine."

"Ivy was right about you." Erin smiled knowingly.

He arched a brow, probably in question, at the woman. "Do tell."

She stood, placing a hand on her brother's shoulder. "*Ancient.*"

Conn chuckled low and stood. Giving Erin a wink, he added, "If only you knew."

Striding from the place, he tempered his anger before encountering the person responsible for this mess.

Hours later, frustration clawed inside of Conn as he surveyed Eric Dunstan's home. Not only was the massive place overgrown with brush, weeds, and trees, but the house was also in dire need of repairs. Anyone could see from the dismal façade. Cracked pottery lined the front, along with abandoned vehicles.

No wonder Dunstan was after Ivy's land. Hers would be a boon to his dull estate.

He continued to pound on the front door. Conn's fury was barely containable after the incident with Ivy. If Dunstan did not agree to leave her alone, he might be forced to take other measures to convince the bastard.

Peering inside the front windows, Conn scanned for any signs of the man. His irritation grew when he realized the man wasn't at home. Clenching and unclenching his hands, Conn fought the urge to roar. The man should be taken out into the woods and thrashed for frightening and hurting his beloved.

Beloved. The mere word slammed into his mind with a force to halt him where he stood. From the moment he had whispered the binding vows and pledged his soul—his blood to Ivy, an overwhelming desire to protect her consumed him. He sealed his fate. But would she be willing to open her heart to him? The circle could not be complete without her own vow.

Tossing aside the thought, he sniffed the air. A foul

scent tainted the area.

"Have you found him yet?"

Conn glanced over his shoulder. Glaring at the man, he replied, "Not here. Why are *you* here, O'Reilly? What of your dealings with the man?"

"I never cared for the way Dunstan treated my sister when he came into the pub. I tossed him out the last time. He was trouble the moment he returned to claim his land," his voice hardened ruthlessly. "To hear what happened to Ivy—"

Conn arched a brow in warning. "*Ivy* is my concern."

Mac raised his hands up. "I understand. My reasons are purely of friendship. You both have made it perfectly clear. But that won't stop me when my friends are threatened."

Inclining his head toward the woods, Conn asked, "What is beyond the trees? The stench is one of flesh burning."

"Sweet Jesus. The old forge." Mac shoved past Conn and ran into the trees.

Conn followed the man cautiously, pushing aside limbs and stepping over fallen logs. Smoke filled his lungs the closer they approached. His Fae senses were reeling by the time they stepped into the clearing.

"Damn! There's a body in the fire pit. It could be Dunstan. Help me get him out," shouted Mac between fits of coughing.

Rushing to the man's side, Conn pushed him back. "It's nothing but charred flesh and bones, but we need to put out the fire before it spreads."

Flames snapped to life as the embers danced off the pit—capturing a nearby brush.

Mac pulled his shirt over his nose and mouth. "The stream is on the other side. How are you going...no time," he stated, wheezing. "Bloody hell." He pointed to a wallet and keys nearby.

Rubbing his eyes, Conn pulled him away from the smoke-filled area. "Get some help. I'll attempt to bring water to the fire. There has to be something around the forge." Picking up the wallet, he looked inside. "They belong to Mike Banister."

"Sweet Jesus," he coughed out.

Conn motioned for him to leave. "Go fetch the Garda and firemen."

"I'm not leaving," barked Mac. "You need help."

"Worried something will happen to me?" Conn coughed, dragging Mac along with him.

"Miracles have been known to happen," he said smiling and then coughed from the effort.

Conn finally pushed him through the trees. "Go!" he ordered.

Hearing the man's footsteps receding, Conn collapsed onto the ground and took in large gulps of air and energy.

Standing, he sprinted through the thick smoke, his eyes burning by the time he made it to the water. Quickly bending on one knee, he held out his hand over the water. "From the depths of the ocean, to the zenith of the clouds, let both be joined and fall over the land burning brightly. Let the water cleanse, soothe, and wash away the fiery embers." Dipping his fingers into the water, he glided them in a continuous circle, until the storm clouds gathered. When the first drop of rain landed on his face, Conn sat back on his heels and waited.

The downpour of rain slashed across the land.

Rising slowly, Conn shook from the energy. He lifted his face to the pelting of water, breathing deeply. Hearing the sound of fire engines, he blinked. Shaking off the last residual power, he bolted back to the forge.

By the time he emerged, there were men surrounding the place, adding additional water to the outlying areas. He spotted Mac speaking with one of the Garda. Making his way to them, he raked a hand through his hair as he approached.

"Conn MacRoich. Strange how you should be here so soon after the break-in at The Celtic Knot."

"Inspector Flynn, my reason was purely one of a verbal warning," countered Conn, handing the man Mike Banister's wallet and keys.

The man jotted down a few notes. "I'll need to speak with you both later."

"You can find me at the pub," responded Mac.

Conn ignored the Inspector as he walked away. Lightning splintered overhead, and he frowned. He was in no mood to sit and answer feeble questions about a man he'd never had contact with. His concern was now finding Eric Dunstan.

"Great timing for a storm." Mac kept his stride even with his as they emerged out of the trees.

"A true miracle," replied Conn, smiling.

Mac shook his head, pulling out his car keys. "Come by the pub later. Drinks are on the house."

Conn eyed the man warily. "A peace offering?"

He snorted. "A temporary truce."

Conn watched the man drive off and rubbed his chin. "He would have made a great warrior." Getting on his motorcycle, he took off down the road.

Lights from The Celtic Knot glimmered as he made his way down the street. The rain had turned to a light drizzle as he veered off the road toward the cottage. As soon as he checked on Ivy's garden, Conn would kiss his beloved goodnight and head to the pub. He would watch over her from afar. In the morning, he would resume his mission on finding Dunstan.

Parking his bike, he made his way to the garden. Halting in front of the place, he cast his hands outward, filling the place with a touch more magic to help the growth. The light shimmered over the ground, hovering over those that needed extra tending. He lifted his hands higher, chanting the ancient words.

"What...*what* are you doing?" Ivy's demanding tone sent a chill down Conn's spine.

"In order to move out of the darkness, one must see the light," he stated in a clear, calm voice.

Ivy stood near his side and gasped. "They're much bigger. How?"

Turning fully toward her, Conn dropped his hands and let her see the power around and within him. No more shadows. No more darkness. He loved Ivy, and he wanted her to see who he truly was—the man *and* the Fae. He tossed aside the risks and prayed the woman who stood before him would accept the knowledge he was going to divulge. Had he not planted the seed already? Now was the time for truths. "I've encouraged them along with magic."

Her gaze snapped to his, never wavering. "*Who* are you?"

Conn took a step closer. "You already know the answer, remember? You said the words the first night you saw me enter the Seven Swans."

Fury shown in her eyes. "Ancient Celt, but that's only because I recognized an *old soul*."

"No. I *am* an ancient. Far more than you can imagine." He swept out his hand. "Older than the land we are upon, older than some of the stars." He took another step closer. "I am a Fenian Fae warrior—bound to this world and the realm of Fae below. We are the Tuatha De Danann—the Shining Ones."

She shook her head, stumbling backward. "Not true. Not real."

Conn reached a hand toward her. "Listen to me Ivy. I speak the truth. You know this to be true in your heart."

"Don't touch me!" Her breathing became shallow. "Is this your way of saying goodbye? Or are you insane? You're using everything that has happened to me recently and fabricated this story. You're twisted."

He withdrew his hand. "Then explain your garden. Explain how certain people have unique gifts and talents."

"I can't, but that doesn't mean I'll accept your nonsense. You're expecting me to understand that you're some kind of mythological creature. For all I know you planted chicken manure to help the plants grow, and you're only sputtering this story about yourself to scare me away."

Clenching his fists, he snapped, "I do not utter nonsense. I do not jest. I speak the truth. And I am not a *creature*."

She rubbed a shaky hand over her forehead. "Get out of here Conn. I don't have time for faerytales in my life. They're best left for children and apparently this *thing* we have between us is not real for you any longer."

A torrent of pain slashed through his soul. She refused to listen to her heart, instead sealing it with fear. "Don't send me away, Ivy," he pleaded.

Tears streamed down her face. "I don't know what to believe anymore."

His body shook. Was it so impossible to accept? "Then let me help you see the light of truth. I will show you wonders that will take your breath away."

"No! Leave," she sobbed and ran off down the path.

Conn collapsed onto the ground. When he lifted his head up to the sky, he couldn't determine if the wetness on his face was the rain or his tears. In all his lifetime, even in times of true sorrow, Conn MacRoich, Fenian Warrior, Prince of the Fae had never shed a tear.

Chapter Twenty-Two

"Loneliness and revelations are often times parallel paths."
~*Chronicles of the Fae*

"Rubbish. Utter crap. *Coward*." Ivy's lip trembled as she rocked back and forth in front of the fire, clutching the pillow to her chest. Deep pain and sorrow engulfed her. She had fallen in love with a lunatic. Her bedroom was now sealed off—sheets stripped with his smell had been tossed into the laundry room. His leather jacket was propped over one of the chairs, but she refused to go near the item.

Neala, sensing her pain, had curled up beside her.

Tears that she had kept at bay, now threatened to spill forth. He did not deserve them, so she squeezed her eyes shut. Never would she again fall prey to his dazzling silver eyes. "It had to be a trick of the fading light. Yes, that's why they glowed."

Yet, it wasn't the first time she'd witnessed the transformation in the man's eyes. Ivy assumed he was special—gifted like her. He made her feel safe, treasured, loved.

She bit her lip. "Oh, Mom...it hurts. I loved him. How do I separate the real from the fantasy?" Her fingers dug into the soft material. "What a mess I've made here. I'm confused. I want to leave. This isn't home anymore."

Dropping her head onto the pillow, Ivy let the tears fall freely. Weariness cloaked her like a heavy blanket. Images from another time floated through her mind as sleep beckoned her.

"Dearest, why do you weep out here in the garden?"

"I don't understand my visions, mama. They can't be real. I see people who don't look like us. They are diff...different." *She hiccupped and rubbed her eyes.*

Her mother cupped her chin. "My sweet daughter, what you see is real. You have a gift."

"Father says it's a curse."

"Bah! He knows nothing. It's fear he speaks. But you, darling, have the capacity to look into the past and capture what others cannot."

She pouted and lowered her head. "What good are they? I don't want them."

Her mother sat down next to her. "You never know, Ivy. One day, you might come to help another, or use them for research. You must trust in the visions, not fear them. Do you truly believe that God and the Goddess would grant you a horrible gift?" Touching Ivy's heart, she added, "Always listen here. The mind has a way of trapping the fear inside."

Ivy nodded her head in agreement and wiped her nose. "Saint Brigid had visions, right?"

Her mother smiled. "And let's don't forget, Hildegard von Bingen. Many sought her counsel, including a pope."

Sighing, Ivy plucked a dandelion from the ground.

"What are you going to wish for, sweet child?"

Ivy smiled wistfully. "For a faery guardian to help

me when I am lost."

Bolting upright, Ivy rubbed her bleary eyes. Stretching out her body, the pain in her neck radiated down to her legs. Neala had moved to a blanket on the couch, and the fire had dwindled to embers. One hand was numb and Ivy winced, trying to bring some blood back into her fingers.

Looking up at the photo on the mantel, Ivy smiled. "Thanks, Mom for making me remember."

Finally standing, she tossed the pillow onto a chair. Gazing out the window, early morning light stretched across the clear sky. Pink tinged the outer edges—a promise of a sunny day and hope surged within Ivy. Fear had seized her last evening—blinding her to what Conn was saying. Yes, a small part of doubt continued to linger, but she was determined to speak with the man further. Glancing at the sketch she had drawn of Conn, Ivy traced a finger over the lines of his features. "Definitely a warrior."

Giving Neala a kiss on the head, she made her way upstairs to prepare for the new day.

An hour later, Ivy wandered along the path to the Celtic Knot. Breathing in the crisp autumn air, she walked into the store and waved in greeting to Roger. Entering her office, she checked on several incoming orders.

"Thanks for giving me a full shift today," stated Roger, as he strolled in, handing her yesterday's mail.

Taking the items, Ivy plopped them on her desk. "You're doing me a favor, so thank *you*. Nan will stop by around noon to give you a break, but if you need anything, please call me on my cell. The order for the Thompsons should be here today. As soon as it arrives, please give them a call. Mr. Thompson ordered a rare copy of Pride & Prejudice for his wife."

Roger saluted her. "Yes, boss."

Smiling, she waved him away. When all her other tasks had been accomplished, Ivy left the bookstore in Roger's capable hands and went in search of a Fae warrior.

****

Anxious and edgy, Ivy tried to steady her shaky nerves. Arriving at Sean's, she didn't know whether to bolt or storm into the house. Reaching for the knocker on the door, she tapped it twice and took a step back. "Oh, please be happy to see me, Conn." Although she half-expected the man to slam the door on her face after the way she treated him last night.

When several minutes ticked by, Ivy slammed the knocker harder. Biting her bottom lip, she waited another full minute, fear snaking its way inside her. Peering to the side, she saw Sean's car, but no sign of Conn's motorcycle. *Perhaps he's heading back to my place?*

"Good morn, Ivy Kathleen," greeted Sean.

Ivy almost jumped out of her skin. Turning around, she smiled at the man. "How are you?"

Moving past her, he opened the door and gestured her inside. "Good, though my bones are aching with the morning chill. I have the kettle on. Care for a cup of tea?"

She glanced around, scanning for any signs of her Celt. "Sure. Would love some."

Sean placed a gentle hand on her arm. "He's gone. Left last night." He walked quietly down the hall.

Stunned, Ivy stared at the retreating man. Finally

recovering her senses, she ran after him and into the kitchen. "What do you mean he's *gone?*"

Her friend refused to meet her hard stare. Instead, he busied himself with the tea preparations. "Exactly what I said, lass."

She swallowed, fearing to ask the next question. "Gone...for good?"

Sean shrugged, pulling out a chair for her to sit. "Yes. I believe so."

Shock and grief ripped into Ivy. The blow of his words was akin to a hammer on her soul. Numbness slithered inside her, removing all her joy. Sean placed a cup of tea in front of her, but she didn't have the strength to lift the item. *Did Conn not understand I was taken aback, reeling from his announcement? Yet, you did order him to leave.* She clutched her fingers tightly together.

"Drink a sip of your tea," urged Sean.

Unclenching her hands, she placed them around the cup—the warmth spreading through her frozen body. "I've mucked things up," she complained.

The man took a seat across from her. "No. You were unprepared for what he told you."

Almost dropping the cup, she squeaked, "He told you?"

Sean took a sip of his tea and nodded. Placing his cup down, he leaned back in his chair. "I am one of the privileged few to know about Conn. He once saved my life."

Ivy's mouth dropped open. Snapping it shut, she took a gulp of her tea, grateful it wasn't scalding. "Do you have anything stronger?"

Sean chuckled. "Aye, but you'll need your wits to

hear my tale of how I met the Fae warrior."

Sighing, Ivy looked away. "You have to understand how fantastical this sounds."

"The world is filled with many wonders."

Turning her gaze back to the man, she put her cup down. "Before you share your story, can you answer me another question?"

"Ask me anything."

"Did you know that I'm Thomas' daughter, *not* his niece?"

Muttering a curse, Sean stood and went to the cupboard. Retrieving a bottle of whiskey, he returned with two glasses. Opening the bottle, he poured a small amount into her glass, but filled his substantially more.

Ivy lifted her glass. "A toast to my *father*." She downed the entire contents.

Sean drained his glass. "I suspected, but never dared to say anything. He was my friend. If he wanted to disclose the information, he would have done so many years ago. Rumors circled around Thomas and your mother, until she married Patrick. I never pried. He retreated into his own grief for many months after she left for America. However, after the first letter arrived with your picture, he transformed. Did you find out when you visited Anne Fahey?"

"Yes. The woman has not moved on with her life. I left with a bitter taste and feeling sorry for her."

He nodded. "I feared she would speak her mind, but couldn't fathom the secret. She cloaks herself in resentment and loneliness."

Ivy trailed a finger over the rim of the glass. "Ever since I've arrived, I've unraveled one secret after the next. It's enough to have me spinning around in complete confusion."

Sean placed a hand over hers. "You've come home to your destiny."

She snapped her gaze up. "I wished my mother had left and brought me back home to Ireland."

Releasing her hand, Sean pushed away his teacup. "I am sure they both had their reasons."

"Ones that went with them to their graves." She leaned back in her chair. "Now, tell me your tale of Conn MacRoich."

"Happily."

For the next hour, Sean shared every detail he knew of the great Fenian Fae warrior with her. Amazed and in awe, Ivy listened intently. She was transported to another time within his story, witnessing the details of a friendship that spanned decades.

"Why did he return this time?" she asked softly.

"This one is his story to tell, not mine."

Nodding her head in understanding, she placed her hands on the table. "The first time he walked into the pub my *sight* showed me the ancient warrior, but last night when he uttered the words out loud, I feared them."

"You were not raised in Ireland, Ivy Kathleen." He spread his arms wide. "The land is filled with magic everywhere—"

"But the church squashed those beliefs," she protested.

Sean laughed heartily. "No, my wee lass. Here, we honor and respect both. Ask Father Connelly. Even the man of the cloth believes in the Fae."

Ivy's eyes grew wide. "No. Really?"

"Most definitely."

"Next, you'll be telling me about the leprechauns," she teased.

Sean held up one finger. "We do have an expert in the village who can tell you all about them. She converses with them often."

Ivy burst out in laughter. "Sorry," she choked, trying to regain her composure.

"Quite all right. But don't make fun of them out in the land. There are eyes everywhere." He tapped a finger to his nose with a smile.

"I'll try and remember the warning. I don't want to offend any wandering leprechauns."

"Ahh…yes, speaking of warnings, I must tell you that Conn and Mac O'Reilly discovered a gruesome find yesterday."

"Wait. Conn and Mac were together?"

"Apparently they've formed a temporary truce. It's the latest news at the Seven Swans." The man shifted in his chair. "As I was saying, they made the discovery of a burnt body in the old forge on Eric Dunstan's property."

Ivy felt the color drain from her face. "Do they…" she swallowed, trying not to visualize the image. "Do they think it's him?"

Sean scratched behind his ear. "Until it's confirmed, no one is speculating. They believe it's Mike Banister who worked for him, since Dunstan has gone missing."

"I don't understand. Why were they out there at the man's place?"

"Apparently, you have strong protectors and after the break-in, they—Conn and Mac went out to confront Dunstan."

Ivy snorted in disgust. "All for an ancient set of keys that might be linked to some treasure or relics."

Sean folded his arms over his chest. "Yes, Conn mentioned them to me. Tales of lost relics and treasures have circulated the village for centuries. Another fable and one that is false. The keys most likely are to a dilapidated castle or building. Yours is one of the oldest in the village."

Curious, Ivy asked, "And the other?"

"The ruins of Castle Lintel."

"Yes...the ones I can see from the store." She shivered. "So Dunstan might have murdered Mike Banister for what?"

"We cannot say for certain the body is Banister's, yet. Eric made a few enemies from the moment he came into the village. For all we know, a fight happened, and Dunstan torched the body to hide the evidence."

"I was one of those enemies," she countered.

Sean patted her hand reassuringly. "Do not fret. The Garda is placing extra men nearby. They know of the threats to you."

Weariness descended over Ivy, and her thoughts floated back to the reason she came to the house. Fighting back the wave of loss, she took a deep breath in and released it slowly. "Sean, where is Conn?"

He lowered his head at her. "May I ask the reason?"

Smiling, Ivy replied. "I'm in love with the Fae warrior."

Sean smacked his hand on the table. "Good, but be warned, he's hurting deeply."

Standing, Ivy walked around the table and hugged

the man. "Don't worry. I pray I can heal his heart."

Chuckling softly, he replied, "You can find him in Dublin. He keeps an apartment on the fringes of the city. I'll fetch you the address."

Placing a kiss on his cheek, she whispered. "Thanks, Sean."

Chapter Twenty-Three

"Candlelight of hope dwells even in a minuscule speck of sand."

~Chronicles of the Fae

Gazing at the old map of Glennamore, Conn let out an exasperated breath. For five, long, agonizing days, he battled his next move. Returning to the village and Ivy was not an option. She no longer wanted him. He was a monster in her eyes. But he had no regrets. It was time she knew the truth.

Then, there was the alternative to return to his own world and make his report. Yes, his quest was now complete. Ivy had stepped out of the shadows—grown, blossomed, and embraced her new life.

What direction could he seek? The loom of fate had not been corrected for her ancestor and this bothered him. There was no way to undo her fate unless he regained his status as a Fenian Warrior, traveled back in time, and rescued the lass. An idea he pondered, but knew the council would forbid him from reweaving the loom. In addition, if he tampered with the string, another would be lost to him.

He took a sip of whiskey from the bottle, contemplating all avenues—possibilities to right one path without damaging another. To argue his case before them. If they refused, he could always do what he deemed was right for the humans. Had he not stated before how foolish the Fae council was in their ways? Always sitting in their chambers dictating laws.

You're not forming any coherent thoughts. They're a jumbled mess.

His mind was numb from too much thought and clouded with far too much whiskey. All in an effort to deaden what he had been avoiding since he left Glennamore—one aqua-eyed lass with a body that made his blood burn. She opened his heart to love, and he fought every waking moment to seal it shut. Nevertheless, he was helpless to the constant invasion of her image, so he tried to focus on the other situation. Her ancestor.

He failed miserably.

"*Ivy, Ivy, Ivy,*" he muttered her name repeatedly trying to banish everything about her from his body and mind. To cleanse her essence that had seeped into his skin.

And again, Conn failed.

Her words shattered his heart that night, sending him into a spiraling, bleak existence. This world meant nothing to him anymore. Gone were the joys he felt in this human world. There was nothing left for him here.

"I gave you *everything*, Ivy Kathleen O'Callaghan. Did you not hear the whispers of my heart to yours?" Raking a hand through his hair, he growled. "Enough!"

Rising slowly, Conn glared at the map. "I shall never love another. If I have to burn my heart from my body, so be it. I'll request missions to the remotest part of the centuries. Give me a sword and place me inside the deadliest battles." Flinging the bottle outward, the glass shattered the framed map of Glennamore.

"I dismiss you from my life."

However, try as he might, Conn was unable to harden his heart, but he gave no care. He would journey for the rest of his life with bitterness and regret. A lesson to be carried until they tossed his ashes upward to the stars.

Storming into his bedroom, he tossed a few items into a backpack. He would return to his own world, give his account, and seek out the Brotherhood. Time to face his own destiny.

Grabbing the keys to his motorcycle off the table, he strode to the door. Glancing once more behind him, he made a vow never to return to Dublin. The place was his beginning and now his ending.

"Let another clean up the messes," he snapped.

Swiftly opening the door, Conn froze.

A lovely vision in a short-kilted skirt and boots turned around and smiled at him. "Hello, Conn."

He blinked, fearing the image would fade. "*Ivy?*" he asked in a hoarse voice.

She tucked a loose strand of hair behind her ear. "I'm sorry. Can you forgive me for the other night?"

"It's been five, long nights," he snapped.

Ivy lifted her chin in defiance. "Yes, but I had a lot to consider. Your announcement was shocking. I had to let everything settle that night. I went to see Sean the next day. He told me where I could find you. Of course arrangements had to be made for the Celtic Knot, and I couldn't get Nan or Roger to cover until—"

Conn dropped his backpack. He needed to feel her—make sure she was real. He grabbed her around the waist with one hand, crushing her to his chest. "Five *agonizing* nights and you couldn't call me?"

She placed a hand on his cheek. "I was afraid—"

"Of me? Was I a monster in your eyes to be feared?"

Shaking her head, Ivy's voice trembled when she spoke. "You are the most beautiful man on this planet, Conn MacRoich. How could you think—"

He silenced her words with a passionate kiss. A rush of emotions overtook all rational thought. Bitterness, loneliness, emptiness—all replaced with euphoria. His kiss was urgent, demanding, and when his tongue invaded her softness, Ivy's moan entered and filled his body.

In one swift move, Conn lifted Ivy into his arms and kicked the door closed. Entering his bedroom, he slowly slid her down his body. Pinning her against the wall, he feasted on her lips, neck, and throat. Stripping her free of her blouse, he gazed at the flimsy black material encasing her beautiful breasts. "So beautiful, so real." Taking his finger, he gently pulled it down, freeing first one and then the other silken globe. His hands roamed over her body, exploring places he feared to never to touch again.

Breaking free, he placed his hands on either side of her on the wall. "Why?" he demanded.

Ivy's breathing was labored as she placed her hands under his shirt. "Why what?"

Conn withdrew her hands and held them firmly by her sides. "Why did you return? Do you accept me knowing who and what I am?"

She squirmed, nudging against him, and his cock swelled more. "Every detail, Fenian Warrior. I'm looking forward to hearing about your life in the Fae realm, and the history you've witnessed. Did you want to hear more?"

He ravished her pout with his lips. "You are mine forever. Do not leave me again," he ordered, trailing a path of kisses over her face. "I will find you, *mo ghrá*, always."

"How I love you, Conn MacRoich."

His body stilled. Her words slammed into him, strong and loving. "You have given me a treasure."

Her smile beguiled him. "Stop talking and take me to bed."

Conn needed no more encouragement. Removing his shirt, boots, and jeans, he tore the bra from her skin and teased his tongue over her pert nipples. Ivy dug her fingers into his scalp, her pleas for more sweeping them both to another realm. He couldn't get enough of her scent—sweet, heady, and filling him once again.

Grasping her hand, Conn pulled her toward his bed. Cupping her face, he breathed his request against her lips. "Indulge me in a fantasy?"

Ivy arched a seductive brow. "Now I'm intrigued. Will you grant me one?"

"Done." Conn kept his gaze on hers as his fingers slid under her skirt and finding lace panties blocking his entrance. "Do they match the bra?"

Her eyes mirrored his own lust. "Yes," she whispered.

He stroked lazy circles over the material, causing her to gasp. "This…this is your fantasy?"

Pinching her most sensitive area, he leaned near her ear. "No, *mo ghrá*." Tearing them free from her body, he spun her around to face the bed.

Ivy angled her head to look at him. "Love the skirt and boots?" she coaxed, wiggling free from the lacy material.

"You have no idea." Bending her over the bed, he lifted her skirt to expose her round, lush bottom. Caressing her soft, ivory skin, Conn fought the urge to take her too swiftly. Unfastening the skirt, he let it slip to the ground. Spreading her legs slightly apart, he gazed over the sight. "Ahh…you present a vision with only your boots on."

"I do?"

"A feast," he replied, with each touch, stroke, and kiss. "I have yet to taste every inch of your body." His finger traced over her tattoo, and he bent down and placed his lips over the area.

Ivy moaned.

"Sensitive spot?"

"Don't torture me. I need you," she begged.

Her words undid Conn and taking his cock, he thrust deeply into Ivy's hot flesh. Exquisite pleasure filled him each time he withdrew and slid back inside her. He watched her hands clutch the furs on his bed, her own desire building. There was no gentleness, only one of reclaiming what he thought lost to him. His love. His heart. His life. All Ivy.

Climbing higher, Conn let the release rip through him, sending him on a wave of pleasure so intense he barely heard his love's own cry when she screamed his name.

He quickly withdrew and brought them both onto the bed and entered her once again. Covering her mouth with his, he drew in her breath and gave it back mingled with his own. This time he took his leisurely time in kindling the desire in them both, kissing the tender side of her breast, behind her ear, and on her shoulder. But she surprised him by digging her fingernails down his back and wrapping her legs around him. When he withdrew slowly, Ivy pushed him harder inside her sending his senses reeling.

"Are you my vixen?" he rasped against her cheek, rubbing his face over hers.

She nibbled on his ear. "Vixen, wench, *lover*. Your heart's desire is mine."

Her raw sensuousness carried him to greater heights than he'd ever known. The fire continued to spread as the tremors of release began. He flicked his tongue over her taut nipple, eliciting a growl from her sweet lips. "Fly with me, *mo ghrá.*"

Conn kept his gaze on his beloved, and when the bright flare of passion exploded within her, he emptied everything he had into the woman he loved.

****

Warm, sated, and happy, Ivy trailed her hand over Conn's smooth muscular chest. She thought him to be asleep, with one hand over his forehead and the other flung out to the side. He was the most gorgeous man ever, and she was deeply in love with the Fae. He had no idea how agonizing those five nights were to her, too. It was torture not to leave after her conversation with Sean and head directly to Dublin. Yet, she needed to think and not feel.

The first couple of nights sleep was elusive. Oftentimes, she wandered downstairs in despair. Her heart, body, and mind ached for Conn. Regardless that he was a Fae warrior Ivy knew she loved him. There was one fear she held close to her heart. He was an ancient, so why did he choose to be with her? He called her *my love*, said she was his, but did he truly love her?

Or was she a possession?

Her hand stilled over the center of his chest. *I don't know what to believe?*

"You have found my heart," uttered Conn softly.

Startled, she lifted her hand. "Sorry, I thought you were asleep."

"I am merely resting." He placed her hand back on his chest. "A Fae's heart is centered to his body, unlike a human's."

All other doubts vanished, intrigued by this new knowledge. "Fascinating. And your blood?"

He opened one eye. "Red is universal in the cosmos."

Ivy shrugged. "I had to ask."

"I'm not an alien."

"Umm...in a way."

Conn moved to his side and propped his head on his hand. "Would you be upset to know that humans were not created on this planet?"

She rolled her eyes. "Are you discounting evolution and man? God?"

His face grew serious. "Absolutely not. I'm stating a fact, which I'll explain in further detail later."

"Why me?" she blurted out.

Conn drew her to him. "Honestly?"

Ivy shook her head, though she held her breath fearing the worst.

"I cannot say, Ivy. From the moment I saw you, everything else shifted within me." He sighed, bringing them both back down against the pillows.

Placing her hand back in the center of his chest, she gazed up at him. "Surely there have been others. You're—"

"Ancient, not *old*," he interjected.

"Is there a difference?" she teased. "Then tell me more."

For the next several hours, Ivy listened with rapt attention to her Celt explain the world of the Fae and what a Fenian Warrior and the Brotherhood meant to him. Shocking as some of the information seemed, she absorbed it all, urging him to divulge more when he would hesitate or become unsure. The man had traveled through time—stood, counseled, and battled with many kings and queens. Her mind staggered, especially when she wanted to know how it felt being whisked from one century to the other. As he discussed his magical qualities, she probed him for examples, and he promptly reminded her about her garden.

"And Bradon Finnegan? You're the one in the painting?"

"Yes," he answered softly, stroking a hand down her back. "Bradon witnessed a skirmish between another of my Fenian brothers and a human. He grew concerned, deeming the warrior was in grave danger and dashed forward. Bradon put himself in front of the blade not realizing the Fae would have swiftly deflected the blow. Stunned by the brave actions of Finnegan, the warrior summoned a Fae healer to mend the man's wounds, though they were not life threatening. From that very day, your ancestor was revered. He kept his secret—a vow he pledged before all three warriors, myself included."

Ivy yawned. "What were their names?"

"Liam MacGregor and my mentor, Aidan Kerrigan. We allowed him to paint the landscapes of our world by sharing stories with him. He had a magnificent talent—one I see in you."

She snuggled closer. "Tell me more of your home. Your world beneath ours."

Ivy closed her eyes when he spoke of the beauty of his home. When he spoke about being away for so long, his voice took on a tone of sorrow. Therefore, Ivy held off with any questions. In time, she believed he would share everything, including painful memories.

This was a time of beginnings.

Rubbing her eyes with one hand, she draped the other over Conn's chest—content and relaxed.

"Sleep," he encouraged.

"Not tired. Hungry."

"No food in the apartment. We can go out."

Ivy bolted up straight. "Let me cook for you."

Conn laughed. "What are you suggesting?"

She scooted onto her knees. "I spotted a market across the street. It had all these different kinds of squashes. I make a fantastic Spaghetti Alfredo Squash with Peas. And I have a special dessert that I know you will like, too."

Conn leaped off the bed and grabbed his jeans. "Tell me what you need."

"No." Ivy scrambled off the bed and rushed to his side. "Let me go get everything. I want it to be a surprise."

He eyed her skeptically. "Afraid I'll get the wrong item?"

She laughed out loud. "Yep." Picking up her discarded clothes, she dashed into the bathroom. Hastily getting dressed, she stole a glance at herself in the mirror before leaving.

Conn stood there holding out her coat. Helping her

put it on, he then wrapped her purse over her shoulder and walked her to the door. "Do not tarry too long."

Ivy stood on her tiptoes and kissed him thoroughly. "Missing you already."

Chapter Twenty-Four

"When a heart bleeds red, all the Fae weep."
~Chronicles of the Fae

Smiling, Ivy hastened across the street to the market. Dusk was settling over the city, and she spotted the first star winking down at her. Had she really spent all day in Conn's arms? Time slipped away as they talked, laughed, and made love. She'd never known such joy.

Happiness filled her as she picked up a small basket to fetch the items she would need for their meal. Looking over the squashes, she found one suitable and wandered inside the store. She gravitated to another area of produce and found shallots and fresh thyme. Moving along the narrow aisle, Ivy picked through a selection of cheeses and selected grated Parmesan. Next on her list, heavy cream and frozen peas—praying they would have them in stock. Quickly locating them, she made her way to the selection of ice cream.

"Bet you've never had a root beer float, Conn MacRoich."

Finding the rest of her items, Ivy's steps quickened to the register. Tapping her foot, she tried to be patient, since her only thought was returning once again into Conn's arms. Her lover. Her friend. Her Fenian Fae Warrior.

Why is it when you're in a hurry, the clerks always want to chat with the customers? Get moving!

Whistling a tune, instead of yelling at the clerk and customer, she tossed in some dark chocolate from one of the nearby baskets.

Five long, grueling minutes passed and finally they were done.

Ivy smiled and handed the woman her basket.

"A fine day. What are you fixing?" asked the clerk, slowly putting her items into a bag.

Her smile faded a bit. "A special meal. Here, let me help you. My boyfriend is starving."

The woman laughed. "A hearty appetite is good in a man. Enjoy your meal."

Handing the clerk her money, Ivy snatched up the bag. "Thanks. Have a great evening."

Glancing both ways, Ivy darted back toward the apartment. Her steps slowed as she approached the building. A tremor of unease crept down her spine. Keeping her nerves steady, she nodded to the man standing off to the side.

"Good evening, Ivy Kathleen," greeted Mike Banister.

The smile on his face never made it to his eyes. "Hello, Mike." *Must get inside to Conn.*

"Can I help you?" he asked, blocking her path to the door.

Ivy shook her head. "Nope. I'm good." She waited for him to move.

He leaned near. "Wrong answer."

Before she had a chance to scream, Mike had a hand over mouth, knocking the groceries from her arms. He shoved a knife into her side. "One word from those lovely lips, and I'll carve a slice from your body and deliver it to your boyfriend."

Ivy trembled, but nodded.

Mike removed his hand from her mouth and yanked her around the side of the building into an alleyway. His fingers dug sharply into her arm.

"This could have been solved easily, if your uncle had not interfered with our plans," he hissed, dragging her farther away from civilization.

Her fear turned to anger. "*You* were the one. You killed him. For what?"

"He interfered with my plans."

Her eyes grew wide with fear when she saw his car, the trunk already open. It would be over for her the moment he tossed her inside. *Think, think, think!*

"What do you want, Mike? Let's just settle this now."

His eyes raked over her body. "You're willing to barter?" His laughter was sinister. "First, I want the treasure. Second, I'll take you, since you're obviously screwing the man in the building."

She stumbled forward. "I don't know *anything* about a treasure. And I'd rather die than have you touch me."

The man shrugged. "Not really your choice, now is it?" Mike pointed to her purse. "I bet you have the keys inside there."

Ivy seethed with fury. "You're an ass. They're nothing. Go back and tell your boss they're only junk. One is the original key to my cottage."

His expression darkened, and Mike leveled the blade against the side of her neck. "*Boss*? Do you want to hear how Eric Dunstan died? Do you want me to show you what parts I carved from the man?"

Ivy felt the trickle of blood seep down her skin, unable to move. "Why?"

"Because he was weak. Only wanted your land. He didn't believe in the treasure either." He snarled. "I was the one who told Eric that the ruins belonged to you. Yet, he didn't think they would amount to anything and brushed aside my ideas. In the end, he fired me, and I had to kill him." He lowered the blade. "The *treasure* will be mine."

You're an insane bastard! "The keys are in my purse. Take them."

He leaned nearer, the stench of his breath choking Ivy. "No, I can't let you go now. I've just confessed. Don't want you scurrying off to the Garda."

Ivy swallowed the bile in her throat. "I won't tell a soul."

His lips twisted in a cynical smile. "Liar."

Ivy knew her time of negotiating was at an end. Regardless of the blade, Ivy clawed at his face, pushing his body away from hers and let out a scream.

"You bitch!"

He smacked her hard across the face, and she fell backward against the stone wall. When he reached for her arm, she kicked and continued to scream. Yet, the man was far stronger. Lifting her up, Mike dumped her into the trunk and slammed the hood.

Pain slashed through her body and lights danced before her eyes. Glancing down, her hands encountered cold steel protruding from her side. Somehow the bastard had impaled her against something in the trunk. Fighting the dark wave of abyss, Ivy continued to scream for help. But the effort cost her dearly as blood spurted forth.

The car lurched forward, and the icy claw of panic took hold of her. Hope faded the moment Mike shoved her into his vehicle, and her nightmare of dying without once again seeing the man she loved consumed her.

"Conn, *please* hear me. I'm hurt. I need…" She sucked in a huge breath and let it out slowly. Her vision blurred, cold sweat trickling across her brow. In one last desperate attempt, Ivy blurted out her heart to another. "Hear my plea Fae. He is…my…*heart*."

Dizziness swamped Ivy as the void of darkness enveloped her.

Love you always…

****

Conn dropped the bottle of wine as Ivy's screams pierced through to his mind and soul.

Rushing to the window, he saw the groceries flung out into the street. With a great roar, he tore downstairs and yanked the door open. Concentrating, he opened his Fae senses and looked in both directions. Nothing to his left, but when he glanced to the right, Conn could see the fading glow of lights from a car. His fists clenched with fury.

With time now his enemy, he tried to control the burning rage as he sprinted back into his apartment. Pulling his boots on, he ran inside his den and pulled forth his dirk and keys. Swiftly leaving his place, he was on his motorcycle in minutes.

Only two people could have taken Ivy. Eric Dunstan or Mike Banister. It didn't matter which man, for one would die. Never in all of his life had Conn wished to seek vengeance. This world was one where he kept the balance between justice—good *and* evil. If there was a death, it was not by his hand, unless he was forced to save those he guided. Now, the humans had taken something he treasured. Something he loved. His beloved.

"*Ivy!*" he bellowed, accelerating to an unholy speed, trying to catch up with the vehicle.

Turning the bend in the road, his anger intensified. They were heading farther away from the city and out into the country. He tried to remain focused, but his emotions were clouded with a rage he'd never experienced.

He shook as he tried to maintain the speed of the bike. Careening around a narrow corner, the area opened and relief washed over him when he spotted several vehicles ahead. Saying a silent prayer, he sped faster along the road. Approaching one of the vehicles, he maneuvered the motorcycle alongside. Seeing an elderly man driving, he uttered a curse and drove off ahead of him.

What if he was wrong? What if they had taken Ivy elsewhere within the city? Shit! Clear the emotions. Focus on the task. You are a Fae warrior.

Sealing all doubt, Conn steadied the ferocity and indecisiveness of his unstable emotions. The wind slapped at his face, but he silently thanked the Gods for keeping the sky clear. As Conn steadily made his way nearer to the other car, he was unsure on what to do without placing Ivy in jeopardy. Without any plan, he had to rely on only one attack.

Stop the vehicle.

As if sensing his presence, the car accelerated. And so did Conn. His motorcycle was built for speed and he weaved nearer. The car swerved, almost hitting him.

Conn slammed on the brakes and then sped up. Intent on slowing the vehicle proved futile as the bastard kept trying to drive Conn off the road.

The battle raged on and Conn sped up.

When he approached the side of the car, the man leveled a gun at him. *Mike Banister*, his mind screamed. Conn ducked the shot fired and slowed. Instantly the bastard put on the brakes, and Conn sharply angled his bike to avoid being hit head on.

The action cost them both. The car lost control just as Conn skidded across the pavement and crashed through the fence, landing below the main road.

Dazed, Conn tried to draw in a deep breath. Pain seared down his back when he stood on shaky limbs. Reaching for his dirk, he sealed off the injury within his mind. He would tend to his wounds later. Steadily making his way back to the road, Conn fought the wave of panic at finding the car on one side.

Running over to the vehicle, he wrenched open the passenger door, but stunned to find no Ivy. His hand tightened on his dirk upon seeing Mike Banister slumped over the wheel, blood oozing from his head.

Storming to the driver's side, he yanked the door open and pulled the man onto the ground. "Where is she?" The man was unconscious and of no use to him.

Scanning the car, he almost missed the item on the floor. Grabbing Ivy's purse, he clutched it to his chest and looked around. Finding the lock to the trunk, he clicked it open and sprinted to the back.

Blood pooled around her body, her face ashen even in the twilight. Glancing down, Conn noticed a metal shard protruding from her side. The bastard's trunk was filled with junk, ranging from broken saws to rusty pipes and shorn off pieces of metal. Fearing the worst, he placed two fingers on her neck and let out an anguished sigh when he felt the faint pulse. It was weak, but his sprite was a fighter.

"Stay with me, *mo ghrá*. Do not leave me." He breathed the words across her face, praying they would echo within her heart.

Taking a step back, Conn raked a hand through his hair. He had no transportation to get her swiftly to a hospital. Even if he did, he feared she would not make it in the hands of doctors. She required something more powerful, no matter the consequences. Conn no longer cared about the laws. The Fae realm was her only hope. He would gladly give his life for Ivy. Since he was unable to transport her there with magic, he knew of another way and prayed it would happen.

Quickly kneeling, he placed his palms upon the ground and called forth a desperate plea. "Here me, my friend. Once again, I require your assistance for a woman who is injured." Conn let the energy swell, build, and pulse outward.

Long, torturous moments passed. Then it came on a light breeze. *I am here Fenian Warrior.*

The horse snickered behind him and Conn rose. After greeting the animal, he made his way to Ivy.

Brushing a lock of hair away from her face, he bent low. "I must act swiftly. Find a safe haven within your mind and stay there. Time will slow. Do not fight against it. I will not leave your side."

Conn straightened. Flexing his hands, he only had moments once he lifted Ivy away from the metal pipe. His magic would reduce her heart rate and breathing, causing the blood flow to decrease dramatically. It was the only way to transport her there.

Calling forth the magic inside him, he breathed in deeply and in one swift move lifted Ivy into his arms. Her strangled cry almost undid him. Gently lowering her to the ground, Conn moved his hands above her body—beginning at the head and traveling down to her feet. Bringing them back over the wound, he concentrated until beads of sweat broke out on his brow. Releasing the long held breath, he cradled her into his arms. "Sleep, Ivy," he commanded.

Conn stood and walked over to a boulder. Standing on top, he waited until the horse approached. Carefully straddling the animal, he secured Ivy within his arm and grabbed the mane. Giving a nudge, they took off at a light gallop across the land.

Onward they traveled through the Irish landscape—starlight, the crescent moon, and magic their only guides through the terrain. Conn held Ivy's motionless body, focusing on the destination. He allowed no other thoughts to drift through his mind. There was no room for doubts from the actions he was destined to make on this night. His mindset was clearly on saving the woman who held his heart—his life.

As the hours passed, their speed increased as a cold blast of air descended from the north.

An owl hooted in the distance, signaling the first sign they were drawing near.

When the lone wolf's cry echoed in the night, Conn angled the horse northward.

The cry of all birds and beasts were announcing the arrival of the Prince.

And Conn uttered a prayer the doors would open for him.

Chapter Twenty-Five

"A sacrifice not willingly chosen can shred its purpose."

~Chronicles of the Fae

The trees welcomed Conn in greeting as he approached. Bringing the horse near an ancient oak in the center, he dismounted carefully while still maintaining his grip on Ivy. Placing her gently on the ground, he swept his hands over her body until he felt the whisper of a heartbeat.

Satisfied, he stood and went to the horse. "Thank you. I owe you my deepest appreciation." The animal snorted and nudged his head against Conn's arm. "Remain here my friend. I shall have someone tend to your needs. Until then, rest nearby."

Conn removed his shirt and boots and knelt on one knee before the giant tree. Placing a hand on Ivy, he held his other outward. "Open the gates from this world to my realm. I, Conn MacRoich, Fae prince have returned."

He gritted his teeth and waited. Stone, cold silence greeted him.

"Open the gates from human to Fae," he uttered with more conviction.

But the gates refused to open for Conn.

He brought Ivy's limp hand to his chest. "I will not

leave you." Kissing her fingers, he released her hand.

There was another way to open the gates to his world. Once again, he faced consequences, and he risked putting another in jeopardy. Yet, it was unavoidable and his last solution. Glancing at Ivy one last time, he closed his eyes.

Fully kneeling on the ground, he quieted his mind—sealed the sounds of the nocturnal creatures and the elements. Conn let the magic swirl around him, weaving a single thought out for another. It traveled through the vein of the land where there were no barriers and sought its destination.

"Abela."

Her gasp sliced through his mind. "What's wrong?"

"I require assistance."

She probed his thoughts.

"Stop!" he ordered. "I am not a specimen."

"What have you done?" her question laced with anguish.

"Please open the gates," he pleaded.

"You have a human."

"She is injured. Her life has been slowed. I require a healer."

"No," whispered Abela. "I'm sorry, but I cannot go against my own people. If you cannot open the gates, then there is reason."

"Not even for your brother?" he demanded harshly.

"Why?" she yelled. "I would gladly assist you, but I don't—"

"I love her!"

A sob wrenched free from his sister. "Blessed

Danu, can it be so?"

"I have spoken the binding vows."

Silence followed and he sensed his sister was pacing.

"Is there nothing you can do?"

"Quiet. I am concentrating," she snapped.

Hope soared within him and Conn kept vigil waiting for her.

Abela's love washed through his mind and body. "We must act swiftly. I shall not open the gates. However, I will part the two realms and create a path for you to move through. I don't know how long I can keep it stable. Once you step through, my magic will escort you along the way. Concentrate on the path in front of you—your chambers. If you sway for even a second, you'll lose the sight and venture into another realm. One where I will not be able to bring you back."

Conn wrapped a single thought of love out to her. "Thank you, Abela."

"Don't thank me yet, Brother. Upon your arrival, seal off the place with your magic. You do realize I must alert the king and queen."

Conn stood. "Have them bring a healer."

The mists descended and swirled around him as he picked up Ivy. He cradled her body close to him and waited. The air cooled and thinned. As the tendrils of vapor parted, a realm between the two worlds opened up for Conn.

"Now," ordered Abela.

Darting forward into the abyss, the pressure slammed into Conn. His steps faltered, but he steadied himself and quickly moved forward. Seeing his chambers looming in the distance, he kept his focus fixed making long strides toward the place. Lights and soft music called out to him from his left, but he ignored their luring song. His lungs tried to adjust to the lack of air and for a moment, he thought to pause and take in deep cleansing breaths. But he shoved the thought aside and his pace increased.

The steps to his chambers became visible, yet, the mists thickened. Time was running out. Abela could no longer maintain the chasm open between the realms. Using every ounce of energy, Conn started to run. Pain slashed through his chest—his arms becoming weak. Dark spots clouded his vision, and he gritted his teeth.

I will not fail!

With one final burst of speed, Conn crossed over into his chambers, crashing against the floor on his side. Taking in huge gulps of air, he lifted his hand and sealed off his chambers. Placing his chin on Ivy's head, he waited until he had regained his strength.

After several moments, Conn stood and went into his inner chamber. Waving his hand outward, the velvet covers fell back on his bed. Carefully, he placed Ivy on the soft linens. Next, he gently removed all of her clothing.

"By the hounds," he hissed, staring at the gaping hole in her side. Snapping his fingers magically, he dressed her in a soft ivory gown fashioned with buttons down the front.

He bent and placed a kiss along her brow. Her face held no trace of color, and Conn held his hands above her body. This time the whisper of her heartbeat took longer. His beloved was dying.

Pinching the bridge of his nose in frustration, he paced with uncertainty at the foot of his bed. Surely his parents had now heard the news of his arrival. What could be taking them so long? He halted. Did they decide not to come? Not to bring a healer? If he opened the door to his chambers, would there be guards to take him away—transport Ivy back to the human realm to die—all alone?

"No," he growled. He glanced at her and grasped the bedpost. "I refuse to believe such cruelty from my own parents."

"I am happy to hear those words, my son."

Conn turned at the sound of his mother's voice. He blinked, unable to move. "And father?"

"What about your father?" she echoed.

He had no time for bantering of words. "Will we be expecting him?"

Ignoring his question, Queen Nuala moved to Ivy's bedside. "What have you done, Conn?" She brushed a finger over Ivy's pale features.

Conn choked back the emotions, but his voice betrayed him. "I have fallen madly in love with a human—one where I have spoken my vows to pledge my heart with hers." He wandered to Ivy's side and sat on the edge of the bed. Lifting her hand, he placed it against his heart. "Never did I imagine such love for another. I am a warrior with centuries of training to avoid all emotional bindings." He lifted his gaze to meet his mother's. "Call it fate, destiny, or purely chance. Her soul called out to mine, and I accepted."

His mother came to his side and cupped his face within her hands. "Love often comes to us unbidden. Even the greatest of Fenian warriors have fallen, and I don't mean that in a negative content."

He swallowed. "Thank you."

She sighed and stepped back. "You do realize there will be a price for what you seek?"

"Payment for her life? From father?"

"Yes," she whispered sadly. "From your king."

"I would give my life freely, if that's what is required."

"I would never bargain a life for a life," snapped King Ansgar storming into the room. Behind him trailed a man in long white robes. The king gestured to the man. "I have brought you your healer."

Standing, Conn made room for the man. Clasping his hands behind his back, he bowed to his father. "Thank you."

"Who is she?" he demanded.

"Ivy O'Callaghan."

His father's eyes blazed with fury. "Your *charge*?"

"My *beloved*," he corrected, daring his father to challenge him.

Silence permeated the place.

"If I may have a few moments with the human female," suggested the healer.

The king gave a curt nod. Conn followed his father and mother into the other room. His mother passed a hand over the table and a wine jug with glasses appeared. She poured some into two glasses, and then handed one to the king and Conn.

"Forgive me, Mother, but I would rather keep my wits."

She eyed him skeptically. "Your wits hover on disaster. Drink and relax. You have been through a great strain. The healer will tend to your wounds, as well."

Arguing with his mother always proved futile,

especially when she smiled. Taking the offered glass, he took a sip. The wine warmed him immediately. Realizing how cold his chambers were, Conn threw out a spark of fire into the fireplace. The blaze brought illumination and took the chill away.

"Explain all," ordered his father, taking a seat by the blazing hearth.

Conn leaned against the stone, the heat barely seeping into his body. "I fulfilled my quest. Ivy has emerged from her shadow of secrets, which were many. Her true parentage was discovered. In addition, she has suffered vicious attacks—one where she would have died without my intervention."

His father drained his glass of wine. "Nevertheless, you have left out one important fact."

"That I fell in love with her? A fact only important to me."

"Wrong. Have you decided to ignore *all* laws?"

Conn watched as his father's ire grew. Challenging him might cost him, but he refused to back down. "It must be a trait among Fenian Warriors. Although, I don't believe love is against our laws?"

Throwing the glass into the fireplace, his father stood. "It was a mistake to place Aidan Kerrigan as your mentor."

His mother gasped and reached for her husband's arm. "How can you speak thus? Did he not save your life during the battle between the old and new religions?"

King Ansgar closed his eyes. Upon opening them, he placed a hand over hers. "Forgive me for my harsh words. You were correct in reminding me." Meeting Conn's glare, he said, "He was one of our greatest, but I cannot fathom why *you* chose a human."

Swirling his wine, Conn then drained his glass and placed it on the table. "Do we choose love, or does it seek us out, Father?"

"Love between a Fae and human is forbidden," he uttered somberly.

Conn raked a hand through his hair. Striding to the entrance of his vast garden, he glanced outward at the magnificent waterfall. "My mind knows the law, but my soul and heart refused to listen." Glancing over his shoulder, he added, "What would you have me do?"

When the healer emerged, all thoughts of their conversation vanished from his mind. The Fae's features held the grim reality, and Conn feared hearing the words. He walked slowly over to him. "Tell me," he gritted out.

"I am sorry, Prince. The female—"

"Her name is *Ivy*," interrupted Conn.

The healer straightened. "My apologies. Ivy has lost far too much blood. In order to heal the wound in her side, she requires more. Furthermore, she has been kept overlong in a suspended state, and her spirit is starting to cross over."

"No!" roared Conn, pushing past the man. He refused to hear his words. Running to her side, he leaned over her. She couldn't die. Not now. Not when he opened his heart to love. He'd given her a piece of his soul, so why not another. He was doomed already. Another sacrifice would ensure her life—forever.

"No," he stated again and lifted his gaze to those watching him from the entrance. "Give her my blood. I've said my binding vows to her. My blood will sustain her."

"It's not done. Do not speak of tainting both worlds," bellowed the king. "I refuse!"

For the first time in his existence, Conn cared less about formalities. He was no longer concerned with rules, laws, and his training. Striding to his father, he met his hard stare. "She is my beloved, Father."

"And I forbid it. Do not think you can sway me." He jabbed a finger into Conn's chest. "You speak like a youngling, not a warrior."

Conn's eyes blazed, but he kept his fists clenched by his side. "Name your price."

Thunder rolled overhead, and Conn realized his father was dangerously nearing the edge of his control.

"I do not barter for a life," the king's tone held a warning.

"You would if it was the queen," countered Conn.

Without giving him a chance to respond, Conn knelt on one knee in front of his father. His sacrifice was needed, and he sealed off the pain to his heart. "I make this one last request for the woman I love. Grant my blood to save her life, and I will renounce my association to the Brotherhood. In addition, I shall take my rightful place as prince by your side, and choose a wife from the royal house of Frylnn."

Hushed silence descended throughout the room.

"Done," accepted the king. "I will await your arrival in the royal chambers." In a brilliant flash, he departed.

"She will never be the same," stated his mother softly. "Her blood will flow with yours—ours and she will live a life not fully content."

Conn kept his head bent. "Then issue her a Guardian to help her through the process."

His mother knelt down in front of him, but he refused to meet her gaze. "Once healed, she'll be returned to her world. You would let her go?"

When Conn lifted his head, his eyes brimmed with unshed tears. "Yes. Her life is more important than my own." He rose slowly. "I would willingly give up everything for Ivy."

His mother shook her head. "A noble gesture. But you have not considered her heart, have you, my son? Without you."

Conn watched as his mother vanished from the room in a soft whisper of light. He had no time to consider his mother's words. Nodding to the healer, he stripped the last of his clothing from his body.

Making his way to Ivy's side, his eyes roamed her features, studying every curve, committing to memory every detail about her. For when the dawn of morning came, Conn MacRoich, Fae prince, would take his place beside his king. Never again would he step foot in the human realm.

In that quiet moment, Conn suddenly realized his sacrifice would cost him the greatest love of a lifetime.

"Forgive me, *mo ghrá*."

Chapter Twenty-Six

"Shards of glass make for a beautiful prism when held up to the sunlight."

~*Chronicles of the Fae*

Beautiful, soothing music floated around Ivy. Buoyed by a sense of peace, she drifted within the warm waters of bliss. Contentment filled her being, and she longed to stay in this place. There was joy, happiness, laughter, and love. She danced and sang, lifted high above the stars and then flew back down. All of these emotions radiated throughout her body, but there was something missing.

It was fleeting each time she paused to ponder its meaning. When the thought was almost within her grasp, it floated away, as if someone snatched it from her mind.

However, she couldn't forget the voice. It beckoned her on several occasions—filling her with stories of long ago. Tales of giants and dragons. Kings and queens. So many questions burned within her to ask, but the words refused to emerge.

So, Ivy happily went on her spiritual voyage, until one day she heard *him* sighing. Oh how agonizing the sound was to her ears. She longed to reach out and give comfort. His torment ached within her, and Ivy became restless. Sadness entered her serene world.

Her fingers stretched and the feeling was unnatural. Heaviness engulfed her as she slowly attempted to open her eyes. The effort tired her, but she waited and calmed her breathing. On the fourth endeavor, Ivy managed to open her eyes fully. Blinking several times, she took in her surroundings. The room was magnificent—reminding her of being in a forest. A huge armoire graced one side of the room with etchings of animals carved into its wood exterior. On the opposite side, an array of multi-colored lights spilled in from a large window through beautiful crystal panels. Her fingers brushed over the soft velvet green cover. And the bed was one fit for a giant. A massive four-poster. She squinted, trying to focus on the post's design, but finally gave up.

It was a simple, but elegant room. But where was she?

Memories flooded her mind, and she cried out in pain, clutching her head.

"Here, drink this," ordered the man, his voice soothing.

Ivy took the goblet. "Too...too many thoughts," she muttered in a hoarse voice and closed her eyes.

"It is to be expected, though you have been asleep longer than we wished." He nudged the cup to her lips. "Drink," he urged.

"What is it? Tastes like cream mixed with almonds and cinnamon."

"A healing tonic."

She snapped open her eyes. "Why am I not in a hospital? Where am I?"

"If you drink the rest, I will tell you." He pulled a nearby chair to her bedside.

"I'm in no mood for negotiating."

The man's mouth twitched in humor. "I now see why he chose you."

Realization slammed into Ivy. "Conn. What happened?" She rubbed a hand over her brow, trying to organize the images. *The encounter with Mike Banister. Being shoved into his car. The horrific pain at being impaled. Darkness.*

"You are in the Prince's chambers. He brought you here after you were injured."

Ivy took another sip of the cool liquid, finding the man's words unsettling. She looked down at her body. "I don't know any prince. Again, why am I here and not in a hospital? Are you a special nurse?"

"It was the only way Prince Conn could save your life."

Gripping the goblet firmly to keep her hands from shaking, she looked directly at the man. "Prince as in prince of the *Fae* realm."

The man smiled. "Precisely. And my name is Kaelan."

Ivy drained the last of the liquid and handed the goblet back to him. "I thought he was a Fenian Warrior?"

"Ahh…so he has shared his status with you."

Ivy blushed. They had shared so much together. Yet, in their time and discussions, Conn never mentioned he was heir to the Fae realm. "Yes, but not his lineage."

Kaelan frowned in concentration. "I deem he withheld this knowledge, since he did not consider himself a prince. Once he took the oath of a Fenian Warrior, he renounced his right to one day rule our world."

Weariness swept through Ivy. "Where is he?"

The healer rose. "He is attending to his duties with the king."

"I'm confused. I thought you said he gave up his right to rule."

A shadow passed over Kaelan's features. "He is no longer a Fenian Warrior. In order to save your life with his own blood, he agreed to leave the Brotherhood and take his place by his father's side."

Yawning, Ivy tried to sit up more fully. "Why are you telling me this and not Conn?"

Kaelan shrugged and left the room.

"Wait, I have more questions."

"Sleep," he ordered, his words echoing in the room.

"I think I've slept enough." Yawning once again, she slid down among the pillows. "What was in that drink," she mumbled, slipping into a deep slumber.

****

Warm lips touched hers, and Ivy bolted awake. She rubbed her eyes and then looked around the darkened place. Bringing a shaky hand to her lips, his scent lingered—one of the woods and all male. A lone candle burned low on a nearby table, yet, no trace of the physical man in the room.

"Where are you, Conn?" she blurted out, tears misting her eyes.

Frustration seeped inside of her as she dug her fingers into the soft velvet blankets. She had no concept of time or day. Her reality was skewed, and the man she loved elusive.

Deciding to take charge, she eased out from the

covers. She marveled at the lovely pale rose-colored gown she wore. However, Ivy's first task was to inspect her injury. Her feet dangled over the edge of the massive bed. Feeling unsure, she opted to slip the gown from her shoulders. Taking a quick look to her left, she proceeded to shove the fabric farther down.

"Sweet Brigid," she gasped, running her fingers over her smooth skin. No bandages. No scars. No pain. Nothing. No physical evidence of her injury.

Stunned, Ivy quickly pulled the garment back over her body. Reaching for the matching robe, she struggled to put it on. Taking in some deep calming breaths, she eased her feet onto the floor. Her balance was shaky, so she used the side of the bed for support. Inching her way along the bed, she finally made it to the end and clutched the bedpost.

"You can do this, girl. If you fall, there's always crawling."

Taking several small steps, Ivy moved ahead. Her steps remained steady and with each one, strength infused her. Reaching the double doors to the other room, Ivy pushed them open. Light spilled into the room from the blazing fire, and she glanced around in all directions. Conn's bedroom was stark in comparison to this one.

Beauty filled her eyes as she slowly made her way into the room. Crystals, amethysts, and various other gemstones dotted several tables, each engraved with Celtic designs. A striking carved hutch filled with glassware, silver goblets, and decanters lined one wall. Mahogany bookcases—their shelves lined with gild-covered books extended down a long corridor, and her fingers itched to touch them. On the walls were vivid colored tapestries depicting scenes of animals and great warriors, clothed in dazzling material.

A large round oak table rested near a window. Her stomach growled when she spied a silver bowl filled with apples, pears, and pomegranates on top. Taking measured steps, she went and retrieved an apple.

Making her way to the fireplace, Ivy paused to inspect the two beautiful chairs flanking the hearth. Carved out of wood and polished to a luster, their armrests resembled stags. Embroidered cushions in hues of green and gold complemented each chair. "Fit for a prince," she whispered, trailing her hand over the high back.

Leaning against the chair, she lifted her gaze. Above the fireplace mantel was a display of armory, mostly swords and shields, but they were magnificent. The room reminded Ivy of a mixture of ancient and fantasy—a blend of both of Conn's worlds.

With a sigh, Ivy wandered slowly to the crystal double doors, her strength increasing with each step. Pushing them open, starlight filled the area, along with the glow of the full moon. Its beam so radiant, Ivy could make out the silhouettes of the trees and landscape. She detected a waterfall nearby, its soothing music filled her, and she stepped outside.

Inhaling deeply the cool, fragrant air, Ivy hugged her arms around her body. Lanterns were placed on either side of the stairs leading downward. She was tempted to cross the marble terrace and descend into the place, but decided to sit in one of the wooden chairs.

Sinking down into the cushions, she took a bite of her apple. "What a magical world you live in, Conn. Why would you ever want to leave?"

Tucking her feet underneath her, she ate in blissful silence and tried to determine the constellation of the stars. They shone mightily in the inky blackness—ones she'd never seen before. Ivy counted over twenty dragons, their outlines blazed more than the other lone stars. "So dragons did exist?"

This was a world within another world. Or maybe it was all in one, and the Fae realm had a touch more illumination? Question upon question built within her mind, and she made a mental list to ask when she saw Conn. "Whenever the man...*Fae prince* decided to appear."

She giggled and leaned back in the chair. Soon, sleep beckoned and dreams of Conn returned.

****

The scent of sweet aroma stirred Ivy awake. Opening her eyes, she tried to adjust to the intense brightness inside the room. Colors of the rainbow danced along the golden floor through the crystal panes. Confused at her surroundings, she tossed the covers off and sat. Rubbing a hand over her brow, she shook her head. Her last waking memory was of sitting on Conn's terrace and falling asleep. Yet, her dreams were filled with him. Her face heated at the images of their lovemaking, and she longed to hold him.

"Did you bring me back to your bed, Conn?" she asked quietly.

Glancing to her right, she saw a gardenia floating in a large bowl. Its heady perfume filled the place. Lying next to the bowl were soaps, lotions, and combs.

Stretching her arms over her head, she longed for a shower or hot soak in a tub. Surprisingly, her body felt rejuvenated after everything she had been through.

Catching sight of the beautiful pale green gown at the end of her bed, she scooted off. Fingering the stunning, soft material, she gathered it into her arms along with a rose-scented bar of soap. Spotting the matching slippers, she opted to go barefoot.

Making her way out of the room, Ivy shielded her eyes from the shimmering daylight. Blinking several times, her eyesight soon adjusted. Walking out onto the terrace, Ivy stood mesmerized at the vision below. Never had she beheld such beauty. Colors so vivid they stole her breath. A golden hummingbird flitted nearby, its wings glistening in the light. Lush trees, flowers, and birdsong filled an entire valley. It wasn't a garden, but paradise.

"What a wonder it would be to paint this bucolic scene," she whispered.

Hearing the sound of water, Ivy took the marble steps leading downward, sighing when her feet encountered the downy softness of the grass. Taking flight like a child, she continued on her journey until she found the waterfall, spilling into a small circular lake. Stone rocks dotted around the area with sunlight touching each of them.

Placing her gown on one of the larger boulders, Ivy stripped from her other one. Leaning over, she dipped her hand into the water and let out pleasurable sigh. "Heated."

Sliding into the water, Ivy closed her eyes. The sensation was exquisite, and soon she found herself swimming to the other side. Giddy and lighthearted, she backstroked to where she had left the soap. After cleansing her body and hair with the rich lather, she swam to a larger flat boulder and hoisted herself on top.

Fully stretching out, she let the warmth of the sun dry her body.

Happy and content with her bath, she curled to her side. Ivy glided her fingers in the water. "Did you bathe in these waters, Conn?"

Sitting upright, she hugged her knees to her chest. "Where are you?"

Her stomach growled, and Ivy removed herself from the stone and quickly got dressed. The material flowed in gossamer waves down to her ankles, hugging all her curves as well. Running her fingers through her hair, she made her way back to the chambers.

Upon entering, Ivy halted. Sitting in one of the chairs was a striking woman. Her golden locks cascaded around her body to her waist. The woman's pale features were accented by the hue of her lavender eyes, and a thin silver circlet of vines surrounded her head. Her pale blue gown shimmered with the light of a thousand stars. She inclined her head to Ivy and stood slowly.

Were all the Fae so tall?

Ivy could have sworn the woman glided across the floor toward her.

"I bid you welcome, Ivy Kathleen O'Callaghan."

"Um…hello and thank you."

She gestured to the large table. "Are you hungry?"

Ivy turned her sight to the table. An array of breads, sweets, cheeses, and fruits were spread out on silver trays. "Oh, my."

The woman's mouth twitched in humor. "I assume that is a yes?"

Smiling, Ivy nodded. "Will you join me?"

Her smile lit up the entire room. "How kind. Yet,

he did mention this quality of yours."

"Let me guess. The *elusive* Conn MacRoich?" Ivy pulled out a chair for the woman.

She let out a sigh. "Yes. My son is attending to his duties with his father."

Stunned and embarrassed, Ivy gripped the chair. "I'm so *sorry*. I didn't know…this is all so new. Besides, I think he owes me an explanation."

Moving toward Ivy, the woman placed a gentle hand on her shoulder. "There is nothing to apologize for, Ivy. Let us start over. I am Queen Nuala, but please call me Nuala. I have come to see how you are healing. Please sit."

Ivy took a seat next to her and tucked her grass-stained feet under the chair praying the woman didn't notice. No matter what Nuala had stated, she was in front of royalty—a queen and the mother of the man she loved.

Nuala handed Ivy a plate. "Are there any questions you wish to ask me?" The queen placed some breads and cheese on her own plate.

Ivy reached across and plucked a small loaf of warm bread, cheese, and grapes. So many burned within her mind. How could she spill them out for the queen? For Conn's mother? In the end, she deemed simple questions the best tactic. "How was I healed?"

"My son's blood helped to replenish and bind your wounds." Nuala poured some wine into a glass and handed it to Ivy.

Taking a sip, Ivy placed it down. "Why didn't he take me to the hospital? They would have been able to do a blood transfusion there."

The queen shrugged. "A question you must present

to him."

Ivy nibbled on a piece of cheese, trying hard not to snort. "And when can I expect to see him?"

The woman gazed into her wine glass. "I cannot say."

Her words came across to Ivy as something else. "Is there more you wish to tell me, Nuala?"

Sadness passed over her features, but only briefly. Meeting Ivy's stare, she answered, "For the moment, Conn is preparing for the coronation that will make him heir to our world."

He doesn't want to see me. Now that he's returned to his own world, I'm nothing. Does he visit me while I'm sleeping and have regrets? He can't even tell me in person. Reaching for her glass, Ivy drained the contents. The wine left a bitter taste in her mouth, and her hand trembled as she placed the glass on the table.

"His chambers are stunning, but might I have another room until I'm healed?"

Nuala folded her hands in her lap. "Forgive me, but these chambers are the only ones for you. My son has ordered you to remain here."

Ivy grasped the arms of the chair. "*Ordered?*" Seething with anger, she glanced away from the queen.

"It does seem harsh," stated Nuala.

This time Ivy snorted in disgust and looked at the woman. "If you would be so kind as to inform Prince Conn that if he doesn't show himself in his chambers by nightfall, then I wish to have someone escort me back to my home."

Nuala smiled slowly. "I shall pass along your message."

"Thank you."

Standing, she cupped Ivy's face. "For now, I have placed a Fenian Warrior near your door. His name is Ronan—a dear friend to my son. If you so *wish*, he is here to show you our world."

Stunned, Ivy asked, "Is Conn aware of this situation?"

Releasing her hold on Ivy, she waved the door open. "No."

"Going against your son's orders?"

Nuala laughed, the sound similar to chiming bells. "You forget, Ivy, I am the queen. All serve me, *including* my son. Furthermore, he can't object to you wandering the grounds, or the library of the Fae kingdom while you're healing."

She grasped the woman's hands. "Thank you. I would enjoy seeing your world before I leave."

Ivy stood and watched as the queen glided out of the room. What if Conn MacRoich decided not to answer her summon? Questions only he could answer, might not be possible. Confusion, hurt, and anger filled Ivy like shards of glass, each one piercing her heart.

Her earlier happiness now overshadowed by the thought of leaving and never seeing her Celt again.

"Hear my words, Conn MacRoich, and hear them well across the winds. You were my friend first, lover second, so please do me the honor of explaining what happened."

Striding toward the door, she flung it open and stared upward into the face of Fenian Warrior, Ronan.

"After you take me on a tour, please show me where *Prince* Conn is hiding."

He gave a curt nod. "I will see what I can do."

Chapter Twenty-Seven

"A fork in the road can alter or hinder your journey."
~*Chronicles of the Fae*

Lunging forward, Conn's muscles screamed as he blocked another blow from Taran's blade. Sweat dripped down into his eyes, but he refused to wipe it away. His body had grown weak with no one to train with and his brothers knew this well. Finbar had joined them after an hour and Conn fought them both. Yet, soon, Darroch and Faelan—two others of the Brotherhood, had joined him in the training lists.

It was now time to end this exercise.

"You fight like a lass," taunted Faelan, deflecting a blow by Conn.

"Did you hear him grunt? By the hounds, never thought to hear those words from the prince," mocked Taran.

Darroch held his sword up to the light. "I don't know if I want the blood of my prince on my blade."

Finbar laughed. "Take pity on him, my brothers. I deem it's the extra weight he has put on. Must have gone weak in the human realm."

"Arrogant asses," growled Conn, swinging his blade outward and surprising Finbar. The Fae stumbled backward and crashed against the stone wall. "One down, three more to go."

"Bastard," remarked Finbar, wiping the dust from his face.

Giving the man a mock salute with his sword, Conn leveled it against Darroch. "Is my blood not good enough for your sword?"

Darroch swung heavily, but Conn rebounded quickly and slammed a fist into the man's face, knocking the Fae out cold.

With a great war cry, Faelan charged forward. However, Conn ducked and tripped the man. Faelan landed against the well. Dazed, he shook his head, but remained seated.

Conn glanced over his shoulder. His smile became predatory. "So we're back to the beginning, Taran. Ready to concede defeat?"

His friend made a slight bow, his eyes never leaving Conn's. "*Never*, my prince."

Arching a brow, he turned and waited for the attack. In a blink of an eye, Taran vanished and reappeared behind him. Nevertheless, Conn was prepared for this tactic and effectively blocked the attack with a backhanded blow. Swiftly turning, Conn delivered a blow to the man's chest, tossing him across the lists.

Finally wiping his brow, Conn glanced around the training yard. "Next time, call more of the Brotherhood to assist you weaklings."

Darroch was the first to start laughing, followed by the rest of the brothers.

As they all stood slowly, Conn went and embraced each one. "I have missed you all. Thank the Gods and Goddesses you didn't bring Ronan." Reaching for a ladle from the well, he dipped it into the water. After drinking the cool, sweet liquid, he wiped his mouth with the back of his hand. Handing the ladle to Taran, he noticed the somber expressions on all their faces.

"Has something happened to Ronan?"

Taran leaned against the well. "No." He looked at the others and then added, "He's been given an important assignment."

Frowning, Conn crossed his arms over his chest. "Do tell."

Taran let out a sigh and dipped the ladle into the well. "He's been chosen to be Ivy O'Callaghan's guardian—in this realm and her world."

"Chosen by whom?" Conn clipped out.

"The queen."

"Many have seen him escorting her about the land, including myself," added Faelan.

Conn's body stiffened in shock. His own mother had betrayed him. But why? And why Ronan? The Fae was one of his dearest friends. Did he not mention to her that Ivy was to remain within his chambers until she was healed and well enough to enter her own world?

"Where did you see them last?" demanded Conn.

"They were walking toward the library."

Conn rubbed a hand over his face in frustration. "There is one more mission that must be completed before the coronation. The king has granted this, along with the Fae council. Furthermore, I shall require one warrior to make this journey with me."

"I will go with you," declared Taran.

"I have no wish to speak for the others, but I would be honored to accompany you," stated Faelan.

"Agreed," announced Finbar and Darroch.

Conn nodded. "Taran shall accompany me on my last quest as a Fenian Warrior. But I thank you all. Now, I must attend to a matter with Ronan."

"Do you deem it wise?" asked Taran.

Glancing upward, Conn stared into the crystal blue sky. "When it comes to Ivy, wise is not the word I would choose."

"Then what word would you use?"

There was only one, and Conn was unable to utter the word out loud. *Love*. Swiftly vanishing, he reappeared near the wooden doors of the library.

Banishing his sword, he changed magically into his royal cream-colored tunic and golden leather pants. Running a hand through his hair, he didn't know what he would say if Ivy was still inside the place. He paced in front of the massive doors, contemplating his words. He had spoken them often. In fact, daily.

Each day, Conn visited Ivy in his chambers—watching over her sleeping form. He filled his empty nights by her side, telling her tales of his homeland and his love for her. Conn knew the time was fleeting. She had to return to her own world, and soon. He had tarried too long—fear keeping him away from her in her waking moments.

He'd whispered his apologies a hundred times while she slept, but now he needed to utter the words for her to hear. The greatest challenge of his life stood behind those doors.

Placing his hands upon the wood, he pushed them open.

Sunlight streamed in from the adjacent windows. He nodded in passing to another Fae, keeping his senses open to her. Walking along the sections of the library,

Conn headed in the direction he knew Ivy would appreciate. The history of the Fae.

Laughter pealed out, the sound filling him. Yet, Conn was unprepared for the sight that greeted him. She sat regally in a large chair with her feet tucked under her, and her face held a rosy glow. Fae children sat around her in rapt attention as she told a story from her own childhood. One of the girls cupped a hand over her mouth and giggled. Another child held up his hand to ask a question.

He leaned against a bookcase, his heart breaking once again. As long as he lived, he would treasure this one last moment of Ivy. Beauty, grace, strength, courage, and love.

"I would have shown you the stars, *mo ghrá*," he uttered softly.

Ivy glanced up and their gazes locked.

Conn straightened and moved slowly across the room. He smiled at the children as he spoke. "I wish to speak to Ivy."

The children all nodded and as they took their leave, they made slight bows to him in passing.

Keeping his hands clasped behind his back, he noticed wariness in Ivy's eyes. "You are well?"

Smoothing out her dress, she stood. "Yes. Thank you for saving my life. But why didn't you take me to the nearest hospital?"

"There was a crash involving the vehicle you were in and my motorcycle. Unfortunately, time was critical, and you required immediate medical attention."

Frowning, Ivy moved forward. "How did you manage to get me here? Magic?"

He arched a brow. "I have friends in the animal

kingdom. I called forth a horse, and we were able to travel the landscape quickly."

"Wow...remarkable." She twisted her hands together. "What happened to Mike Banister?"

"You no longer have to worry about him."

"He died in the accident?"

"Yes," Conn lied.

Ivy nodded. "Good. Less work for the police."

He shifted slightly. Did she know how much he ached? "Do you find my chambers comfortable?"

A flash of humor crossed her face. "They're more than comfortable. You have an entire forest and waterfall contained all for your pleasure. Don't get me started on your book collection, though I couldn't read most of them."

"They provide the necessary solitude. The books are a collection of the many languages over the centuries. I am sorry I did not pull out those in English for you to read."

She started to reach out to him, but hesitated. "You never shared everything about yourself. Why?"

"At the time when we were together, I was a Fenian warrior, *not* the Fae prince."

Ivy took another step closer, her scent surrounding him. "What changed?"

By the Gods, he wanted to touch her skin. He ached to devour her sweet lips, smother her face with kisses, and whisk her away. "In order to save your life, I made a bargain with the king. I have left the Brotherhood and will take my place as heir to the throne."

Her eyes misted with unshed tears. "Yes, the healer Kaelan told me this, but he didn't tell me there were *strings* attached to this deal. So, you can never return to…above? With me?"

"No," he replied in a hoarse voice.

"Too much for a prince to love a human?"

Her words were like a dagger to his heart. "It is not my decision."

A single tear slipped down her cheek. "No, I suppose you could not go against your family, laws, or whatever. But thank you. I owe you so much for giving me courage to step out of my shell."

He clenched his hands tighter behind him. "It was there within you all the time. It only required coaxing."

She swallowed and standing on her tiptoes, Ivy kissed his cheek. "I will love you forever, my *Celt*. Be happy."

Conn was unable to move, words of love frozen inside his heart. His mind screamed at him, but he locked them far away. "I shall remember you always," he whispered.

Raw hurt glittered in those aqua eyes he adored as he watched her turn and walk quietly out of the library.

And Conn let out an anguished moan.

****

"Are you ready?" asked Taran, coming alongside him at the forest's entrance to the human world.

Conn glanced sideways at his friend. "Do you have the required information?"

The warrior snarled and pulled out his dirk. "The bastard is currently residing in the northern part of Ireland. A town called Cragan."

Removing his sword from its sheath, Conn held it up to the light. "Remember, Mike Banister is mine."

Taran's voice hardened ruthlessly. "A shame I

cannot take a slice at the man."

"Regrettably, his death will not come by my hand."

His friend snarled. "Where?"

"Undecided." Conn gestured the Fae forward. "Lead onward."

In a flash, both warriors passed into the human realm. Light rain greeted the two men as they emerged and steadily made their way to the small town. The gray light only added to the dismal atmosphere of the place. A dog darted out from behind a garbage can, giving them only a passing glance as he ran across the street. If Mike Banister wished to disappear from the Garda, he chose a perfect place to withdraw.

"He keeps a small place around the next bend," uttered Taran, keeping his focus steady.

"Weapons?"

"An arsenal."

"Back entrance?"

"Door and large kitchen window."

"Any visitors?"

"None since he's arrived."

Conn's smile became sinister. "Good. All the more easier to displace him permanently." He wanted no trace to lead back to Ivy once she returned to the village.

As they approached the road leading to Banister's house, Conn motioned for Taran to go around the back. With stealth-like moves, Conn made his way to a cluster of trees and crouched behind them. Keeping his gaze and concentration on the front, he waited for Taran to magically seal off the back exit.

When he heard the falcon's cry, Conn vanished and reappeared inside the house. Instantly, an alarm sounded.

"Shit," he hissed out, drawing forth his blade. Mike Banister appeared with a loaded rifle aimed right at his head. A wicked scar across his brow was evident in the fading light.

"Wrong choice of weapon to bring to a fight," stated Mike.

The man's words seemed worn, thin, and hollow, used so often by shallow men.

"Ahh…but I disagree. Perfect to where I'll be sending you." Conn moved toward the bastard.

"Stop!" he ordered. "Take another step, and I'll splatter your brains against the walls."

How easy it would be to snap the neck of the bastard. Conn would never forget the damage to Ivy's body. A muscle twitched in his jaw, and he fought the urge to end this standoff.

"Now this is what you're going to do—"

"I'm listening," interrupted Conn.

"Shut-up!" he shrieked, spittle flying outward. "You and that dead bitch have ruined all my plans."

"She's not dead."

The man's face contorted. "Good. Then I can find her *after* I've disposed of you. You are forthcoming with all this information. I will remember to tell her right before I carve her heart out of her chest."

Conn's blood boiled, and his hand gripped the blade tighter. "Wrong. Where you are going, you'll never set eyes on Ivy O'Callaghan again."

"You're an arrogant bastard."

Conn's expression stilled and grew serious. "I am my own arrogance, and I grow weary of this sparring of words."

Taran had quietly moved in behind Banister, allowing Conn the advantage he needed. "Do you think you can fight both of us?"

Surprised by Taran's outburst, Mike reacted and half-turned.

Bringing his sword in an arc, Conn used magic to freeze the man where he stood. Stepping forward, he removed the rifle from his hands and flung it into the corner.

The man's eyes grew wide, and he struggled to break free.

Conn waved a hand in the air, releasing him. Mike stumbled, fear registering on his face. "What...who are you...*monsters*?"

Taran rubbed a hand across his chin. "Did you hear what he called us?"

Conn leveled an icy stare at the man. "There is only one monster in this room. You." Shoving him hard against the wall, he leveled the cold steel against the man's throat.

"Devil's spawn," gasped Mike. "Kill me now."

"No, Banister. You shall not die by my hand. Your destiny awaits...in another time, another place." He leaned close. "What you did to Ivy will be repaid to you a thousand fold. She will never have to endure seeing you again."

Fear shown in his eyes. "What are you saying?"

"Atrocities, slavery, war—the Crusades were horrific in many ways. That is where I'm sending you, Mike Banister."

Before the man had a chance to utter a protest, Conn whispered the ancient words and created an opening within the veil. The clang of steel, shouting, and dust filled the room as the vortex opened. Taking a step back, he knelt and held up his fist. "So let it be done."

Snakelike tendrils gripped a hold of the man, and Mike's screams lingered long after Conn sealed the veil. Breathing heavily, he waited until the last fiber of energy left the room.

Taran approached by his side. "Impressive. Never thought to send the bastard there, and so swiftly. You've mastered parting the veil extremely well. A shame you're abandoning us."

Conn stood. He looked at his friend and clasped a hand on his shoulder. "The Brotherhood will always be a part of me. Trust me, I have no desire to rule a kingdom or take a wife whom I will never love."

The man shook his head. "Then you're doomed to a life of misery."

Conn's voice was resigned. "Then I will learn to seal off the pain."

Chapter Twenty-Eight

"Hidden scars always find a way of tearing open, if you heal them too quickly."

~Chronicles of the Fae

Hearing the bells chiming in the distance, Ivy leaned against the crystal doors to the garden. Though the sun warmed her skin, she was unable to stop the chills from entering her body—her heart. Each time she tried to close the door on Conn MacRoich, a memory from the past ripped open the hurt.

She'd spent the entire night tossing and turning within his bed, recalling every detail of their conversations, including the last one from a few days ago. Ivy wanted to scream at him when she saw him. Yet, when he stepped away from the bookcase, she stopped breathing. Gone was the man in leather, replaced by the Prince of the Fae realm. And her heart grew heavier.

He'd bargained his own life for hers. Could his pain mirror hers? Her love for him consumed her—making it impossible for Ivy to breathe at times. However, a part of her ached to hear what he never professed. Words of love.

He may have called her his love, but it wasn't the same. Perhaps he never fully loved her.

Glancing upward, she shook her head. "You bring

me into the light, but take back the most treasured gift you gave me. *You.* Or was it only a piece, Conn?"

Ivy wrapped her arms around her body. This was not her world. It was his. The longer she stayed, the more the pain would consume and destroy her.

She turned at the sound of soft knocking. Sighing heavily, she wandered over and opened the door. "Good morning, Ronan."

"Good morn to ye, lovely lady."

Ivy gestured him inside. "The bells sound beautiful. I've never heard them before."

"Aye, they are."

Collecting her slippers off the terrace, she asked, "What are they for?"

Silence was her answer, and she turned around. "Conn?"

"His coronation is today." He retrieved her silk shawl on one of the chairs and held it out to her. "Where would ye like to venture today?"

Her heart pounded so loud, she thought it would burst. Squaring her shoulders, Ivy grasped the material to her chest. "There's only one place."

"Excellent. Where?" he asked.

Ivy draped the material around her shoulders. "Take me to Conn's coronation." Shock registered on his face, but she held up her hand. "I only require to stand at the back for a few moments."

"I dinnae deem it wise."

Ivy grasped the warrior's hands. "Grant me this one last request, please? If I must give him back to you, I would like to witness some part of his coronation."

He closed his eyes on a sigh. "Now I understand why my prince could not resist your charm."

"Thank you," she whispered.

As they made their way out of Conn's chambers, Ivy glanced over her shoulder at the massive room, trying to etch every detail into her memory.

Closing the door softly, Ivy placed her hand on Ronan's outstretched arm. He led her along the corridor and down the marble steps. She traced her fingers along the vines circling the banisters. Sunlight, bells, and birdsong greeted them as they left the royal house. Moving the length of the inner gardens, they passed fountains and canopies flowing with ribbons. The scent of lush flowers filled her with each step.

Ronan escorted them around a bend on the path and through a stone archway covered in roses, gardenias, and lilacs. Beyond, the area opened up and she witnessed another crystal palace. This one in hues of green and gold with massive turrets on either side. Banners fluttered in the light breeze—each depicting a dragon.

With each step, they drew closer, and her nerves tingled. She bit her lower lip, but held her head high. Approaching the steps, Ivy took a deep breath in and released it slowly. The place reminded her of a magical castle. She counted four turrets, glistening like icicles against a sapphire sky. "It's stunning. Beyond words."

"Aye. 'Tis the Cathedral of Trees."

"Excuse me, but this doesn't look like it was carved from any tree."

"They are *inside*." The warmth of his smile echoed in his voice.

"Incredible."

"Can ye manage the climb?"

"How many?" She turned her gaze upward to the

open doors.

"Ninety."

Ivy rolled her eyes. "I'd rather not."

In a flash, Ronan transported them before the entrance of the cathedral.

Swaying slightly, she firmly grasped his arm. "You could have warned me."

Ronan chuckled low. "My apologies."

"Why ninety steps?"

"For the nine dragons that came with our people. They are the elders, the timekeepers of the Veil of Ages. Though they have left us, they dwell in the cosmos, along with their descendants."

"I'm in awe of your people." Releasing her hand, Ivy moved forward.

The cathedral was vast and filled with many of the Fae. They gathered around trees that did indeed tower inside. A soft glow of lights flickered from all the branches. Casting her sight upward, she smiled. The ceiling resembled the night sky, glittering with the brilliant light of stardust. It was a place of worship and called out to her. She ached to move forward and join the crowd.

When the first trumpet sounded, she focused her gaze to the center. In the far distance, standing under an arched trellis covered in vines, stood Conn. Her Celt was magnificent in his royal blue sleeveless tunic edged in silver and gold. Silver bands encircled his upper arms, and Ivy fought the desire to be near his side.

Ivy recognized his mother standing apart from him. She had her hand on a man's arm. His features were similar to Conn's, and Ivy believed him to be the king.

She stood motionless, watching as Conn took his

place in front of his parents. She swallowed, trying to force the lump away.

As the second trumpet blared, Conn knelt. The king took the thin crown from the queen, and placed it on Conn's head. Ivy barely registered the words spoken, but she felt them within her own heart. Bells chimed loudly and Conn stood. Beautiful song burst forth in a chorus of many voices. Offering her own words of prayer, she took a step back.

Fighting the tears that threatened to spill, she whispered, "I will *never* forget you. Years will pass, but by no means will there *ever* be another."

"He did not tell ye?" asked Ronan softly, stepping beside her.

Ivy kept her gaze steady. "Tell me what?"

"That he was a prince? Left the Brotherhood? Gave his vow to his king?"

She sighed. "Yes, he told me everything. But he left out the most important words I had hoped to hear."

"Which would be?"

Ivy let the tears fall freely. "Not once did he ever tell me he *loved* me."

"It is difficult for ye to comprehend, since humans require the spoken words. However, a Fae professes their love within the mind, heart, body, and soul."

She shook her head in dismay. "And as a human, those same spoken words would resonate in those very places you mentioned."

"If I can offer some insight, Conn did truly love ye, Ivy."

Turning toward the Fenian Warrior, she placed a hand on his arm. "Nevertheless, it wasn't meant to be. Please return me to my home. I do not belong in this world—*his* world."

"As ye wish, my lady. But first, preparations must be made for your journey back to the other world."

She glanced once more into the cathedral. "Will they take long?"

"No. I must send a message to another Fenian Warrior. Time moves differently in your world than ours. I must return ye to a certain point in time."

Ivy frowned. "How long have I've been gone?"

"Many months, but dinnae fear. When I take ye back, it will only be a few weeks."

"But who took care of my cat, Neala?"

He chuckled softly. "She was cared for by your friend, Sean Casey. Conn mentioned the feline when he brought ye to our world."

"Good. I am ready," she uttered softly.

With a wave of his hand, Ronan transported them to the gateway in front of the giant oak trees.

Ivy clutched a hand to her chest, trying to ease the pain of leaving. Unable to stop the flow of tears, her vision blurred.

Ronan placed a gentle hand on her shoulder. "The warrior has informed Sean Casey of your arrival. He will help to spread the story of your recovery from the accident. The timeline has resumed."

Wiping away her tears, she turned to Ronan. "Thank you. Your world is beautiful. I appreciated the time you took in showing me everything and being patient with all my questions. I will miss you."

Ronan placed a fist over his heart. "I am your guardian, Ivy, in this world and yours. If ye should ever require my aid or have a question regarding your health, please call forth my name."

"*Health?*"

The warrior smiled and nodded. "Your blood flows with the Fae. Ye will find that ye will heal quickly."

She rubbed a hand over her forehead. "Good grief. Anything else I should know?"

"Only time will tell."

"Thanks." Taking a deep breath in and releasing it slowly, Ivy inclined her head toward the trees. "Take me home."

****

Fresh snow draped the trees in a blanket of white creating a magical effect around her cottage. Holding her mug of tea against her chest, Ivy stared out the kitchen window. Several weeks had passed, and the melancholy refused to leave her side. It kept her company and at times, held her prisoner in her own home. She'd tried fighting the ache within, but its claws had settled deep inside her heart.

Therefore, Ivy kept busy at the Celtic Knot. Nan and Roger had proved to be diligent and hard workers. They'd maintained the store to a pristine and profitable condition during her short absence. Preparations were now being made to hire a local storyteller for the children on Saturday mornings, and Ivy let Nan oversee the interviews.

Peter Gallagher had returned and given his account to the Garda. The villagers were furious with his involvement, but soon took a softer approach for Nan's sake. When he walked into the Celtic Knot, Ivy patiently heard his apology, and then sent him on his way. Her wounds had not healed, making forgiveness extremely difficult to give the man. Perhaps in time, she told him.

The Garda had even questioned her when Mike Banister suddenly dropped off the planet. When they asked her about Conn, she informed them that he had returned to Dublin and should seek him out there for further questioning. They would never know the truth—Conn was gone forever, and Banister vanquished to another time-period, so Ronan had shared with her.

Her days might be filled to the brim with work, but the nights were a disaster. The utter loneliness and torment of never seeing Conn entered her during those long, dark hours. Her life would never be whole, and Anne Fahey's words came back to haunt Ivy.

"I don't want to become a bitter old woman," she cried out.

Neala rubbed against her leg, and Ivy blinked. Placing her cup on the counter, she bent and scooped up the soft feline. Nuzzling her close to her face, she sighed. "I must find a way to move forward from all this encompassing grief, my friend. It's not healthy. And I'm beginning to hate Sundays with nothing to do."

The cat purred within her arms.

Giving Neala one more scratch behind her ear, Ivy gently put her down and went to retrieve her coat. Brushing her hand over Conn's leather jacket hanging in the closet, Ivy had found she couldn't bear to get rid of the only item of his in her home. Letting out a sigh, she closed the door softly.

Making her way out of the cottage, she paused by the garden gate. Her beautiful garden flourished even in the harsh weather. She would be forever grateful to Conn for transforming a broken mess into a stunning paradise of flowers, vegetables, and herbs. Her refuge.

Trailing her fingers along the wood, she smiled.

Moving onward, Ivy followed the path to the one place she had never inspected. The stables. Her steps hastened as she approached the place through a cluster of pine trees, the snow crunching under her feet. Halting before the structure, she gazed upward. "Wow. Did you mean to have a lot of horses, dad?"

Approaching the two stable doors, she let out a sigh of relief. "Good. No keys needed." Lifting the latch, she pushed them open. Stale air greeted her as she stepped inside. Yet, the place was in spotless condition. Ivy walked down the center, counting ten stalls—five on each side. The place was equipped with everything required in keeping a horse.

Instantly, an idea was born.

Twirling around, Ivy almost squealed in delight. Cupping a hand over her mouth, she tried to stifle the laughter—the sound foreign to her ears. Inspecting each of the stalls one more time and taking note of everything else, Ivy quickly made her way out of the place.

Entering her house, she picked up her phone and sent a text to Sean. Not waiting for his reply, Ivy grabbed her purse and headed toward her car. Maneuvering the car carefully out and onto the main road, she tried to contain her excitement.

While in the Fae realm, Ronan had shown her a pasture where many horses were grazing. At the time, Ivy was still recovering, and he refused to let her ride. She pleaded and sobbed, saying it would be good for her health. Bribing a Fenian Warrior didn't work either, so she had to be content with watching the magnificent animals from a distance.

What she longed to do was ride a horse through the Irish countryside. And there was one horse she was determined to find. The one that had saved her.

Steering onto the path near Sean's home, Ivy parked off to the side. Quickly shutting off the engine, she opened the door and stepped into a pile of soft snow. Shaking her head, she carefully made her way to the front door.

The man greeted her on the front steps. "I was about to head to the Seven Swans. Care to join me?"

Beaming up at her friend, she replied. "Love to."

"Good. I'll drive," he stated over his shoulder as he went back inside his house.

"Scared of my driving?"

Sean returned and locked the front door. "Always."

She grabbed his arm. "At least I can chat while you drive."

As soon as they got inside, Sean turned toward her. "It's good to see a smile on your bonny face."

"I'm tired of this heaviness in my heart," she uttered softly. "Did you know I was out to the stables for the first time today?"

He laughed and started the engine. "No. I assumed you had already inspected them on your first tour with Peter."

Ivy snorted. "He never showed me the place." Waving her hand about, she added, "They're amazing. Did he…*dad* have any horses?"

Glancing in both directions, Sean turned the car down the main road. "Yes. He had several many years ago. It was his goal to teach horseback riding lessons. Sadly, after you and your mother left Ireland, Thomas abandoned his plans and sold the animals."

Ivy peered out the foggy window. "I plan on acquiring a horse. It's a beautiful place and should have one...or two."

"Excellent news. Thomas would approve. How have you been feeling?"

She eyed him skeptically. "I'm very well, thank you. You don't have to fuss over me. You're as bad as Erin. She's constantly bringing me food and touching my head to make sure I'm not running a fever." Ivy pointed to her body. "Remember, Fae blood inside me."

"Yes, but—"

"Stop," she interrupted. "I'm having a happy moment. Don't spoil it for me."

Smiling, he nodded.

Turning into a parking space near the pub, Sean turned off the engine. As Ivy exited the car, light snow fell softly on her face. Lifting her head, she welcomed the dusting of flakes.

Making their way inside the warmth of the Seven Swans, Mac waved at Ivy and Sean in greeting. The place was packed with villagers, and Ivy noticed a band setting up in the back. One of the musicians winked at her. *If this was some other time, I might have considered winking back, but not now and maybe not ever.*

Ivy leaned near Sean. "Let's grab a booth away from all the noise."

"Are you sure? They play a mean fiddle, along with great storytelling."

She shook her head. "Baby steps, Sean. I'm learning to take them slowly toward civilization. Now let's take a seat, so you can tell me where I can find someone to help me tame a wild horse."

Chapter Twenty-Nine

"When the stars are aligned, anything is possible."
~Chronicles of the Fae

Leaning against a pillar in the Hall of Remembrance, Conn stared at a paneled mirror. Though golden light reflected all around its borders, he gritted his teeth. He'd saved Ivy, but the other he had failed. At least that's what he kept telling himself. The seer refused his request to witness the events afterward for Ivy's ancestor, saying the O'Callaghan clan had once more taken their place in the light.

The image wavered and flowed and time moved forward. Nevertheless, it would never continue with him.

He'd hardened his heart from all emotion, even when he visited the royal house of Frylnn. His decision to wed the eldest daughter was granted by her father. Instead of sealing the pledge with a blood rite, he left the palace. Conn had no desire to set eyes on the woman until the wedding ceremony. He knew her well and deemed her to be an excellent choice for his people. His father would be pleased.

Conn glanced at the summons in his hand from his king. No doubt to discuss terms of the union. Crumbling the missive, he tossed it into the air and watched as the paper vanished.

But the idea of marrying without the bond of love left a bitter angst within him. For as long as he lived, there would only be one who claimed his heart. She might be departed from this world, yet, her essence still lingered. Her voice, *her scent* filled him each time he stepped through the door to his chambers.

"*Ivy*," he whispered, her name on a prayer.

Cautiously moving forward, Conn raised his hands outward and a group of mirrors appeared. He had sealed them off the moment she'd left the Fae realm. Deep sorrow had filled him in the beginning, and he sought refuge inside the hall—reliving every detail of their time together, and then cloaking them.

His hand wavered, aching to unveil them one more time. But he closed his fists and turned away. Too many memories haunted him here, ripping apart his soul. Clenching his jaw, Conn stormed out of the room.

As soon as the doors were sealed, he made his way through the marbled archway and across the bridge. Approaching the palace of his parents, he nodded to a guard as the Fae opened the gilded doors.

Stepping through, he went directly into his father's solar. Placing his hands behind his back, Conn waited to be acknowledged.

His father glanced up from his reading. "Why are you standing thus? Take a seat."

"I have other appointments to attend to."

King Ansgar's eyes hardened. "What angers you, Conn?"

"I have no desire to speak about my emotions. And for the record, I am not angry."

His father rose slowly from his chair. "Is this how we shall be from now on? With our conversations consisting of clipped sentences? I have no wish to see you become a martyr."

"*Martyr?*" echoed Conn. "Have I not done what you have asked of me? I am fulfilling my duties. A bride has been chosen, and I'm positive we can come to terms with a date by next full moon."

"And can you be happy?" uttered his mother softly coming into the room and standing beside his father.

Conn held her gaze. "I have given my pledge, but desires—*happiness* was not on the bargaining table."

"So you'll rule as a hardened king once I am gone?" snapped his father.

Fury crawled to the surface within him. "I will do my duty, but do not ask me to be happy."

"What of love?" asked his mother.

"The only woman I ever loved is forbidden to me," snapped Conn.

His father pointed a finger at him. "Another poor decision on your part."

Conn clenched his jaw so tight he feared it would snap. Unclenching his hands, his voice took on a chilling tone. "She was the best *decision* I've ever made in a millennium. Be content with your marriage pact and an heir to the throne."

Without asking for permission, Conn flashed his hand in the air and vanished. Entering his chambers, he removed his royal tunic and tossed it on the floor. Flinging open the doors, he halted. Ivy's presence surrounded the entire area—from terrace to the garden paths and even the waterfall.

On a groan, Conn transported himself to his stables. Seeking out his horse, he mounted the animal and took off to the only place he could find solace.

****

"You may be the King of the Fae, but you are as stubborn as your son," protested Queen Nuala.

"Stubborn?" he barked. King Ansgar paced in front of his desk. "Did I not allow his woman to live?"

"The *woman* has a name," she corrected, clasping her hands in front of her. "You make her sound meaningless. Since when did humans become lesser than a Fae?"

Taken aback, King Ansgar halted. "Have I ever stated they were?"

"No, but your actions prove otherwise."

The king wandered over to a large window. Placing his hands on either side of the stone, he cast his gaze outward. "It was not my intentions. I have only wanted the best for our son. He never listened to me in his youth. Joined the Brotherhood over my objections. Our conversations were always fraught with terse words. Each time a suggestion or order was given, he countered it, or bent it to suit his needs."

"He may have disregarded your orders as a father, but he would not do so with his king."

King Ansgar turned around and folded his arms over his chest. "Are they not one in the same?"

Queen Nuala smiled. "Not for our children, dearest."

He groaned. "Do not speak to me of Abela. I still have misgivings about her becoming a priestess. A royal princess has never undertaken such a cause."

His wife moved toward him. "Did it ever occur to you that our children were destined for greater? The loom of the Fae has come to a crossroad within the stars."

Narrowing his eyes, he glared at his wife. "You've spoken to the seer."

She held her head high. "Yes."

"Yet, she refuses to speak to me?"

Queen Nuala placed a hand on his chest. "Because you refuse to see with your heart, my king. You're ruling our children with your mind. Controlling their actions. Wanting to carve out their futures. It is not yours to do so."

"I only wish for the best," he uttered softly, looking into the eyes he loved so well.

"Must I remind you that twins have never been born in the Fae realm? They were destined for a greater purpose. One dark, the other light. A balance of both realms."

"Is this what the seer has told you? Are you able to share her message?"

She nodded. "If you pull too hard on Conn's thread, the entire kingdom will suffer from this unsteady path. Our son met his destiny the day he made the decision to save Dervla. If he had chosen another, his quest would have never seen him return to take his rightful place as the future king."

Stunned, the king leaned against the stone wall. "So all of this—his trial, his failure to save the right human all had to do with *Conn*?"

Tears glittered in her eyes. "Yes."

He pinched the bridge of his nose. "But she—Ivy is a human."

"And what about the Dragon Knights? They are part human *and* Fae."

"It was different. We required guardians for the dragons. Mother Danu gave her blessing."

322

She cupped his face. "Our children are unique. They will change both worlds for the better. The Dark One may have been vanquished, but I sense another presence looming far out there. We shall need the strength of a stronger Order of the Dragon Knights and Fae, including the humans."

King Ansgar grasped her hands and placed a kiss inside each palm. Releasing them, he tipped her chin up with his finger. "The seer did not see this. *You*, my love have had the visions."

Her smile spoke volumes. "You know I cannot speak of this."

"You are my queen, but also the daughter of a seer. Tell me, what am I to do?"

She brought her arms around his waist. "I would never begin to tell my king what to do."

He leaned down and brushed a gentle kiss over her mouth. "Then tell your husband—your lover what he should do."

"Go speak to your son as a father and *not* as his king."

****

Conn let his horse set the pace, galloping over open hills with the sunlight streaming all around him. A cool autumn breeze invigorated him on his journey. The vastness of the place poured out before him, urging him onward.

Heading toward the southern gate, he nudged the animal away from the giant oaks and toward the flowing stream. Bringing them to a place shaded by several birch trees, Conn dismounted.

"Go drink, my friend. You have earned it." Giving his horse a firm pat, Conn fisted his hands on his hips and drank in the scene. The stream lapped gently over smooth stones on its passage to the western ocean. The gateway to *Tir na Og*.

Striding over to one of the trees, he collapsed onto the soft grass. Bringing his knees to his chest, he stared outward. Swans glided past him, oblivious to his presence. He tried to clear his mind—to bring himself to center within his body, mind, and soul. Yet, there was too much chaos and his emotions clouded.

Would he ever find peace? If turmoil were the price for Ivy's love and saving her life, he would gladly do it all over again.

A lone doe ambled on the other side of the water. Her lazy movements settled a small part of his inner battle. He brushed a hand over the ground and wildflowers bloomed, reminding him of another.

"Serene and beautiful," commented his father taking a seat near Conn.

He eyed his father skeptically. "A place of solace."

"Yes. Often times we would find you here when you were very young."

Conn frowned. "How young?"

His father rubbed his chin in thought. "The first time, you were five summers."

"I don't recall the memory," he stated and turned his sight back to the swans.

"You were angry. I refused to let you go to the lists with the other warriors. You stomped your foot and vanished before my eyes. It was the first time you defied me."

"And not the last," Conn replied dryly.

His father chuckled. "No, though I would not expect anything else from my son."

Conn stood. "I have no wish to displease my king."

"I have always been proud of you."

He turned toward his father. "Why are you here?"

The king stood and placed a hand on Conn's shoulder. "Cannot a father wish to speak to his son?"

Conn arched a brow. "Speak plainly, father. Mother might be used to you answering questions with a question, but I refuse."

Releasing his grip, his father surveyed the area. "Tell me about your Ivy."

Shocked by his words, he narrowed his eyes. "Why?"

The king moved toward the stream. "I shall like to hear how a Fae prince *and* Fenian Warrior fell in love with a human."

Confused, he snapped, "What purpose would it serve? She is no longer a part of my world."

His father glanced over his shoulder. "Nonetheless, she will always remain a part of your heart. Did you not state that you spoke the binding words to seal your souls together?"

Conn fought the wave of pain threatening to spill forth. Unable to answer, he clenched his hands.

"If you did so, then you know the battle you shall always face." His father turned back around. "It will tempt, torment, and create havoc within your very being. We are Fae. When we love, it consumes us at times." He took a step closer. "Again, tell me about the woman you love."

"She is my breath, my heart, my soul," uttered Conn in a strangled voice.

"As well as your blood. Yours mingled with hers when you saved her life."

"Why are you doing this?" demanded Conn.

"Because your father has been a fool. Yes, I was furious upon your return. We had not seen you in so long and then you arrive under guard. We—no, let me rephrase. I had hoped this final quest would make all right between us. You'd come back and accept your place here." He let out a sigh. "You can imagine my fury when I heard you'd secretly entered the realm with an injured human. I was not pleased. I forced you to make an ultimatum."

Conn held his arms outward in exasperation. "What do you want me to do?"

His father gestured toward the trees. "Go bring home your future wife before it destroys you."

Stunned, Conn gaped at his father.

"It does no good standing there like a forlorn goose. Do not step foot back in this kingdom until Ivy O'Callaghan is by your side."

"What about the house of Frylnn?"

"Let me deal with the repercussions. It would have made a miserable match."

Conn couldn't move. He raked a hand down the back of his neck. "I don't understand. What changed your mind?"

"A conversation with the woman who holds my breath, heart, soul, *and* blood. Your mother. She reminded me of the true nature of our people."

"And that is what?"

"Love. Without it, we are a hopeless race."

Holding out his arm to his father, he waited. However, he surprised Conn by embracing him. "I only have one request when you both enter the realm."

"*Anything.*" Joy infused his words.

"To meet her alone. If she is to be the future queen, I must speak with her first."

Conn laughed, the tone sounding foreign to his ears. "I can assure you, Ivy will charm you the moment you see her."

Chapter Thirty

"A Fae's love can turn tears of joy into brilliant crystals."

~*Chronicles of the Fae*

"So many books and not enough time to peruse them all," complained Ivy, pushing the giant ladder to an area of the library in the cottage she had yet to explore. Climbing the steps, she pulled out one of the books. Flipping it open, she snorted. Glancing at the others with identical spines, she noted the brass plate on the shelf. Her uncle had amassed an entire collection on Greek mythology, but it didn't do her any good, since it was all in Greek.

Replacing the book, Ivy noted an area tucked in a corner. There was a collection of books all tied together with a plaid ribbon. Reaching as far as she could, she grumbled a curse when her hand barely touched the spines. "I'm not getting back down."

"Do you want me to give you a push?"

Ivy's hand slipped. "Damn! You scared me."

"You shouldn't be attempting to push the ladder while you're standing on it," scolded Erin.

Ivy narrowed her eyes at her friend. "And friends *knock* before entering."

Erin shrugged dismissively. "I saw you through the window. Thought you could use some help."

"What did you bring today?" Her friend just couldn't understand that she'd lost her appetite. Even explaining about the grief did no good either. Erin was determined to feed, talk endlessly, and remind Ivy that she needed to step back into life.

"Cheesy Mac and Cheese with bacon and a salad."

"I'm gaining weight with all these meals you're preparing. A salad would have been fine."

"You're *not* a rabbit."

Ivy chuckled softly. "But I do like vegetables."

Erin set the package of food down and gripped the ladder. "Hold on."

She pointed to the books in the corner. "I only need to go a foot over."

Her friend complied and pulled the ladder in front of the books she specified. When Ivy pulled them out, dust engulfed her. Sneezing, she almost lost her balance.

"Sweet Brigid, be careful. I can't break your fall."

"But you could soften it," teased Ivy, wiping the dust off the top of the books with her fingers. However, the books no longer held her interest. It was the ancient looking box setting way in the back. "Erin, I'm going to toss these down to you. There's something else behind here."

"All right."

After gently dropping the books to Erin, Ivy stood on the top rung and stretched outward. Tugging it forward with her fingers, she was surprised by its beauty. The large box looked like oak, its luster shining through the layers of dust. "Grab me a cloth, towel, *anything*."

Erin quickly left and returned with a kitchen towel.

"Do you need help?"

Ivy glanced over her shoulder. "I think I can manage." Wiping off the dust, she gasped. Etched on top was a four-leaf clover with the initials S.D. carved underneath. Carefully making her way down the ladder, Ivy's hands trembled as she made her way over to the desk.

Erin handed her a towel. "It's beautiful, but what do the initials mean?"

Ivy swayed. Lights danced before her eyes. The vision slammed into her with such force, she had to grab the sides of the desk.

The man stood before the blazing fire, clutching a letter. Tears streaked his face. His hand shook as he held the item outward, the flames snapping at his fingers. At the last moment, he drew it back and crumbled it within his fist.

"I will never forget our love. An ocean isn't far enough."

Ivy watched through the haze as the man moved to the desk. Opening up the box, he smoothed out the paper. Folding it, he stuffed it in the envelope and tucked it inside the box. "This was to be yours on our wedding day. Now, it will only hold what could have been."

Placing a hand on top, he wiped the other across his face. "Enough! You have your life to live and I have mine. Be well, Sara."

The vision blurred, and Ivy sucked in a huge breath of air. "Water," she gasped, struggling to fight the pain inside her and stay focused.

Erin grabbed the bottle of water at the other end of the desk. "Drink," she ordered, placing it into Ivy's cold hands.

Taking slow sips, Ivy blinked and stumbled over to a nearby chair. "That was horrible."

Erin knelt beside her. "What happened?"

"I saw him...my father." Her voice trembled. "He had a letter from my mother and was ready to toss it into the fire. The intensity of his pain was overwhelming. I've never experienced emotions on that degree with a vision."

"Do you think it has anything to do with the box?"

Ivy glanced at the item on the table. "Absolutely. It belonged to my mother. The initials are for Sara Donaldson. My father made it for her. It was to be a gift for their wedding day."

"I'm sorry, Ivy."

She shrugged and took another sip. Standing, Ivy made her way back to the desk. Picking up the towel from the floor where it landed after her vision started, she wiped the dust from the top. Flipping the latch back, she carefully opened the lid. Scents of her mother filled her, but without any visions. The box was crammed full of letters, and Ivy feared to touch any of them.

"Sweet Jesus," muttered Erin. She placed a hand on her arm. "Do you think it's wise to read them?"

Ivy closed the lid. "I don't know." Leaning against the desk, she stared upward at the empty space on the bookshelf. "It's so sad. Am I doomed like they were?"

Her friend nudged her. "What are you saying?"

Mixed emotions surged through Ivy, and she glanced sharply at Erin. "Must my life mirror my parents? Am I destined to live in sorrow, pain, *and* regret?"

"Conn left you," snapped Erin and moved away from the desk. "Time to move on."

"And find another man? You don't understand."

Erin grabbed the bag of food and started for the door. "There's plenty of other fish in the ocean."

Ivy pounded her chest. "I am still in love with him. I have no desire to find another man to take Conn's place inside my heart."

The woman's steps stilled. Glancing over her shoulder, her eyes were filled with sadness. "Then I guess you'll be living a life filled with the things you don't want."

"Just like my parents," stated Ivy.

"I love you, my friend, so don't make the same mistake they did. Find your true happiness." Erin dashed back to Ivy. Embracing her, she whispered, "Grieve, get angry, cry your heart out, but return to the living." Stepping back, she smiled. "I'll go put this in your fridge."

Ivy reached out and squeezed the woman's arm. "Thanks."

As Erin strolled down the hall toward the kitchen, she shouted. "I expect to see you at least every other day at the pub. I can't keep taking these daily long breaks to make sure you're fed."

"And here I thought you had added catering to your list of duties."

"Good to hear your sass has returned."

Sighing, Ivy rubbed her eyes. Wandering back to the table, she placed her hand on the lid. "I believe it's a wise idea to peruse these letters, regardless of what you may think, Erin O'Reilly."

****

Neala snuggled closer to Ivy, purring softly. The fire blazed and snapped as Ivy continued to pull one letter after the other out of the box. Some detailed her life in vivid images, sharing even the minuscule things—a bump on the head, always running barefoot, her first report card with all A's, the time she wept over the death of a dragonfly—the list was endless. However, some letters Ivy refused to continue reading. They were personal and intimate. Her mother poured out her heart with love, longing to be back in her father's arms.

Nevertheless, it was not meant to be.

Pulling Conn's jacket more firmly around herself, she glanced around the place. There had to be hundreds of letters and notes strewn about the place. When she first started reading them, she placed them on the table, but after several hours, the neat pile had fallen onto the floor. Sometimes, there would be a note mentioning a particular picture of Ivy, and then, lengthy letters filled to the brim about her. However, Ivy sensed the frustration of her mother's life within each of them. The woman didn't belong in the states. Her mother's soul would always yearn for Ireland and Thomas. But she stayed away, hoping Ivy would have a better life away from Glennamore. In addition, Thomas—*her father* had agreed.

"How wrong you both were."

Frowning, she reached for the particular one where her mother worried for her stepfather. In the note, she had become concerned when he thought she was leaving him and returning to Glennamore. Her mother had come home one afternoon with Ivy and found Patrick with a loaded gun. In his confusion, he thought she was leaving and wanted to end his life. Placing Ivy safely in her room, she convinced him to put down the gun, but only after she made a solemn promise never to leave him. Ever.

"So you made a promise to stay with him, because he what? Wanted to end his life?"

Ivy tossed the letter down in disgust. Gazing into the flames, she bit her lip. In truth, she couldn't pass judgment on any of them. She lived inside her own glass house and didn't dare cast stones at others. Though her stepfather was cruel at times, he did support Ivy and her mother. Never once did he lift a hand to them. He confined his abuse to words.

"You were a man haunted by your own fears each time you saw me." Ivy shuddered and stretched her legs out. Collecting all the discarded letters and notes, she placed them back within the box in an orderly fashion. Setting it back on the table, she rose and went to the window.

The morning clouds had vanished, bringing forth a day with no threat of rain or snow. Digging her hands inside the pockets of Conn's leather jacket, she fought her own wave of despair as she stared out into the trees. She leaned her head against the cool glass pane. "Time to cast my sight to the present. The past is gone. The future has yet to be written."

Hearing Neala yawn, Ivy glanced over her shoulder. "I can assume you agree?"

Neala jumped to the back of the couch, her tail swishing back and forth.

Curious, Ivy went and picked up the feline. However, the animal let out a hiss and escaped from her arms.

Fisting her hands on her hips, Ivy watched as the cat sauntered into the kitchen. "Excuse me? Is it something I said, or are you tired of my sullen behavior?"

Shaking her head, she removed Conn's jacket and walked into the kitchen. Apparently, Neala decided to flee the place through her small door. "Just remember who feeds you," she shouted.

The afternoon sun beckoned Ivy, and she went to retrieve her coat and riding boots. She longed to clear the dusty cobwebs from old memories.

Grabbing her keys and a small purse, she stepped outside and locked the back door. Though the threat of Banister was gone, she felt the need to continue to carry the old keys with her. Making her way along the path to the stables, she paused before her garden. Red roses that were bigger than her hand trailed over one of the trellises. Ivy could smell their intoxicating aroma from where she stood.

"Thank you for this, Conn...always."

Quickly brushing aside the memory, she steadily made her way down the road. A falcon's cry echoed above, and she shielded her eyes to catch a glimpse of the bird. Birds in nearby trees sang in harmony, flying about from one branch to the other. A sense of wonder and peace settled within her, and her steps quickened.

Coming to a halt in front of the stables, Ivy's heart froze. Time ceased to exist. The world tilted, and she found it difficult to draw in a breath. Her champion, her best friend, her *Fae* lover stood next to her horse.

"Conn," she uttered softly.

He turned slowly toward her. Her eyes roamed over his features—from his black tight pants, fitted leather vest, silver armbands encircling his massive tattoo-covered arms, and up to a face chiseled from the Gods. His silver blond hair hung loose to his shoulders. Yet, it was those eyes that held her captive.

"Conn," she stated with more conviction. "Are you real?"

His smile stole her breath and soothed her weary soul. He patted the nose of her horse. "How did you ever manage to tame the beast and bring him into a stable?"

Ivy's lip trembled. "I named him, Drust, after a ninth century king of the Picts. Sean and Mac helped me find him outside of Dublin."

His laughter filled the place, sending goosebumps down Ivy's body. He stroked the animal once more and then started to move toward her. "Did you know that Drust was a rival of the Scottish King, Kenneth MacAlpin?"

She nodded. When he stood merely inches in front of her, she lifted her head up to meet his gaze. "You're really here."

"Yes," he whispered.

Ivy could feel the breath of his word against her cheek. "For a day? Week? Month?" She swallowed. "How *long*?"

Conn grasped her firmly around the waist. "For as long as you want me, *mo ghrá*."

Tears tumbled free as he captured her mouth, swallowing her cry of joy. The kiss sang through Ivy's veins, mending the wounds and scars inside her heart and soul. When his tongue sought hers, a firestorm of desire swept through her, and she wrapped her arms around his neck for support.

Breaking free from the kiss, Ivy swayed. "What happened? Are you no longer the prince?"

Conn brushed his thumb over her bottom lip. "I am still the prince. Apparently, my parents had no wish to see me become a hardened Fae. The king has ordered me to bring you back to our world."

Ivy's eyes widened. "Why?"

He cupped her face, his eyes glittering like the stars in the sky. "Because I love you, Ivy O'Callaghan. The moment my body entered yours, I sealed my fate. You became mine. Though I have never mentioned the words to you, my actions spoke volumes. The Fae realm cannot rule without love at its core. One day, I shall be king, and I want the woman who is at my side to be the one who carries my heart."

Her entire being burst with joy. Never did she believe to hear those words of love, or to set eyes on the man again. She brushed a lock of hair away from his forehead. "I never stopped loving you. You were inside my mind, body, and spirit every waking moment, as well as within my dreams."

His lips recaptured hers, demanding more. "Ivy, *Ivy*, I've been lost since you've left."

"Oh, Conn, how I love you."

Lifting her into his arms, he brushed kisses along her neck. "Marry me, Ivy? Become my princess—my future queen?"

Placing a hand on his cheek, her heart pounded. "I'm human. Are you prepared to share a brief lifetime with me?"

Amusement flickered in the depths of his eyes. "You are only *half*-human now. When my blood entered your body, you became part Fae. Your lifeline

337

has been extended. Furthermore, in my world, time moves at a much slower pace."

Surprised, Ivy responded, "Now I understand fully what Ronan meant by my healing. While only the other day, I sliced my finger cutting tomatoes. It healed instantly. To say I was shocked, is putting it mildly. I wonder—"

"No more talking," he ordered, striding toward the pine trees.

She laughed. "Where are we going?"

He arched a brow seductively. "Home. To our chambers and into my bed."

Chapter Thirty-One

"A thread on the loom of life varies, as does a grain of sand. Each one is uniquely different."
~Chronicles of the Fae

Gliding his fingers over Ivy's lush bottom, she nudged against him in her sleep. Instantly, his cock throbbed, and he longed to sink deep within her again. By the Gods, Conn had never known such desire.

The moment he returned with her in his arms, he ripped her clothes from her body. To touch her skin against his own. To taste what he dreamed never to feast on again. He fought the raw, pulsing tide of desire, but Ivy urged him on with her own passion.

Their day was spent in joyous union, exploring, whispering, and cherishing each other's body. As the first star dusted the evening sky, Conn prepared a meal of honeyed bread and eggs, content to watch her nibble on her food, while she chatted about the store, Drust, and finding the letters her mother had written. He felt her frustration in her words, even when she talked about not being able to find out the meaning behind the two keys. There was senseless violence over items that possibly meant nothing. And when she worried about leaving her animals, the bookstore, and the villagers, he reassured her that all had been taken care of, including aid from Sean.

Conn listened with captivated attention. Every nuance about Ivy he found fascinating. When he swiped a crumb from her bottom lip, desire boiled to the surface once more and they made love right there on his table.

Sleep was elusive for him, his need so great. Nevertheless, his sweet Ivy required her own.

He placed a hand behind his head and stared at the ceiling. There was a final step before they were to be married. She had to meet the king. He'd purposely held off telling her, but come morning, he would have to present Ivy to him.

"You're thinking far too much. Or maybe Fae don't need to sleep." She yawned and placed a hand over his heart.

"Contrary to what you may believe, Fae do require rest," he replied dryly.

Ivy grasped his chin and forced him to meet her gaze. "Then why aren't you resting?"

He took hold of her fingers and kissed each one. "In the morning, you are to appear before the king."

She narrowed her eyes. "For what purpose?"

"His one request was to meet you before we were to be married."

"Sounds like a reasonable demand. Tell me about him."

Conn shifted and leaned on one elbow. "Fierce ruler, demanding, strict, arrogant, stubborn, loyal, and devoted to my mother and our people."

Ivy smirked. "Sounds like you."

Taken aback, he sat up. "We are *nothing* alike."

She arched a brow in question. "You might want to re-think that statement."

He snorted and looked away.

"I'll reserve my final judgment after our meeting. Should be interesting."

Conn snapped his attention back to her. "You're not afraid?"

Sitting up and scooting near him, Ivy presented Conn with a glorious view. "Nope."

Nodding slowly, he gestured to the feather pillows. "You should get more rest."

Her eyes raked boldly over his body. "I've rested enough."

Her rosy nipples teased him in the fading candlelight. "Come here."

She smiled wickedly. Surprising Conn, she immediately straddled his waist and eased her body down over his swollen cock. Wrapping her arms around his neck, she trailed her tongue over his lip. "Better?"

Groaning, he fondled her breasts. "Yes."

Ivy moved in slow, torturous movements, until they were swept away on a tidal wave of pleasurable bliss. Conn's release so powerful, his vision blurred. Wrapping an arm around her waist, he brought Ivy down upon the covers. Nuzzling her neck, his last coherent thoughts were ones of love.

Blissful, deep sleep beckoned, and Conn followed.

When the deep pounding refused to relent, he let out a growl. Had he not just fallen asleep? Ivy stirred in his arms. "Make them go away," she mumbled.

Refusing to move from the warmth of her body, Conn snuggled her closer to his. Yet, the infernal pounding continued.

"By the hounds of Cuchulainn," he roared.

Gently moving Ivy aside, he bolted out of the bed

and stormed to his front door. Yanking it open, he glared into the face of Ronan. "What do you want?"

Ronan's lips twitched with humor. "Good afternoon. Did ye forget about Ivy's appointment with the king?"

"Of course not," he snapped. "Wait, did you say afternoon?" Conn glanced over his shoulder at the sunlight dancing through the crystal panes.

"Aye."

"Shit." He rubbed a hand vigorously over his face. "Inform the king she'll be there within the hour."

Ronan turned to leave, but paused. "The next time ye greet someone at your door, ye might want to put on some clothing. Ye were fortunate I persuaded your mother that *I* should be the one to fetch ye and Ivy, and not her."

Conn grumbled a curse and slammed the door. He could hear the warrior's laughter all the way down the corridor.

Entering his inner chamber, he found Ivy sitting up. Her tousled appearance, swollen lips, and body called out to him. Striding over to her, he placed a kiss along her brow. "Sorry, but we've managed to oversleep. Something I've never done in *my* lifetime, until I met you."

She giggled and wrapped her arms around his neck. "It would seem we're making this a habit. I'm sure your father will understand."

Conn let out a groan as he lifted her into his arms. "Again, you have yet to meet the Fae king."

Ivy nibbled his earlobe. "Where are you taking me?"

"To my inner bathing chamber."

"What about clothes?" she asked, trailing a path below his ear with her tongue.

He found it difficult to concentrate. "The wardrobe…has been stocked with dresses. More can be made to your liking when you see the Fae designer."

"I love the clothing here. Makes me feel sensual," she purred against his skin.

Entering the bathing chamber, Conn waved his hand outward. Warm water appeared inside a huge copper tub. Originally, his idea was to have her bathe quickly by herself. But with Ivy, he found his plans often changing.

Stepping inside the tub, they both let out a sigh as he submerged them in the soothing, warm water. If his father had waited this long, he could wait another hour. Or two.

****

Ivy chose a pale blue gown after nervously inspecting ten other dresses. She wanted to greet the King of the Fae looking her best. After all, he was her future father-in-law. She cupped a hand over her mouth to stifle the laughter threatening to spill forth. "Would you ever have imagined this life, Ivy?" Biting the inside of her cheek, she stood up from the marble bench and paced in front of a large mirror.

Earlier, she'd protested to Conn that he didn't need to prepare his father. She was quite comfortable going into the room by herself. Heated words were exchanged, and Ivy pondered if there was more to what Conn was telling her about his father. Was the king a monster? Maybe he disliked humans and only agreed for Conn's sake. Ivy shook her head at the silly nonsense. Her future husband had become more protective than ever.

Glancing into the mirror, she lifted her chin. Her cheeks held a rosy glow, and her lips were red and swollen from all the kisses she had shared with Conn. The woman gazing back at her was one in love and it showed everywhere. Her face heated more, and Ivy pressed a cool hand to her forehead and strolled away from the mirror.

Dizziness blurred her vision, but she quickly recovered and leaned against an archway. "All I want is a decent night's sleep," she said. If only she was able to sleep fully and without the nightly dreams. They had started when she returned home from the Fae world. It was always the same recurring dream. A child's whisper—calling out to its mother. Over and over again, the plea to be heard. In the beginning, Ivy believed it was herself. Yet, the voice didn't sound like hers.

"Ready?" Conn gently touched her shoulder.

Ivy jumped from the contact. "Sorry. Deep in thoughts."

He put his arms around her waist. "You have nothing to fear."

She shook her head and leaned against him. "I'm not. I keep having this recurring dream."

Conn drew her back. "Nightmare?"

"No, not at all." Noting his concern, she gave him a reassuring smile. "I'll tell you about it later. Take me to meet the king."

He stared at her for a few more moments, and then placed her hand in the crook of his arm. Approaching the entrance, the gilded doors opened.

Peeking inside, she asked, "You never mentioned

this, but do I curtsy? Bow?"

Conn cupped her chin and kissed her soundly. "Neither. I will await you outside."

Ivy gave him a wink and turned to enter the massive chamber. The doors closed quietly behind her.

If she thought Conn's chambers expansive, they were miniscule compared to his father's. Glancing around, she noted the dark, forest green colors. Two long corridors branched out on either side of the chamber. It was as if she had stepped into the woods teeming with twinkling lights and golden colors. Giant tapestries adorned the surrounding walls, each depicting a scene with a Fae. Massive bookcases towered upward, their shelves lined with books that would take a lifetime to read. Scrolls, quills, and books were scattered across a large polished desk with the king's chair big enough to hold two people. A giant globe of the kingdom rested on a stand with four golden dragons as the legs. The object slowly moved in a clockwise rotation, and Ivy longed to study the world. The heady scent of flowers and earth filled her as she continued to observe the chamber in all directions.

The blaze from the hearth at the end of the room called out to her, but she kept herself rooted to the center.

Ivy knew the moment the king entered the room. His presence surrounded her making her skin tingle. He seemed to materialize from one of the tapestries. Ivy's mouth gaped open and then she quickly snapped it shut. A mirror image of Conn, though older and with shorter hair, walked toward her.

"Greetings, Ivy Kathleen O'Callaghan, and *welcome* to our world. I am King Ansgar." His voice had depth and authority as he stood in front of her, his hands clasped behind his back.

Straightening her shoulders, she smiled fully. "I'm honored to be here, though this is not my first time in your beautiful home."

His smile was disarming, so like his son's. "You are correct, and this isn't the first time we have met."

She arched a brow slightly. "Were you there when Conn brought me to his chambers after I was injured?"

The king nodded.

"Then I am indebted for your kindness and generosity. If your son had not brought me here, I would have surely died."

He gestured outward. "Walk with me."

King Ansgar led her down the corridor on the right. More tapestries lined the walls in an array of stunning colors. Entering another larger chamber, the king led her to a large balcony overlooking a lush garden. Ivy could make out the hills in the background, decked in autumn colors. A variety of roses, foxglove, lavender, iris, and honeysuckle—their blossoms larger than any she'd ever seen spilled over large archways leading to other areas of the garden.

"Beautiful," she whispered, placing her hand on her chest. Inhaling deeply, she released it slowly.

"A favorite of the queen's as well."

Ivy kept her focus on the landscape. "Is there anything you'd like to ask me?"

His laughter was rich and warm. "You do realize I was against this union in the beginning?"

Ivy glanced at him sharply. "Yes. But you changed your mind."

King Ansgar rubbed a hand over his chin. "We

don't change our minds, Ivy. I was led to another path of light."

"Are you worried I won't be good enough for Conn? Or are you concerned because I'm human and will one day rule by his side?"

This time, the king roared with laughter. "Perceptive. A quality I admire in you—one of many."

Turning fully toward the king, she asked, "Which are?"

He stepped closer. "Love and loyalty to my son. You have given him your heart. It reflects in your eyes and aura, basking you in a rose glow." Sighing, he placed his hands on the stone ledge and turned his sight outward. "The queen informed me that your lives have been interwoven. A destiny that began centuries ago. I might have been against this marriage, but in truth, I only wish happiness for my son."

Ivy reached out and placed a hand on the king's arm. "I love him with every fiber of my being. Even if you banish me from this place, I will *always* love him."

The king pushed away from the wall. "One day, Conn shall rule a kingdom that is older than the ground we walk upon. Nonetheless, in order to rule, he must have love within his heart. And he cannot govern a people if you are not by his side."

For the first time, Ivy pondered the possibility of the Fae—the people not accepting her. She twisted her fingers together. "There is so much to learn and prove to the Fae."

Frowning, he crossed his arms over his chest. "The first lesson I will pronounce is that the Fae love the humans. Our blood has mingled with them before and you shall learn more in your teachings. As long as you love the prince, our people will become yours. You have already endeared yourself among them."

Startled, Ivy asked, "How? I've only met Ronan, and the queen."

He chuckled softly. "When the Fenian Warrior was escorting you about the land, he was introducing you to our people."

"You knew?"

"No. On orders of my dear wife, the queen."

"I do not give out orders, only requests," corrected Queen Nuala gliding into the room. She grasped Ivy's hands. "I believe the king has sequestered you long enough in here. Welcome, again, to your new home."

The warmth of her touch filled Ivy. "Thank you."

The queen released her hands. "I've come to inform you that Conn awaits you in the Hall of Remembrance. There is some knowledge that must be illuminated for you both."

"Would you care to enlighten me?" King Ansgar asked in a warning tone.

"Later, my love."

Reaching for his wife's hand, he placed a lingering kiss inside the palm. "Do not keep me waiting."

She smiled fully. "Never."

The king nodded slightly toward Ivy. "The wedding is in two days. I shall see you then."

Surprised, Ivy sputtered, "Bu…but King Ansgar, there's so much to prepare and…and I haven't discussed anything with Conn."

He took her hand. "There will be no argument. In addition, from this day forward, please call me, Ansgar."

In a brilliant flash, the Fae King vanished, leaving

Ivy dazed.

The queen took Ivy's arm. "Have no fear, the entire kingdom will be more than willing to assist with the festivities."

"I suppose so." Anxiety settled within her.

"Good." She patted Ivy's hand. "Close your eyes. It will help when I transport you into the hall."

Ivy's breath seemed to solidify in her mouth, so she nodded. She felt a slight tingle, but it was over in seconds.

The queen whispered, "You may open them now."

Delighted, Ivy looked around. "Amazing!"

Conn was at her side in two strides. "Did it go well with my father?"

"He's as charming as you, so yes."

Placing a protective arm around her, he moved her along the corridor. "These are images of my life we are witnessing."

"Do you know what this is about?" she asked keeping her voice low, fascinated by the moving pictures.

"No."

They stopped in front of one of the panels. The image remained blurred. Queen Nuala approached and stood beside it. When she spoke, she kept her gaze on her son. "When you rescued Dervla, you unexpectedly set in motion a series of new threads on many lives. Even the seer did not foresee what would happen."

Conn let out a growl. "Old knowledge, mother."

"Do not interrupt," she ordered in a voice of authority.

Queen Nuala waved her hand over the picture. Instantly, the image came to life.

Fascinated, Ivy moved away from Conn. Everyone was arguing in the far corner of the open field, but it was the figure standing behind the tree that captured Ivy's attention. She was drawn to the person, as if she knew their identity. Ivy lifted her hand outward.

"Do not touch the panel," ordered Conn softly.

"I know her," she stated in a low voice.

"As you should," said the queen. "For she is your ancestor."

Ivy's fingers ached to touch her, and the room faded away. Light bounced off the reflection and knowledge of her ancestor flooded within her. Time bent and folded, weaving a pattern of not only her ancestor's life, but of the others that followed. Their journey was one of strength, courage, bravery, and love. All streaming through time to bring about one culmination.

"This is where it began, but it did not end here. We were the hidden, but strong. We were forgotten, but forged a new path. Darkness shrouded us in secrecy, but the light shone brightly on our path." Ivy swayed, as deep heaviness descended all around her.

"Open your eyes, *mo ghrá*," whispered Conn, cradling her in his arms.

Ivy blinked and gazed into eyes blazing like she'd never seen before. She cupped his cheek. "I saw them all."

Queen Nuala touched her head. "Your ancestors, beginning with the first one in the image?"

"Yes. And you were wrong, Conn."

He frowned. "What do you mean?"

Ivy pushed away from him, though remained seated in his lap. "Her lineage was kept strong *and* in hiding. She watched knowing she was not meant to be the one saved. She married secretly and well—to a druid, I believe." Ivy rubbed her head, trying to sort out all the knowledge. "She had the gift of sight, too."

Conn glanced sharply at his mother. "But I was put on *trial*. Made to witness an event that shredded the fabric of many generations."

His mother shrugged slightly. "At the time, we did not fully see its purpose. Contrary to what many believe, even the Fae make mistakes. It was all part of the process."

Ivy placed a calming hand on Conn's chest. "We were destined to meet."

Placing his forehead on hers, he sighed. "The stars were aligned."

She giggled. "You could say, right?"

Conn looked up at his mother. "Did you know this would happen with Ivy—the vision?"

The queen took a few steps back. "My son, not only is Ivy your future wife, but she will become the next seer. I did not fully understand my own vision until she was brought into this hall."

"What?" they both exclaimed in unison.

Then Queen Nuala brushed a hand over them both. "And I deem it wise to name your firstborn daughter after the woman who brought you both together. *Sorcha.*"

Conn and Ivy exchanged looks. "Daughter?" they asked in stunned voices.

"Yes," confirmed the queen, giving Ivy a pointed look. "She's been calling out to you in your dreams."

Ivy clutched her abdomen. "I'm *pregnant*. My *daughter* is speaking to me?"

Conn muttered something in his ancient language. Lifting her into his arms, he stood. "If you don't mind, I think we'll retreat to our chambers."

"Good idea," muttered Ivy.

Queen Nuala smiled. "Your father has requested that Ivy stay inside the royal chambers with us until you are married."

Conn snorted and gave Ivy a wink. "I'm sure you can convince the king that it would be wiser if she remained with me. As I've already stated, I've shared my binding vows and blood with the woman who holds my heart."

Giving no time for his mother to make a retort, Conn whisked them away in a glorious flash of light.

Chapter Thirty-Two

"Wisdom is gifted to those who seek with an open mind and heart."

~Chronicles of the Fae

Conn gently laid Ivy on the bed. He glanced around his inner chamber and laughed. "I never recognized my own future until this moment."

Ivy shifted on the bed. "What do you mean?"

He pointed to the massive headboard and the bedposts. "Take a look at the carvings."

"Yes...they're vines."

"Vines of *ivy*," he corrected, sitting down on the bed.

Touching the carvings, Ivy smiled. "You had your own vision."

Conn shrugged and gathered her into his arms. "Fate had a way of weaving my destiny when I chose to carve this bed. It was born of a desire to learn more about the human world. I spent many moons carving the pieces and putting them together."

"How old?" she asked, trailing a hand across his chest.

Bringing her hand to his lips, he kissed the vein along her wrist. "Over a thousand years ago."

Ivy surveyed the carvings. "The wood shines like it was made only a few days ago."

353

"The thread of your life began within me when my hands carved the first piece of wood."

"Although, *love* was not what you considered in your life." Sighing, she scooted off the bed and went to stand before the crystal paned window. "So much to comprehend. You. Being a seer. Carrying a child—*our daughter*."

Conn rose and went to her. His chest constricted with fear. Kneeling in front of her, he placed his hand over her abdomen. "Tell me you're happy, Ivy. If any of this displeases you, I will happily change the stars to give you anything." Noting the shadows that haunted her eyes, he added, "I cannot bear to see you in any pain."

"I'm not," she reassured, smiling fully. "I love you Conn. Just trying to process all this new information can be daunting." She paused, biting her lower lip. "Are you happy with the news, especially to find out I'm pregnant?"

On a moan, he wrapped his arms around her waist. "My love for you is deeper than the cosmos. It fills me more than I can explain. You now carry another precious gift within you besides my heart. *Our child*." Standing, Conn cupped her face. "When we are married, I shall proclaim my binding vows out loud for you to hear."

When she lifted her head, love radiated within her eyes "And you shall hear mine."

Conn lifted her and brought her back to their bed. "You do realize your life is now in this world?"

She gave him a speculative look. "So I gathered. I've already been formulating a plan."

"Do share," he urged, kissing the soft spot below

her ear.

Ivy let out a pleasurable sigh. "I would like to make Nan and Roger co-owners of the bookstore. If Nan wishes, she can also stay at the cottage. I believe it's time she moved away from Peter."

"What about the one year contract?"

"I'm gifting it to the people—Nan and Roger, so I believe it's all within the legal parameters. Actually, I won't sign over the deed until my one year is up. I'll have Sean draw up the papers."

Conn skimmed her thigh with his fingers. "Impressive."

She arched under him and nipped him on the chin. "It's intriguing to think that you knew so many of my ancestors. What would Bradon Finnegan have thought if he knew that one day, you were fated to meet and fall in love with his descendant? Wish we could find that lost painting."

Conn's hand stilled. Bolting upright, he used magic to quickly dress them both for cold weather.

"You have got to stop doing this," she protested, her eyes narrowing at him. "I prefer to dress myself. In fact, I was getting ready to take off said clothes."

He held out his hand. "Curious as to what the keys may open?"

Ivy's eyes widened in alarm. "You've figured it out?" She jumped off the bed and ran over to her purse. Pulling them out, she handed the keys to him.

"I've been attempting to put the puzzle pieces together." Conn watched the play of emotions on her face.

Jabbing a finger into his chest, she ordered, "Show me."

Grabbing her around the waist, he whispered against her cheek. "Close your eyes."

In an arc of light, he brought them both outside the ruins of Castle Lintel. A light dusting of snow covered the place, creating an illuminating glow in the fading daylight. Unprepared for the weather, he quickly made sure Ivy was cloaked in hat, gloves, and a warmer coat.

"Just *present* the clothes, instead of dressing me," she protested once again.

Conn ignored her grumbling and handed the keys to her. "Stay here. I'm going to check inside the area which would have been the main hall."

"Nope. I'm coming with you," she argued, stepping past him and entering the main portion of the castle.

"I can freeze you where you stand."

Halting, she looked over her shoulder and gave him a scathing look. "Fine. But when all is secure, come and fetch your *weak* maiden."

Conn reached for her hand and squeezed gently. "As I was planning." Kissing the tip of her nose, he vanished and materialized inside the Great Hall.

Damp cold greeted him as he stood and looked around the place. The ruins were remarkably intact as he cautiously made his way over to the large hearth. How many times had he feasted here with Finnegan? If he closed his eyes, he could make out the voices—boasting of stories, smells of rich food, and lively music. Placing a hand against the stone, he smiled recalling the fond memories. "So many my friend."

Walking to the far right end of the massive fireplace, he felt around the sides of the crumbling stones and wood paneling. Pushing with his fingers, he continued to explore the area until he felt one of the larger stones move under his touch. Conn shoved harder the next time and was rewarded with a click. The panel to the right moved a fraction. Musty air assaulted his senses, along with Ivy's shouting and demanding he come fetch her.

Waving his hand upward, he brought her forth inside the hall and to his side. Grasping her firmly against his chest, he arched a brow. "Happy now?"

Ivy shoved at him. "You could have warned me."

Conn silenced her further protests with a kiss. Breaking free, he pointed to the gap in the wall. "A secret passage."

"To where?" she asked, trying to see inside the hole.

"We're about to find out."

Holding his palm upward, Conn blew across the opening and light illuminated the dark interior. Surveying the place inside, he noted stone stairs leading downward. Grabbing the paneling, he tore it free from the wall. Noting the descent, he turned toward Ivy. "Stay here. The stones are damp. I cannot risk injury to you, *mo ghrá*, or to our child." He was keenly aware of her scrutiny, but prayed she would comply.

Surprising him, Ivy squeezed his hand. "Be careful."

"Always," he reassured and started to descend the stone stairs.

Conn continued to expand the area with light, and as the stairs veered to the left, he followed them and then came to a halt. He stood before a massive rotting door. Pulling out the keys, he attempted to put one inside the lock. Yet, it wouldn't budge. Fumbling for the second one, he sucked in a breath and inserted the key inside. Instantly, he was rewarded when he heard it give, and he pushed the door open. Bringing forth the light inside the place, he breathed a sigh of relief.

Chuckling softly, he glanced around the aging chamber. "So this is where you stashed your wine, Cramar." The Earl of Lintel was known for his vast collection, but had kept it a secret from everyone, including his children. He died before revealing the cellar, causing an uproar among his many sons.

Scanning the area to make sure it would be safe for Ivy, he went to retrieve her. Conn found her pacing by the open paneling.

"Care to see what I've found?"

"Yes!"

He gathered her into his arms and brought her to the wine cellar. "Impressive, but this all belongs to you. One of the keys unlocked the secret that held the whereabouts of the lost wine." Conn leaned against the wall and folded his arms over his chest. "For decades, the Earl of Lintel's sons searched everywhere, including the caves in the hills. They believed their father had stashed all the wine away from the castle. There weren't any building documents to refer to and the earl never disclosed where he kept his immense collection."

Ivy perused the area. "Why not?"

Conn moved away from the wall. "Because the earl deemed he would live a long and hearty life."

"And did he?"

"No. He died in a riding accident at the age of thirty-five."

Ivy continued to move along the cellar. "I wonder

if the wine is any good?"

"It most certainly was when last I drank from a bottle."

She regarded him for a moment and then shook her head. "I keep forgetting the life you led."

Conn stepped in front of her. "Nevertheless, it did not truly begin until you walked into my life."

She wrapped her arms around his waist. "So this was the treasure after—" Slipping free from his arms, she made her way to an alcove. "Conn…"

"Yes, I see it, too." Bringing the light farther inside the tiny place, they both stared in awe.

A long wooden box stood upright in the back corner. Conn pulled forth the smaller key. "Care to wager that this key belongs to the box?"

Ivy grabbed his arm. "I say yes, and if it does, you will grant me a day at the waterfall."

His smile turned wicked as he stepped near her. "And if it doesn't, you will have to watch me swim in the water by the stones."

She smacked at him playfully. "Not if I'm naked on those stones."

Conn roared with laughter. "Deal."

Stepping inside, he pulled the box from its hiding place, removing the cobwebs that graced its exterior. Taking it over to a table, he held the key out for Ivy. "You do the honor."

Her hand trembled as she took the key. Glancing down, she swiped at the dust. "It's beautiful."

Conn watched as she fitted the key inside the lock. The latch opened and Ivy lifted the lid. "Could it be," she whispered, bringing forth a long leather pouch. "Move the box off the table, please."

Complying, he asked, "You know?"

Ivy glanced at him sideways. "Didn't you mention that Bradon Finnegan loved to stay here?"

"Yes," he responded slowly.

"I really shouldn't without gloves, but I'm too excited. Grab the other end" Gently, Ivy undid the bindings and unrolled the leather pouch. The colors of the painting stood out within the cellar.

"By the Gods," uttered Conn in shock.

"It's not the lost painting of *The Meeting of the Warriors*, but another one," gasped Ivy looking up at him.

He shook his head. "Correct, because I have the original hanging in my chambers."

"What?"

Conn shrugged. "I'm sorry, but after Finnegan's death, he stated that it was to be gifted to me."

Ivy glared at him. "You never said anything, and I didn't come across the painting in your chambers."

Staring at the images in front of him, he nodded slowly. "It's in an alcove between two bookcases. I kept meaning to show you."

"Then what is this one, and why didn't Bradon ever display it anywhere? Actually, it's more stunning in color, design, and landscape."

Sighing, Conn lifted his head. "The fourth warrior is Rory MacGregor. At the time, he did not believe Finnegan should be painting or sketching *any* Fae. He deemed it could bring about harm to his people and ours. In truth, Rory was in a dark place. He'd recently returned from the past in Ireland where the new and old religions were raging a war. We, the other two warriors tried to convince him otherwise, but he would not hear of it. Brushed us off that day and never came back." Casting his gaze once more to the painting, he added, "Finnegan drew his exact likeness from that very first meeting. A true and gifted man."

"They are all striking men, including you." She lifted her gaze to meet his.

"I will show you the other painting when we return."

Ivy slowly rolled the painting up within the leather. "You do realize how valuable this lost artwork is, Conn?"

"Millions," he stated, tying the ends of the pouch. Gently placing in back inside the box, he closed the lid. "What will you do with it?"

Her expression stilled and grew serious. "Hang it next to the other one." She took his hand and wove her fingers through his. "Take me home. We have a wedding to plan."

Bringing their joined hands to his chest, he lifted the box into his other arm. Leaning near her ear, he whispered, "Close your eyes."

Her laughter filled him as they left the ruins of Castle Lintel.

Chapter Thirty-Three

"The prince bestowed the princess with a crystal pendant of his tears as a wedding gift."
　　　~Prince Conn's gift to his wife, Princess Ivy

Ivy glanced at the reflection of the woman staring back at her from the looking glass. Gone was the frightened girl who arrived in Ireland months ago, and in her place was the future princess of the Fae. Gowned in a shimmering white sleeveless dress with pearls and crystals, she looked ethereal as the dress flowed down her body, trailing behind her. Her Fae attendants had woven more tiny seed pearls within her hair, and her face glistened with a rosy color, making her eyes more colorful.

There are those who say faerytales do not exist. They are only for the young, but Ivy now knew better. She'd stepped into her own tale of adventure. Unbelievable? To some, yes. Even in the early hours of dawn, she'd had her own doubts of the world she'd entered. However, one glance at the man—the *Fae* lying next to her, banished all her fears. He was her prince and soon to be husband. In this life and the next.

Glancing down, she placed her hands over her abdomen. "My *wee* Sorcha. I so love your father, and you already fill me with such happiness."

Turning away from the mirror, Ivy went to brush

her fingers over her cloak. Queen Nuala had presented the item to her earlier in the morning. The material was woven from a special thread used by the Fae and adorned with white rose-tipped feathers. Many hands had worked on the cloak, infusing their love inside with each stitch. When she brought it out, the material shimmered.

Giddy with happiness, Ivy slipped her feet into the soft satin slippers and walked toward the open doors to the balcony. Soon, the attendants would return and escort her to the Cathedral of Trees.

"*Conn*," she breathed his name on a sigh.

Noting the first star in the evening sky, the air grew warm around her. The colors in the garden became distorted—muted, and she rubbed her eyes. In an arc of bright colors, a young woman in white appeared on the steps of the balcony. Her ebony hair flowed around her in soft waves to her waist. A silver circlet of vines surrounded her head. The woman radiated beauty, love, and the looks of another.

Startled, Ivy blinked. Recognition flared inside her, and she took a step forward. "You're Conn's sister."

The woman smiled fully and came toward Ivy. She inclined her head slightly. "Yes, and you're the woman who captured my brother's heart."

"I'm delighted you're here. Conn mentioned you, but stated you weren't able to leave the temple."

Her musical laughter filled the place. "As if anyone could keep me away from my brother's wedding. Please call me Abela. If you would permit me, I would like to escort you to the Cathedral of Trees. When a Fae is given to her intended, the priestess leads the procession. I have asked for the honor. In addition, the

363

other priestesses will follow us inside the cathedral."

Overcome with emotion, Ivy nodded.

Abela lightly touched Ivy's cheek. "Oh, little sister, how I have longed to see this day. It is a celebration like no other. You have given my brother the greatest gift. Your love and in doing so, filled his soul with love. Now here is my gift to you."

Ivy stared at the crystal teardrop pendant dangling from a silver chain. Various colors of blues and pinks sparkled inside. "It's exquisite."

Placing the pendant over Ivy's head, she then stood back. "They are Conn's tears. Never before had I heard him weep. When a Fae weeps, we all mourn or celebrate in joy. Since we are twins, our bond is much stronger. I made this gift, so you will always understand the depth of his love. It is eternal. Forever, Ivy."

Swallowing, Ivy held the teardrop up to the light. "From this day forward, all his tears will only be of joy."

The woman moved away from Ivy. "I am blessed to see this day. My heart is full." Raising her hands outward, a bouquet of flowers appeared in her arms. They were woven together with vines of ivy.

Abela presented them to her. "Roses and gardenias. I heard they were a favorite of yours."

Ivy clutched them to her chest and inhaled their heady aroma. "Lovely."

The first bell sounded in the distance and both women turned their heads.

"It is time," announced Abela.

Ivy went and retrieved her cloak. Fastening the material around her shoulders, she clasped it closed with a Celtic brooch. Taking one last look at herself in the mirror, she picked up her bouquet and nodded to Abela.

As they descended the steps, the song of many voices filled the air. A sense of peace surrounded them as they made their way through several archways alive with flowers. Onward they continued, past the flowing stream where swans glided across the blue water oblivious to the celebrations.

Pausing before the bridge, she took a deep breath and released it slowly. The glittering cathedral steps loomed before her. The blare of the first trumpet heralded their arrival.

Abela glanced over her shoulder. "Have no fear, little sister. You're now infused with Fae blood. You will be able to manage the steps."

Nervous laughter bubbled forth from Ivy. "Reading my mind?"

The woman arched a brow, similar to her brother. "*Never.*" Yet, her mouth twitched in humor.

As they reached the steps, Ivy cleared her mind of fear and doubts and followed Abela upward. With each step, strength infused her and soon she was at the top. Her heart beat rapidly, but she knew it wasn't from the climb. No, it was only for one reason. *Conn.* Her nerves prickled with anticipation.

Clutching her bouquet of flowers, Ivy held her head high and stepped into the cathedral. Beauty and song filled her. The Fae tossed out flower petals along her path, and some blew kisses her way. Each step drew her closer to the only one she ached to see. Starlight dusted down upon everyone, creating an ethereal atmosphere.

Abela's voice rose in joyous song with the others

and onward the procession continued. As the crowd parted, Conn stood at the center. Magnificent in his royal golden tunic and pants, he radiated pure masculinity. Smiling fully, his one look seared a path straight to her heart. "How can a heart have so much love?" she whispered.

Abela nodded to her brother and took her place beside the king and queen.

Conn moved toward her. Everyone else faded from her view as she took his outstretched hand. Strong, warm, safe. Ivy smiled.

Bringing her hand to his lips, he whispered, "You are a vision. Beauty beyond words."

"And you steal my breath," she uttered softly.

Lightly brushing his fingers across her pendant, he regarded it with a glint of wonder. "Need I ask whose tears?"

"Abela gave it to me as a wedding present."

"Hmm...I favor a conversation with my wee sister."

Ivy clutched the pendant. "Are you angry with her?"

Conn took her hand and placed it in the crook of his arm. He then led them to the center underneath the vine-covered trellis. "Not in the least. It is *my* gift to you, too. But there are times when I wonder if my sister has made a wise choice in following the path she is on."

"Remember, it's her journey. You and I have already taken ours."

Taking her hand, he brushed a kiss along her knuckles. "Before we say our vows, we shall kneel for Mother Danu's blessing."

She nudged him lightly. "Your mother informed

me of what to expect. I will hear or feel her words."

"You are not frightened?"

"Never, with you by my side, Conn."

As they both knelt upon the moss-covered ground, the area warmed considerably, and the roof of the cathedral opened to reflect a starlit night sky. Moonlight swept down on them encasing them both in her radiance. The power of the Goddess wove through Ivy and around Conn. Her love entered Ivy's soul, whispering her approval of the union. Joy infused Ivy's spirit as she closed her eyes on a prayer.

Upon opening them, they waited for the High Priestess to come forward. Conn took her hand as they both stood before the woman. A twinkle of moonlight caught his eyes as he glanced at her.

The priestess's words echoed within the place—ancient and mystical.

"You have both come freely to the Mother and to the Fae. We, your people, rejoice in your union. Prince and warrior stands before us. Both shall remain in your lineage and travel through your descendants along with a new bloodline. A time of renewal and change is on the horizon."

The priestess turned to Ivy. "Child of the humans, we welcome you. Your strength, courage, and love radiates within and throughout the realm. We welcome you—your gift, and the new seed of life you carry within your womb. May your union be fruitful, multiply, grow in wisdom and love. Even in death, your souls shall remain sealed with your thread of love for the other."

Retreating to the other priestesses, she bowed before them.

Ronan and Taran approached. Each made a slight bow. Ronan was the first to step forward. Kneeling on one knee, he withdrew his sword and placed it on the ground in front of Ivy. Confused, she glanced sideways to Conn.

"What are you doing?" Conn inquired his gaze intent.

"As I am the guardian of the princess—"

"Wrong," corrected Conn. "She is mine."

Ronan's expression stilled and grew serious. "That may be, but as a Fenian Warrior and former *guardian* to the princess—to Ivy, I am bound by honor to pledge my sword, loyalty, and life to her. Ye already have my allegiance, my friend. This I ask of your wife."

Conn held his arm outward. "Granted, old friend."

Ronan grasped it firmly. "Thank ye." He regarded Ivy with kind eyes. "Will you accept my pledge, Princess Ivy?"

"Yes," she uttered softly.

Standing, Ronan gestured to the other Fenian Warriors who had stepped forward. "We have come to witness this union and pledge our vow."

A gasp echoed throughout the cathedral as the Fenian Warriors knelt in front of Ivy. She glanced outward at the gathering, unable to form any words. Hundreds of warriors in a display of loyalty bowed down to her. As one voice, they uttered their pledge as Ronan had done. Rising and lifting their swords, they all saluted Conn and then vanished.

"Impressive," mumbled Ivy.

"Indeed." Conn squeezed her hand. "Walk with me."

Smiling, she complied and he led her to a quartz

fountain, the water gently bubbling up from the middle. He took her flowers and set them on the ledge.

Taking both of her hands within his, he placed them on his chest. Her gaze never wavered as she stared into his silver eyes. "Until the mists descend and I depart from this life to the next, you shall always have a part of me. I weave my love freely—blood to blood, my heart to yours. Blood to blood, my soul to yours. Blood to blood, my body shall forever shield and protect you in this realm and to the next. I bind you with these words to me always." His voice raw with emotion, he added, "We shall walk into the land of forever as one love."

No longer could Ivy hold back the tears. She let them fall freely. "My love for you resembles a Celtic knot. There is no beginning. No ending. Time will pass. Worlds will crumble and fade away, but you will always be with me. My love is eternal." She paused and stepped closer. "My love is as vast as the universe from which you descended."

Conn placed his forehead on hers. "I will show you the stars, *mo ghrá*."

Her lip trembled as she placed her hand on his cheek. "But you already have, *my Celt*."

His lips came crashing down on hers, stealing the breath and moan from her lungs. Ivy clung to him, lost in a dazzling world of light and sensations. His tongue plundered deeply, and she surrendered.

She barely registered the rousing shouts of the gathered Fae. Bells chimed, along with trumpets, but they faded as Conn swept her away with his passionate kiss.

When he broke free, Ivy swayed from the

emotions. Wrapping a strong arm around her waist, he teased the vein along her neck. "After the first round of toasts and the main feast has ended, I am taking you to our chambers." His eyes roamed over her body. "This gown hugs parts of your skin where I desire to taste."

She eyed him skeptically. "Your mother has informed me the celebrations will last three days. I don't expect she'll be happy if we leave after a few hours."

Conn tipped her chin up with his finger and winked. "Ask me if I care?"

Ivy rolled her eyes. "I'm doomed if we have sons that mirror your stubbornness."

Lifting her high, Conn roared with laughter.

Chapter Thirty-Four

One week after the Wedding Feast

Warm air and soft skin surrounded Conn as he slowly awakened to a new dawn. Opening his eyes, his heart burned at the sight. He would never tire of the vision of his lovely sprite nestled next to him. Each morning brought new joy. She radiated a beauty that brought him to his knees—him a feared and noble warrior. One that spanned a millennium and more. And this frightened Conn. Nevertheless, without Ivy in his life, there would be none.

An empty existence.

The past week was one filled with festivities and seeing old friends. Sean wept with joy when they appeared and told him they had married. Thrilled with happiness, he promptly handed over a hissing Neala, who had objected being pulled from the comforts of her mistress's cottage. Ivy's horse had behaved himself, though it was the feline that gave Sean fits.

Conn's mouth twitched with amusement recalling the visit to the Seven Swans. As Ivy mentioned their elopement, Erin shouted in glee and promptly pulled their best single malt from the shelf for a toast. And then promptly told him if he ever hurt Ivy again, she would rip certain body parts from his body. However, Mac stood rooted to the bar floor gaping at him. Yet, in leaving, the man shook his hand and wished for all the best.

Leaning on one elbow, he studied her sleeping form. Pouting lips, swollen from all the kisses he bestowed on her. Lashes that framed eyes that entranced him. A dimple in the left cheek, enhancing her looks each time she smiled at him.

Her hand was cradled under her cheek, as she snored softly. Conn prayed his daughter would resemble her mother.

Daughter. The very word sent his mind spinning.

Rising quietly from the bed, he draped a cover over her shoulders. Striding through his chambers and onto the terrace, he braced his hands on the ledge. Fear lodged inside of him. *Will I be a good father? Will she find flaws within me? Will she love me?*

Then Conn remembered his mentor, Aidan Kerrigan. Regret filled him. "Why didn't I ever seek you out after you left? I am sorry, my friend." He lifted his head to the light streaming down. "Let my words carry to you across the void."

"Talking to the elements, husband?" Ivy approached near his side and slipped an arm around his waist. Her simple touch soothed an ancient ache.

"Old friends, long gone," he replied, burying the memory.

"I'm a good listener, if you need to talk."

He trailed a finger down the front of her open robe. "I'd rather do other things, now that you're here."

Her laugh was sensual and full of promises. "What did you have in mind?"

By the Gods, how he loved the sound of her voice in the early morn. Husky, rich, and ready for him. He lifted her onto the ledge. "Remember the first night under the full moon?"

She twined her fingers into his hair. "How could I ever forget? It was glorious, powerful, and full of desire."

Conn pushed the material away from her shoulders, exposing her luscious breasts. "In all of my life, I had never lost control as I did on that night." His finger brushed across her rosy nipple, eliciting a sigh from her lips. "I fully intended to take you right there."

Spreading her legs farther apart, she held his head back. "Why didn't you?"

"It was not a path I was prepared for at the time," he concluded. "In truth, I feared the power you had over me. You brought this warrior to his knees."

Ivy removed her hands from his head. "Am I your weakness?"

"On the contrary, you are my strength. I had to walk my own destiny."

"Which is?" Ivy inquired, placing her hands on his arms.

"Love and accepting my place here in the realm."

Her brow furrowed. "Will you miss being a Fenian Warrior?"

He chuckled softly. "No. We are moving in a new direction. The warriors have been appointed under my command as of yesterday. The Fae council no longer has a say in what they do. My position will be in terms of advising and overseeing their missions."

"So, in other words, you're still a part of the Brotherhood," she stated dryly.

"Yes, but I cannot travel through the veil to assist others," he assured her, kissing her tenderly. "I can only slip through a few hundred years."

Ivy wrapped her arms around his neck. "Good. There is one more question."

He nipped along her neck. "Yes?"

"Why does everyone in the Brotherhood have last names? I've met so many of the Fae, and they only have first names."

Meeting her gaze, he replied, "Think of the Fae as belonging to certain *clans*, or royal clans. We call them houses—"

Her eyes danced with mischief. "Like the House of Frylnn? Your sister spoke of this one to me."

Conn tweaked her nose. "Let us not mention that particular one. Again, I must have words with my sister."

Ivy laughed. "Continue."

"As I was explaining, each of the Fae here in the realm belongs to a certain house. Whereas, the Fenian Warriors were given surnames in order to live above in the human world. Names were chosen from noble clan families—ones loyal to the Fae and the Dragon Knights."

"Fascinating. Explain to me again about these knights."

Sweeping his gaze outward, he replied, "The order was founded thousands of years ago. Strong and loyal people were selected and joined with a house of the Fae. Furthermore, special gifts and powers were bestowed to them."

"A marriage? Union of both worlds?" Ivy interrupted.

"Correct. They were the guardians of our dragons. But when the war between the new and old religion began, the dragons were hunted and slain. As a final attempt to save the last one, the Dragon Knights were ordered to take her to Scotland and safeguard her in the waters of Loch Ness, where she dwells to this day."

"Who guards her?" she asked softly.

A golden hawk made lazy circles in the sky and Conn studied its flight. "A new order of Dragon Knights. The MacFhearguis clan."

"Another lesson I've learned today."

Conn snapped his attention back to Ivy. "Would you like to meet Adam and Meggie MacFhearguis today?"

"To Scotland?" she asked, her eyes growing wide. "I thought we could never leave here."

He snorted, looking past her to where Neala sat on a patch of grass in the sun. "So I've been ordered. However, for reasons I cannot fathom, I deem it important to make a visit."

Ivy started to pull her robe around her shoulders and Conn halted her progress. Cupping one breast, he leaned near her cheek, "The day is young, and I have plans for you by the waterfall."

Her smile turned seductive—inviting. "I'm all yours."

****

Many hours later, Conn stood with Ivy before the bridge leading to Aonach Castle. Sunlight danced along the snow covered ground, adding a magical look to the stone fortress. He looked behind him, sending out his greetings to the Great Dragon. She quickly acknowledged his presence. Bowing his head slightly, he stared back at the home of the current Dragon Knights.

"It's positively stunning," declared Ivy, pulling off the hood of her cloak. "How old did you say this place was?"

"Over eight hundred years."

"How many knights?"

"Only two. Father and son—Adam and Jamie," he confirmed. Though all appeared well, Conn sensed an undercurrent of a growing power within the structure.

"Should we proceed?" Ivy asked, tugging on his arm.

Focusing on her words, Conn nodded.

Entering through the portcullis, Adam MacFhearguis stood at the entrance to the castle. Approaching the man, Conn took his outstretched arm in greeting.

"'Tis good to see ye again. Archie stated ye would be arriving." Adam glanced at Ivy. "Greetings, my lady, or shall I call ye Princess?"

Smiling, she replied, "Ivy will do."

Adam immediately took her hand and placed it in the crook of his arm. "Ye must share the secret of how this great Fenian Warrior came to break so many rules and how you enticed him to the marriage bed."

Ivy laughed and caught Conn's glare. "Easy. He fell in love with me."

Adam roared with laughter. "Let us go into the Great Hall. Meggie will be along shortly. She is feeding the wee babe."

"Ha! He's a monster. Eats as much as *two* babes," shouted Meggie as she descended the stairs. "And don't get me started on his wailing."

Meggie went straight to Conn and touched his face. "I am beyond happy to hear the news." She turned toward Ivy and grasped her hand. "I'm delighted to meet ye. We have pestered Archie relentlessly about ye."

"Thank you," responded Ivy, smiling.

"She actually wept when Archie delivered the news," replied Adam dryly, removing his son from her arms.

Conn took Meggie's hand and placed a kiss along her knuckles. "Another fine son."

She sighed and glanced at her son. "Yes, though his birthing was rough. Even Jamie feared for his life at one point."

Ivy brushed a finger across the sleeping babe's face. "What's his name?"

Meggie stepped away and put an arm around Adam. "Alexander Conn MacKay MacFhearguis."

Stunned, Conn stared at them for a few moments. "I am...honored."

"As ye should be for saving our lives. And when the other babies arrive, they shall be honored with the names of Rory and Liam."

"More?" squeaked Ivy.

Meggie laughed and took her arm. "According to our other son, Jamie, we will be blessed with two more sons. Let us move into the Great Hall. I have some food, wine, and beer set out."

"Where is Jamie?" inquired Conn, stepping into the hall.

"Down by the loch. He should be here shortly," answered Adam, placing Alexander in a cradle by the hearth.

Ivy's eyes grew wide. "He's only a child."

"One that is growing daily," countered Meggie,

gesturing for Ivy to take a seat next to her.

Conn frowned. "What are you not saying?" His question was aimed at Adam.

Adam raked a hand through his hair. "Our son has grown since your last visit. There is a restlessness about him. As if he is waiting for someone or something to happen. We now train with real blades."

"I sensed the growing power the moment we arrived. It is within Jamie."

Adam handed Conn a beer. "He shares only his wisdom, but naught about himself."

"We vanquished the evil," uttered Conn, taking a sip of the beer.

"Mayhap my son is growing into his own power. He will lead a new order of Dragon Knights one day."

"True, but I will bring this to the attention of the Fae council."

"Prince Conn!" shouted Jamie from the entrance.

"Wow," muttered Ivy. "How old is he again?"

"Four winters," stated Meggie quietly.

Conn stood, watching as the lad strode into the room. "Yet, he possesses the body of an eight year old, and the mind of an ancient."

Standing slowly, Ivy moved toward Conn. Her face paled, and he wrapped an arm around her waist. "He has witnessed the birth of the stars and their destruction. It will take another to lead him away from the darkness. One, whose light will be a beacon in the abyss," she uttered softly, wiping a hand across her brow.

"*Mo ghrá?*"

"I'm all right," she reassured him.

"We shall talk about your *vision* later," he whispered against her ear and placed her in his chair.

Reaching for the lad, he embraced him firmly. "Soon you shall be taller than me, Jamie."

"Time will only tell," he said.

For the next several hours, Conn and Ivy recanted their story of how they met and news of the Fae realm. Archie soon joined them, and he proclaimed a special toast in honor of the new marriage and bloodline. Food, drink, and laughter surrounded the hall, until Alexander woke wailing and Meggie carried him off.

When Conn caught Ivy stifling a yawn, he deemed it wise that they should leave. Goodbyes were made, along with a few tears from the new bond the two women had developed. Conn assured Meggie that they would return, and she stated she would hold him to his word.

Conn led Ivy out into the bailey. Yet, before he had a chance to summon the power to leave, Jamie ran toward them.

He stood before them both, but his gaze met Conn's. "A destiny welcomed. A future yet to be opened. A destiny foretold. A future yet to be written. Guard her with your life, Warrior Prince."

A tremor of unease slipped within him. "I will always protect Ivy," Conn stated firmly.

Jamie's eyes burned with that of the fire dragon within him. "Nae. Your daughter. *Sorcha.*"

Not once during their visit did Conn or Ivy mention she was pregnant, and Jamie's words sliced like a knife to his heart. Why would he concern himself with his future daughter? What path did he see?

To his shock, Ivy stepped from his embrace and placed a hand on the lad's shoulder. "She will be safeguarded."

Jamie broke into a full smile. "Be well, Princess."

Conn reached for her hand and gave a curt nod to the lad. "Until the next time, *Dragon Knight*."

Epilogue

Conn stared at the ripples cascading over his luscious wife's body as she swam naked through the water and under the waterfall. He had spent an hour cherishing every inch of her body, until her screams echoed throughout his garden. It was her first request upon returning from Castle Aonach, and he happily complied with his wife's wishes. He wanted to banish the uneasiness he sensed on his visit, and the words Jamie MacFhearguis imparted.

"*Sorcha?*" he growled, smacking the stone with his hand.

Startled by his outburst, Ivy sputtered in the water. "What's wrong?"

Rubbing a hand vigorously over his face, he dove in after her. Rising up before her, he wrapped his arms around her warm body. "Nothing."

She pinched his arm. "You're lying."

"Really?" he responded dryly. "Are you sure?"

"Yes. Your eyes are always a dead giveaway. They shift to pure silver. Remember, I've witnessed one or two of your lies."

He laughed, bringing her closer to his body. "My apologies, but I have no wish to disturb our pleasurable time here with my concerns."

Shaking her head, Ivy's lips thinned. "Sorry, but we're in this together. Husband and wife. Prince and

Princess." Brushing a lock of wet hair away from his brow, her tone became softer. "I understand Jamie's words bothered you. I'm not entirely happy about them, nor do I understand them fully. Even my vision was unclear. Was it his future? Our daughter's? Will they meet? I cannot say. However, we cannot fight the path. A connection was forged. Did you not speak of the threads on the loom of fate? We are not to tamper with them."

Conn groaned. "This is our *daughter* we are discussing." He placed a gentle hand over her abdomen. "I have no wish for her to suffer any trials."

Her fingers trailed over his silver armbands. "I don't either, but I can't live her life—only my own. Does this bother you that they might be fated to meet?"

Smirking, he glanced away. "We don't have to ever return to Castle Aonach. The problem is solved."

Ivy grasped his chin and forced him to meet her gaze. "Seriously? Our daughter has yet to come into this world, and you're behaving like an overbearing father. You can't alter destiny. Besides, I like the MacFhearguis clan—all of them. I can't believe how upset you are over the boy's words."

"His words are ancient. He is destined to become the strongest Dragon Knight that has walked the earth. In keeping with the old tradition, he consults the Great Dragon. I pray she will help to guide him, along with his father."

"Then let it go," she urged softly.

How he longed for advice from Aidan Kerrigan, especially on parenting. *A future yet to be written, stated the lad. Not if he can see another for his daughter.* "The veil weaves in many layers, leaving more than one path to follow. I will consult the Fae council in the morning."

She shrugged. "Only *time* will tell. For now…" Ivy rubbed against him. "Let us be happy."

He brushed a gentle kiss along her brow. "I've never been happier, wife."

"Good." She smacked at him playfully. "Now stop frowning."

Bemused, he said, "Only an afterthought."

Ivy laughed and hugged him. "You are the most interesting man I've ever encountered. Perhaps it's your Fae blood," she teased, leaning back and trailing her fingers down his arm.

He quirked a brow. "And the *only* one you shall ever have. Fae *or* human."

Licking the beads of water off his chest, she said, "I can barely handle you."

"Are you complaining?" he asked, rocking them gently within the water.

A rosy blush stained her cheeks. "Never."

Brushing his hands over her hips, Conn pulled her against his growing length. "My love for you is endless, *mo ghrá.*"

"See how our destinies were forged." Ivy placed her hand over his heart. "Two bodies, two hearts, one love of a lifetime."

Conn's heart was bursting with love for her. His lips brushed against hers as he spoke, "Did I not promise you I would show you the stars?"

Ivy wrapped her legs around him, buoyed by the water and his strength. "Yes, you did, my Celt."

He roared with laughter. And with a wave of his hand, Conn brought the starlight down around them, enclosing them in shimmering mist that blazed with the light of a trillion stars.

When Ivy gasped in delight, he smothered her sighs with a soul-searing kiss.

****

Outside the shimmering mists, a darkness continues to grow. A force so vile that only one warrior can stop the evil when it is unleashed. And only one woman can bring the light that will shine on this man's soul.

Glossary of the Fae Realm

CATHEDRAL OF TREES: A place of worship and where royal ceremonies are held.

COURTS OF THE FAE: Special chambers where the Fae Order discuss and advise on the laws of the realm.

FAE APOTHECARY: A place where one can purchase or create medicinal herbal remedies. Or consult a healer.

FAE COUNCIL: A group of nine Fae members who proceed and advise over the laws, especially those governed by the Fenian Warriors.

HALL OF REMEMBRANCE: A place where the Fae can visit to reflect on their life's journey through mirrored images.

LIBRARY OF THE ANCIENTS: All the knowledge that the Fae brought with them to Ireland.

PLEASURE GARDENS: A vast, luscious, sensual garden where the Fae may find others for sexual pleasures.

ROOM OF REFLECTION: The Fae prison.

A Note from the Author

I have always been fascinated with Celtic mythology, so it only made sense that I would develop and expand the world of the Fenian Fae Warriors. Theirs was a world rich in legends, colors, and senses. I've based my own fictional account on the legend of the Tuatha de Danann—one of the invasions of Ireland. They were known as the Shining Ones or the *Fae*.

The Tuatha de Danann were defeated in two battles by the Milesians, whom historians and scholars alike agree were probably the first Gaels in Ireland. It was agreed that the new invaders (Milesians) and the Tuatha de Danann would each rule half of Ireland. Therefore, it was that Amergin of the Milesians chose that half of Ireland which lay above ground, leaving the Tuatha de Danann to retreat below. They were led underground by Manannán mac Lir, God of the Sea, who shielded them with an enchanted mist from mortal eyes. As time passed, they became known as the Sidhe (Shee), or Ireland's faery folk.

I hope you've enjoyed Conn and Ivy's story. Conn first made an appearance in *Dragon Knight's Sword,* Book 1 in the *Order of the Dragon Knights*. When he strode forth within a crowd to the heroine, Brigid O'Neill, I knew he would be destined to become a main character throughout the series, including having his own story.

Next in the *Legends of the Fenian Warriors* is Rory MacGregor's story—*Oath of a Warrior*. His is a tale of a hardened warrior who seeks the pleasures of many a lass, but seals his heart from any and all love.

A word about the author...

Award-winning Scottish paranormal romance author Mary Morgan resides in Northern California, with her own knight in shining armor. However, during her travels to Scotland, England, and Ireland, she left a part of her soul in one of these countries and vows to return.

Mary's passion for books started at an early age along with an overactive imagination. She spent far too much time daydreaming and was told quite often to remove her head from the clouds. It wasn't until the closure of Borders Books, where Mary worked, that she found her true calling—writing romance. Now, the worlds she created in her mind are coming to life within her stories.

Visit Mary's website where you'll find links to all of her books, blog, and pictures of her travels.

http://www.marymorganauthor.com

50691169R00223

Made in the USA
San Bernardino, CA
30 June 2017